Warburg in Rome

Books by James Carroll

Warburg in Rome

JAMES CARROLL

Houghton Mifflin Harcourt   BOSTON · NEW YORK   2014

www.hmhco.com

Library of Congress Cataloging-in-Publication Data
Carroll, James, date.
Warburg in Rome / James Carroll.
pages cm
ISBN 978-0-547-73890-1 (hardback)
1. World War, 1939–1945 — Jews — Rescue — Fiction. 2. World War, 1939–1945 —
Civilian relief — Fiction. 3. Rescue work — Europe — History — 20th century — Fiction.
4. War relief — Europe — History — 20th century — Fiction. 5. Rome — Fiction. I. Title.
PS3553.A764W37 2014
813'.54 — dc23
2013046582

Book design by Brian Moore

Printed in the United States of America
DOC 10 9 8 7 6 5 4 3 2 1

For Lexa

Hear this, all ye people;
give ear all ye inhabitants of the world.

— Psalm 49

Contents

Prelude

The Name

DAVID WARBURG HAD received the notice the evening before, an order to appear, setting this early appointment. He'd come downtown just as the sun was turning the dark city pink. From the window of his office on the third floor of the second most stately building on Pennsylvania Avenue, he'd watched the morning ease fully into its own. The Washington Monument took the light, a garment. At five minutes before the hour, he set out.

The broad, polished corridors would be bustling soon with Treasury Department functionaries, but not yet. He strode to the central marble staircase, a gleaming gyre below the soaring translucent dome. One hand in his trouser pocket, his jacket back, one hand riding the railing, he skipped down two steps at a time, coming to the grand second floor, which was dominated by the diplomatic reception room and, adjoining that, the secretary of the treasury's suite of offices. Cool it, he told himself. Swinging left toward the ornate double door, he slowed his pace.

Last night, Janet had been certain that this meeting with the secretary himself promised something, as she put it, "really good." But Warburg was wary. It had irritated her that he'd declined to match her high spirits at the news of this summons. In the past, pointer in hand, he'd briefed Mr. Morgenthau on debt security legislation and congressional vote counts, but he'd never been formally introduced to him. This summons had come without explanation, which was enough to spark Janet's wishfulness — another steppingstone toward the day they would get married.

Warburg couldn't acknowledge it to her, or to anyone, but he was appalled to find himself a seat-of-government paper pusher as the war built toward an inevitably savage climax. The latest report was that German troops were marshaling on Hungary's border, Budapest another morsel soon to be devoured in a Nazi rampage that was not impeded by the Red Army offensive on the Dnieper. Warburg was that rare, able-bodied man of twenty-eight not in uniform. Dancing at midnight on the Shoreham terrace thrilled Janet, but it embarrassed him to be seen there, even with such a beauty. She was happy just to rest her cheek against the lapel of his suit coat, as they softly swayed to the orchestra's mellow rhythm. He felt tenderly toward her, but tenderness was a flimsy bridge across the yawning gulf that had opened between them, whether she knew of it or not.

On his office wall, where Janet did not see it, Warburg had posted a floor-to-ceiling map of Europe, with yellow pins denoting General Mark Clark's stymied army in southern Italy, still the only Anglo-American force on the continent. There were also pins to the north and east, red ones, marking the Soviet offensive lines. Green pins, concentrated between the Danube and Vistula Rivers, marked places reported or rumored to be the Germans' forced labor, transit, and prison camps. Warburg had been tracking the Nazi killing sites for months, though it had nothing to do with his official work.

The war, darling, he'd say as they were dancing, *by the time it's over, Europe will be a charnel house. Did you hear me?* No, of course she didn't, because he'd said it to himself. It was not Janet's fault that he'd become obsessed with the slaughter lands to the east, nor was it her fault that he found it impossible to speak with her of his obsession. And, later, the face powder on his lapel would not come out.

Right out of law school, Warburg had been conscripted like most men, though the draft, in his case, was not into the Army. When, in the spring of '42, the law school dean, a former New Dealer named Harold Gardner, had taken the job of general counsel at the Treasury Department, he had taken a handful of newly minted lawyers with him, including Warburg. "Don't be ridiculous," the dean had said to Warburg, swatting away his initial demurral. Warburg had already filed enlistment papers, effective at the term's end, itching to join the fight. But Gardner was insistent: "Washington is where your country needs you, David." Warburg still refused, but Gardner chided him: as a lawyer in uniform, Warburg would never see service overseas in any case. He'd be a JAG mandarin, bringing acne-faced AWOLs to court-martial, at Fort McClellan in Alabama or someplace worse. In fact, Gardner had promised to see to it.

And so Warburg had joined the fray in Washington, becoming one of the samurai bureaucrats in the thick of the vast legislative re-invention of federal finances made necessary by the explosion of war spending. The rolling congressional authorizations for the war bond program was Warburg's particular portfolio. As it turned out, he'd already been central to the raising of more than half a billion dollars in war funding, which helped keep inflation down and the war economy booming. Not bad service, that. But alas, judging by the markers on Warburg's wall map, Hitler wasn't as yet much hindered.

At the treasury secretary's reception area, a primly dressed woman promptly showed Warburg into the ornate inner office. Harold Gardner was there, sitting with Morgenthau in matched leather wing chairs in an alcove where one large Palladian window overlooked the White House. There was a clear view of the President's mansion because only the faintest pale lime of early buds tempered the stark black-and-white branches of the late-winter trees. A third man was seated on an adjacent sofa.

The three men came to their feet at Warburg's arrival. Henry Morgenthau Jr., a slim figure whose tanned baldness struck an elegant fashion note, was nearly as tall as Warburg. Yet Gardner was the first to stretch out his hand, putting his responsibility for this meeting on display. He let his affection for Warburg show, saying as he turned to Morgenthau, "David was the best we had in New Haven." But before the secretary could reply, or even grasp Warburg's hand, his desk buzzer sounded, and he went to the telephone.

"Friendly greetings to you, Felix," Morgenthau said grandly into the mouthpiece. Gardner and the other man resumed their seats, but Warburg remained standing, as if holding a hat.

"Thanks for calling back," Morgenthau said. "Too early? Of course not. I've been at my desk for an hour. Same as you." Morgenthau listened, then laughed. "How is Frieda?" He paused, then added, "Give her our love." There would be a performance aspect to this conversation. "The reason I called—I have one of your young relations here with me right now." Pause. "That's right. I'm about to brief him on the job I'm giving him. A very important job, and I wanted you to be the first to know. Yes. In Rome, once liberation comes . . ."

Listening, Warburg thought, Whoa, what's this? He exchanged a quick glance with Gardner, catching his all but imperceptible nod. Rome? Gardner had insisted more than once that Warburg was indispensable on Pennsylvania Avenue, with three new bills a month coming off his desk. "The Appropriations Committee," Gardner had barked repeatedly, "is clay on your potter's wheel. Can't do without you."

". . . the War Refugee Board," Morgenthau was saying. "*My* War Refugee Board. Once Mark Clark captures it, Rome will be the nerve center and the escape hatch both. And your young man will run things."

Warburg took this in with apparent calm, but it was shocking news. The absolute opposite, he realized at once, of what Janet was hoping for.

War refugees. Everyone in Treasury was aware of Morgenthau's having badgered Roosevelt into long-overdue action on refugee relief, such as it was. "Refugee" was a generic euphemism, since those in the know—certainly including Warburg, whose gaze drifted to his wall map dozens of times a day—understood full well that the urgency applied to Hitler's particular target. Jews.

For months, Morgenthau had been sounding death camp alarms inside the government, finally forcing Roosevelt's hand by threatening to go public with the still secret cables coming in from Geneva. Elsewhere in Washington, and even in certain hallways at Treasury, the War Refugee Board was seen as the product of a Jew's special pleading for Jews.

In Warburg's own shuttling between Treasury and Capitol Hill, the WRB was not much discussed, and overseas operations of every kind were beyond his purview. Hell, overseas operations were beyond Morgenthau's purview, but that had not stopped him. Picking up on the secretary's spirit, Warburg had made a point to get his name added to the special cable circulation list, the weekly Geneva reports with their growing drumbeat of transfers, deportations, and disappearances. Green pins, to Warburg. Jewish pins.

And now what was he hearing? He himself to be appointed to the work? Rome? Warburg could not —

"David," Morgenthau said abruptly, but into the phone. "David Warburg," in answer to the other party's question. Morgenthau's tanned face had gone white, the skin at his mouth so taut it barely moved when he repeated, "Yes, David."

All at once Warburg realized with whom Morgenthau was speaking — *Felix!* — and what was happening. A feeling of alarm made him momentarily lightheaded. He had to stifle the impulse to interrupt, to explain. It was an old feeling. Glancing again at Gardner, he saw the pleased expression on his mentor's face begin slowly to darken as he, too, realized from the change in Morgenthau's demeanor and voice that something was wrong.

"Really? No, I'm quite sure. David Warburg. Yale Law School . . . highly regarded. Our man on the Hill . . . about thirty, I would say . . . I see, but . . . Well, let me look into it. Yes. Right away. No chance, you say? All right, Felix. I apologize for the confusion. I'll clear it up . . . Of course. Thank you."

When Morgenthau placed the receiver in its cradle, he pressed down on it for a long moment as if to cancel what he had just heard. Then he looked up at Warburg. "He's never heard of you. Felix Warburg has never heard of you."

Warburg knew how important it was to meet Morgenthau's gaze, to return it steadily. He said, "I've heard of him, of course."

"'David is not one of our names,' he said." Morgenthau looked at the man on the sofa. "Do we do that, Rabbi? Establish a roster from which family names are taken? Jacob? Moses? Moritz?"

"I would think 'David' is a good name," the man said.

Morgenthau looked back at Warburg. "I approved your appointment thinking you were of the Warburgs."

"I am, Sir." He smiled pleasantly. An old trick. The way to be at ease is to be at ease. "But the Burlington Warburgs," he said, "not the New York Warburgs. My father was a butcher. Not a banker." A line Warburg had used before. In fact, he'd used it with Janet's parents.

"Did you know this, Harold?" Morgenthau asked Gardner.

"No, Sir. I just assumed . . ." Gardner met Warburg's eyes, and his expression said, You *let* me assume.

"Burlington?" Morgenthau asked. "Burlington, Vermont?"

"Yes, Sir."

"How'd you get to Yale Law School?"

"Middlebury College. Basketball scholarship. It wasn't until I got to New Haven that I even knew about the New York Warburgs." Quite pointedly, Warburg refused to meet Gardner's eyes. Was the imagined elite family connection why the law school dean had made him his favorite? Of course. Nor had Warburg been so naive as to have been ignorant of that. Warburg, like Oppenheim or Lehman or Loeb — the exception Jews. Rich. But David Warburg had not established those rules. "I never pretended to be what I am not," he said. Again Warburg's easy smile, a stance that cloaked what his seniors might take as rebuke.

"I'm not suggesting anything like that, young man," Morgenthau said. "But damn. We need Warburg's money. It seems crass, I know. But there it is. We need his influence with the community. I'm in a box here, you know that, don't you? The President gave me the Refugee Board — and no independent funding. I can't sign a canteen chit without State and War cosigning. Damn!"

"But are you a Jew?" the man on the sofa asked Warburg.

"I beg your pardon?"

"Are you a Jew?"

Unaccountably, Warburg thought of the prayer shawl his father had offered him when he was sixteen, white wool with black stripes. His father had called it a *tallit,* said it had been his own grandfather's, and that it was time for David to have it, for his bar mitzvah.

"Were you bar mitzvahed?" David had asked his father.

"Yes. I wore it." He had held the shawl out to his son.

But David had stepped back, saying, "Have you been to temple since?"

His father had shaken his head no, all at once mute with what could only be read as shame.

"Well, I can't do that," David had said — the fierce integrity of youth.

His father forced his shoulders into a shrug, unable to hide his disappointment. "No matter, I suppose," he said, and again indicated the cloth. "Maybe the stripes are black as a sign of mourning." He then turned and walked away. His father never mentioned the *tallit* again.

Now Warburg shifted to look down at the man on the sofa, saying nothing.

"This may work whether or not you are a Warburg," the man explained. "It won't work if you're not a Jew."

Silence thickened the air. What was this? The WRB postings abroad were staffed from Treasury, three from the legal office alone. Istanbul. Lisbon. Algiers. Warburg doubted that any of them were Jews. There simply weren't that many Jews in the department. Why would Rome be different? Why, for that matter, was Warburg being brought into this now at all? Weeks earlier, when the President had first approved the rescue project, Warburg had asked to be a part of it, but Harold Gardner had said it was out of the question. Warburg, with his credibility on the Hill . . . his potter's wheel.

Morgenthau left his desk to return to the alcove and sit. He gestured for Warburg to sit beside the third man. "Forgive me. The phone rang before introductions were complete. Warburg, this is Rabbi Wise. Rabbi, Warburg. *David* Warburg. One of *our* names, if not theirs." He laughed, dispelling the tension.

But the rabbi's name was what registered with Warburg. Stephen Wise was the head of the American Jewish Congress, famous as the leader of the "Stop Hitler Now!" rallies that had helped Morgenthau push Roosevelt off the dime. Warburg joined him on the sofa, extending his hand. "It's an honor, Rabbi. We all appreciate what you've been doing. I read Gerhart Riegner's cables." World Jewish Congress cables that Wise had steadily funneled from Geneva to Washington. Indeed, Warburg had copied out lines from one of the Riegner cables and placed it under the glass on his desk. Without prompting, he could have recited it there and then: "Never did I feel so strongly the sense of abandonment, powerlessness and loneliness as when I sent messages of disaster and horror to the free world and no one believed me."

"So are you?" Rabbi Wise was not deflected.

Warburg answered, "I'm too tall to be a Jew. Jews are no good at basketball — so I was told growing up. At Middlebury they forgave me my name because I had a deadeye set shot. I told you my father was a butcher. But he did not keep kosher. He was called Abe, but he was not a temple-goer. I was not bar mitzvahed, because neither of my parents was observant and I didn't see the point. My parents did not insist. So what does that make me?" Warburg asked. "Once I'd have said it makes me plain American, but what would Hitler say? Hitler, of course, makes the difference." Warburg let his gaze drift to Gardner. "I didn't know it for certain until I got to Yale, but yes, I am a Jew."

"Temple-going doesn't matter," Morgenthau said. "Hell, I raise Christmas trees on my farm in Dutchess County. I wouldn't know a Seder from a sedan. No offense, Rabbi." Morgenthau, too, looked at Gardner. "I like your young man."

The Files

I T WAS WELL after midnight when the tall, dark-haired woman used the cast-iron key to unlock the stout wooden door of the Villa Arezzo on the Aventine Hill. She had found the old key in one of her father's boxes. The click of the lock made her wince. She pushed the door inward, but slowly, hoping to dampen the creak of the hinges. Since before her father's time, the palazzo had been the Rome headquarters of the Croce Rossa, the Red Cross, and as a child she had played here, although never in the thick of night. Now, for a long time, she stood in the once grand foyer, not moving. Her own breaths seemed loud in her ear, but otherwise, no sound. No one here.

Marguerite d'Erasmo was the twenty-four-year-old daughter of a French mother and an Italian father. He had been the director general of the Croce Rossa. He had died before the war broke out, but he was still revered here, and it had been the most natural thing in the world for his daughter to don the blue uniform, and she'd been wearing it since the war began. By 1943, last year, she was head of the Women's and Children's Committee for all of Italy.

But only weeks ago, everything changed. When Mussolini was overthrown and the king announced Italy's withdrawal from the war, the Germans had swiftly moved south and the Wehrmacht stormed Rome. Not so fast, Berlin was saying. The Red Cross offices were promptly taken over by rough-mannered German soldiers.

In the beginning, they hovered in the corners of the faded palazzo with their weapons holstered, leaving Marguerite and her colleagues to do their work. But soon enough the soldiers were replaced by newly arrived functionaries of the German Red Cross, although they, too, wore the familiar field-gray uniform. They ordered the Italian workers to get out. Marguerite had been one of those to protest, but the German in authority had pulled a pistol from inside his tunic and leveled it at her.

Even in the darkness, Marguerite efficiently made her way up the familiar grand stairway to the second-floor room, which was quartered by four large desks — one had been hers. The room, with its window, was brighter than the corridor, and she stood at its threshold for a moment, taking in its shapes. There was her typewriter, still on her desk — just what she needed. Good. But first, something else. She pulled the door closed behind her, shutting it without a sound.

In shadow, the room seemed like a chamber in a mausoleum. Along one wall, evoking burial vaults, stood five metal file cabinets, each with four drawers. Still there, apparently unchanged. Good.

She crossed to the armoire in the corner, opened it, and found — sure enough — the pair of large canvas satchels that had long been stored there. She picked up the bags, went to the center file cabinet, and quietly pulled open its top drawer. The well-ordered look of the folders told her they'd been untouched — thank God. She began to stuff the first canvas sack with files and papers, the census records of certain Red Cross internment camps, located in the environs of Rome and to the north.

After Mussolini had mistaken the fall of Paris in 1940 for a sign of Hitler's imminent triumph and thrown in with him, a mass of refugees poured into Italy from beyond the Alps, fleeing Italy's new ally. They came by the thousands: fugitive conscripts, able-bodied men avoiding work camps, Communists, anti-Vichy Frenchmen, opponents of the Nazi-friendly regimes in Slovenia and Croatia, and — notwithstanding Italy's own racial laws — Jews.

Throughout that year and the next, Marguerite knew, Jews came from the Balkans, Greece, Romania, Austria, Poland, and France. They came through mountain passes and by boat, landing in any number of the dozens of harbor towns along the peninsula's pair of long coastlines. Mussolini's government turned a near-blind eye to such fugitives, allowing them to be helped by the Red Cross, as well as by churches, convents, and schools. Marguerite and her colleagues had grown frantic when, soon enough, those foreign refugees were outnumbered by native Italians, displaced as the Allies began bombing industrial centers like Milan, Turin, Naples, and Bologna. Many thousands were made homeless by the air raids, with ever larger numbers of terrified city dwellers fleeing into the countryside. The Red Cross was overwhelmed.

Those in the camps were desperate, but Marguerite's focus had narrowed. Red Cross officials throughout Italy, fully aware of German policy, had long since stopped recording Jewish identities in their census lists, but names and places of origin were still registered. Italian relief workers had taken to referring to the foreigners who'd been first to seek haven as "old refugees," a euphemism for Jews, but the Gestapo, once unleashed, would not be fooled. Family names and birthplaces would be tip-offs. The particular file drawers containing "old refugee" records were what had brought Marguerite here tonight. It had been one of her jobs to keep these files collated and updated. She realized what a danger they posed.

Days before, Rome had been jolted by news passed from mouth to mouth that more than a thousand of the city's Jews had been hauled into trucks in the old ghetto by the Tiber. Urgent word spread for surviving Jews to hide, and doors in every neighborhood had opened to them. Meanwhile, outside Rome, hundreds more Jews were being dragged away from Red Cross camps, and Marguerite had no doubt that the Gestapo elsewhere was making use of the organization's census lists. But they would not use these!

She quickly emptied the contents of four drawers, filling both satchels — the records of several thousand people. Stuffed, the sacks were heavy, but the padded leather handles enabled her to lug them across to her desk. She placed them carefully to the side, then took her chair. After looking back at the door to be sure she had firmly closed it, she snapped on the gooseneck lamp, found the Geneva-stamped International Red Cross forms, fed a page into the typewriter, and made the keys dance. She drafted orders under her own name for a mother-child survey of Italian-run displaced persons camps in the regions from Tuscany to Veneto. Next to the Geneva seal, she embossed the page with her certification die. It was time to get out of Rome, and this credential — together with her blue uniform and more than a little luck — would make it possible. She would move from town to town collecting official data on children — and filing everything else in her mind. These orders would justify her steady northward progress, aiming at her eventual transport across the frontier into Switzerland. At Red Cross headquarters in Geneva, all that she had learned in Nazi-controlled Italy would matter to someone. It was the only thing she could imagine doing.

No sooner had she sealed and pocketed the self-created visa than she heard it — the big door downstairs, the sound for which she'd had one ear steadily cocked. She switched off the gooseneck lamp. Darkness. She listened. Again she heard it, a second banging of the door. Someone entering the building. She heard a man's voice, then laughter. Then "*Sehr gut!*"

Instinctively, she plunged down into the small space under the desk, curling herself tightly. Her exceptional height notwithstanding, she was lithe. Calm, she told herself. If she remained in this black hole, she would be all right. She clutched her knees and froze. That she could hear them jostling in the entrance foyer below meant they were not attempting to be quiet, therefore not sentries, not searching. Soon the noises grew muffled. Then fell to silence.

Marguerite remained where she was, not moving. The odor of the desk's underside hit her — raw, unfinished walnut — and suddenly she was taken back to another place, the cavern of another desk. She had often crouched like this under her father's roll-top desk, which was a feature of his study in the family villa in Parioli, the patrician Roman neighborhood where Marguerite had grown up. She loved to hide under her father's desk right before he returned home each evening, knowing he would stop there first to check the day's mail. She would pop out and squeal, then collapse into giggles. He would always fall back, feigning surprise, then relief. "*La mia principessa!*" At that he would sweep her up into his arms, making her feel, simultaneously, that she was flying and that she was safe.

Marguerite's father had lost his position as Red Cross director upon the publication of his 1935 report documenting the use of mustard gas by Italian forces in Ethiopia. Both he and Marguerite's mother were widely denounced as traitors. Even Marguerite's schoolmates had used the word: *Traditore!*

Later that year, she was told that her mother and father had been killed in an automobile accident. Though only a girl of fifteen, she knew that her parents were murdered by black-shirted thugs. After the "accident," the Grand Council of Fascism expropriated the d'Erasmo villa in Parioli and seized the family assets. Marguerite, orphaned and disinherited, moved in with the Cistercian sisters at her school. An exuberant, expressive youngster until then, she became shy, withholding. She came of age as if she were a nun.

So silence like this came naturally. And since this was the abject posture of prayer, her most familiar entreaty took form from her unthinking lips: *Remember, O most gracious Virgin Mary, that never was it known that anyone who fled to thy protection* . . .

Suddenly sounds burst from below again, only now what Marguerite heard was the laughing voice of a woman. Then she heard the pop of a bottle being opened, champagne. The Germans had entered the room directly beneath her, the public reception chamber, furnished with tattered fainting sofas and Turkish divans. The voices of at least two men. More laughter. "*Glück,*" one cried, "*und lange Leben!*" Revelry. New arrivals. More women. Germans and their local *Liebchens* having found a love nest.

The sounds rose and fell, squeals of delight and feigned resistance, drunken snorts, a pathetic bacchanal. Marguerite uncurled herself to leave the cavern of her desk, hefted the two canvas satchels, one in each hand, crossed through the darkness to the door, opened it an inch, and listened. The men were singing now, *Ein Prosit, ein Prosit* — a toast, a toast! And Marguerite took the cue.

She went out into the corridor, away from the elaborate central staircase, toward the innocuous-looking door that opened onto the back stairs, originally for servants. The bags slowed her going, but she went down deliberately and quietly. In short order she was through the first-floor utility room, out into the cluttered service alley that ran behind the building, then onto the broad Via di Santa Prisca. The war-time blackout meant no streetlights, so at this time of night the street was a desolate vacancy. It ran downhill, a winding channel to the nearby Tiber. Marguerite moved as quickly as she could, was soon at the river, down onto the unseen quayside. There she emptied first one sack of files, then the other, into the rushing water that only moments before, a short way upstream, had run past the now *Judenrein* Jewish ghetto.

PART ONE

War

A Mighty Endeavor

D AVID WARBURG WAS alone—alone with his thoughts. In the shadowy tin tube he tried to picture the armada far below and well to the north—something like a thousand warships and merchantmen, if the rumors were to be believed. Legions more of landing craft swarming shoreward like water beetles, the tides breaking into waves of men hurling themselves against fire-spewing bunkers. Fortress Europe stormed at last, the great drama unfolding since dawn today.

During the fuel stop at an outcropping of rock in the Azores only hours ago, Warburg and the dozen others had clustered around the shortwave at Base Ops—a thrown-together canvas shanty on the edge of the steel-mats airstrip that stretched pretty much across the entire island. "The President, the President!" a gas jockey had yelled at concert pitch, and sure enough. Men huddled and hushed. Once the radio static cleared, the unmistakable patrician vowels floated in upon the crackling air, America's most familiar voice, with its most reassuring cadence. "Last night," FDR began, "when I spoke with you about the fall of Rome . . ."

The fall of Rome had been everything to those particular listeners, until then the essence of their concentration, anticipation, dread, and hope. Now they were being told that Rome was mere prelude, an overture to the music that mattered. ". . . I knew at that moment that troops of the United States and our Allies were crossing the Channel

in another and greater operation." Greater than Mark Clark's liberation of the Eternal City, the first Axis capital to fall to the Allies? When
Fifth Army tanks had rolled onto the tarmac of Ciampino Airport,
Warburg's plane had taken off from Fort Dix field, the wheels-up he
and presumably everyone else on board had awaited for weeks. In the
Azores, they had still been two thousand miles shy of Rome, yet — so
the President implied — the pages of history were turning already. The
real operation was far to the north. Bloody Italy had always been a
feint.

"It has come to pass with success thus far. And so, in this poignant
hour, I ask you to join with me in prayer." *Ahem*s and shuffling, even
in the radio shack. Hats came off. The President's tone slipped into a
chute of the properly lugubrious. "Almighty God: our sons, pride of
our Nation, this day have set upon a mighty endeavor . . ." Warburg's
gaze went involuntarily to the next man, a bald sergeant whose freshly
bared head was bowed, his eyes closed, lips moving. To Warburg, the
President's pieties rolled on in packages, hardly registering.

But then a phrase leapt out of the sanctimony as Roosevelt said,
"Help us to conquer the apostles of greed and racial arrogancies . . ."
Arrogancies? Was that a word? *Racial* arrogancies? Warburg squeezed
closer to hear what this could be, but Roosevelt had slid smoothly into
the slot of his most solemn petition. "Some will never return. Embrace
these, Father, and receive them, Thy heroic servants, into Thy king-
dom."

Arrogancies. Racial arrogancies. These hours later, the phrase was
still hovering in Warburg's mind. Wrapped in a blanket against the
freezing altitude, he now sat on the narrow metal bench that ran along
one wall of the stripped-down fuselage. The C-54 Skymaster, once
reconfigured for cargo, was carrying passengers again, but apparently as ballast, the men distributed so as to keep the craft in balance.
No matter who they were — brass, civilian VIPs, seat-of-government
functionaries — the cargo was what mattered. In addition to the twelve
or fifteen figures harnessed, like Warburg, on the twin benches, the
plane held pallets of sacks and boxes stacked to the ceiling, running
fore to aft and stamped USA QM. Cartons of C rations, evaporated

milk, flour — thirty thousand pounds of Quartermaster supply, a first gesture of relief for starving Rome. The plane's windows were blacked out, with the only light coming from three yellow-hued naked bulbs hung at intervals and filling the cramped space with eerie shadows that, early on, had made Warburg think of Plato's cave.

The starboard passengers were entirely cut off by the wall of cargo from those on the larboard bench. On Warburg's left, a man had been steadily hunched over a book, as if there were light enough to read. On Warburg's other side, an eternal sleeper was pressed into the corner, hugging himself against the cold. Under his own blanket, Warburg wore the heavy olive parka that had been supplied as they boarded the plane in New Jersey, and under the parka, the gray suit and tie of his kind. Most of Warburg's fellow passengers had spent the long transatlantic hours as intent on their stoic hunching as he was. Only bursts of steamy breath made clear that the otherwise impassive hulks were even alive.

Before taking off from the Azores on this last leg of the flight, the laconic pilot had craned in from the cockpit to apologize for the temperature that was soon to plummet again, but saying, "Cargo's what counts. This man's army don't give a shit for men," he'd drawled, adding, "God help those bastards up in Cherbourg."

Warburg reached into the thickness of his clothing for a pack of cigarettes, but when he brought it out, he found that it was empty. He crushed the foil and cellophane, thought better of dropping it, and stuffed it back in his pocket. At that, the man on his left rose from his apparent stupor, leaning over with a pack in his fist, a magic trick. He shook it once, expertly producing a pair of cigarettes. They each took a light from Warburg's match. "Thank you," Warburg said.

"Forget that cargo, the canned food," the man said through the smoke-marbled steam of his breath. "The tins pop their seals when they freeze — salmonella here we come." He snorted gruffly, a bear in his GI blanket coming out of hibernation. Warburg too, in his blanket, must have seemed oafish, when in fact he was as thin as he was tall. His neighbor was not a bear, Warburg thought, but a defensive tackle on the bench. For a man who had sat silently for so long, he was suddenly animated, as if he himself had popped a seal. "Think about those beaches," he said. "Those Kraut pillboxes."

"Yes," Warburg said. "Good luck to our guys."

"Amen," the man said, and he patted the book in his lap, an odd act of punctuation. He took a drag on the cigarette, studied it while exhaling, then brought his eyes directly to Warburg's. "What brings you across?"

Warburg dropped his glance to the glowing ember of his cigarette. This was the first time he'd been asked to explain himself. "I'm with the Treasury Department," he said, aiming to let it go at that.

But the man pressed. "To Rome for the Allied occupation? Let me guess. 'Eye Sea,' isn't that what they call it? Invasion currency. Legal tender to be used by civilian and/or military personnel in areas occupied by Allied forces. You giving out the funny money?" Such jovial gruffness seemed forced, but that may have been a function of the man's having to speak above the roar of the engines. The image of a football player, however, no longer seemed apt. Warburg recognized the deliberate display of insider lingo, a standard bureaucratic gambit. Tag, you're it.

"Not exactly." Warburg smiled, doing a bit of forcing himself, but staying with his cigarette. It was true that Treasury was tasked with providing specially printed military currency, and the black-and-blue banknotes had been rolling out of the Bureau of Engraving's presses for weeks. But Warburg's mission was far from that. Since the late-winter meeting in Morgenthau's office, he'd counted the days until this one — while steadily moving the pins on his map and memorizing dispatches from Geneva, Lisbon, Budapest, and Istanbul. At night he'd slavishly bent over Berlitz manuals in Italian and Yiddish, ahead of quizzing by tutors early each morning.

Janet Windsor had lost patience with his obsessive unavailability. He'd tried to describe what he was learning from the Riegner cables, occasionally reading them to her. One telegram began, "It is the eleventh hour of the reign of death," but Janet interrupted him and left the room. For the first time, they quarreled, and before long stopped seeing each other. There would be no wedding. After that, when he pictured Janet, readily conjuring her alluring figure, her moist lips with the sly hint of her tongue, he felt sad. But his fierce desire for her, once thwarted, had become tangled as much in relief as in grief. He regretted that his thoughts had turned back to her now.

"And you?" Warburg asked, veering away from that thicket of loss.

The man beside him dragged deeply on his cigarette. "I have Italian. It might help. I guess they need a lot of help."

"I guess they do," Warburg said, though without being sure who "they" were. He had a "they" of his own. One report had put the number of displaced people in Italy alone at half a million, the number of orphaned children at twenty thousand. *His.* Warburg let his eyes fall to the man's shoes. Civilian, black.

The man said, "Churchill's 'soft underbelly of the Mediterranean' turned out not to be so soft, eh? I thought I'd be back in Rome three months ago."

"Back?"

"I went to school there." When the man added, "Here's hoping Normandy is no Anzio," it was with the air of a man changing the subject.

Warburg was grateful that the noise was too loud for further talk. Smokes extinguished, he and his bench-mate fell back into the lull of their mutual isolation. Hours later, the plane's downward lurch snapped everyone alert, and the blackout shades on half a dozen small windows were lifted. At that, early-morning light divided the fuselage's interior into bright wedges. Warburg lifted the shade behind his ear and pressed his face to the cold glass, taking in coastline, tidy landscape, church-centered villages, squares of forest, rolling grassland, a pastoral scene all pretty and seemingly innocent. Yet the lingering haze of dawn made everything gray, like film shot for a Movietone newsreel. As the C-54 went into its descent, circling what he took to be Ciampino Airport, he saw several AAF planes ahead of them, tracking the same spiral down. As they went lower, Warburg made room at the window for the man next to him.

An amazing sight below — the airfield. Across the vast expanse of tarmac, aircraft and trucks vied with one another for space, with only the narrow crisscrossing runways clear of vehicles. Even there, the succession of planes, gliding in from alternating directions, was steady, so the landing strips were uncongested only by comparison.

"Bedlam," the man next to Warburg said, nodding at the airfield. Against the noise, the man was again speaking at the top of his voice. "Which is from 'Bethlehem'— did you know that?"

Warburg looked at him. As Warburg had done only moments before, the man was shrugging off the parka that, at altitude, had kept him warm. "Bedlam Royal Hospital," the man continued. "The London insane asylum. Original name, Saint Mary's of Bethlehem."

Warburg thought of taking up the etymology challenge, but let it go, answering only, "It does look like madness down there."

The man bent over, bunching his coat to stow it. When he straightened, it was to remove as well his black suit coat, exposing a collarless white shirt with French cuffs, the links of which sparkled gold. He bent over again, this time to draw out of his valise an odd black garment with slings into which he slipped both arms, like a plainclothes cop donning a shoulder holster. Or like a proper T-man.

When the man reached behind his neck to snap a button, Warburg saw the clerical collar and realized he was witnessing the vesting of a Catholic priest. While he slipped his arms back into his suit coat, Warburg's impulse was to look away. But the priest was grinning, as if he enjoyed being watched. He spread his arms and said, "From Clark Kent to Superman." The way to cut off mockery is self-mockery. Warburg knew enough to see the small red tab at the collar as a sign of some rank. The priest put his hand out. "Also known as Kevin Deane. Nice to meet you."

"Hello, Father. I'm David Warburg."

"Oh, really? Warburg. I'm from New York. We have to talk, when we're down and can hear ourselves." With that he turned back to the window.

And so did Warburg, thinking, Here we go again.

Before sunrise that same morning, the second dawn after Rome's liberation, Marguerite d'Erasmo awakened from her first sound sleep in days. She untangled the bedclothes, flicked on the table lamp, rose, and went straight to the curtain that sheltered a corner of the room. She was in the garret of an old boarding house in Trastevere, the Tiber- side neighborhood where many of Rome's workers, artisans, students, and pensioners lived. This was the mansard flat she'd lived in before fleeing Rome months before. It had been kept for her by Signora Paoli, the building's aged *portiere,* who'd greeted her with an embrace upon her return the night before. Now, pulling the curtain aside, Marguerite found the oversized copper tub — still there. She hadn't dreamt it.

Originally a livestock drinking tank, the tub had been hoisted up to the building's attic when pipes for running water were installed to that level — not so long before Marguerite had found the place two years ago. The narrow trough was the furthest thing from a claw-footed lounging tub, but she remembered how the wooden back rest, sloping just so, had made it comfortable enough. Unlike the fine ladies' *vascas* in the rooms where she'd bathed as a child, Marguerite had learned to love this elongated animal waterer for its simplicity and for accommo- dating her tall, thin frame at full stretch. Brooding trances, warmth on her skin, lung-searing steam, peace — such were her prior associations with the tub, but this morning it looked all at once like a ready casket. She closed her eyes for a moment. Unaccountably, her nostrils were seized by the stench of urine, as if, in her absence, those farm animals had been here to reclaim the thing.

She reached for the left wall faucet and turned it. The tap sputtered, ran cold at first, gradually offering tepid water, and then, to her amaze- ment, hot. Scalding. Only then did she lean into the depth of the tub to plug the drain hole with a fist-sized lump of cork. This would be her first bath in weeks. Waiting for the enormous tub to fill, she fell back onto the bed, as if for a languid reverie. She let her arms and legs swing, as if trying to stay afloat, as Carlo's face broke into her mind.

The ache came screeching back. What were those first feelings of hers? The single-minded woman for whom he had been only the ex- otic Savoyard, with his mountain-man tangle of red hair and beard; how drawn she'd been by the political defiance that had made him a fugitive, the fire that she had taken to be all courage and virtue; her beau ideal of the responsible life in an age of wickedness — where was the unchastened woman of such perceptions now? Once, with her eyes closed like this, she could pretend that the fingers between her legs were his, as she had in the beginning imagined eventually giving herself to him. But the beginning was a lie. Who was she to have believed it?

This was no dream. Days before, she had left Trieste without Carlo, hidden in the stinking hold of a fishing boat that took her to Ancona. *Remember, O most blessed Virgin Mary . . .*

That she was changed forever by what had happened in these months since she'd fled Rome, after the Nazi occupation, was the base fact of her new condition — yet still an astonishment. She opened her eyes. At the window, the first glow of dawn had come. At this moment, in the rough hillside hut above the village of Vranjak, would come the soft rapping on her door as she lay in a shepherd's bed of quilted furs. Carlo's habit was to wake her at just this hour — since she was the sunshine, he always said. She knew that he had come this early at first hoping to make love to her. She had let him kiss her, had kissed him fiercely back, but no more than that. Marguerite had never been with a man. Until him.

Now the intolerable weight of hurt and guilt might have nailed her to the bed, but the tub was soon to overflow. Again she got up, this time stripping off her underwear and the soiled red bandanna she wore at her throat. She used the kerchief, despite his having given it to her and despite what it meant, to hide the hideous bruises there. Yes, despite. In her nakedness, there was no hiding the purple marks on her face, shoulders, and arms.

She slid into the trough, stifling a yelp at the heat. She stretched almost fully out. Down, the tide lapped at her clavicle. Her small breasts floated. Holding her nose to go under, the water swamped her, which was all it took to release her gasping sobs.

Leaving Rome months before, Marguerite — despite what she had already seen — had in no way been prepared for the mass of lost and desperate people she'd encountered as she moved through towns and villages.

As she'd hoped, her blue uniform and embossed Red Cross visa secured passage through German checkpoints and gained her access to the improvised camps that kept springing up. Her woman-and-child survey became real. She'd lost count of the hollow-eyed wives whose husbands were dead or forcibly taken off to labor camps in Germany; of the children alone, or doggedly holding hands; grandmothers clinging to a rosary. Despite the German occupation, desperate refugees were streaming into northeastern Italy from Slovenia and Croatia, where conditions, apparently, were even worse. Using a code of her own devising, she compiled lists of names and noted the locations of the camps, and the monasteries, convents, and schools that had been given over, in particular, to Jewish refugees. Always, she moved north. Geneva had become a fantasy destination, and the Red Cross headquarters where she would make her report drew her like the magnetic pole.

But the onset of winter had made passage into Switzerland impossible, and then, in Vicenza, an industrial city between Venice and Milan, Marguerite was caught in January's Allied bombing raids. Night after night the waves of roaring aircraft came, reducing whole neighborhoods to rubble — and reducing her sense of the great world to the narrow streets and hurt buildings around the Villa Rotonda, a decrepit Renaissance palace that had long served as a school, but was now a discreetly ad hoc hospital, where she found refuge.

Situated on the crest of a low hill, the villa was licensed as a sanitarium for lepers and syphilis sufferers, and was rumored to harbor victims of plague, which was why nearby Wehrmacht contingents left it alone. Actually, there were only a few actively infected patients in the place, and their afflictions, their skin lesions and blisters, were a kind of feint. The whispers about plague were manufactured. In fact, the Rotonda was devoted to caring for Italian resistance fighters for whom Vicenza was a center. Stymied through February and March, Marguerite found herself working as a nurse's helper, and that was where she met Carlo. It must have been the sustained madness of the bombing terror that so blinded her to what else marked him besides exotic charm.

Carlo Capra was the most dramatically beautiful man she had ever known, with his fiery red hair and beard, deep-throated laugh, eyes that caressed whatever they fell upon. He was shorter than she, but his limbs were supple, and, as his wound healed and he took his exercise in the solarium off the ward, she saw him return to a native feline grace. Bringing him trays, changing his bed linens, sitting with him as he slept and ate, she had never experienced such easy intimacy with a man. She was not prepared for the feelings he stirred in her, nor for rediscovering her own inbred wit—the playful, unselfconscious girl she once again became in his presence. "Our Socialist Barbarossa" she called him one day.

"Not Frederick Barbarossa!" Carlo countered. "Not the emperor who held the Pope's stirrup!"

"Redbeard, then," she shot back. "The pirate." He was delighted and reached for her. She skipped away from him, almost a dance move, a serving girl in a dockside tavern, and they laughed. How long had it been since her step had been so light?

Afternoons, they sat together with late-winter sunlight slanting in through the white curtains of the solarium, she in a narrow, straight-backed chair, he in a wicker love seat. In that otherworldly room she confided what she had experienced since Rome, both the suffering in the camps and the paradoxical lightness of feeling that came over her when she could somewhat assuage the pain of others. With needy children, she told him, she was spontaneous again. They readily took to her, and when she offered comfort, she felt comforted herself. Their wary mothers trusted her. On the road, practically a fugitive and sur-rounded by danger, she had discovered within herself the unlikely gift for functioning with equilibrium and efficiency inside a full-blown, unending nightmare.

Carlo understood. He knew suffering, and he knew danger. And he knew that functioning in the midst of horror, and surviving it, can bring a strange kind of joy. Having met her at that level of recent feel-ing, he then took her deeper, into the well of past feeling where their bond of intimacy was even stronger. Marguerite was able, for the first time, to turn inwardly back to her late father when Carlo told her the story of his, a Turin labor organizer, the editor of a Socialist newspaper who had been tortured by the Fascists and later killed in Rome's notorious Regina Coeli prison, the very place Marguerite's father had been held for a time. She'd had no idea, until she began to speak of it to him then, that her own parental grieving was so unfinished. Unknowingly, while talking, she moved from her chair to sit beside him in the love seat.

She told him of her recurring dream — how it was given to her to speak the mystic word that would bring her father and mother magically back to life, but then, before working the trick, she always woke. She could never remember what the magic word was. From the time that dream began, her parents' being dead was her fault. She prayed the *Memorare* — *Remember, O most gracious Virgin Mary* — again and again but all she could do was forget and be forgotten.

And she spoke to Carlo, most astonishingly, of how grief can be marbled with rage. It was a surprise to her, that afternoon in the solarium, when she found herself weeping as she talked, and equally surprising that he had been holding her hand. The first man ever to do that.

More than once, as she spoke to him of her father, it seemed Carlo was finishing her sentences in speaking of his own father. Yes, rage! When he confessed that a kind of lust for vengeance was what had taken him into the hills as a *Partigiano*, she was not appalled. That he seemed in that moment dangerous made her feel close to him. She was dangerous, too.

Carlo was at the Rotonda for the five weeks it took the badly infected flesh wound that had brought him there to begin to heal. In that time, once their bond of trust was established, he spoke to Marguerite of what he would return to, his Partisan unit based near the Sava River at the border of Slovenia and Croatia, territory that had been under Mussolini's control until Italy's capitulation in 1943. Since then, Germans had moved into the region, but the pressing conflict was with the Ustashe militia of the Nazi-friendly Croat state under the "petty Hitler," Ante Pavelic. Carlo could not pronounce Pavelic's name without a sneer.

It was when Carlo described the Ustashe death camp created expressly for children that Marguerite first imagined going to Croatia with him. She had heard of the Jasenovac concentration camp, where Serbs, Jews, and Roma had been gathered since early in the war. That many were being routinely murdered there was assumed, but now she understood who the murderers were. Still, she had not known of Sisak, the nightmare sub-camp Carlo described, saying it was a few dozen miles down the Sava from his base, in what he called the Partisan Fourth Zone. That evil Sisak could have sparked an impulse in her she was too guarded otherwise to admit — the impulse to be with Carlo — seemed shameful to her now.

But what he had described, how it cried out to be exposed! Thousands of children being held, as young as the age of three. He said they were being put to death in gas vans that made endless circuits on a huge former racetrack, a rubber hose channeling exhaust fumes back into the closed trucks crammed with little ones. He said that Ustashe guards had turned the gassing into a raucous game, with two or three of the tightly sealed vans roaring around the oval at the same time, as if it were a Grand Prix event. The winner was the truck all of whose young captives died first.

Sisak was not on any Red Cross list Marguerite knew of. Nor was any concentration camp anywhere in the German Reich, or in occupied Europe, known to be devoted only to children. If she were to make a report to Geneva, how could she not take along evidence of that? So she went with him.

Across those weeks, beginning in early April, moving from Italy into Croatia, Marguerite had left behind her pretense of Red Cross neutrality to assume, if not a formal place in Carlo's band of Partisan fighters, the role of fellow traveler, witness, helper. Carlo's men maintained one of the hand-along points in the fugitive chain for those fleeing the Balkans, helping Jews or Serbs or Gypsies or downed Allied pilots or simple deserters to make their escapes. From Budapest to Zagreb to Sobota to Ljubljana to Trieste, and then by boat to Ancona, Pescara, Bari, or other ports in the Allied-controlled south of Italy. Knots of frightened people arriving in the dark, departing in the dark,

carrying bundles, the men in long coats, the women wearing babush-
kas. Few, if any, children.

Where was Sisak? She wanted to see something of it for herself, but
Carlo said it was too risky. At one point, against his wishes, she made
her way alone to Zagreb hoping to contact the Yugoslav office of the
Red Cross — her colleagues. What did they know of the death camps?
But all she found at the appointed address was a bombed-out ruin.

She approached a woman in the street, but the woman spoke neither
Italian nor French. Marguerite mimed the acts of eating, sleeping, an
inoculation in the arm. She displayed her Red Cross credential with its
insignia. At that, the woman led her to a Franciscan monastery off the
city's main square. There, a timid, brown-robed friar took her into a
parlor, where she waited. After what seemed a long time, a man of authority came, another friar, but large, brusque, and with a face whose
features were organized around a dramatically pronounced harelip.
The notch at his mouth went all the way to the base of his nose, splay-
ing his nostrils. The deformity drew Marguerite's sympathy. *Whatsoever man that has a blemish,* the Scripture says, *he shall not approach
the altar.* She had never seen a lame or disfigured priest before, and
instinctively grasped with what dogged will he must have pursued his
vocation. That facial badge of suffering reinforced the trust she'd have
felt toward any priest. She was direct with him.

In answering her, the friar spoke in fluent Italian, but his voice was
high-pitched and had a distracting nasal resonance, an effect of the
cleft palate. While speaking, he had to continually wipe saliva from
his mouth, drainage from an open nasal cavity. He seemed unselfconscious, though, and flourished a white handkerchief as if for emphasis.
And emphasis there was. The Franciscan monastery was itself a center
for relief, the distribution of food and medicine, the rescue of the desperate ones. The friar knew whereof he spoke, and his handkerchief
fluttered as he became more agitated. Jasenovac, hah! The rumors
about Jasenovac were lies, Bolshevik propaganda. The friar had never
heard of a camp at Sisak, and insisted that in areas controlled by the
Ustashe government, children were being well cared for. He had been

to every refugee camp in Croatia and was certain that conditions were as positive as was humanly possible.

In the Serb-controlled areas to the east, the priest said, the story was very different. "The Serb Communists are beasts," he snarled, with a sudden pitilessness that dismayed her. His account, which contradicted everything Carlo had said, confused her. For Marguerite, his authority as a priest was near absolute. Robes like his, belted with a triple-knotted cincture — one knot each for poverty, chastity, obedience — spoke of righteousness. The saliva, eluding the handkerchief, dribbling pathetically from his chin, somehow added to his credibility.

When she returned to Vranjak, Carlo sharply rebuked her for having gone to Zagreb. When she told him what the priest had said, he only stared at her. His contempt could not have been plainer. "What priest was this?" he asked at last.

"I don't know his name. His face was deformed — his mouth. I never —"

"Vukas."

"What?"

"You spoke with Vukas!" At that, Carlo turned on his heel and left her. She didn't see him again until the hour of the wolf the next morning, when he came to the hut where she was sleeping. He had never come to her before dawn, in the darkness, nor had he ever entered without that soft knock of his. But this time he was above her, shaking her awake. "Come," he said. It did not occur to her not to do so.

They set out into the hills. Marguerite had to hurry to keep up with him. He strode ahead, certain of the trail. He carried a rifle, and across his shoulder was slung a leather bag. The forest was frighteningly dark, but as they moved the sky brightened, and before long they left the woods behind, ascending above the tree line. Mist rose from the gnarly grasses. It seemed to Marguerite that she and Carlo, trekking across the wild terrain, were its only living creatures.

From behind, she watched as Carlo's bobbing dark hair took on its familiar red hue, as if dawn came first to him, the pirate's privilege. They crested the peak of a high hill just as the upper edge of the sun cracked the far horizon. Like a hunter hiding from that light, Carlo threw himself on the ground, and Marguerite imitated him. He pulled binoculars from his bag, peered through them, at what she could not tell. But then, in the shadowy valley below, she made out the structures of a small hamlet centered on the cupola of a church, the snake of a road, and the gash of a river that cut the landscape in two. Beside the river — then she saw it. The large oval of a racecourse, a dirt track defined by fence rails running all the way around. Inside the oval was an expansive shantytown of shacks and tents. The sun had yet to illuminate the valley, but without being told, she knew what she was seeing.

Sisak.

Carlo said nothing. They waited. The mist evaporated. A glacier of sunlight crept down from the far hills, bringing the valley to life. People began to stir in the shantytown. An approaching truck appeared on the distant stretch of road, followed by another, and another. This convoy swooped into the scene, followed by a pair of large black autos. Suddenly all was bustling at the racecourse. Carlo leaned on his elbows and put the binoculars to his face again. After a time, he handed them to Marguerite, with the single word *"Selezione."*

With the added clarity of the binoculars, Marguerite was able to see that the racetrack was strung around with coiled barbed wire, off the razor edges of which bounced the first rays of the now unfettered sunlight. At the center of the track stood the dominating figure of a brown-robed friar. Beside him, joined to his arm by a leash, was a tall, lean dog. Even at that distance, Marguerite could sense the ferocity of its snarl — a Doberman pinscher. Each time the friar snapped the leash, the dog lunged forward.

The friar conducted the selection as a maestro does a concert, waving with his free hand a white handkerchief, like a baton. Figures tumbled out of the backs of the trucks, and others lined them up. They were children, some very young, some teenagers. They were being put into rows by adults, some of whom were dressed in brown robes, other Franciscans, and some in the black uniforms of the Pavelic militia, with the telltale red-and-white-checkered crest emblazoned on their shoulders, on the peaks of their caps. Ustashe. The children were channeled toward a makeshift table, over which the large friar presided as if it were an altar. Marguerite adjusted the focus wheel on the binoculars, shifting to his face. The fissure in his mouth beaded with saliva. Vukas. The priest from Zagreb.

She lowered the binoculars, but Carlo pushed them back toward her eyes. "No," he commanded. "Watch!"

Vukas directed the traffic, more policeman now than maestro. Each child was presented to him. First Vukas jerked the dog's lead, sending it with flashing teeth at the child's face. When the child responded with horror, the friar pulled the dog back. It seemed a test, a way of measuring the child. The friar then bent forward, performed an examination of some kind, seeming perversely to chuck the chins of the little angels. With a wave of that handkerchief he sent the child off one way or another — toward the shanties inside the oval or back onto the tarp-covered bed of an adjacent truck. Terrified of the dog, the children bolted away. From the distance, the priest, except for his dog, seemed almost to have a kindly air. Onto the heads of some he placed a hand, as if in blessing, but then Marguerite saw that those were the ones pulled aside and loaded again into the trucks. What, were the selected ones chosen by the blemished priest for being unblemished?

The death race. Three trucks. No, four. Loaded with boys and girls, toddlers, teenagers. Soon the canvas rear flaps of each truck were stitched tightly closed, the cords fixed with rods. A length of firehose was attached to the exhaust pipe of each truck and fed into the bed.

Still staring, Marguerite said, "Can't you stop this?"

Carlo replied, "I am stopping it. That is what I am doing."

But not this morning. Not this race. When at last the trucks lined up on the track, Vukas held his arm aloft, now using the handkerchief as a starter's flag. His head fell back in laughter, and from his twisted mouth a great uproarious cry of triumph must have come. The flag fell and the trucks leapt forward, gunning up to full speed. Vukas let his dog go, and it began to chase after the trucks, to devour them. Because of the intimate view through the binoculars, it seemed Marguerite should have heard the roaring engines and the howling dog, but she did not. Indeed, the rigid silence from across the span of distance — the trucks, the laughing, the dog, and God knows what sounds being emitted by the throats of children — lent the scene its ghostly unreality.

Around and around the trucks raced. At each pass, Vukas and the knot of his underlings could be seen to cheer like students at a football match. A soldier appeared with a tray of earthen-gray beer steins. Vukas seized one and held it aloft. All did the same, foam splashing. Vukas cried out some ritual phrase, and the others echoed it in reply. And all at once, maestro again, he began waving that white handkerchief, as if this were a rathskeller and the time had come for drinking songs.

The friars' brown robes swayed in time to the music, countered by the metronomes of rosary beads hanging from their cinctures. *Ein Prosit, ein Prosit!* As the trucks thundered around the deadly circuit, the priest and his cronies drank and sang. Laughed, drank, and sang. The dog, at last, collapsed at Vukas's feet, and the friar bent down to pet it, *Good dog.*

Later, in a clearing in the forest where they'd stopped to rest on the way back to Vranjak, Carlo said, "I am sorry. But that is your priest."

Marguerite nodded, but, awash in anguish, as in night terrors, she had nothing to say.

Carlo solemnly untied the knot of the red bandanna at his throat and removed it from around his neck. She did not resist as he put it around her neck, saying, "Now you are one of us." He tied the kerchief for her and adjusted it as if it were an item of apparel, nothing more. "The red," he said then, "in Red Cross."

Marguerite's eyes filled. An abyss had opened inside her, and she was falling in it. The feeling was, she would fall forever.

Carlo touched her cheek. She touched his hand. As if that were the signal he'd been waiting for, he kissed her. She was defenseless against him. No, she was defenseless against herself. She returned his kiss, and then, momentarily, matched the press of his body with her own as he pushed her down onto the grass. But when she closed her eyes, the feeling of falling gave way to something else, and Carlo assumed it was desire, what he had been waiting for. "*Ora!*" he whispered urgently. Now!

But she stopped him. To his "Now!" she said simply, "No!" Her eyes were once more wide open, seeing everything, including how the obscene violence at Sisak had sparked his erotic desire for her. The authority of her abrupt recognition was absolute. When she had firmly shut her eyes, the face she had seen in the dark was not Carlo's, as it should have been, but the grotesquely twisted visage of a rabbit's lip. Vukas. The devil priest. That he, not Carlo, was the man inside her mind carried the jolt of a slap. Vukas was the meaning of her "No!"

Carlo, unaware of all this, pulled back, rose quickly to his feet, snatched up the rifle and bag, and strode off, resentful. He was apparently indifferent to whether she followed. Follow she did, but in a fog of confusion that had yet to lift. Marguerite d'Erasmo had glimpsed her fate. Wrong about a priest, she would be proven wrong, in another brief and ugly interlude, about the only man she had yet imagined loving, when he was shot dead — not by Fascists, but by her.

She came up from under the water, choking.

The man on the bicycle lunged out of the rampant foliage and down the narrow path from the Villa Borghese, the vast Roman park looming above the northern margin of the ancient city center. Giacomo Lionni had been a named fugitive on the Nazi list for seven months, since October 1943, and on that verdant plateau he had survived. The German occupiers, apparently spooked by the Borghese throng of riffraff, had left its precincts alone. But now the Germans were gone, as he'd seen for himself the day before. *Gone!* Yet he rode like one in danger of being caught.

An unwelcome glow of first light low in the sky emphasized the last of the night's shadows, and, on his bicycle, he clung to them — all but invisible. As Lionni sped down to the Piazza del Popolo, his sudden impulse was to let go of the handlebars — no hands! — as if he were a boy instead of a half-lame man nearing fifty. The heavy canvas roll slung across his back made balance a more delicate project than usual, but this was a flight of pure joy. *The Germans are gone!*

The two-wheeled conveyance was its own delight this morning, since the German occupiers had outlawed bicycles. Partisans had used them to hit and run. Therefore, *Biciclette Proibito!* How Romans had snorted at the Fritz hysteria, even while obeying.

The piazza's central fountain was dry, and no cars were passing through, not because of the early hour but because of the gas shortages. Yet the plaza was far from vacant. Ghostly figures had preceded him down from the overgrown acres of the Villa Borghese with its tents, tin shanties, and open fires. In these first mists of dawn, the otherwise silent piazza hummed with the deep, plaintive moan of the specters' collective longing. Their apparently aimless circling was in fact purposeful, for they were in search of food.

Soon market trucks and carts from what few vegetable plots remained within reach of the city would be crossing the plaza toward the center of Rome. With luck, well-placed members of the plaza throng would be able to snatch a potato or a round of bread. Or perhaps a merciful farmer might toss down an overripe melon, a bruised cabbage, a handful of beans.

This was the second day of the Americans' arrival, and housebound Romans could begin to believe that the horror on the other side of the window was gone. The SS and the Gestapo, the black uniforms, knee-high jackboots, lightning bolts, death's heads, eagles, swagger sticks, red armbands, and broken crosses — all gone, replaced by a quite different breed.

American and British soldiers had stormed into the undefended city like bearers of bread, circus ringmasters — that was their mood. Straw-haired farm boys riding tanks like tractors, straddling gun turrets like jockeys, declared their supremacy by hitching their helmets at their belts, bareheadedness a victor's boast. The GIs offered Lucky Strikes and Hershey bars in return for straw-wrapped bottles of Chianti, embraces, and what they'd already learned to call *baci* — kisses. The honking of jeeps, the clanking treads of flower-bedecked half-tracks, and the whoosh of double-propped P-38 Lightnings — would it not all be music to which Romans could dance as if they had never cheered Il Duce?

As Lionni wheeled into the Via del Corso, a church-lined boulevard that ran from the Piazza del Popolo to the base of the Capitoline Hill, his mind went, as it often did, to the stories his father had told him about this street. Because it ran straight as an arrow for more than a kilometer, the Corso, beginning in the Renaissance, had been used as a horse track during Carnival—hence its name, for racecourse. But for several hundred years, the climax of pre-Lent Corso festivities included the sporting event Romans most loved: the punitive footrace of the Jews. They were outfitted in conical hats and clownish robes and forced to compete against one another, up and down pavement littered with horseshit from the earlier races. Eventually one staggering Jew was declared the winner, and wrapped in purple. His prize was the privilege of kissing the Pope's shoe. The fucking Pope!

Lionni approached the Corso's terminal point in the Piazza Venezia and its palazzo balcony—fucking Mussolini! But he was gone, too. Out of Rome's shadows would come the zombie witnesses to all that the vast throng of Il Duce's former minions would want to forget or deny. And wasn't Lionni himself summoning the most damning of those witnesses? As soon as he'd seen with his own eyes the American commanding general, Clark, standing yesterday on the hood of a jeep beside the Arch of Titus, surrounded by correspondents with notepads, Lionni had rushed back to his old building to haul his now permitted bicycle out of the cellar. Thus began his frantic round from one Jewish hiding place to another, all over Rome. He knew the secret hidey-holes because he himself had arranged for most of them, beginning more than two years before. The circuit took him into the night and through it, and finally back to the Borghese gardens for his tarp, which he'd rolled up and slung on his back. Dawn had come too quickly, making him late for what he had to do next.

But the Jews he'd encountered on the Appian Way—or rather, beneath it—came back into his mind. As dusk was falling less than twelve hours ago, he had banged on the door of a neglected old wayfarers' chapel, in the floor of which was a forgotten entrance to the ancient tunnels where fugitive Christians had once hidden from the pagan legions—the so-called catacombs. Last October, Lionni had ushered several dozen Jews down into that network of caves through this very chapel door, and he was certain they were still down there.

But no one was answering. "It's Jocko!" he called, banging so loudly the door shook on its hinges. "Jocko! Jocko!" He was not surprised that they wouldn't show themselves after all these months, but surely they would do so if they knew it was he.

At last the chapel door was pulled slowly open, exposing a gaunt old man ready to be shot, having risked this because he had less to lose than others. Seeing Lionni, the man fell into his arms. "Jocko!" he whispered again and again, as if greeting the Messiah's cousin. Lionni went down into the caverns, passing through alcoves and burial rooms, all the while saying, "The Americans have come. All is well in Rome." Women clutched at his hands, children stroked his coat. "The Americans have come," he repeated. "All is well in Rome." The simple phrase came haltingly from Lionni's lips because what he beheld in the cramped, ill-lit tunnels and cells — pale-eyed ghosts, scarecrow women, stooped men, terrified children — made him weep. Again and again the Jews embraced him, uttering blessings. In the one spacious chamber, red lanterns had been hung on either side of an improvised ark and its Torah scroll, and when he saw it, Lionni knelt. He was not a religious man, yet sobs racked him, bending him over, so that his forehead scraped the limestone floor.

Hour after hour through the night, Lionni had seen such Jews emerge pale and blinking from attics and cellars in Trastevere, cloisters of walled convents, rectories, monasteries, back rooms of shops, ateliers of the Corso, courtyards of the Via Margutta. "The Americans have come," his mantra, repeated in Italian, but also in Yiddish, for those from across the Alps. "All is well in Rome." And then came the antiphon: "Jocko! Jocko!"

At each place, Lionni appointed someone to make a careful list of the names of those who were emerging, the beginning of the roster of survival that he would check against the roster of hiding he'd compiled months ago, before he himself had had to disappear. Assuming, of course, that the original roster, and the one who kept it safe, had survived. All may indeed be well in Rome, but for Lionni the horror was far from over. The Nazi death machine was still grinding toward its worst, and Lionni was still looking for a wooden shoe to throw.

Hence this ride on his newly precious bicycle. He pumped harder, rising from the seat for heft, pushing through the Piazza Venezia.

Slung across his shoulder and secured with ropes across his chest was the rolled-up canvas that had served Lionni as his fugitive domicile on those all too frequent occasions when, warned, he had slipped out of one basement room or another until, with the milder weather, he'd wound up in the open-air Borghese acres. But that was over now, and it wasn't for a tent that he needed the canvas this morning.

He was headed for the walled complex of buildings not far from the central railway station, the Termini. The Ministry of Transport was the headquarters of the national railroad, which Mussolini had so famously run on time. How Il Duce accomplished that Italian wonder was less well known: he would order the engineers of tardy trains to be flogged.

Lionni was making his move in the small window of time between the Germans' departure and the return of Italian security, whatever it would amount to under Allied control. Since the Nazis had disbanded the Carabinieri, today at least there would be no civil law enforcement of any kind. So he was counting on the ministry's offices being penetrable.

Soon Lionni passed groups of American soldiers bivouacked on the grassy apron of several great villas, once and future islands of privilege but for now mere campsites. Lionni waved at one of the guards, who happily raised both arms in return.

In the last weeks of the occupation, Lionni had become obsessed with the Ministry of Transport. He had surreptitiously observed it, pretending, variously, to be a street sweeper, a railroad lugger, a garbage man — always in the same billed worker's cap and soiled blue smock. He became familiar with the entire perimeter of the compound.

Now, by the time he reached the enclosure's back side, the soft light of true dawn bathed the rough wall. A lingering cloud of mist promised rain. In this light Lionni would be fully exposed, but he had no choice. He knew from earlier visits that this rearmost wall had been built of remnant cement blocks — jagged, odd-shaped, or broken —

resulting in just the protruding foot ledges and handholds he would need. Dismounting his bicycle, he pushed it behind a pile of disused pallets and crates. He stood back to assess the wall.

It was twice his own height, and though formidable was not insurmountable. But along the top of the wall were embedded shards of broken glass which glistened in the fresh sunshine. Green and brown predominated, every edge a threat. Quickly untying and unfurling his erstwhile tent and bedroll, Lionni doubled the canvas over again, then hurled it up and onto the thorny crown of the barrier. Pushing and rearranging pallets and crates, he made a stack against the wall, then scrambled onto it. Lionni prided himself on his agility, despite his shortened leg, the result of a badly set bone break in childhood. From the top of the pile of lumber scraps, he slapped himself against the wall, found the ledges he needed, and clambered skyward. Atop the wall, the heavy canvas might prove just thick enough to protect his body from the shards of glass. He hurled himself up, vaulted to keep his weight from settling, then plunged into the compound, finding it, as he expected, to be deserted.

Master of Ceremonies

T HE C-54 BOUNCED and bounced again when it hit the runway. Inside the plane, aft, a stack of wooden crates broke loose from its cords, causing cartons to crack open, spilling dozens of cans, which then banged forward like cannon shot as the plane decelerated. Several struck Warburg's feet—unexpected pain.

Turning sharply, the plane pulled quickly off the runway, causing more cartons to spill. "Captain Marvel has to get us out of the way," Deane said, "the rate these birds are coming in."

"I'm impressed, Father." Warburg grinned at the priest, drawn to him. "You seem to know your way around."

"*Savoir-faire*, my friend. French for 'savvy fear.'" Then Deane matched Warburg's grin with one of his own. "I hate flying." He held up the book he'd been reading more or less the whole way across. A prayer book, with ribbons dripping out of its gold-edged pages.

As the plane slowed, the roar of the engine faded, and Warburg could speak almost normally. "So you prayed us across."

"So you're a Warburg."

"Not the way you mean," Warburg said. "I'm from Vermont."

"Oh, well, there are Warburgs in New York."

"I've heard."

"Felix Warburg has helped Archbishop Spellman with the New York Foundling Home. Mrs. Warburg is on the board of directors.

She's very nice." Deane's easy smile was the one he used in Park Avenue salons.

"You work with Archbishop Spellman?"

"Until this week I was his MC."

"Master of ceremonies?"

"Yes, but not the way the Toastmasters mean it. In the Church, the master of ceremonies is just that. On the altar, at the big guy's elbow, I hand him the chalice when he's ready."

"And off the altar? Trusted assistant there, too, I'll bet. Chief of staff or something."

Deane lowered his head, a self-mocking bow.

Warburg said, "I've heard that it was Archbishop Spellman who finally shut up the anti-Semite priest Father Coughlin. Would the master of ceremonies have been involved with that?"

Deane's failure to reply read less like discretion than modesty.

"Was that you?" Warburg pressed.

"Coughlin is a disgrace. The archbishop didn't need me to tell him that."

"And if you don't mind my asking, Father, what's so important in Rome that the archbishop has sent over his right-hand man?"

"Are you kidding? If Secretary Morgenthau can send across his Man Friday, why shouldn't Spelly?"

"Spelly?"

Deane laughed. "What do you call Morgenthau when he's not looking?"

"Mr. Secretary."

Then they both laughed.

The plane halted, and in short order fore and aft hatches were thrown open. Bright light poured in at opposite ends of the cargo hold, with flotillas of dust motes dancing in the sunshine. Crewmen leapt aboard, ignoring the passengers, who were trying to gather their belongings as the offloading of crates began. It wasn't until the pilot came from the cockpit and barked orders that the cargo handlers pulled back, and a roughly hewn lumber stairway was pushed up to the forward hatch so the passengers could get off. Warburg followed Deane out into the morning, each man with a single valise, both men over six feet tall. The priest and the Treasury official made a pair, although the priest appeared to be older by a decade or more.

Deane carried his prayer book under his arm. When he saw Warburg taking note of it again, he said, "The Roman breviary. Known to my kind as 'the wife.'" He grimaced, and smiled.

Having left their plane behind, they crossed an open stretch of tarmac and soon found themselves in a man-high maze of stacked canned-goods crates and burlap sacks, and also of ammo boxes and pyramids of shells. The supplies had been successfully offloaded from dozens of planes like theirs, but there was no claimant in sight and no operations command. Clearly the only drill here was to empty out aircraft and get them gone. Unhelmeted soldiers hustled down the aisles of cargo with urgency but no evident purpose. The C-54 passengers were misfits in this corner of Ciampino. Ignored, they snaked in single file along the narrow lane of the open-air warehouse, following one another dumbly. Those in uniform — bars, brass leaves, and silver eagles on epaulets and collars — tossed salutes back at the occasional dull-eyed GI who'd bothered to salute first. These soldiers had been through hell, and looked it.

It was not a terminal to which the passengers were headed, but a massive hangar, the near corner of which had been converted into some kind of personnel processing center, with Army clerks behind counters fashioned of planks set across stacked crates. Forms were being stamped and queued soldiers coursed through successive lines. Compared to the apparent anarchy of the outdoor depot, the hangar scene exuded an air of relative order, and Warburg was drawn to it.

But as he, Deane, and the others were about to leave the tarmac, a large canvas-sided truck came wheeling in from behind the hangar, nearly running them down. A man and a woman leapt down from opposite sides of the truck cab — the woman being the driver — and all at once there was an outbreak of argument. A pair of clipboard-wielding

NCOs pushed back against the truckers, and then MPs materialized. They, too, got rough with the pair, whose furious shouts fell strangely on Warburg's ear until he realized that this was Italian. His Berlitz was useless.

Since the American soldiers patently had no idea what was being said, Monsignor Deane stepped in front of the MPs with upraised arms. "*Per favore! Per favore!* Hold on, folks. Calm down! *Calmi! Calmi!*" The easy authority of his intervention—his size, the striking black of his suit, his Roman collar, the rich tenor of his voice—had its effect, and the contretemps faded. All yielded to the priest. He engaged the two Italians. It was quickly apparent that the woman was in charge. After a set of rapid-fire exchanges, Deane turned to one of the Army clipboard holders, a sergeant. "They're the Croce Rossa, the Red Cross."

Only then did Warburg notice the faded symbol on the truck's canvas, the familiar cross the color of dried blood. The truck, too, had been through hell. Warburg's gaze, now set loose, went to the woman. The first thing to strike him was her bruised face, an eye half closed in its blackened well. Tall and thin, her knee-length blue skirt and blouse hung loosely on her body. Her calves were strikingly unshaven. Taking in her face again, he saw, apart from the bruises, its emaciation, a hint of weary glamour in the way her cheekbones protruded. There was also an accidental glamour in the angle at which her beret was cocked, keeping the other side of her face in shadow. Because of bruises there, too? Her pale lips made clear that she wore no makeup, but the crescent under her eye was dark enough to seem penciled in. A red sliver of what he took to be an undershirt showed at her throat, reminding Warburg, oddly, of the priest's crimson collar tab. The woman, suddenly aware that Warburg was looking at her, met his gaze with such directness that, despite himself, he returned it. For a long few seconds, they stared at each other.

"They are here to pick up food," Deane was saying to the sergeant, "for an open-air orphanage." Deane turned to Warburg. "She said there are more than a thousand untended children holed up in the Quirinal gardens — lame, lost, abandoned. They just congregated there, without adults. She has to get them milk and bread."

"We got no orders for that, Father," the sergeant said. "My orders are to watch out for black market operators."

"It's Monsignor, Sergeant," Deane said easily. Without knowing the subtleties, Warburg recognized the pulling of rank.

"Sorry, Monsignor. But we don't sign anything out of here until the major shows."

"When will that be?"

"Who knows? Look around, Father — I mean Monsignor. Sorry. You see any officers? Logistics staff meeting, probably. We're supposed to have motor pool support here by now, but do you see any vehicles? Typical."

"Meanwhile, Sergeant, these Red Cross folks have orphans to feed. She said the kids are living on *castagne* — chestnuts. Raw chestnuts. Look here. What's on that one pallet alone? Fifty boxes of Carnation Farms? Come on, Sarge. That's milk."

"No can do, Monsignor. Not feasible." He flashed his clipboard. "*Capiche?* No signature, no release."

Warburg stepped forward. "I'll sign that. I'm David Warburg. WRB." Having pronounced the initials with authority, he counted on them meaning nothing to the soldier. But he flashed his leather credentials folder with a flourish, then held it before the man's face, requiring him to examine it. "That's the secretary of the treasury's signature there. And you see the service grade — GS-19, Sergeant. Think brigadier general. Let's call this *my* shipment." Warburg was trumping not only the sergeant, but the priest. "Evaporated milk. Civilian disposition. It's *meant* for the children. You can let this one pallet go. By the time the Red Cross comes back for anything else, standing orders will have been issued. You'll receive a commendation. Where do I sign?" Warburg took the clipboard out of the soldier's hands, leaving him to roll the words "brigadier general" across the craps table of his brain. Warburg pulled a fountain pen out of his inside pocket, uncapped it, and waved it at the bottom of the page, a wand. Handing the clipboard back, he said, "Now get these people some help loading that stack onto their truck."

"Yes, Sir."

"And get them some of that flour."

The sergeant turned and barked orders at his crew, the chain of command kicking the dog.

Monsignor Deane spoke briefly to the Italians and moved away toward the hangar, where in one cleared area the C-54 passengers' luggage was being offloaded. As Warburg moved to follow Deane, the woman half reached out a hand and surprised him by saying in English, "Thank you, Sir."

"You are welcome, Miss," he said, struck again by her face. Battered as it was, he saw that she had healed somewhat. The bruising was not fresh. On impulse, as if this were the breakup of a conference on Pennsylvania Avenue, he pulled out his wallet, withdrew a business card, and handed it to her. "If I can help," he said. She took the card and pocketed it without a word. Without seeing its useless letters and numbers, his office in Washington.

A few minutes later, outside the pedestrian door on the hangar's far side, Warburg rejoined Deane. The sun had climbed in the sky and was asserting itself, a hot day coming. The rumble of jeeps, small trucks, and animal carts competed to ignore the shrill whistles of numerous MPs. Warburg put his suitcase down beside the priest's.

"Hey, by the way," Deane said, "nice move back there with the Red Cross people."

"You set the pick, Father. Or should I say 'Monsignor'?" Warburg smiled.

"Pick-and-roll, David. Like a couple of point guards. And why don't we make it 'Kevin'? Since you're not in the club."

"The club?"

"The Church."

"What if I'm a convert?"

"Are you?"

Warburg laughed, but also, at the base of his spine, shivered. Convert? "No. No."

"You still play b-ball?" the priest asked.

Warburg shook his head. "Not in years." A pair of exceptionally tall men, recognizing each other — a different club. "But you were no point guard."

"Neither were you. Not bad for a pair of posted forwards, then."

After a beat of silence, Warburg said, "What did you make of that woman?"

"What about her?"

"Bruises. On her face and neck."

"Get used to bruises, David."

Warburg turned to the priest — was there a hint of condescension? But he saw only a matter-of-fact clarity in Deane.

Pushing toward them through the mess of traffic was a large black sedan. Its horn was blaring. "This is me," Deane said. Fixed to the car's front bumper were a pair of gold-and-white flags. "You need a lift?"

Warburg shrugged. "I guess my reception committee didn't show." In fact, he felt a familiar stab of resentment, the goddamn Army, the goddamn State Department, both primed to ignore the WRB.

"Where are you going?"

"Clark's headquarters, wherever that is."

"So you *are* brass. We'll find it. Hop in."

The driver, on the other side of a half-shut glass screen, was dressed in a chauffeur's cap and suede gloves, even in June. They set out along the multilane main road to Rome, but it was so pitted with unrepaired shell holes and so congested that the driver turned off. Soon they were a lone vehicle following a narrow road hugging a meandering stream.

With Warburg ensconced beside him in the back seat, Deane explained that he'd spent four years at the North American College in Rome, earning a doctorate in theology at the Gregorianum, the pontifical university. He loved Italy. He loved Rome. He hated what Mussolini had done to it. Never mind the Krauts.

He fell silent and looked out the window. The fields around them were barren and unplanted — battleground, not farmland. The road also twisted through battered villages of ruined buildings and burnt huts. The faces of villagers lifted at their passing. Those vacant expressions may have been what prompted the priest to open his book. Deftly, he flipped a ribbon, and his lips began to move silently.

After passing yet another battered town, Warburg couldn't help interrupting him. "The church belfries are all destroyed," he said. "Every church we've passed. The Germans attacked the churches?"

"Just the towers. Because of lookouts and snipers. It's the first thing that approaching artillery targets. Belfries. Steeples. And not just the Germans. That's our propaganda. The Allies do it, too."

"How do you know this?"

"My job has been to keep the archbishop briefed."

"On the war?"

"The battle for Rome. It was touch and go here for months. After Clark blew up Monte Cassino, the Church was as afraid of the Allies as of the Germans. With good reason, actually. The only destruction you'll see when we get to the city was caused by our own B-17s."

An awkward silence settled between them. Deane went back to his breviary. After some moments, though, he lifted his eyes to stare straight ahead. "WRB," he said.

Warburg did not reply.

"You said WRB."

"That's right. War Refugee Board."

"Morgenthau."

"Yes. I told you, I'm with the Treasury Department. I'm setting up in Rome."

"Where?"

"To be determined. A lot to be determined."

"But the 'Board' . . . the name is 'War Refugee,' but actually your work is about . . ."

What is it with this word, Warburg wondered, that makes people hesitate before using it? He finished Deane's sentence. "About the Jews. Yes. If we put the word 'Jew' in the name, Roosevelt couldn't possibly have approved it, and Congress would have howled. But Jews are the point."

"I know what's happened to Jews."

"What's *still* happening, Father."

"I share your concern, David," Deane said, but with the air of a man steering away from what he's thinking. "In fact, you and I have a lot in common. Call it coincidence. You've come here for the War Refugee Board. I've come for Pontificia Commissione di Assistenza. Catholic Relief Services. Have you heard of us?"

"Of course."

"Boils down to the same thing—refugee assistance. Archbishop Spellman provides most of the funds for the Vatican relief agency. We've raised millions in the States, a nationwide campaign, still at it. Now that Rome is open, we're betting the farm. Call it the Belmont Stakes, third race in the Triple Crown. I'm Spellman's jockey. I'm to be the Commissione's deputy director." Something in the way Deane announced this implied it was to be his official role—but perhaps not his only one. "Maybe I can help you."

"I'd appreciate anything we can do together," Warburg said, but carefully. He could not put his finger on the source of his unease with this guy. Everything he said carried an echo of the unsaid. Warburg added, "My operation is not off the ground yet."

"My operation's been going strong since Emperor Constantine." A crack, but there was no levity in Deane as he made it. "We're feeding people across the continent," he continued. "Every Catholic parish in Europe is a franchise soup kitchen of the Holy See. And we've been poised for this moment. With the liberation of Rome, the walking dead will start to climb out of their graves. All the feeding and caring that's been done up to now is mere prelude. As the liberation line moves north behind Clark's red-hot rake, you'll see. Tens of thousands. Hundreds of thousands. Not just Jews."

Warburg heard the echo of Morgenthau's D.C. critics: the Nazis are oppressing millions—why single out one group? "Relief is one thing," Warburg said. "I'm still thinking about rescue. That's what the R in WRB means to me."

"What can you do from Rome?"

"More than I can do from Washington."

"We protected them in Rome," Deane said. "You'll see."

"By 'them' you mean Jews? By 'we' you mean—the Vatican?"

"No offense, David, but you may not know much about how the Holy See and its dependencies operate. A mark of the Catholic Church is unity."

"Does that include bishops? I've been paying attention to Budapest, waiting to hear some moral instruction from the archbishop there. He seems friendly to Hitler, to put it mildly."

"We were speaking of Rome."

"Yes. I've been paying attention there, too. Do you know of the Cistercian nunnery in the Via Sicilia?"

"No. There are a thousand convents in Rome. If the Cistercians are helping, so are many others. 'Nunnery,' by the way, is a pejorative word. Elizabethan slang for 'brothel.'"

Warburg ignored the correction. "I know that Jews are coming out of hiding all over Rome today," he said.

"Including out of Vatican City itself," Deane said coldly.

"I hadn't heard that."

The two stared at each other for a long moment, a thick silence. Finally Warburg said, "Look, I understand that no Jew will have escaped this nightmare without some Catholic having helped. That's obvious." He paused before adding, "I'm also aware that far from all Roman Jews were protected. You know of last October's arrests, when the Vatican said nothing."

"Yes. Tragic. Deeply tragic. I wish it could have been prevented. But every able-bodied Italian male has been hunted by the Gestapo through these full nine months. Thousands of *them* are in slave labor camps, too. The terror has been total, David."

"And also quite particular, Father. We know by now that there are slave labor camps and there are death camps. Not the same thing. The Pope criticizes Allied bombing, but not Nazi horrors."

"Yes. Knowing the Allies will not take his words out on innocents. Unlike Hitler." Deane slapped his prayer book shut.

The car slowed, entering another village. This one was different: a throng of people clogged the small fountain square. The sun had climbed in the sky, and the piazza was awash in the full morning glare. On one side, rubble from a collapsed building had been pushed out of the road. Ripped mattresses and broken bits of furniture were strewn about. Deane's driver leaned on the horn. As the vehicle breasted through, men and women had to hop away from the bumper, and when their eyes took in the Vatican flags, some shook fists. Some faces twisted with curses.

The driver snarled a phrase back toward his passengers, and Deane explained, "A Red town. Communist."

All at once, the car was adjacent to the fountain, and there the crowd was more compactly gathered. In its midst, balanced on an improvised pit of smoldering coals, was a steaming open kettle. Beside that stood a naked young woman, each of whose arms was being pinned by other women.

Deane craned forward toward the driver and asked his question: What's going on? But the driver was gape-mouthed and did not reply. He dropped the car out of gear, but it continued to inch forward. Most of the people, several dozen, were too intent on the naked woman to notice the car. A heavy bearded man had shears at the woman's head, hacking at her hair. Her submissiveness was total. Out of the nearby cauldron rose the fumes of boiling tar, and to the side, a clutch of boys were wrestling with chicken carcasses, stripping them of feathers.

The car was still rolling slowly forward when Deane opened his door. Warburg did the same with his. What the hell—?

When the car stopped, the two men got out and, mirroring each other, moved silently forward. They towered over the people in the square. Their height and the sight of Deane's clerical garb subdued them. Now the papal flags fixed to the car's bumper could be seen to fully register. The man with the shears stopped cutting, and the women holding the girl loosened their grip. She slumped to the ground, hiding her nakedness in a crouch. With one hand she covered her scalp.

"*Che cosa?*" Deane asked.

"*Puttana dei tedeschi!*" one of the women snarled.

While Deane spoke to her, and then exchanged unpleasant words with the man holding the shears and with others in the crowd, Warburg removed his suit coat and went to the girl. He stooped and draped his coat around her. Coaxing her to her feet, he turned her toward the car. A large bald man blocked his way. "Move!" Warburg said. The man stepped to the side. While the priest continued his rebukes, Warburg led the girl away.

The intimidated chauffeur had not stirred from his seat. Warburg gestured for the girl to get into the back of the car. He followed her in and closed the door. Taking that as his signal, Deane abruptly walked away from the crowd, got in on his side, giving the girl her space, and softly closed his door — no parting rebuke needed. He quietly commanded the driver, "*Vada!*"

A few minutes later, out in the deserted countryside again, Deane ordered the vehicle stopped. The girl seemed in shock, slumped, as unmoving as marble, eyes shut. Deane, addressing Warburg over her head, said, "They call it pitchcapping here. Goes back to the days of witches. '*Puttana.*' Slept with some German. 'Horizontal collaborator.' I'm afraid there'll be a lot of payback now. Especially from the Reds."

Deane got out, went back to the trunk, opened it, and opened his suitcase. He returned with a white garment over his arm. He gently told the girl to get out. When she did, he looked away while handing her the robe. Rousing herself, she donned it, the hem falling to her ankles, the pleated yoke settling on her shoulders. Once unfurled, the linen could be seen to be trimmed with lace and red piping. But for her bloodshot eyes, moist nostrils, and soiled cheeks, she looked all at once less the shorn victim than an uncoiffed angel — a nun in her undergarment.

Moments later they were under way again. The girl was sitting in the front seat. Deane had instructed the driver to learn from her about friends or family who would take her in, either in Rome or on the way there. Warburg had his suit coat back. He was staring into his own reflection in the window. How ludicrous it seemed now, that quotation under glass on his desk back in D.C.: "Never did I feel so strongly the sense of abandonment, powerlessness and loneliness . . ." What did he know of such things? And who was he to have lectured poor Janet about them?

Janet. It was she he was seeing in the window's reflection — her gorgeous body, languid in the tanning sun by the swimming pool at her parents' place. But not naked. She had never been naked with him. He felt a rush of chastened gratitude now, a belated appreciation of her modesty.

"Real love, compared to fantasy"—Dostoyevsky's line came to Warburg's mind—"is a harsh and dreadful thing." That Red Cross woman at the airport, he suddenly thought, she would know that. Her body, too, had struck him.

"The poor girl," Deane said.

Warburg turned from the window, facing the priest. "Maudlin," he said.

"What?"

"In the airplane you spoke of Bedlam. The other insane asylum in London is called Maudlin. The one for women. Original name, St. Mary Magdalen. Maud. Maudlin."

"How the hell do you know that?"

"English major." In a different context, Warburg might have grinned, making a crack about Russian novels, quoting goddamn Dostoyevsky. Instead he let his eyes drift to the girl in the front seat. Mary Magdalen. But this child was no whore. How unfair his associations were.

Deane thought he saw a question in Warburg's eyes, and answered it: "My surplice."

"Your what?"

"A vestment for hearing confessions." Deane might have laughed. But no. This was too sad.

In any case, though there were questions in Warburg's mind, the garb cloaking the girl was not one of them.

Marguerite d'Erasmo was walking among the children at the Quirinal gardens. Dozens of children, perhaps hundreds, impossible to count— toddlers clinging to the hands of older siblings, adolescents, boys, girls, androgynous waifs. Empty-eyed and silent, except for the rattle of coughs and sniffles. The children wore the home-woven garments of peasants, tattered aprons, or the soiled plaids of school uniforms. Today the sun would burn, but the youngsters would remove none of their clothing for fear of losing it, because what they wore was all they owned. Mostly they were unshod, and many limped with pain from the sores on their bare feet. Some were sunburned, with flushed faces, and some were pale as toadstools. Some sat blank-faced and unmoving, others clustered around pits in which the nighttime coals smoldered. Boys in twos and threes threw their fingers in games of morra. Boys at play in every circumstance!

How the throng of young ones had come to congregate here was a mystery to Marguerite, but the rest of their stories she knew well — the flight of families from battle-ravaged towns to the south and bombed cities to the north, captured fathers, kidnapped mothers, the hidden children left behind in barns and cones of hay, from which finally they joined the snaking lines of desperate Italians on the march toward Rome. In wartime, children are invisible except to one another, and here their companionship had become a condition of survival. The gardens were a kind of no man's land into which, until yesterday, adults were all but forbidden admission. Adults were dangerous.

Thoughts of Sisak came unbidden to Marguerite, the trucks roaring around their oval circuit, the dog, the devil priest cupping the heads of toddlers, selecting them. But she had tried to dispel the thoughts with her *Memorare* — a prayer no longer, but an incantation: *O Mother of the Word Incarnate, despise not my petitions* . . .

Now that the open-air kitchen had been established in the corner of the gardens nearest the former palace — stock pots sterilizing water for reconstituting the evaporated milk, onto which lumps of bread were being set afloat for ladling into tin cups — Marguerite was permitting herself actually to look at these little ones. Near the serving tables, a crush of youngsters pushed forward, but elsewhere the children seemed indifferent to the food. Awake and aware of the day, they had assembled themselves with apparent purposefulness, but their herding was unthinking. They seemed blind to Marguerite, for whom they made room like sheep dumbly ovaling a shepherdess. Her own senses were far more concentrated than usual, but were tethered, in truth, to the herd at Sisak.

Quirinal, she told herself, you are in Quirinal. When she came upon a girl who had curled her willowy body into a fist, beneath the canopy of a prostrate shrub, Marguerite stooped. The stench of urine rose from the child's filthy frock, which unaccountably made Marguerite think she knew her. The girl's hands were at her mouth, where she furiously gnawed at her fingernails. Marguerite gently took the girl's fingers, thinking as she did of her own father, how it always reassured her to have him reach for her hand.

If Marguerite's father came to mind now, wasn't it because he was the one to whom she longed to tell the final story of Carlo, as if then she herself would understand?

Should she have known that such male fierceness, enough to draw her at last, could have been fueled only by the demonic? In Croatia, she thought she'd come to share equally in Carlo's hatred for Ante Pavelic, the Fascist warlord. Wasn't she like Carlo in despising the Ustashe crimes, centered on Jasenovac? If only half of what was said about the place was true, yes, it paired Pavelic with Hitler. To say nothing of Sisak. Nothing of the Franciscan.

But now Marguerite understood that what she had felt, even that deadly morning after seeing the children in the gas trucks, was cool compared to the furnace that burned in her red-bearded pirate. Having attached herself to his guerrilla band in the rough borderlands between Yugoslavia and Italy, she saw now that she had been merely a child at play, not knowing it was play for her alone. Until Trieste.

The brigade numbered fifty men. In its boldest strike yet, they had slyly come down out of the hills in pairs or threesomes. A third of them set up ambushes on the roads leading into the seaport city, while the rest lost themselves in its plazas and courtyards, like stevedores or sailors on leave. Carlo had left Marguerite behind in Vranjak, to stay with the other women.

As was typical, he had said nothing of the unit's project, but a terrible premonition after he'd gone convinced her that disaster awaited them. She had followed, moving through the night along the simple road, understanding that all she had to do was keep going downhill. She arrived in Trieste at dawn, just after the trap was sprung, and Carlo's contingent of thirty Partisans had captured the entire militia barracks while its fighters were still asleep. Marguerite came upon the scene at the great piazza on the water's edge just as the gunfire began. The shots echoed off the proud neoclassical palaces that lined three sides of the square, a vestige of the city's Habsburg grandeur, though by now many of the buildings were in ruins. Assuming a battle, she crouched, moving forward slowly toward the noise.

But she was wrong. There was no battle. As she stepped out of the shadowy arcades, it was readily apparent who was who, because the men of Carlo's brigade were dressed, as always, in dark peasant gear and the red kerchiefs that were the sole gesture of a uniform, donned just before action commenced so they could recognize one another. Their prisoners, though, were as they had been when asleep—men mostly in their underwear, sleeveless shirts, tattered white drawers, bare feet. Those who were clothed wore the black shirts of the Ustashe—that red-and-white-checkered crest for a shoulder patch. Dozens of prisoners, unresisting, were surrounded by rifle brandishers. They lay face-down on the cobblestones or knelt with their hands clasped above their heads.

Marguerite did not understand what she was seeing, and at first could take in only the sound. The Partisans, her comrades, were firing their weapons unopposed, short machine-gun bursts, single gunshots in quick succession. Red-kerchiefed brigade members were dragging bodies to the water's edge and throwing them into the harbor. Then Marguerite saw the familiar figure with rampant red hair and beard. Carlo was moving slowly through the knot of prisoners, placing the snout of his pistol at one head after another and firing. Carlo was the group commander. This was his operation. His victims were, to him, the villains of Sisak. "I am stopping it," he had said to her on the hill above the racecourse. "That is what I am doing." A massacre.

The Quirinal girl refused to open her eyes. Marguerite coaxed her with soft words, to no avail. Sweat poured off the girl's face, and Marguerite recognized the fever. "Come, my sweet," she said, and scooped the child up. She was perhaps eleven or twelve, weighed next to nothing. She mounted no resistance, was conscious, but was wholly indifferent to her own condition. Marguerite carried her to the medical tent, where equipment, pristine white cloths, gray woolen blankets, and bottles of various fluids were just being unboxed. A nursing sister was in charge, and she welcomed Marguerite. The sister took the girl into her arms, saying, "Now we begin. One child at a time."

Carlo looked up from the man he had just executed, turned, and saw her. Their eyes locked for the briefest moment. Oddly, he lifted his pistol and aimed it at her. Then he threw his head back and laughed. She turned and ran into the alley from which she'd come.

I fly unto Thee—the verse she'd habitually prayed while running within the walled garden of her childhood home in privileged Parioli. But the Trieste air was wet and murky, this was a quayside slum, and she was no girl at play. She tripped and fell. She got up, running. The alley narrowed. At a fork, she went right. She saw her father's face, then the wreckage of his automobile, which she had never seen and never stopped seeing. *Papà! Papà!*

Marguerite's task in life had been to draw her treasonous parents back from the fires of hell by being good. And so she was. Essential to being good was the recitation of her prayer: *I fly unto Thee . . . in Thy mercy hear and answer me.* As she fled now, recitation was automatic, yet she knew the prayer was as useless as the magic word of her dreams.

When Carlo caught up to her, he seized her arm, and for the first time hurt her. He threw her against a wall. "*Tesoro mio, Tesoro mio,*" he began, but she covered his mouth with her hand. In his right fist he held the pistol.

"Treasure? What treasure?" she demanded. "How could I not know this about you? How could I think you are good?"

He holstered the gun and pulled her hand away from his mouth. "I *am* good. Here." He pushed his face against hers. The stench of alcohol hit her. She had seen Carlo drunk once, twice, but from a distance, in gatherings in the larger building in Vranjak—a raucous intoxicated stranger. She twisted her head but he clamped her face between his hands, pushing his tongue at her lips. One hand fell away from her face to pull at her clothing.

"Carlo! Stop!"

He replied by drawing back to throw a fist at her face, a blow that failed to land. He straightened up.

"Who are you?" she demanded.

Instead of answering, he looked one way and then another. The lane was deserted. He took her hand and began to pull her toward a nearby alcove, the doorway of a blighted building. Again she resisted. Once more he swung at her, and the blow landed, a fist at her jaw. By the time her head cleared, he had pushed her into a dark corner and her skirt and pants were at her ankles. One of his hands was inside her shirt, pulling at her breast; the other was between her legs.

His lips at hers, she opened her mouth, an instinctive trap. She bit him, hard.

"*Cazzo!*" he cursed, and punched her again. She fell back. He pushed her down on the alcove stoop. The smell of urine, there it was. Sailors and roustabouts relieving themselves here. He unfastened his belt and trousers and then was on her. *How could I have crossed borders with him?* Her question was no longer about Carlo or Croatia, but about herself.

She closed her eyes and an old instinct took over — detached escape, as if hers were the mystical body. She simply left her body, there in that filthy corner, removing herself from all physical sensation. Numbness. Nothing. Null. No. She let her eyes drift to the blue sky at the roofline. *I fly unto Thee.*

All at once she was unresponsive, cut off from everything, including him. Marguerite felt only the sigh of wind in the air above, where she was floating now. She felt the pulse of breath from the fluttering of birds' wings. She saw the small white flakes of ash from freshly stoked fires, carried in faintly gray currents of smoke. *I fly unto Thee.* Eyes shut, Marguerite soared past the risen sun to the far corner of the cosmos, meeting *Papà, Mamma,* kneeling with them at daybreak and saying the words of the *Ave Maria.*

He was pushing into her when she sensed a change in him, his real-ization that she was gone, utterly gone. She was an unmoving sack of wheat, a soft mannequin, a corpse. Yes, detached from physical sen-sation. But also she was supremely attuned to the mechanisms of his body. She had not known it, but his erotic charge required the negative pole of her resistance. Now that her fight was gone, so was the elec-tricity of his assault. A woman with no history of erotic love, yet she understood that his erection was failing. His eyes searched for hers, found them, and she saw the shock of his recognition — her vacancy.

She sensed his defeat. Now he was really dangerous. He fell on her again and pushed into her with what was left of his stiffness. That he was nearly limp made him pump more furiously, grunting like a goat. Yes, she had imagined the moment of intercourse, but never like this. His erection failed fully. He was out. He began blindly to strike her with both fists, landing blows on her head, face, and shoulders. Then, with both hands around her throat, he began to choke her. His mighty fingers and thumbs closed together, sealing off her air. Now I die, she thought.

In the Quirinal gardens, having finally faced her anguish, she bolted. Flight again, but this time with a purpose.

A few minutes later, after a fraught ride at the wheel of the Red Cross truck, cutting through narrow streets and congested squares, she was on her knees in the chapel of the Casa dello Spirito Santo. Here, at the Cistercian convent on the Via Sicilia, she had studied as a child, and then, after her parents' death, and moving in, she had come modestly to womanhood. Here, the girls had condemned her parents, and here, she had learned, above all, to be good. Neither playfulness nor laughter had come with her to this place, but the place had saved her.

The ancient chapel, with its stone tower and arched portico, was at-tached by a pair of classical colonnades to the school on one side and the cloister on the other. The monastic enclosure included freestand-ing structures as well — a stable, a laundry shed, a chicken coop, priv-ies, and the priest's small house. The sprawling complex of buildings all faced a central courtyard, a configuration that walled off the bustle of the street, where a nondescript multistory façade revealed nothing of its hidden inner world. Out there, only a copper-green plaque on the weary wooden door gave an indication of what was inside: "This building," its inscription read in the precise formulation of the Lateran Treaty of 1929, "serves religious objectives, and is an extraterritorial dependency of Vatican City. All searches and requisitions are prohibited."

Into the chapel from the courtyard outside came noises of girls and boys at play, amid milling clusters of perhaps two dozen figures whose presence, as she'd passed them, had registered as a low hum of talk. They were refugees, having just come out of the monastic crypt — free. The sound of laughing children should have been an antidote to what drove Marguerite here, but was not.

Inside the vacant Romanesque chapel, all was otherwise quiet, solitary, and cool. The windows were narrow and high, with glass in mainly violet hues, leaving the space perpetually dark but for the flickering red altar light and the blue candles at the feet of the Madonna and Child. On this prie-dieu, Marguerite had once known the consolation of prayer. But now the Madonna seemed indifferent to everyone but her Son.

From behind Marguerite came the faint rustle of the priest taking his place in the confessional booth. A moment later, she rose and crossed to the penitent's kneeler. "Bless me, Father," she whispered in Italian.

"*Vi benedica, Signorina.*"

Through the screen she could make out the priest's profile, still the most familiar face in the world. His hawkish nose and dramatic brow, the protruding jaw of a friendly wolf. "*C'est moi, mon père.*"

He brought his head around to peer intently through the shadow. How his eyebrows still met above his nose, one solid bridge of bristly hair. But having not seen him in almost a year, she was startled, even in the dark, by how old he seemed. And indeed, a man in his seventies, he *was* old. Time was being harsh with him. "*Ma princesse?*"

"*Oui.*"

How naturally the French came to her. He was known as Padre Antonio, but she knew him as Père Antoine. That the sisters of Casa dello Spirito Santo had French origins, and a French chaplain, was what had first drawn Marguerite's mother to their school, she herself being French. The priest had been Marguerite's tutor. On Tuesdays and Thursdays for most of a decade, she had come to his cottage. Not tutorials in the beginning, only chocolate and easy chatting about everything from the birds of Provence to the heartbreaking *Vol de Nuit*, the novel by Antoine de Saint-Exupéry, which had made its real impression when she saw the film version, starring Clark Gable — her father's treat during an Easter holiday. That she had returned to Spirito Santo to discover that Père Antoine had himself seen the movie — and approved of it — had seemed miraculous to her.

But the talks between girl and priest had become burdened after the car wreck. Through that year and the year after, Marguerite had desperately wanted to transform her status from boarding student to postulant, entering the convent as a nun. If that was not being good, what was? At first it had mystified her that Père Antoine discouraged this holy inclination. For a time she thought he considered her unworthy. Only gradually had she understood that he was right. Hers was an impulse of pure flight — a *vol de nuit* if ever there was one. Père Antoine continually insisted that she was already good. And he was there to remind her of who her real father had been — the great Angelo d'Erasmo — and that his Red Cross was what, in fact, she had always wanted for herself. The priest, her second father, returned Marguerite to her first. The Red Cross was her vocation. If the organization could not be an actual home, that was all right, since its purpose was to help the homeless ones. Her wound had become her strength.

And now — after Quirinal, Sisak, an alcove in an alley — here she was again: flight and grief, *vol de nuit*.

"I have sinned, Father."

He did not reply, but faced away, showing her his profile once more. If she had come to him like this, on her knees in the ancient shadow, then he would display the confessor's impersonality. As she wished.

She had closed her fists and was pressing them against her sore mouth, so that when finally she whispered again, "I have sinned," the sound was stifled at her knuckles.

Tears coursed down her face.

"My child," the priest whispered, "you must speak."

But her silence was broken only by the quick, moist intake of breath at her nose. After a long time, Père Antoine whispered, "What happened to you?"

She shook her head, but he did not see.

Lionni pushed his bicycle into the same courtyard less than two hours later. In the enclosure now were perhaps a dozen pale-faced Jews in various poses of relaxation — smoking men, kerchiefed women, a finger-sucking girl, a pair of boys kicking a wadded-up rag as if it were a ball. They were sitting on hay bales or the old wagon, or lounging against stacked mattresses that had been brought from the crypt to be aired out. These released fugitives who owed Lionni so much did not recognize him. For his part, Lionni was so taken with the sight of the old priest standing at the threshold of his hut that he let the bike drop and ignored his charges to run with his broken gait to the white-robed old man. The priest stood with arms wide open, hair flowing back from his face like a prophet of old. But prophets were not known to grin as Padre Antonio was grinning. Lionni banged into his embrace, jolting both of them, with the priest clasping his arms around the small figure as if to squeeze the air from his lungs. "My friend, my friend."

"Padre, the Messiah has come. The Messiah has come!"

"I thought it was only the Americans, Jocko!" The priest jostled Lionni with affection and relief.

"No, Padre. The Messiah, I swear."

"The Messiah, you say?" Padre Antonio clapped the smaller man's shoulders. "Good! We can ask Him if He has been here before. If He says no, I'll be first to cover my head with the *tallit* and blow the *shofar*. If He says yes, I'll baptize you myself."

"Ah," Lionni said, "but what if he refuses to answer?"

"That means He's a Buddhist and we are both in trouble." They hugged again.

From the courtyard, the priest ushered Lionni into his house. The larger of the priest's two rooms served as oratory, parlor, kitchen, and one-man refectory. In its center stood a scarred deal table below a suspended oil lamp, which now, in midafternoon, was unlit yet still stinking of kerosene. Aged biscotti tins were spread out on the table, arranged, as Giacomo Lionni had routinely arranged them months before, in alphabetical order of the surnames inscribed on nearly a thousand index cards. Each of a dozen tins held about a hundred and fifty cards, and each card contained the name, age, and coded location of one person.

At the sight of the tin boxes, Lionni gasped and fell to his knees. Before the Torah scroll in the catacombs he had knelt also, but this vision was just as sacred. When, in October, the Gestapo had descended like locusts on the streets around the Great Synagogue, they had used the addresses of the rabbi's tithing roll to locate Jews. When Lionni had then learned that the Germans were looking for him, his nightmare was that the refugee lists he had compiled would somehow help the Nazis. Desperate, he hauled the boxes here to Casa dello Spirito Santo.

The priest said quietly, "Yesterday, when I learned of the Americans, I brought your boxes out of the stable. I knew you would be coming for them."

Only now did it hit Lionni what he had asked the priest to risk. If the Nazis had found these boxes, they would have killed the old man. Or, rather, they would have killed him after he refused, under torture, to decipher the cards. Lionni's group was called the Delegation to Assist Hebrews, and this was its archive. The priest had become the de facto manager of the Jewish network of hiding places and escape routes. Updates, changes, hastily arranged transfers, new places of refuge, old ones suddenly unsafe — the flow of information had come here, to him, him alone. Across Rome, the parish priests, monks, nuns, and schoolmasters who protected Jews necessarily knew little of each other, but all knew of Padre Antonio. He was perhaps the most dangerously committed man in Rome. And here he was, alive.

Lionni came to his feet, then let his hands drift reverently above the tins as if blessing them, or as if drawing a blessing from them. "This will enable us to know who is missing still," he said. "We can know who survived, and who . . ." He let the sentence hang, unfinished. "By tomorrow I will have the beginning of a list of those who are showing themselves. Praise God, Padre! From all over the city they are coming out. I have seen it!" Lionni let an arm sweep back toward the court-yard, the crypt dwellers released. Then, once more, he embraced the priest. "By keeping their names alive, you kept *them* alive. Thank you."

"It is me who thanks you, Jocko. For *your* being alive. For being here."

"You are good, Padre. You are good."

"No. No." Like one bursting with a secret he could no longer conceal, the priest abruptly said, "In the winter, I concluded that one of the convent serving girls was preparing to betray us, to inform the Nazis that we had Jews in the cellars here. On the street, repeatedly, I had seen her cozy up to a blackshirt, holding his hand. A Fascist thug, I thought, sent, no doubt, to pump her for what she knew about those in hiding."

The priest's agitation made Lionni interrupt. "Padre—"

"No. Listen. Listen! Just as I was about to confront her, she brought the young man to me, now wearing peasant rags. He was not a thug but her brother, and he had just deserted *la milizia*. She had told him he could trust me. He asked me to help with his escape. Of course, I did. But Jocko, Jocko . . . here is the truth." The priest went to a box in the corner, opened it, and withdrew a long chef's knife. The blade glistened as he held it up. "I stole this from the kitchen. I had decided to kill the girl because I suspected her treason. She who trusted me. I was going to kill her with this knife and dump her body in the river. That simply, I had become like the Nazis. If I am not a murderer, it is only an accident."

"No, Padre. You were protecting us."

"From a trusting lass?"

Lionni saw what the priest was confessing—how the lethal Nazi abomination had spread, a universal corruption. Lionni fell silent. The

priest lifted the knife. "I keep this now as a reminder of what I am."
He remained unmoving for a long moment, then put the knife down
beside the tins. "So Jocko," he asked at last, "where did you yourself
find to go?"

Lionni laughed. "Here, there, everywhere."

"I prayed for you. Every day. Every hour of every day."

"The Gestapo was looking for me, and so I could not come to you."

"I know that. Indeed, the Germans did come here, a number of
times. You should have seen our holy abbess deal with them. If any
males dared to so much as approach the cloister, she stormed, they
would be anathema. '*Anathema sit!*' she cried. It frightened the Catholics among the Germans, but it *terrified* the Protestants. And the atheists could not get away fast enough." The priest was grinning with delight. "Luckily there were no Jews among the Germans, or they would
have known how little there was to fear in excommunication."

Lionni replied with brusque solemnity, "You know where the German Jews are."

Of course he knew. But mostly the priest held the knowledge off. Some
nights, though, it had spiraled down on him, and he would get up
from his cot and go out into the cool air of the yard, across to the
stable, where he would clear away the straw, only to sit with his hand
resting on the tin surface of the topmost biscotti box.

Sometimes he brought his lantern with him and opened the box
for the mental exercise of decoding the encrypted place names on the
cards. The primitive key required transposing letters of the alphabet,
plus two. Fraterna Domus . . . Santa Sofia . . . Villa Rosa. Sometimes
he picked out cards at random to whisper the fugitive's name aloud:
"Alatri, Bemantani, Molari, Gargiulo . . ." He intended to pray for
them, but after each name he would add "*ora pro nobis,*" as if praying *to* them. The scurrying of stable mice and rats was antiphonal
response enough—his litany of saints. "Levi, Mavante, Wasserstein
. . ." And, always, Padre Antonio ended his supplication with "Lionni,
Giacomo . . . *Omnes Sancti et Sanctae Dei, intercedite pro nobis.*" Dear
Jocko, and all ye Holy, Righteous and Elect of God, intercede for us.

But why should they? From all evil, Good Lord, deliver us. And who had delivered them, God's elect, into the hands of this evil, if not we ourselves?

Padre Antonio—Père Antoine—had been a young priest in Paris during the time of Dreyfus, and had he not himself cheered on, if from the side, those rabid monks and clerics who spouted Jew-hating slogans? *Death to the Dreyfusards, damn the deicide people, down with the Jews!* Even as a young *curé*, Antoine understood the ways in which anti-Semitism was useful to the Church, a way to reconnect with the French masses. That he had seen nothing amiss in this—weren't the Jews the enemies of Christ?—was now a source of wrenching shame. At last it was clear where it all had led. *In die judicii, libera nos Domine.* On the day of judgment, Good Lord deliver us.

"Seeing you, Jocko, is like seeing my brother whom I feared lost at sea."

"After months on the raft," Lionni replied, "the sailor is saved, but when he explains himself to his rescuers, the words come out as gibberish. He regards his rescuers as cruel for not understanding, but then he realizes they regard him as insane. Language fails, Padre—which is insanity."

"Or perhaps silence, Jocko. Holy silence."

The men stared at each other, a direct look, which was unusual in Rome, where for a year no one had dared look another in the eye, afraid of what he would see—or what would be seen. Yet Padre Antonio could have held Jocko's gaze forever.

Lionni, though, abruptly shook his head. "I must talk with you," he said. "I need your counsel."

A few minutes later, having moved the biscotti tins aside, they were bent over the map Lionni had pulled from inside his shirt, the railroad plan for the region north and east of Modena. "Here you see, in red, the rail lines that are still working. These marks indicate rolling stock destroyed. Here you see fuel dumps, and here the yards where locomotives are repaired."

"Where did you get this, Jocko?"

"It fell from heaven," Lionni said. "And here—" he poked the map decisively—"is Fossoli, near Carpi. You know Fossoli?"

The priest nodded. "The POW camp for British soldiers captured in Africa."

"Yes, but since last year an internment camp for 'enemies of the Fascist state.' Police Order Number Five."

"*Quinto*," the priest said. The November decree ordering the arrest of all Jews in Italy.

"At first," Lionni said, "they were prisoners of Italian Fascists, not the Germans. The Fascists insisted that the Jews would be protected from the Nazis. 'Internment,' they said, not 'deportation.' But then, in February, the Germans took over. The trains began to roll, heading north. Thousands of deportees—who knows how many?—between February and the end of May. Last week."

Lionni picked up the chef's knife and stabbed the map with it, a punctuation for the word "Now!"

The priest jumped back. Lionni released the knife and it fluttered, its point stuck near the place marked *Carpi*. Lionni forced a dead calm into his voice. "Now," he said again, but softly. "German forces in the area are in disarray. Fossoli is still well above the line of Nazi retreat. In the camp, there remain only its last prisoners, the special classifications—Jews in mixed marriages, their children, those of undetermined racial impurity, and the Jews who've been forced to do the work of the camp. Jews the Germans chose not to kill until now. About four hundred people."

"How do you know this?"

"The Italian guards have just been sent away by the Germans. These Italians brought the news to Rome, yesterday, the day before. The Allies have pushed the Germans back from Pisa, and the Wehrmacht prepares for retreat throughout the province of Modena. The Germans intend to hold the line in the west—Torino, Milano—not here. The commandant is ordered to close the camp quickly. The remaining Jews are to be transported. Finally." Lionni pulled the knife out, then pounded the map with his closed fist. "It has not happened yet. We must stop it."

The priest said nothing, only stared at the map, its black and gray hash marks.

Lionni moved his hand to a spot away from Fossoli. "Here," he said, "the rail tracks run to the Po. This bridge across the river. The only railroad bridge to the north in the entire area. Destroy the bridge and the deportation stops."

"And . . . ?" The priest raised his dramatic eyebrows.

"The Americans."

"And . . . ?"

"Now that they have their airfield at Ciampino, the bridges of the Po will be in range of their Air Force. They will be bombing the bridges in the west to cut off German supply lines. We must make this bridge to the east an American target."

"Are you personally acquainted with General Clark, Jocko?"

Lionni drew himself up to his full height and faced the priest. "You, Padre. You. Go to the Holy See. General Clark will listen to the Holy See."

Father Antonio snorted. "But will the Holy See listen to me? I have been across the Tiber repeatedly, looking for an open defense of our Jews. Nothing." Set loose, the priest could not stop. "The Vatican is riddled with Fascists. Those who are not Fascists are cowards."

"But surely, Padre—"

"No, Jocko. Listen. When I asked the monsignors to help with our Delegation, they instructed me to have nothing to do with a Jewish organization. They even ordered me to expel all Jews from *here*, from Spirito Santo. They told me that I . . . I! That *I* would be the cause of the Pope's being taken prisoner by the Gestapo."

The priest stopped. Lionni said nothing, letting his silence convey his contempt for the Church. Padre Antonio said quietly, "I was stupid to go to the Vicariate. Once the monsignors were aware of me, they came after Spirito Santo—'a Vatican dependency,' they said. They issued a solemn *trasferimento* decree requiring the sisters to abandon their convent and yield the monastery to Vatican authority. But the monsignors did not know Mother Abbess. She simply pretended the order had never come. The Jews were protected again, not just from the Nazis but from the *monsignori*."

After a moment the priest added, "Expect nothing from across the river!"

The two men were not aware of her—Marguerite standing on the threshold between the rooms, stooped slightly because her height nearly matched the door frame's.

She had been sleeping on the priest's cot, collapsed in the exhaustion that broke her in the chapel. Lionni's arrival had awakened her, and through the closed door she had listened. Now, from her place behind the men, she spoke: "I know an American. An important one."

THREE

Handkerchief

C OLONEL PETER MATES came to with a jump. What had startled him awake was the unfamiliar feel of the sheets. After all these months — satin! This was his first morning in the poshest suite of the freshly requisitioned Hotel Barberini on the Via Veneto, and he hadn't slept alone. The woman he'd picked up on the boulevard was sitting on the edge of the bed adjusting her shoes. Already corseted in a flesh-colored girdle and brassiere, the fasteners of which had slowed him down the night before, she had her back to him. He had no idea now what her face looked like, never mind her name. He did remember the overpowering aroma of her cheap perfume — or was that a present sensation?

Mates threw the splendid sheets back, found his shorts on the floor, and retrieved his wallet from his trousers. He withdrew a handful of lira notes — five bucks — and faced back to her just as she was pulling her dress down from over her head. A tawny-skinned, pretty girl, it turned out, but with bad teeth and much too young — younger, he realized with an efficiently deflected stab of guilt, than his youngest daughter. A pair of rivulets marked her cheeks. Apparently she had been weeping.

He took his silk pocket-square from his uniform jacket on the chair and handed it to her. She dabbed her face, then dropped the cloth on the bed. He gave her the bills, which she took without a word and folded into her dress. When she'd left his room, he heard her stifled yelp of surprise from the next room, followed by a man's soft voice. Only then did he remember that he'd been assigned a suite-mate — the Jew from Treasury. He began to dress.

Mates was new to Rome that week, like all Americans, but he had lived here before, years ago. All winter and spring, from the OSS base in Brindisi, he had fervently anticipated this return.

Having carefully knotted his uniform tie and put on his tailored field jacket, Mates retrieved the slightly soiled silk square from the bed, whiffed it for a hit of the girl's perfume, and studied the thing.

Parachute silk. Months before, he had used his survival knife to cut it from the ballooning canopy, iridescent in the moonlight, after his one drop — a souvenir of having lived through the most harrowing six minutes of his life. Mates had been commander of the Special Ops unit supplying Yugoslav Partisans with night drops. Though at fifty he was a decade over the airborne age limit, he'd cut orders for his own mission, a rendezvous with the deputy to Marshal Tito, the guerrilla leader. The meeting wasn't strictly necessary; what had he been trying to prove? The silk square was his only answer. He'd found a Brindisi seamstress to hem it with cross-stitches — a rakish item now, but also a secret reminder of how scared shitless he'd been that night.

He folded the square back into his left breast pocket, ready to be brought out again for further women of Rome.

"Good morning," Mates said as he entered the sitting room that separated the suite's two bedrooms. The Jew did not reply at once, and Mates took in the high ceiling and lavish French doors whose lace curtains billowed in the morning air. The fellow was sitting at the writing desk in the window alcove, his pen poised above a sheaf of papers. "You were asleep when I got here last night," Mates continued. "I hope I didn't wake you up. Or *we*, I guess I should say."

"Actually, Colonel, I was dead to the world." Warburg stood. "I'm David Warburg."

"Mates. Peter Mates."

The men shook hands.

Mates was just tall enough to dislike being the shorter man. He said,

"Sorry if the girl disturbed you just now." He touched his mustache, a hint of male conquest.

"She seemed sad," Warburg said, suddenly aware of the girl as a third female victim—a quick lesson in war.

Mates grinned. "Not sad last night."

Warburg said nothing.

"You're from Treasury, I'm told."

"Yes. And you are C-A-D, which is why they put us together, I guess."

"Civil Affairs Division. Not cad." Mates waited for Warburg to pick up on the crack. He did not. Mates took in Warburg's white shirt and gray trousers. "We should get you some tans."

"Not necessary. I'm outside the chain of command."

"Lucky you."

"But I will need some help getting what the chain supplies. General Holton, Clark's exec, told me I could depend on you."

"Christ, Warburg, I just got here."

"So did we all, Colonel. Perhaps that's why you haven't seen the general's order yet. I have a copy here somewhere." Warburg sat, opened a file folder, and picked up a sheet. He handed it to Mates, who read in silence.

After a moment, Warburg said, "I appreciate your help. I'll be easier to supply than Marshal Tito was."

"Tito? Never heard of him."

"General secretary of the League of Communists of Yugoslavia," Warburg said.

Mates recognized Warburg's parry, a show of knowledge he should not have had. Mates wondered if this fellow was OSS, deep cover, as he himself was now. But there were no Jews in the OSS, not that he knew of. "What's Treasury's brief in Rome?"

"Refugees," Warburg answered. "Join me for coffee downstairs, I'll lay it out for you."

Mates handed Holton's letter back and made a show of checking his watch.

Warburg dropped the page on the desk and picked up another. "Here's a list of what I'll need."

Mates did not move, pointedly declining to take the page.

Warburg said, "Beginning with a jeep and driver, someone with Italian. Someone who knows Rome."

Still Mates did not respond.

Warburg said, "Today, Colonel. I need it today. This morning."

"Forget it, my friend." Mates produced a pack and withdrew a cigarette.

"Every CAD resource at my disposal, Colonel. So Holton says, and Holton speaks for Clark. You have a jeep and driver. Let's start there."

"Whoa!" Mates froze, the cigarette halfway to his mouth. "This *is* deadly. My jeep? My driver? My canoe? My scout? Next you'll want my squaw."

"No, Colonel," Warburg said, annoyed, "not your squaw." Warburg stood, and now he was the one to look at his watch. "I have to be at the Swedish embassy at ten-thirty. Why don't you come? It'll be the most efficient way for you to get the picture."

After a long moment, Mates lit his cigarette, inhaled, waved the match, then said through the smoke, "Who says I need to get the picture?"

Warburg smiled. "Tito."

Mates smiled, too.

Warburg clapped the colonel's shoulder. "Come on. We have time for coffee. I'll buy."

They arrived at the embassy as a pair. Warburg was not unhappy that a senior American officer at his elbow, like an aide, enhanced his appearance as a man of status.

The ambassador was a septuagenarian named Urban Sundberg, and Warburg had done the research. Sundberg's family firm had emerged from a base in Malmö shipbuilding to become a leading manufacturer of marine pumps. When the Swedish Navy appropriated the company early in the war, the Stockholm Admiralty was happy to have Sund-

berg in Rome—part salesman, part spy—for as long as the Axis had
maintained its winning tilt. Now the Fascist-friendly diplomat was a
living reminder of Sweden's misplaced bet. Warburg was here to collect.

Entering the ornate drawing room to greet Warburg and Mates,
Sundberg was blinking. He stepped gingerly across the fringed lip of
an Oriental carpet, maneuvering a gold-handled walking stick. His
long, thick silver hair brushed his collar. In his free hand he carried
Warburg's leather credentials folder and the business card that Warburg had presented at the front desk.

"Mr. Ambassador, I am David Warburg. I am with the United States
Treasury Department. This is Colonel Peter Mates."

"Greetings, gentlemen," Sundberg said, but uneasily. He fumbled
the cane and credentials to free up a hand to shake. Then he gave
the leather folder to Warburg, but slid the business card into his coat
pocket.

"I have asked for coffee to be brought. If that is agreeable." He gestured at the bentwood chairs flanking a low rectangular table. Without
waiting, he took a seat.

The Americans, too, took chairs. "I'll come to the point," Warburg
said. "On behalf of my government, I put before the Swedish Ministry
for Foreign Affairs a formal request for a diplomatic—"

Sundberg's hand shot up. "Mr. Warburg, I have no authority—"

"You have authority to send a protected cable to Stockholm. I am
not asking you for decisions, Mr. Ambassador. Merely for the trans-
mission of adjuration. The United States respects Sweden's scrupulous
neutrality. As a consequence of that neutrality, Sweden has at times
been positioned to act in the middle range of diplomacy, the ill-de-
fined region between the sanctioned and the morally imperative. That
is the case today. Knowing Sweden's record as we do, we are here to
press a matter of utmost urgency to my government."

"But Sir, the Foreign Ministry, surely communication from Washington to Stockholm is the proper—"

Warburg shook his head. He was about to invoke Roosevelt, but

Mates cut in: "Mr. Warburg is speaking for Washington." The colonel's imperative tone was a fist on the table. When he then added, "I am speaking for General Clark," a second fist fell, surprising Warburg. Clearly, Mates was a quick study. And, equally clearly, he disdained this quisling.

Sundberg nodded. "Please, then . . ."

"This week," Warburg resumed, "your Foreign Ministry will receive the nomination of a Swedish businessman to the post of special envoy, representing the monarch of Sweden to the regent of Hungary in Budapest. My government expects the nomination to be approved. My government seconds his nomination. That is what you are to communicate."

"I will be expected to know what your government's interest is."

"Jews."

The word hung in the air.

"Jews?" Sundberg asked. His eyes glazed in a way that made his thought plain: *Warburg, Jews—of course.*

"Yes, Jews," Warburg said. "Since the German occupation of Budapest two months ago, Jews are being transported. Since one month ago, between ten and fourteen thousand Jews have been transported each day. You know the contemporary meaning of the English verb 'transport,' perhaps." Warburg let the silence gather for a moment before adding, "In Budapest the new special envoy will be in a position to issue the *Schutz-Pass* to Jews, identifying the bearers as Swedish citizens. He will rent buildings and authorize those buildings as Swedish extraterritorial properties—libraries, schools, cultural organizations where the Swedish flag will fly. In those buildings, Jews will be immune."

"With respect, Mr. Warburg, no one will believe the Jews are Swedes. The Hungarian police will not be fooled by flags."

"They will be paid to believe. They will be paid to be fooled. Handsomely paid. That brings me to point two. I want the name of the Budapest bank licensed for Swedish diplomatic transactions. I want a numbered account from which a Swedish envoy can draw unrestricted funds. Once I have that bank name and number, I will see to a sizable deposit in that account. The first of whatever sum is required to sow belief and foolishness throughout Hungarian officialdom."

Sundberg looked over at Mates. The American colonel was staring at him. Sundberg looked back at Warburg. "Yes," the Swede said, aware of what was required. "My country received thousands of Jews from Denmark less than a year ago."

Warburg said nothing.

There was a faint rap on the door, which was then pushed open by a servant in gray trousers and morning coat, carrying a tray laden with a silver coffee set. Ambassador Sundberg barked at him in Swedish. The man put the tray on the table and quickly left the room.

Warburg joined Sundberg in ignoring the coffee. "And point three," Warburg said. "Convey to the ministry, if you will, that the United States, taking into account Sweden's cooperation on this matter, will not pursue its inquiry under the terms of the Hague Convention."

"Inquiry, Sir?"

"The Hague, 1907. Concerning neutrality."

"Sweden's neutrality has been scrupulous, the very word you used a moment ago." Sundberg's face darkened with the sudden recognition that Warburg had been speaking sarcastically.

"*Permittenttrafiken*," Warburg said. "More than one hundred thousand troop-carrying Wehrmacht railroad cars through Sweden to Norway from 1941 into this year."

"The transit agreement is suspended."

"Yes, now that the Nazis no longer need Swedish rail, but when they needed it, they had it. Additionally, the Treasury Department inquiry extends to various Swedish commercial enterprises that have, in violation of neutrality laws, entered into contracts with belligerent powers, including Rome."

"Commercial enterprises, Sir?"

"Including yours. Fines. Requisition. Prison. Those are the penalties."

Sundberg's mouth opened to speak, but no sound came out.

"I am expressly authorized to inform you, and the Foreign Policy Council of Sweden, that the U.S. Office of Foreign Asset Control is taking steps to freeze certain Swedish accounts in American banks, and in Swedish banks doing business in the United States, pending the outcome of procedures."

"Procedures?"

"Nominating procedures for the special Swedish envoy, a Mr. Raoul Wallenberg." Warburg stood up, and so did Mates. "I suggest you start composing your cable, Mr. Ambassador. Dispatch it. Each day, Sir, between ten and fourteen thousand souls perish."

Sundberg's expression of helpless surprise slowly gave way to a look of open hostility, which prompted Warburg to add, uncharacteristically, "If they have souls. What do you think?"

"Jesus, Warburg, what was that?" Mates asked outside, as they took the stairs down from the Swedish palazzo. The sun was already high in the sky, a canopy of glare.

"A little one-on-one, Peter." On the sidewalk, Warburg stopped and faced the other man, who, remaining elevated by a pair of steps, looked him in the eye. "Dribbling. Head feint. Lay-up. Did you play basketball?" Mates did not answer. Warburg said, "Sundberg and his ilk backed the losers. We have to give them a way to join the winners — and that way is Jews."

"But these rumors about Jews," Mates said. "I'm old enough to remember the Great War propaganda, the Hun roasting babies on spits, all that."

"I'm not talking about propaganda," Warburg said. "Nor about rumors. Maybe you didn't hear me, Colonel." Warburg could not stifle his feelings. "Between ten and fourteen thousand every day."

"Yes, 'transport.' But to what? Concentration camps are bad, but they're all over German-occupied Europe, in Italy, too. You believe that ovens-and-gas-chambers stuff?"

"You don't?"

"Why don't I hear about it on Voice of America then? Why not on the BBC? Or Murrow from London?"

"You tell me, Colonel. Answer your own question. Why don't you hear about it?" Warburg faced away from Mates, to contain himself.

On the broad Via XX Settembre, traffic was breasting around a stalled trolley, a tangled clot of vehicles — autos, horse wagons, and pushcarts. Pealing church bells sounded from near and far. A loudspeaker truck was passing slowly by, its amplified voice enthusiastically wailing words Warburg did not understand, although he made out *"Grazie"* and *"Il Papa."* At the nearby curb sat the jeep, the driver lounging with a cigarette.

Mates grasped Warburg's shoulder from behind. "Look, I'm trying to understand. I don't get it. So Sweden goes to bat for you in Budapest."

"Not for me."

"But in Budapest? You get Jews in Swedish custody? Then what?"

"Find a way to get them here to Rome," Warburg said. "Then to Naples. Get them on empty troopships heading back to the U.S."

"You're serious."

"We have people working on a route through Romania, down to Istanbul. We have refugee camps being built in Algeria. We have people working on this in Portugal. But the priority — *my* priority — is getting refugees to the States. Roosevelt has authorized it. He sent the WRB here to get Jews to America, the one place we know for sure where they will be safe." Warburg stared at Mates, openly assessing him. Then he said quietly, "I could use your help, Peter."

"Impossible. You're dreaming. No way to get troopships."

"Not for Jews, you mean."

"No. That's not what I mean."

"So, you think I should just pray for the Red Army to hurry up, moving west?"

"If you think the Reds would be better," Mates said. Then, as an afterthought, "Pray? Do you pray?"

"No." Warburg turned and led the way to the curb, where the jeep waited. The driver, a stocky, acne-faced NCO, snapped his cigarette butt away. Warburg opened the door and started to climb into the back seat, but Mates stopped him. "Wait a minute, David." Instead, Mates mounted the jeep first, taking the rear seat, gesturing at the one

in front, the commander's seat. "The jeep is yours. And say hello to
Sergeant Rossini, your new driver and translator."

The formidable walls ringing Vatican City left no doubt as to the enclave's status as a separate principality, its ruler's status as a man apart.
To Kevin Deane, inveterate Bronx Irishman, the sweetest fact about
the world's smallest sovereign state had always been its size: at barely
more than a hundred acres, eight Vatican Cities would fit nicely inside
New York's Central Park.

Frederick Law Olmsted's New York greensward was, in fact, a fitting comparison, since two-thirds of the papal territory in the heart of
Rome was given over to gardens, this central one of which, beginning
in an hour and for the rest of the afternoon, would be reserved exclu-
sively for the Holy Father.

Deane, now a properly cassocked prelate himself, hurried through
the lavish green lawns, shaped hedges, and flower beds. He'd have
preferred a more leisurely stroll, especially in the heat, but he feared
being late. A distracting knot of anxiety tightened in his chest. It was
less than an hour past high noon, and the light was piercing — no such
light in New York City. This was Old World light, he thought, aware of
his bareheadedness, and why shouldn't Roman priests wear the broad-
brimmed clerical hat that made them look as if they were balancing
the ringed planet Saturn on their heads?

Perfumes of nectar and pollen filled the air, trumping the cologne
he'd slapped on his cheeks moments before in his cramped apartment
in the wing behind him. Because of Spellman, Deane had been offered
a large suite of rooms atop the Palace of the Congregations, on Via
della Conciliazione, the boulevard sloping from St. Peter's Square
down to the Tiber, just outside the Vatican's perimeter. But, also because of Spellman, Deane had known to display his humility, request-
ing more modest quarters adjacent to his office — quarters *inside* the
Holy See. Where you stand in the hierarchy depends on where you
sit on the toilet. Thus Deane's three small rooms were in the so-called
Apostolic Palace itself, a mammoth complex of linked buildings, the

grandest of which held the papal apartments and fronted on St. Peter's Square. Toward that building's garden entrance Deane strode now, the place where the Pope and his chief aides — and *their* chief aides — lived and worked.

This was the rear façade of the palazzo, yet it was decorated with fluted pilasters, an elaborate cornice, and a crowning balustrade. A Swiss Guard stood rigidly at attention at the doorway, pike in hand. Costumed in golden silk, the Cortés-helmeted soldier looked like a Christmas ornament. He stiffened slightly in a salute that Deane knew to ignore. Every guardsman was already briefed on the new American monsignor, his appearance and his position.

Once through the doors, Deane's vision blurred momentarily in the shadows of the cool interior. He picked up his pace, soutane spiraling at his ankles, to hurry along an apparently endless broad corridor. Deane was entering the inner sanctum, heading for Cardinal Luigi Maglione's rooms — luncheon at the table of the secretary of state of His Holiness the Pope.

A butler somehow knew of Deane's approach and opened the carved oak door ahead of him. Deane entered an apartment that would have set the hearts of Park Avenue decorators aflutter, only here the marble-topped tables, gilded frames, and Murano glass chandeliers had been in place for centuries, a show of the real that was not for sale. Immediately to his left was the entrance to a darkened personal chapel, from which cool air and the aroma of incense drifted. On the right stood an intricately inlaid walnut table holding half a dozen birettas in red-trimmed black and various crimson hues. Hanging from pegs on a multibranched hatrack were three broad-brimmed *cappelli romani* — the Saturn hats. There was also a silk top hat and a pair of gray suede gloves. The butler had his hand out, and Deane realized at once that his own bareheadedness was a faux pas. He winked.

Deane strode into the palatial main room of the cardinal's apartment as if he belonged there. This was the legendary weekly luncheon hosted by Maglione, with diplomats resident in Vatican City the featured guests. Deane knew this gathering to be the engine of the Holy

See's reputation as a purring machine of espionage, and he arrived with all antennae upright. Light streamed in from high Venetian windows through which the dome of St. Peter's could be seen, looming like a tethered dirigible. He wheeled right, toward a dozen men, all but one in cassocks. They were standing in groups of three and four, holding apéritif glasses and cigarettes. Mostly their robes were black with red accents, like Deane's, but three wore purple-band cinctures, and of those, two wore matching purple skullcaps — bishops, therefore. Not a screaming scarlet cassock in sight — good: Cardinal Maglione was not present yet, which meant Deane was on time.

A burst of laughter came from one of the groups, centered on a short, portly man, one of those wearing the purple sash: Domenico Tardini, the director of the Pontifical Relief Commission — Deane's boss in Rome. Tardini was an apostolic protonotary supernumerary, a position reserved for key papal aides. Given the tenor of their last encounter, the day before, Deane was surprised when Tardini waved him over.

Tardini was standing with the short man in striped pants, waistcoat, and cutaway. Deane realized from his coal-black hair and facial features that he was Japanese. What's this?

But then it hit him. With the liberation, the Allied diplomats who'd taken refuge from the Germans in Vatican City would have just switched places with Japs and — Deane looked around — Krauts? As Deane approached Monsignor Tardini, the Japanese man turned away to join a separate conversation. A tray-bearing waiter appeared at Deane's elbow, remaining immobile while Deane bowed before Tardini to kiss his ring. "Most Reverend, Sir."

Monsignor Tardini was still grinning from whatever had prompted the laughter Deane had heard, and he continued to smile as each of the other men greeted the American, fluent Italian all around. Only then did Deane turn to the waiter to take the single tulip glass. He sipped it and recognized the bitter Cinzano, a drink he had always avoided in Rome.

"We were speaking just now of your compatriot," Tardini said in Italian, the grin growing bigger again.

"Oh, Monsignor?" Deane replied, skating over the frozen under-
current. "And who would that be?"

"The much reported soldier, one Sergeant O'Hara, who yesterday
stood on his Sherman tank at the Colosseum, gestured at the ancient
ruin, and said"— Tardini paused long enough to indicate that, even in
Italian, one could invoke a stage-Irish brogue —"'Glory be to God, the
Germans bombed that, too?'"

Once more, guffaws all around, including the Japanese man, though
he remained half turned away, clearly avoiding Deane.

"Very interesting, Monsignor." Deane raised the glass to his lips but
did not sip. "And who reported this?"

Another prelate said, "The BBC, naturally. Who else?"

Deane shook his head. "Lord Haw-Haw on Radio Berlin, I'd have
thought." He was the soul of *buon umore*. At the mention of Berlin,
the Japanese dignitary turned toward Deane, who immediately met
his eyes. "Or Tokyo Rose, perhaps." Deane's grin said, Just joking. He
nodded at the diplomat, who once more turned quickly away.

Now Deane allowed himself a hefty swallow of the drink he held.
Foul taste, just as he recalled, but the familiar jolt of alcohol was welcome. He turned his smile on Tardini. "And if the GI's name was
O'Hara, Most Reverend Monsignor, we can be sure he had the nuns in
school, and therefore knows full well what the Colosseum is."

Monsignor Tardini stared at Deane for a long moment. With the
insult upended, an unwelcome air of unease had blown in. Tardini
sought to dispel it by putting a casual hand on Deane's forearm and in-
troducing him as the new vice director of the Pontificia Commissione
di Assistenza. The clerics would have needed no further explanation,
since all were aware of Spellman, his generous sponsorship of the Pontifical Relief Commission — and his blatant ambition to be named papal secretary of state. Deane knew that his own status here depended
on his being Spellman's man. Normally, the thought of Spellman as
Maglione's successor would have provoked laughter among the Italian prelates, but Maglione was sickly, and at war's end power politics
would shift. The Church might need an American at the Pope's elbow, and His Holiness was unpredictable. It cost the Vatican insiders

nothing to curry favor with the wily Spellman, and therefore with his man here. Hence the implication of affection in Tardini's introduction. Deane knew better than to take it personally, especially after yesterday.

Before the limp-handed introductions were complete, a flurry of arrival noises drifted in from the apartment entrance, and, like leaves to the rising sun, the gathering turned. Cardinal Maglione, a scarecrow figure made even more stick-like by his bright red, shoulder-caped vestments, swooped into the room at the head of a small parade of other men. Deane had laid eyes on the great prelate only across the distance of the nave of St. Peter's, and he wondered why Maglione seemed so familiar. Then he realized he was looking at El Greco's *Saint Jerome*, if shorn of the beard.

Despite Maglione's grotto-eyed gauntness, he seemed vital and happy, with his hands alternately upraised, as if greeting pilgrims, and then tugging at his watered-silk cincture, which seemed not quite to fit. Indeed, the air of recent weight loss clung to him. Yet his broad smile was surprisingly engaging. When he met Deane's gaze, he stopped for an instant, a kind of recognition, then moved on. Behind Maglione were two more bishops, three dark-suited laymen, and, bringing up the rear, a lean cleric in an unadorned black soutane, another El Greco figure, but this of a young man.

Protocol brought Maglione to Tardini, who deftly kissed the ring, the single *baciamano* that this gathering would require. The cardinal ignored Deane and the others, instead turning back to announce his party. He gestured the laymen forward, but was suddenly speaking in a language that momentarily threw Deane. Only upon hearing the name "von Weizsäcker" did he realize it was German.

From then on, Deane's major project was to stifle the cold resentment he felt. The initial current of interest he'd sensed coming from Maglione was perhaps a breed of embarrassment, stirred by recognition of his being American, for the prelate had arrived with Ernst von Weizsäcker, the German ambassador to the Holy See, and his deputy, Albrecht von Kessel, both dressed alike in dark business suits. Von Weizsäcker had a full head of white hair, dramatically combed straight back. He carried himself with an exaggeratedly upright posture and took in his surroundings with one eye half closed, as if missing its monocle. Maglione's flamboyant introduction of the pair was greeted with a chipper round of applause.

Deane knew of both Germans, especially von Weizsäcker, the patrician Prussian who had served as Hitler's secretary of state. Berlin had posted him to the Holy See just as the German vise closed on Rome in September. In briefings at Spellman's office, Deane had heard that von Weizsäcker had then lodged Germany's formal protest against Catholic sheltering of "criminal elements," by which, of course, he meant Jews. It was a protest he'd have made to Maglione, yet here was Maglione kissing his heinie — and covering it. Now that the Allies held Rome, the Kraut diplomat was himself a criminal element, taking refuge under the skirts of Holy Mother the Church.

Deane stood to the side, near one of the grand windows, sipping his Cinzano as if he liked it. He watched as the gathering reordered itself around the Germans. In addition to the diplomats, and two or three of Maglione's Curia flunkies, the arrivals included a bespectacled, cape-wearing German bishop. That would be Ludwig Graz, Deane realized, the rector of the German national church in Rome. Positioned a step behind Graz, ready to take an order, was the dark-complected El Greco figure, the young priest in black.

The strings of conversation had easily reknotted into German, reminding Deane of the Vatican's astounding multilingualism. He chided himself for not seeing this coming. Von Weizsäcker and von Kessel, to avoid arrest by the Americans, would have taken over Vatican apartments just vacated by American and British diplomats. Deane had to remind himself: the Vatican was neutral in this war. His Church was neutral.

The day before, when Deane's wires had unexpectedly crossed with Tardini's, the short-circuit was sparked not by the diplomats, but by the place where they were housed. Like the Allies before them, the Axis envoys would now be lodged in Santa Marta, the hospice compound on the opposite side of St. Peter's Square from the Apostolic Palace, beside the Gate of Bells. Santa Marta was one of the first places in Vatican City that Deane had asked to be shown.

The group of buildings, surrounding a courtyard containing a statue of the Madonna and Child, was constructed in the late nineteenth century to house victims of a cholera outbreak, and then served as a hostel for pilgrims. Deane's guide was one of the sisters of St. Vincent de Paul, the nuns who've been running the place for the half century of its existence. The sister wore the cobalt-blue habit of her order, but what really made her distinctive were the starched white wings of her headgear. From the neck up, she looked like a swan about to take flight.

She had assumed that the American wanted to be shown the VIP quarters, the apartments on the top floors of the five-story building where the diplomats lived—the "guests of the Holy Father"—or perhaps the rooms on the lower floors that housed union leaders, cousins of Victor Emmanuel, or former associates of Mussolini's who had defected after Il Duce's overthrow. A mélange of political misfits had been resident in the place throughout the war. But no, Deane had asked her to show him the cellars.

Santa Marta had provided a home not only for the well-connected, but also for a multitude of anonymous sanctuary seekers, with the dank cellars reserved for the last to come when the Germans took over Rome. In crypts that once served as the cholera morgue were hidden the most desperate of the refugees, the ones the Germans had most wanted. And, assuming they were still there, the ones Deane wanted to see for himself.

The nun gathered the hem of her robes as she wound down the staircase. The rosary hanging from the white cincture at her waist clanked against the iron handrail. Deane had to duck to keep from hitting low-wattage light bulbs and was soon walking at an ever more stooped angle. The subterranean complex below the nineteenth-century edifice implied an archeological calendar, less cellars than caverns that once opened into pagan mausoleums, catacombs, the Vatican necropolis.

As Deane followed the nun through several arched thresholds, he thought of André Gide's *Caves of the Vatican*, a work of bitter satire that ridiculed the blind wanderers amid the cloisters and catacombs of faith. But since the novel had been published, in the early twentieth century, the popular image had taken hold of a deeply buried labyrinth of dank tunnels coursing under Vatican Hill. Fanciful but false. Caves suited the anti-Catholic imagination. Instead, what Deane found was a mundane series of cement-paved corridors, lit and clean, with whitewashed walls. Stout wooden portals to which his escort paid no attention closed off numerous rooms and hallways, leading he knew not where.

Deane sensed that this underground realm was actually far from mundane. That human beings had lately been unspeakably hounded in the heart of Europe still left him short of words, and he was unable to shake the nagging worry that he was himself somehow tied to it. Whatever defined the facts of the Jewish condition north of the Alps, here, in the very heart of Catholicism, that condition had to have been different. Complaints of Roman Catholic unconcern, or worse, about the fate of Jews had to be untrue. Deane thought of that Jew on the airplane to Rome. He wished the man, Warburg, were at his side now, both of them seeing with their own eyes that the Church had not failed this test.

Finally the nun led him to an arched entranceway, sealed by a pair of peaked wooden doors; in the center of each was a closed iron grill, suggesting that once a prison had operated here. This was the heart of the labyrinth. With little effort the nun pushed the doors open; they were unlocked. A broad, rectangular room, low-ceilinged but bright, stretched before them. Several dozen cots were ordered in four rows, with blankets tucked into mattresses. Washstands, straight-backed wooden chairs, and cloth-draped shelves stood along the walls. Bundles sat at the feet of the narrow beds, but only here and there. A pair of Vincentian sisters, each with her winged headdress, were busy folding blankets, cleaning up a recently abandoned space.

Despite the impression of tidiness, a faint stench of overcrowding remained. Perhaps a dozen people were seated or stretched out on various cots, at a remove from one another. The nun explained in unadorned Italian that, until a few days before, more than one hundred people had been living in this space, including children. And this, she said, was only one cellar room among several that had served as dormitories. All but the few "guests" before them had promptly left when the Americans entered Rome.

"And these?" Deane asked.

"They are sick. Or they are not Romans, not Italians. They are perhaps travelers from abroad. Bohemia. They have no one to help them. They have nowhere to go. But they must leave. The bishop said they must depart."

Deane left the nun's side to approach an elderly woman who was sitting on the edge of her cot. Her head was covered with a firmly knotted scarf, and her possessions were bundled at her feet. Tears streaked her face. To Deane's surprise, a rosary was wrapped around her cupped hands. Her lips were moving through the *Aves*. Deane gently touched her shoulder. "*Vi benedica, Signora*," he said. She ignored him.

He returned to the nun. "What bishop?" he asked.

"Bishop Salerno. I asked Mother Pascalina for confirmation, but she said I was to defer to His Excellency."

"I'll speak to the bishop, Sister. We will let these people stay as long as they want."

The nun did not reply.

"And the rosary, Sister. Why is she saying the rosary?"

The nun looked at him blankly.

"If she is Jewish. You told me this is where the Jews have been hidden."

"Yes, Father," the nun replied, "but they are baptized Jews. The Jews who come to His Holiness for protection, they are baptized."

Within moments, Deane presented himself unannounced at Tardini's office on the far side of St. Peter's Square. The gatekeeper in the outer office, an aged Jesuit, recognized Deane from his welcome visit that morning and did not try to stop him when he brushed past, opening Tardini's door without knocking. The stout prelate was seated at an overlarge desk. Standing beside him was a nun whose white habit was set off by her black veil — a Dominican. Both she and Tardini looked up at Deane with startled expressions. The nun had been leaning at Tardini's side. She held a pencil, with which she had apparently been ticking off items on some document. Seeing Deane, she reached down to the document and turned it over.

"Please excuse my interruption, Most Reverend, Sir," Deane said. But he, too, was startled. A nun at the prelate's elbow? And what's on that paper?

Tardini stared impassively at Deane, then forced a smile. He said, "No, no. We were just finishing."

At that, the nun scooped up the document, and other papers, from the prelate's desk and quickly moved away. She left the room without raising a glance toward Deane.

Tardini's desk was positioned in front of tall windows, open to the square. Again Deane said, "Forgive my intrusion, Reverend Monsignor."

A cigarette sat smoldering in an ashtray, and Tardini smothered his impatience with his reach. "What is it, Father?"

"I've just come from Santa Marta," Deane said. "I've just been told that the Jews we've been protecting here in Vatican City are converted Jews. Catholic Jews. Can that be so?"

Through cigarette smoke, Tardini dumbly blinked up at the American monsignor. "What? What?"

Deane said, "I have heard the point made again and again, Monsignor. I've made it myself. Many dozens of Jews have been given sanctuary within the walls of the Vatican. This is the great rebuttal to the charge of the Holy Father's indifference to Hitler's crime against Jews. And now I learn that the Jews here are baptized?"

"Some are baptized, Father. Certainly. That must be true. Among so many."

"But all? Or most? How many?"

"And some are the spouses of the baptized. They themselves are not Catholics. They are unconverted Jews. Many wives and husbands."

"How many?"

Tardini shrugged.

"Monsignor, I have heard Archbishop Spellman describe the Vatican's extraordinary—if discreet—rescue of Jews. He describes it to Jewish leaders in New York. He described it to President Roosevelt, when Roosevelt asked why His Holiness has not condemned the Nazis for—"

"Roosevelt has no right to ask . . . What has Roosevelt done?"

Aside from the invasion of Normandy? But Deane checked himself. "No one says the Vatican rescue is of *baptized* Jews."

Tardini carefully returned his cigarette to the ashtray. He picked up a pen, capped it, and placed it beside a curved felt blotter. His lips were pressed together. "Dear Father Deane, Herr Hitler does not care if the Jews are baptized." He leaned forward. His left hand trembled slightly when he raised a finger. "Do you think Hitler cares if they are baptized? They are *still* Jews. Catholic Jews, too, must be protected. And as it happens, the *convertiti* are mainly the ones that come to us. They trust us."

"*Convertiti?*" Deane said. "*Conversos?*" The Inquisition-era word was a slur, carrying an implication of blood impurity. Deane thought of the other word for converted Jews—*Marrano,* meaning swine.

"Yes, Father—if you will, *conversos.* We have a special obligation to Catholic Jews."

Once again Deane thought of the American Jew. How would this strike Warburg? But he knew. "Excuse me, Reverend Monsignor, but our obligation is to all."

Tardini shrugged, an eloquent world-weariness, more than a touch of impatience. "If we could help all, we would. And our paramount obligation is to do nothing that would make matters worse. As it is, we help those who come to us."

"And send a message to other Jews about the benefit of conversion. Accept baptism, and we will protect you. Is that it?"

"Did you see a baptistry in Santa Marta? There are three hundred and twenty-nine parishes in Rome. I am told that most of them are hiding Jews. No one demands baptismal certificates."

"I was asking about *here*. The Holy Father's household."

"And you have your answer." Tardini snuffed his cigarette, picked up his pen. Dismissed.

Now, looking across Maglione's drawing room at the jovial knot around Tardini, Deane had to stifle an urge to call out to von Weizsäcker and von Kessel, to ask if they knew that at Santa Marta they were sharing a residence with Jews. Rosary or not, the people downstairs from you are Jews! But he checked himself. If he could harbor an impulse to expose the cellar Jews to these Germans, it was because now the Germans were powerless, the Jews were safe.

Deane watched the Axis diplomats with their self-satisfied bowing, clicking of heels, and clinking of tulip glasses, but the disgust he felt was more at his fellow clergy, so thrilled to be in the company of these shits.

"You are the American monsignor." Someone surprised Deane, coming from behind him, speaking accented English and touching him on the elbow. "We've heard of you."

Deane turned and found the young German priest standing there. He had come from the table where the apéritif was being poured, and in addition to his own glass he was holding a fresh drink for Deane. "Here. Champagne. It's better." He took Deane's empty glass and handed it to a passing waiter. Though the unadorned black of his cassock marked him as junior, the priest carried himself as if he were a regular at Maglione's lunches. He'd entered with Archbishop Graz, the ranking German Catholic in Rome. Clearly this priest had made himself essential to the boss, a recognizable clerical type, the skilled factotum — from the Latin for "do everything." But then, Deane thought, I should know.

"Thank you. I'm Kevin Deane." He raised his glass.

The German clinked it. "Roberto Lehmann."

"Roberto?"

Lehmann laughed. "*Sí.* I was born in Buenos Aires. But I am from Mainz. My mother is Argentinian. My father was an importer." The German's oiled hair gave him an exotic, Valentino-like appearance.

His soutane was a well-tailored worsted. His fingernails were mani-cured.

"You are from New York."

"Indeed so. Bronx Irish Catholic. Your English is good."

"Necessity." Lehmann smiled. "I learned your language yesterday."

"General Clark would be flattered. Soon American slang will be heard in the streets of Rome," Deane said, "if not on the Third Floor — the papal apartments."

Lehmann smiled. "I know where the Pope's quarters are."

"Well then, perhaps you can answer a question."

"I hope so."

"I brought a personal gift from Archbishop Spellman for His Holi-ness. The archbishop instructed me to leave it with the papal valet. But yesterday a German nun headed me off—"

"Mother Pascalina."

"Yes."

"The Holy *Hausfrau*," Lehmann said.

"What's the story on her?" Deane asked. "She seemed to have real authority. She insisted on talking to me in German. Is it possible the woman speaks no Italian?"

Lehmann shrugged. "What was the gift?"

"An electric razor."

Lehmann laughed, and then so did Deane, despite himself. He'd tried to tell Spellman to send something else, but the archbishop said the Pope loves the latest gadgets. "His Holiness shaves every morn-ing, too," Spellman added. "He puts his pants on one leg at a time, Kevin."

"He wears pants?" Deane said, but Spellman did not laugh.

The German again touched Deane with easy familiarity. "So Amer-ican—a razor with a motor. As for Mother Pascalina, she was the Pope's housekeeper in Berlin when he was just the papal nuncio. She came with him here to Rome. Not *Hausfrau*, actually, but *Oberhaupt*. Mother Pascalina is from Freistaat Thüringen, the home of the Dober-man pinscher." Lehmann laughed again, then made a show of looking left before adding quietly, "You can be certain she took the razor for herself. The mustache nun."

Deane made no comment, but thought it odd that a nun was the assistant to the Pope. And Tardini, too, depended on a nun. Was that Dominican sister also an *Oberhaupt*?

Lehmann offered a cigarette to Deane, who took it. Lehmann flipped his lighter, a fancy gold trinket with a cross engraved on its side. Holy smoke, thought Deane.

Exhaling, they looked out the window at the swelling crowd of pilgrims below. "It is good that Rome was spared from destruction," Lehmann said. "The world owes that to him." Turning, he used his glass to point at von Weizsäcker.

"How is that, Father?"

"The ambassador convinced Field Marshal Kesselring to base his Panzers outside the city. There were no major Wehrmacht setups in Rome. You say 'setups'? Therefore, no targets for your Air Corps. Nothing for your bombers. On June 2, after meeting with von Weizsäcker, Kesselring chose to abandon Rome without a fight, leaving the way open for Clark."

"So it was humane German goodwill that fended destructive American bombs and artillery."

"Yes. That is sure."

Deane said, "I suspect that Cardinal Maglione would say Rome was spared because of His Holiness. Look at the signs there." In the square below, banners were being unfurled: *Grazie, Sancta Papa!* A huge poster showing the face of Pius XII was being dropped from Bernini's colonnade. Deane asked, "Whose idea was it to invite Romans to come here to thank His Holiness for the liberation? It's already being described as a spontaneous assembly. But haven't you heard the loudspeaker trucks? 'Come to St. Peter's to thank the Holy Father.' That's Cardinal Maglione."

"You object?"

"Of course not. Although I think a word of thanks to General Clark might be in order. Not to your ambassador — in point of fact."

Squinting through his cigarette smoke, Lehmann turned from the window to eye the prelates and the German diplomats. He said coldly, "His Holiness would have been taken prisoner by the SS were it not for von Weizsäcker."

Deane said, "And Ambassador von Weizsäcker came to his enlightened point of view with help from . . . ?"

"Yes. Archbishop Graz. Protecting His Holiness. Protecting Rome. It has been our daily work. Our daily prayer." Lehmann brought his eyes back to Deane, whose own were there waiting.

"I know the game you play, Father," Deane said.

"Because," Lehmann replied, "you yourself are a master."

"Tell me, is it true what they say about Regina Coeli?"

"The prison?"

"Where, three days ago, as your humane soldiers began their retreat, they lined up Partisan prisoners and trade union leaders against a wall and shot them."

"I have not heard that."

"At La Sorta, more than a hundred were lined up and forced to kneel. They were shot in the neck, from behind."

"Is that what they say?"

"Yes. And they say that from the Ponte Milvio, where the emperor Constantine had his vision of the cross, there are corpses hanging today."

"Constantine was from Germany, did you know that?"

"They say the Via Cassia has been sown with mines. Dozens of horses shot where they stood on the streets."

"I have no idea if it is true. Of course, it could be."

"Where does that leave your humane German goodwill?"

"Would you care to compare legends of atrocity, Monsignor?"

It seemed to Deane that the German was daring him to mention Jews.

Lehmann waited. When it was clear that Deane would not reply, the German went on, amiable again. "The point now, of course, is to emphasize the diplomacy role the Holy Father can continue to play, perhaps in partnership with your Archbishop Spellman."

"And with your Archbishop Graz?" Deane asked. "You're thinking of the mediation fantasy."

"Why do you say 'fantasy,' Monsignor? No one in the world is better placed than His Holiness to bring about a truce between the Allies and my country. Ambassador von Weizsäcker has spoken of just such a thing to Archbishop Graz. And with your Spellman reaching out to Washington . . . Archbishop Spellman's position—"

Deane cut Lehmann off with a sharply raised hand. No speaking here of Spellman's position, nor of his ambition, toward which the sly Kraut was aiming his arrow. "A German truce with the Allies?" Deane said. "Not *all* of the Allies, surely. Isn't the idea for Washington and London to join forces with Berlin against Moscow, making Russia our *former* ally? Isn't that it?"

"Are you aware of the Red Army's rampage, moving west?" Lehmann asked. "The Catholic Church is civilization's only hope against such godless brutality. And if I may add, Germany and Hitler are not the same thing."

A faint gong sounded, and a pair of elaborately carved doors at the far end of the room swung open. The two dozen men began to move as one into a second equally opulent chamber. Tray-bearing waiters appeared on either side of the doorway, collecting glasses and cigarette butts.

With Cardinal Maglione at the head of the long, elaborately set banquet table, the men took their places according to precedence—Deane and Lehmann near the foot of the table. All remained standing. The cardinal intoned a Latin blessing. Everyone but the diplomats crossed himself and said "Amen." With a rustle of chairs, they were seated. They snapped open their linen napkins.

Deane's gaze went to a gold-framed object on the wall behind Lehmann—a blanket-sized print of an early-Renaissance map, sepia tones, faint blue meridian lines, a faded red compass rose. Not a print. An original. It showed the world, with the boot of Italy at dead center. A crescent-shaped swath of land to the left, across an ocean—a best guess of the shape of the New World. Something about the primitive cartography struck Deane as odd.

All eyes turned to Maglione as he lifted a long-stemmed crystal goblet of red wine. Everyone knew to imitate him. The cardinal said, "*Al Papa.*" In Italian he continued his toast: "He saved the city of Rome. All Rome today will thank him." Then he added, in Latin, "*Defensor civitatis.*"

Deane caught Lehmann's eye and winked. So much for the spontaneity of Rome's outpouring of gratitude.

As Deane sipped his wine, his gaze went back to the map on the wall: marking the blank place where the United States of America would eventually take form were the words *Terra Incognita.*

FOUR

Intercedite Pro Nobis

ARGUERITE D'ERASMO WAS sitting on an uncushioned wooden bench in a narrow corridor on the top floor of a worn-down building that seemed to have been built as a school, but had, in Fascist times, been given over to routines of some bureaucracy. Around her, Americans were hurrying to and fro. Every male stared at her as he passed, but she refused to raise her eyes.

They were bareheaded and carried themselves with the urgent tempo of messengers, but they wore the rumpled brown uniforms of combat soldiers, and their boots bore crusts of mud. Letting boots occupy the field of her concentration meant they could never find her eyes. Men.

Fish. Her mind jumped sideways — no, back. For a moment she was in flight from Trieste, in the hold of the fishing boat. In the notch-like corner she had made herself even smaller than this. The reeking space was crowded with other bodies, although in the dark of the bulkhead she could not see them. Sounds of whimpering, breathing. The stench of vomit. And urine, always urine. Someone's pleuritic cough. They were fellow fugitives, each with a separate desperation.

Yet no one's desperation could compare with hers. Wasn't that why, when she felt a rough metal protrusion breaking the surface of the wall where her face was resting, she had rubbed against it, scouring the skin at her cheekbone where his lips had touched her, where his fist had fallen. Her facial bruise began to bleed. *Despise not my petitions.*

On the street downstairs—here in Rome, two hours before—an American sentry had refused to allow Père Antoine and Giacomo Lionni into the building with her—not even the priest. When she produced the calling card the tall American civilian had given her at the airport, and had then paired it with her stamped Red Cross credentials, the sentry took both and disappeared. When he returned, he was accompanied by an officer who returned her credentials, but not the card. He gestured her into the building, then held his hand up to stop the others. No admittance except for the woman. That should have told her.

Instead of taking her to an important office, the officer led her to a stairwell and down a shadowy flight to the cavernous below-grade floor, isolated and dark. As she followed him around a corner, he all at once turned on her. "Signorina . . . ," he began, but with misery in his voice, not threat. She knew what he was up to, her new expertise. He took his wallet from his trousers. His fingers were like sausages. He opened the wallet and removed a bill of a currency she did not recognize. He held it delicately before her face, letting the green paper dangle from his thumb and forefinger, while with his other hand he fumbled with the buttons at his fly. There was nothing of force in him, only the expectation of compliance. Weren't all *le donne di Roma* starving? Hadn't they all become whores? Or had he seen something in her that led him to assume that she would gratify him?

Her face must have carried the answer, for she could see him realize the mistake he'd made. His eyes widened. He stepped back from her. Once, it might have shocked Marguerite to find herself—to find women—so routinely victimized, but no longer. War.

Did this man know what she could do to him? She had already been thinking of herself as two distinct persons. He had seen the first: victim. Now he saw the second: killer.

With his fat hands atremble, he stuffed the money back into his pocket. He turned abruptly, wanting to get away, but also saying, "Follow me."

She went behind him down a corridor, then up a long, winding spiral of stairs, passing one level after another, to the top floor of the building. At a wooden hallway bench already half taken up by three rough-looking Italian men, he pointed for her to sit. He disappeared into the adjoining office, and moments later reappeared. With gestures — pointing at his wristwatch, then at the door — he indicated that this was where she should wait. He started to head off, but she raised a hand, stopping him. "If you please," she said in curt English. "The card." He glanced at the Italians beside her, discounted them. Sheepishly, with his fat fingers he searched in his pockets for the business card she'd given to the sentry. He found it, handed it to her, and was gone. Pathetic man. Pathetic men.

At last the door opened, and a squat soldier came out. Stripes marked his sleeve. He cast his eyes over those on the bench, finally settling his gaze on her. He said, "*Signorina? Che cosa volete?*"

"Yes," she answered, a sharp English word. "I am here for Mr. Warburg. He knows me. He gave me this." She offered the card, aware that if this Warburg were as important as he'd seemed at the airport, her escorting officer would never have crudely dangled money in her face. This soldier ignored the card and instead pushed the door half open with a sweeping gesture aimed at her. Marguerite stood but made no move to go where his hand pointed. With his partial blocking of the threshold, she would have had to brush against him.

To Marguerite's left was the glass panel of another door, and she glimpsed her reflection in it. In an instant of self-measurement, she saw the wholly unfetching, loosely draped skirt of a Red Cross worker, a white blouse closed at her throat, and the oversized blue sweater that cloaked her breasts. Only the red neckerchief at her throat gestured at style, but that was for the sake of the bruises on her neck. She saw the gash, still marking her left cheek, where she'd rubbed her face against the metal of the boat.

The soldier waited, but she did not move. He shrugged, then led the way into the room.

There were four desks, each piled high with cartons, and each, but one, being worked by a man in dusty olive. At the rearmost desk sat a man in a gray suit, white shirt, and necktie, his black hair sharply parted and slicked back. A cigarette hung from his lips, a ribbon of smoke rising into his squinted eye. He was leaning back in his chair, a foot stuck in the bottom drawer of his desk.

He swiveled, saw her, and tipped forward in his chair. In short order, he hung up the phone, came around the desk, and stretched his hand out to greet her.

Marguerite stifled her disappointment. She had come on the remote chance that he could help with the mad scheme, but now she felt that the chance was gone. At the airport depot, he had conducted himself like an American of rank, but this cluttered space, shared with military nobodies, sealed the conclusion she had come to in the corridor: yet another poseur. That he seemed glad to see her did not help.

"Hello, Miss," he said.

She took his hand, contact that made her aware of all she was withholding. She said, "Hello, Sir."

"How did you find me?" he asked. "I only realized later how useless my card from Washington would be."

"No. Not useless. On the Via Veneto, General Clark's headquarters. Someone knew you."

"Right. They put me here." He grinned, sweeping his arm around the cramped room.

But she was not grinning. "'War refugees,' you said at Ciampino." His eyes were nothing like Carlo's. "I work also with refugees."

"Yes, I saw that. You were right to demand that milk. Quirinal, was it? How are the children?"

"Not good. Not good."

"If you've come for more food, I can help, I assure you I can help—"

"No. No. I have not come for that." She read his question: Then what?

But he said, "Of course, even a dunce would have seized on the importance for my work of your being Red Cross. Back in Washington, I tried for weeks to contact the Red Cross in Rome, but we concluded that the Germans shut you down months ago."

Marguerite only stared back at him.

"But obviously," Warburg said, "in Washington we knew nothing. I should have taken your information when I met you at the airport." He picked up a canvas-cloaked bundle, freeing a chair. The other men in the room were busy at their chores with boxes and papers. Lists, she saw, pages with columns of names. On a makeshift bulletin board, such papers were being posted beneath hand-lettered headings: *Casoli, Cremona, Lipari, Malo* . . . Familiar town names to Marguerite, the locations of what had been Fascist holding camps.

Warburg handed off the bundle to the soldier, saying, "Clear the room, Sergeant. Give the men a smoke break." An order, a wave of the hand, and, like that, Marguerite and Warburg were nearly alone. A man of authority after all. The soldier who had shown her in was waiting at the threshold for an order.

"Here," Warburg said. "Sit."

"I prefer not to sit."

"Oh." A look of mystified helplessness crossed his face, but it went as quickly as it came. He stepped back to the desk and leaned over to snuff out his cigarette in a cluttered ashtray.

She said, "I have colleagues . . . downstairs. They were not admitted."

"Well," Warburg said, "let's go downstairs, then." It was unusual not to be taller than the person she was speaking with. Marguerite's father had told her again and again that her gawky height was proof of royal blood, and only gradually had she realized he was teasing. He had not lived long enough to reckon with a daughter who was taller than he.

"Shall I bring my translator?" Warburg cast a glance at the soldier in the doorway.

"I can translate," she said.

A few minutes later, Marguerite and Warburg were closeted in a small room on the first floor, waiting for Père Antoine and Signor Lionni to be shown in. Alone, the American man and the Italian woman had found it impossible to speak. No matter what he said to her, she responded with barely more than the hint of a shrug. Finally the door opened, and a soldier showed in the white-robed priest and his diminutive partner, a Roman version of Quixote and Sancho Panza.

The surprise came when Lionni, speaking through Marguerite, told Warburg his name.

"I beg your pardon?" Warburg said.

"Lionni. Giacomo Lionni."

"Lionni? I know of a man called Jocko Lionni. You?"

Lionni nodded.

"The Delegation to Assist?" Warburg said, checking the astonishment he felt in seeing this small man. "You are the head of the Delegation to Assist Hebrews, correct? I have lists that originate with you. We've been trying to find you. My God, Lionni, we thought you were dead."

After Marguerite translated, Lionni grinned. "That was what the Germans were supposed to think."

Warburg clasped Lionni's hand. "You gave us what we needed to persuade Washington to send us."

"Us?" Marguerite asked.

"Me," Warburg answered. "The War Refugee Board in Rome—just me. For now. This is just a start of American help." He faced Lionni. "We know what you've done."

After Marguerite's translation, Lionni pushed the priest forward. "Not what I have done," he said, then waited out the translation before adding, "Padre Antonio. The rabbi of the Delegation since October." Lionni spread his infectious grin again.

After the brief translation, Warburg turned to the priest. "I'm honored, Father. I know of your work, too. A monastery on Via Sicilia, yes?"

The priest nodded.

"Thank you," Warburg said.

Lionni stepped between them. "But we are here to speak with you of something else." Again, the translation; again, the next sentence. "Not refugees," Lionni said. "Slaves. Soon to be smoke." Without waiting, Lionni pulled out of his shirt the folded paper. Opening its creases on the table, he slowly smoothed each newly exposed line with the fleshy part of his hand. Lionni wanted Warburg to sense this map's importance.

The Italian placed the tip of his forefinger. "*Conosce Fossoli?*"

Marguerite: "You know Fossoli?"

Warburg nodded. "Former POW camp. Holding pen for points north. Prisoners overwhelmingly Jewish."

An efficient tattoo, needles of a man's Italian and a woman's accented English, painted the picture of what Lionni wanted. Four hundred still alive. Ready for the railroad cars. Warburg focused on the map and saw the hatched line over the Po River.

He looked up. "So you think the Army Air Corps drops the bridge, that solves the problem?" He was addressing Lionni, but he was staring at Marguerite.

She translated. Lionni shrugged. "Solves one problem," he said. "The other problems we take in order."

It had never occurred to Warburg that more could be done than the arrangement of an exodus for those who had, by dint of luck or wit, already eluded the Nazis or escaped them. They were running. His job, he'd thought, was to give them a place to run to. Islands of Swedish sovereignty in Budapest. A Danube channel. A gateway out in Istanbul. Equivalents, perhaps, in other cities. But here was a proposal to catch the Nazis in the act. Once.

But Warburg checked himself. He faced Lionni. "So we get the bridge blown. The rolling stock cannot roll. The prisoners cannot be taken north. The Germans still have them. Then what?"

Lionni leaned forward, and Marguerite imitated him as she translated. "The senior SS have already departed the camp, ahead of the broad German retreat. The prisoners are the left-behinds, and their guards are left-behinds, too. You say 'left-behinds'?"

"What do you mean?"

"Not combat soldiers. The German guards are themselves wounded. Weak. Very young. The guards are fewer than twenty."

"How does he know this?"

"He knows."

"Wounded. Weak," Warburg repeated. "Still with weapons, no? Still with orders to clear the camp. If we prevent them from evacuating the prisoners, what do you think they do then?"

Lionni stared hard at the American. Finally Lionni spoke, an un-punctuated forced march of iron words. Then he stopped.

Marguerite translated very slowly, her eyes cast down; someone else speaking through her. "'What then? What then?' If we had thought in November 'What then?,' thought what was to come in December, we would not have been here in January. If we thought 'What then?' in January—no February. The Jews of Rome lost the luxury of 'What then?,' the luxury of a future tense. The Jews of Fossoli have at most four days unless something is done. Is that a future, Mr. Warburg?"

When Warburg replied simply, "No," Marguerite conveyed the negation even more simply, with a shake of her head.

When a breeze swept into the room, the corners of the map on the table flapped up. Warburg shuddered with a terrible recognition: he was a man of phony rank, impotent. "You understand," he forced himself to say, "I am not with the U.S. Army. I have nothing to do with target selection. Nothing at all to do with combat. Or bridges."

Instead of translating, Marguerite said to Warburg, "But they know of you at General Clark's headquarters. You yourself have the rank of general."

Warburg was aware of blood rushing to his face, a blush. This woman had witnessed it when, outlandishly, he had pulled rank on intimidated NCOs at Ciampino.

"You are here to help refugees?" she asked quietly. "Or only to bury them?"

Her words fell like a blow on Warburg, and he saw the names again—*Regio, Fiorello, Chiara*—the names he had studied on the reams of paper in the boxes in the cramped room on the top floor of this building, and before that in Washington. Until this moment, Warburg had not really understood what he had come to Rome to do. *Giannino Salvucci. Leona Modena.* Them.

Actual names had lodged themselves in Warburg's memory, but

suddenly they were mere names no more. The sight of the stooped but fierce Jew, Lionni, made Warburg long for the sight of other Jews. He wanted to picture individuals among the throng who were now his people, but as yet he had no faces. All he had were names.

Padre Antonio leaned forward with a raised finger. *"Mes amis,"* he began, and with his French he put Marguerite more at the center than before. She would have to translate into Italian and English both. The priest said that in addition to the absolute value of lives saved at Fossoli, the meaning of such an act for the thousands whose faith in humanity had been shattered would be impossible to calculate. Warburg understood him, and despite being moved, could not help imagining such a grandiose plea being put to Clark's commanders. Their eyes raised to the ceiling: the nobility of what humans could be capable of, if only they weren't human. It was the thought of those commanders that opened what was, in this room of his mind, the only other door — Peter Mates.

Standing by the river in the midst of an early-evening fog, Warburg remembered Burlington, where the air was always damp. By the time he returned there after college, both his parents had died, and it fell to him to clean out the old house. He came upon the prayer shawl in one of his father's boxes, and he had no idea what to do with it. There was no question of tossing it in with other odds and ends of clothing and household wares to be carted off. First he took the *tallit* to Burlington's modest Beth Israel synagogue, in a former Masonic lodge, but he'd found it impossible to enter the place. He thought of giving the *tallit* to one of his father's friends, but none of them were observant either. He thought of burying it, which he'd heard was proper, but that seemed wrong. In the end, concluding that it was the most respectful thing he could do, he took the shawl down to the lakeside and reverently unfolded it, taking the tangles out of its fringes. He stretched the cloth flat and, throwing it the way a fisherman does a net, let it sail out into the air. The cloth billowed, settled on the surface of the lake, and sank slowly until it was gone.

Now, staring into the river, Warburg thought of the rolls of the missing and the lost that were plastering the walls of his own attic office. *Salvucci . . . Modena.* Wasn't that the point of all the lists, a desperate refusal to abet the reduction of Jewishness to anonymity? To protect each name was to defy the Nazi effort to obliterate identity. Each name—a Jew!

At the memory of his sending the prayer shawl out onto the open water of Lake Champlain, Warburg felt a flare of shame. His grandfather, and perhaps others before, had covered their shoulders with that cloth, a sign of devotion. Warburg's father had declined to wear the *tallit* himself, yet had made it a solemn gift to his only son, offering a link to their past and to their people. And he, David Warburg, had said no. In the end, his notion of respect was mistaken. Therefore, why shouldn't he feel this remorse, having once cast that past and those people upon the waters, to drown?

"Hello, Warburg," Mates said as he joined him at the rail, elbows on the metal, facing the dark chop of the Tiber. Just there, the current was set against itself by the stout base of Ponte Fabricio, the oldest bridge in Rome, and the backwash stirred up a crusty black froth. Warburg had proposed this place for their meeting because the woman told him to. He said, "Thanks for getting here, Peter."

"What's so urgent?" Mates looked up at the dusky sky as the first drops of a light rain fell. "Damn," he muttered, then turned up the collar of his field jacket.

"I have some people I want you to meet," Warburg said. With that, he turned and headed out into the congested embankment boulevard.

"Hell," Mates called, "I have a meeting of my own. You're making me late."

But Warburg ignored Mates to thread through a snarl of traffic. Across the way, in front of a church, Lionni and Marguerite were waiting.

Warburg sensed the difference in Mates when he saw the woman, the forward slant of her beret that failed to hide her bruised cheek.

"This is Signor Lionni, Signorina d'Erasmo," Warburg said. "This is Colonel Mates."

Mates shook hands with Lionni, but Marguerite stood back. Mates looked at her. "D'Erasmo?" he asked.

"Sì."

Mates seemed about to say something, but Lionni interrupted, and Marguerite translated: "We must leave the rain."

Without a further word, Lionni led the way past a monumental half-column, vestige of Rome's long-lost grandeur, into the thick of a crowded neighborhood whose ruins were more mundane.

Moments later they were in a small room on the second floor of a nondescript community building. Glass-enclosed shelves held rows of books. Framed etchings showed intricate landscapes. In anticipation, Lionni had already come up here to lay out his map on the round central table. Books at the corners held the paper in place. The window blinds were shut tight. A cone-shaped light fixture hung over the table, setting shadows in motion as they approached, but illuminating the map like an unfurled sacred scroll. Warburg saw that the letters on the cover of the book on the corner nearest him were Hebrew. He glanced again at the shelves — Hebrew. The etchings showed an ancient hilltop city, palm trees, camels, a fantasy Jerusalem.

Mates did not disguise his impatience as he pushed in front of Warburg and barked a command in an imperious Italian. Lionni immediately responded, with equal authority, and quickly the two engaged in a series of no-nonsense exchanges.

Lionni again punctuated his explanation with sharp stabs of his index finger, identifying locations on the map. Amid the torrent of words, Warburg recognized "Fossoli," "Nazi," and "Po," but otherwise understood nothing.

Yet Mates's reaction, soon enough conveyed by a slow wagging of his head, could not have been plainer: No.

Lionni stared at Mates, his harsh intensity fading into supplication. "Please, Sir," he said in English. "Please."

Instead of answering Lionni, Mates looked over at Warburg. "What in God's name, Warburg? What?"

Warburg said, "Our bombers are dropping bridges all over northern Italy, Colonel. Why not that one?"

"How many reasons do you want?" Mates held up his five fingers. "The Fifth Army push is toward the Arno, not the Po, west not east — one. The Krauts are mauling our guys up there, so tactical air corps are doing close ground support, not interdicting transport — two. Twining's B-29s are finally in range of gasoline farms in Austria and Bavaria — three. Even if you blow that particular bridge, the poor creatures in that camp get killed on the spot instead of being sent north — four."

Warburg interrupted him. "The Waffen-SS have already left the camp. A minimal contingent of unseasoned guards, not heavyweights."

Mates ignored him. "And what are we talking about here, three or four hundred people? That's breakfast for Kesselring; every fucking day he's killing ten times that in combat — number five. And six" — having closed his five fingers into a fist, he seemed ready to shake it at Warburg — "you and I are Civil Affairs, not Operations. Tell your friends we have nothing to do with targeting. Quit posturing, for Christ's sake. Who are you trying to impress?"

"The OSS, Peter. Your outfit."

Mates stepped back. "Says who?"

"Your Special Ops command at Brindisi — you've set targets from Trieste to Belgrade. You could set this target."

Mates seared Warburg with his stare. But Warburg did not flinch. He said, "And now, using Civil Affairs as cover, you're my OSS minder. Assigned by General Donovan himself."

Mates laughed. "You have an outsized sense of your importance, my friend, if you think Donovan gives a shit about you. Or your —" He glanced at the unmoving Italians, and thought better of what he'd almost said. Instead, he lowered his voice. "Not 'targets,' David. 'Drops.' From Brindisi, I set drops. I had no authority over ordnance. Never set a target. Anyway, the Special Ops air force is defunct."

"You can call in chits with Clark, Peter," Warburg said. "There would be no antiaircraft guns in the Po Valley. An undefended stretch of river of no tactical significance. Not a formation of B-29s. A single P-51 would do fine. One unescorted sortie, one five-hundred-pound bomb. Less than an hour's fuel. If you won't make the case, help me to do it. Get me to the wing commander. We have to stop this transport.

These are not just any four hundred people. Right now they are the most important four hundred men, women, and children in Europe."

"Oh, really? Name two."

Warburg shot back, "Giannino Salvucci. Leona Modena."

Mates shrugged. "That makes my point. Drop the bridge, halt the transport—the Nazis just line them up in front of a ditch they were forced to dig themselves, and open fire."

"Not if, simultaneously, the world's attention is drawn to Fossoli, the plight of women and children, the Allies riding to the rescue." Warburg touched Mates's chest, adding, "General Clark would love it. A Movietone newsreel."

"Bullshit. Women and children are in duress from the Balkans to the Baltic. Who's going to make noise about these poor people?"

"The Pope."

Mates laughed out loud. "The Pope? Jesus Christ, Warburg. Jesus Fucking Christ. Which is the point. If the Lord Christ himself was in Fossoli, the Pope would still not breathe a word of it. Haven't you noticed? After the Nazis massacred those saps at Ardeatine, the Pope condemned not the Nazis but the Partisans, for bringing it on themselves! Yesterday, with two hundred thousand people on their knees in St. Peter's Square, including lots of teary GIs, he blessed the Krauts for sparing Rome, without a word of thanks to us. Up there on his balcony, above it all. He speaks German at dinner. He loves Berlin. He's pulling for the Führer."

"No, Peter. He's not." Warburg thought of that priest on the airplane. Warburg himself had expressed skepticism about the Church, but then there was Padre Antonio. "Catholics are helping Jews. What are *you* doing?"

"My small part to beat the fucking Germans. End the war. That's how we help the Jews."

"Who's the Fifth Bomber Wing commander? Just get me to him."

Mates glanced over at the woman, who was as unmoving, and as attentive, as the Jew beside her. She met Mates's eyes, held them with a bitter resolve. He looked back at Warburg and said, with a lowered voice, "It's because of her, isn't it? You're doing this because of her."

It was Marguerite who answered, in her clean, cold English. "He's doing it because of the people in Fossoli — as *you* should."

Mates studied her for a moment, then said, "You're Red Cross?"

"Yes."

"There was a man named d'Erasmo who was Red Cross director here."

"My father," Marguerite said.

"Your father . . ." Mates began, then stopped.

"They killed him," she said.

"I know," Mates said. "He was a brave man. A hero."

"And you, Colonel?" Marguerite said.

Mates deflected her by pulling his cigarettes out of the pocket of his blouse.

He offered the pack around, and all took cigarettes. Warburg snapped his lighter and offered it in turn. By the time a canopy of smoke billowed at the metal light fixture, Mates had changed his mind. "Killian. I know him."

"Good morning, Father." Deane pushed away from his desk to stand up. The German priest strode into the office with the skirts of his cassock aswirl. "*Benedicamus Domino*," Roberto Lehmann said. The two shook hands.

"Please," Deane said, gesturing at the supplicant's chair. Then he pulled his own chair halfway out from behind the desk. Both men sat.

"His Excellency sent me," Lehmann said.

"Archbishop Graz."

"Yes. You and I began a conversation. We should bring it to completion. The archbishop has met with the British ambassador. We have assurances of Mr. Churchill's support. London is enthusiastic. His Excellency thought it expedient to keep you informed."

"About what?"

"The Danube Federation."

Deane glared at Lehmann, a deliberate refusal to respond. This was not a phrase he knew, but what it implied was clear, and explosive. Only a month earlier, back in New York, he had sat in Archbishop

Spellman's walnut-paneled office listening to General William Donovan, in full uniform, embrace what Spellman had just proposed. Not the Danube Federation, but what Spellman called the Habsburg restoration. For two years, Spellman had been awaiting the right bet on which to place this priceless chip — that the legendary head of the Office of Strategic Services was a Vatican-friendly Irish Catholic, ready to let Spellman deal. And deal he had.

The Vatican scheme was simplicity itself. After Germany's defeat, and presented with a powerful local civic groundswell in the heart of Europe, what if the Anglo-American alliance promptly recognized the restoration of the dynasty under the long-deposed Archduke Otto of Austria? It would be a central European *Catholic* monarchy — as if World War I had never happened — and, more to the point, it would be a powerful bulwark against the Soviet Union.

In discussing the plan, Donovan and Spellman had finished each other's sentences, as if Stalin were already thwarted, as if Donovan's OSS operatives had already produced the civic groundswell demanding the return of the Catholic monarchy. When Spellman had asked if President Roosevelt would approve the project, Donovan had waved his hand, saying, "The President and I were law school classmates." By then, Donovan had come to think that the Habsburg restoration was his idea.

And now Lehmann was about to propose it as if Archbishop Graz had conceived the plan. Danube Federation, Habsburg restoration: same thing. Whatever it was called, Deane knew the strategy had in fact originated with Cardinal Maglione, who commissioned Spellman to raise it with Washington. Maglione insisted to Spellman that he had imposed a pontifical oath of silence on his inner circle — secrecy was of the essence. Was Graz part of that circle? And did Lehmann know of Deane's own connection, how General Donovan and Archbishop Spellman had turned to him at the end of their meeting? Had Lehmann been told that, under cover of refugee aid, Deane's real purpose in Rome was to set up the Vatican-OSS ploy, ready to spring it as soon as Germany was defeated?

Lehmann said, "Archbishop Graz has seen to His Highness the

Archduke Otto being named a knight of Malta, which will be announced by Cardinal Maglione this week. That is what I have come here to tell you."

Deane was stunned to hear this. Consecrating the archduke would be an obvious tip-off. It was way too premature to go public with the Habsburg ploy: Stalin would snuff it out. A Vatican elevation of the archduke now would ruin everything. But Deane had to go at this aslant. He said, "And as a knight of Malta, the archduke will qualify for a Vatican passport. Is that the point? Since the Germans made him stateless."

"Not the Germans." Lehmann smiled thinly. "Among Germans, the crown prince is beloved. Among German Catholics. Also Germans of Austria, and of South Tyrol, and of Bohemia. German-speaking Catholics will be the source of union for the restored Habsburg Empire."

"Father, may I ask you a direct question?"

"But of course."

"Does Ambassador von Weizsäcker know of the initiatives Archbishop Graz is taking in this regard?"

"The ambassador knows the war will end."

"Is he looking for a way to end it on German terms?"

"Not on Stalin's terms — there's the point. Von Weizsäcker can say only so much. He and trusted colleagues in Berlin need assurances. Archbishop Spellman and Archbishop Graz can become partners in obtaining them. That begins here, with you and me."

"You want Archbishop Spellman to intercede with Washington."

"Yes. Precisely. Calls for the unconditional surrender of Germany must change. There is no point in any German — I dare to say it — moving against Hitler unless there can be some assurance —"

"Of a deal."

"A new alliance. Aimed at thwarting Stalin. In defense of the Danube Federation. The German high command, set free, would formally recognize Archduke Otto at once."

"Von Weizsäcker is part of an anti-Hitler cabal? Why would he have been sent here by Hitler just as the Wehrmacht took the city? Wasn't Weizsäcker the senior German in Rome when the Gestapo arrested

Jews across the river in October? What was it, two thousand Jews, counting children?"

"Not that many. Von Weizsäcker disapproved of that. We all did."

"What does German disapproval sound like? We missed hearing it in New York. And where are they by now, do you suppose? Rome's Jews?"

"Labor camps. Italian labor camps."

"Poland, Father. The Roman Jews were shipped in boxcars to Poland."

"Monsignor, the ambassador has put himself in a delicate position. There are others in this delicate position with him. Surely you do not require the situation to be made explicit. That a figure of the ambassador's seniority is in Rome now, here in the Vatican, means there is space for maneuver. Neutral space, Monsignor, made available by — and within — the Church. For this moment, His Holiness has been waiting. But nothing happens without some signal of interest from Washington. Spellman could obtain such a signal. We know of his good relations with President Roosevelt." Lehmann stood. "Tell the archbishop of New York that Maglione's days are numbered. The time is propitious, given General Clark's arrival in Rome, for an American at the Holy Father's side. Spellman could succeed Maglione. The Holy See with an American secretary of state."

"You're offering the post to Spellman?" Deane's contemptuous smile was kind compared to what he felt.

Lehmann shrugged. "I am only saying — it could be arranged."

"As long as the American helps with a separate peace. Did I get that right?"

"Monsignor . . ." Lehmann eyed Deane coldly. Then he said, "The Holy Father approves of this initiative. He and von Weizsäcker have spoken. The Holy Father cannot ask directly, but he would welcome Archbishop Spellman's exertion of influence."

"How long are you ordained, Father?"

Again Lehmann answered only with his stare. For a young priest he seemed to have an unusual capacity not to be intimidated. But something told Deane that was a pose. Deane, too, remained silent.

Finally Lehmann said, "Why do you ask?"

Deane had a regrettably large capacity for being intimidated, but not by a slick popinjay like this. "Who appointed you to the office of ... what do you call it? The arranger. Is it some element in Berlin? The German national church in Rome? The Holy See? Or perhaps the Holy Ghost?"

"No appointment. My inquiries are informal."

Deane stood up, ending the meeting. Without fanfare, he opened the door for the German, who strode through it.

That should have been that, but in the cramped anteroom that served as the foyer for his and three adjoining curial offices, Deane glimpsed the gray flannel trousers of a seated man, one leg crossed over the other. A wingtip shoe in need of polish. Though the man's face was obscured by a protruding file cabinet, Deane thought at once of the fellow in the airplane. Why? Something as simple as the crease in a trouser leg—sharp enough to focus a camera on. But Father Lehmann had also stopped before the visitor, which prompted Deane to follow him out into the anteroom.

Yes, Warburg. But with him was a slender woman in the blue beret of the Red Cross, its distinctive red patch. She and Warburg had come to their feet. Lehmann had taken the woman's hand, and he was now leaning down to kiss it, like a courtier. A clerical Casanova, he put his lips to the lightly held fingers with such grace that the woman, even averting her gaze, seemed as natural with it as he. Coming back to full height, the German said, in mellifluous Italian, "With gratitude, Signorina, for your tremendous works of mercy." He held on to her hand presumptuously until, at last, she said, "*Grazie, Padre.*" For an instant more, the German priest held her hand. Then he dropped it, and was gone.

Deane stepped toward them. "Mr. Warburg? My goodness, I didn't expect to see you here. If you'd called, I'd have arranged to meet you in one of the Pope's parlors, so you'd be impressed with my importance." He knew his joviality was coming off as forced, but what the hell. "Instead, you find me out"—he gestured around the cramped space—"a back-office clerk." Deane and Warburg shook hands, but turned toward Marguerite as they did so.

"Monsignor Deane, this is Signorina d'Erasmo of the Roman Red Cross."

"Yes, of course," Deane said. "From the airport. The milk."

"Yes."

"The children at the Quirinal, are they . . . ?"

"We've begun, Father," she said.

Deane nodded, then pointed them through the doorway into his small office. "*Prego. Prego.*"

Deane had to bring a second side chair into his room. When the door was closed and the three of them were seated in the space in front of his desk, he turned to Warburg. "What is it, David?"

"Shall I come right to the point?"

What a relief the straight-line question was after the serpentine labyrinth into which the German priest had led him. "Please."

"Do you know what the Delegation to Assist is?"

"Yes. Delegazione per l'Assistenza degli Emigranti Ebrei. The organization to help Jews."

"A Rome-based organization *of* Jews, Monsignor. But in the months since the Nazis took Rome, a priest has been its rabbi. Did you know that?"

"No. What priest?"

It was Marguerite who answered. "Père Antoine Dubois, the chaplain of the Cistercian Convent of the Holy Spirit. He has been the record keeper. The only one, during the occupation, who knew . . . everything."

Warburg said, "For obvious reasons, the Jewish leader of the Delegation was a particular Nazi target. He entrusted his records to Father Anthony. But the Jewish leader has come out of hiding now, with an urgent request. He has identified a concentration camp near the town of Carpi, in Modena. The Germans are in retreat there, pulling back across the Po River. All but a few hundred captive Jews have been transported north, and the rest will follow soon. We need your help in preventing that."

"My help? What can you possibly mean?"

"An American air wing commander, approached through a friend of mine, agreed this afternoon to bomb the crucial railroad bridge, making the last German transport impossible, but only on one condition."

"What?"

"That the Holy Father draw attention to the camp. It's called Fossoli. If His Holiness were, for example, to offer public prayers for those innocents in jeopardy at Fossoli —"

"That's fantasy. Since when do German guards take signals from the Pope?"

"The Germans are not the point. It's the American air wing commander who needs assurance that His Holiness is concerned for these people. Apparently he's a Catholic, and would be . . ."

Into the gap of Warburg's hesitation, Deane thrust, "A sucker for word from His Holiness."

"Not 'sucker.' A strategic point, in fact. Why should a commander, distracted from his battle order and without authority from his own superiors, seek to help some when so many are in jeopardy? It's a matter of setting the Fossoli prisoners apart from all the other victims. The Pope could do that. He prays for victims in the abstract every week. This time, he could get specific. Just use the word 'Fossoli.' It might save them."

"You believe that, David?"

"Yes, I do," he answered, a bit too quickly. He continued his brisk argument. "The American commander needs to think His Holiness will do it. It would have to happen immediately *after* the raid, lest the Wehrmacht be alerted. All I need from you is the promise that it *can* happen."

Deane shook his head. "So then this particular American Army Air Corps command — what, announces an Allied operation coordinated with the Holy See?"

"This is purely humanitarian, Monsignor."

Deane stared at Warburg, not speaking. Finally he said, "Carpi is across the Apennines. Clark isn't taking on those mountains again. He's headed to Florence, not Modena. And anyway, say the train *is* stopped. What happens on the ground? What about the German guards? Who arrives to unlock the gates at Fossoli?"

Marguerite had been staring at the hand in her lap, as if thinking of the German priest who had kissed her there. But now she raised her head. "I do. The Red Cross does. When a *campo* is abandoned by a mobile combat unit, the Red Cross takes it over, cares for the victims. We have done that since Sicily."

"Yes, Signorina, Fascist camps, Italian camps," Deane said. "When the Fascists fled. But these are Germans. Even withdrawn to the far side of the Po, Germans can be expected to control that valley for some time. Carpi can hardly be on Mark Clark's map yet."

"The roads everywhere are clogged with refugees," she countered. "Germans do not want to deal with such desperate ones, especially pushing north. We will have more freedom now than before, for sure. Retreating Germans simply abandoned POW camps in the south. They opened prisons and insane asylums, setting inmates free, just to sow chaos. And, pulling out, they regularly allowed the Red Cross to move in. I have a passport. I have a truck. I have persons."

"The Delegation to Assist Hebrews."

"Yes."

Deane looked at Warburg, who said, "It's true. The Delegation's leader is gathering a group of Partisans, remnants of an underground that formerly operated in the area around Modena. They will converge on Fossoli."

"Partisans?" Deane said. "Or the Haganah?"

"What?"

"Breakaways from the British Army, the Palestine Regiment. Jews. Hasn't Signorina d'Erasmo explained this to you, David? She will have Jewish fighters in her truck." The priest looked at her.

Marguerite just shook her head no.

Warburg said, "I thought the Church's problem with the Partisans was that they are mainly Communists, not Jews."

Deane knew better than to touch that pairing. He simply stared at Warburg, who said, "And what has you Catholics so exercised about Zionists?"

Deane did not want this, yet he pushed back. "So exercised about protecting the Holy Land, the font of Christian faith?"

"Protecting it from Jews?"

"Suppose," Deane said, "the Air Corps drops the bridge. And then, before the stymied German guards at Fossoli can kill the prisoners, the famously neutral Red Cross arrives with a force of Jewish commandos."

Warburg said, "That's your fantasy, Monsignor. The Modena fighters are a shadow of what they were — old men and boys, probably. If there are Jews among them, that is incidental. The Nazis decimated the Partisan groups in the region months ago. Otherwise, they'd drop that bridge themselves. If there are Palestinian Jews jumping off the Jewish Brigade wagons of the British Army, they are barely out of Rome. They could never get to Carpi. Miss d'Erasmo's truck will have food and medicine, not fighters."

Deane shrugged. "The Delegation to Assist Hebrews may have been interrupted in Rome by the Nazi occupation, but it was put in place by the Haganah. Funding. Organizing. Leadership. All from Palestine. Your man — what's his name?"

Something prevented Warburg from answering.

Deane ignored that. "He *is* a Zionist. The Delegation to Assist Hebrews is Zionist."

"You have your nerve, Monsignor, saying that so dismissively. The Delegation has been the only defender of Jews."

Deane did not respond for a moment. Then, "Any Vatican involvement with Zionists would raise a serious problem for us with London, but that would be the least of it. What matters here, whether you see it or not, is where such an enterprise would leave the Holy See's neutrality." Deane had to push away a thought of the conniving Lehmann, but it was true — wild events were overtaking every careful plan. "Much as it has made me wince as an American, the Pope's neutrality may be essential to the war's endgame."

"But we are not talking about Zionism. We are talking about a few hundred wretches who may or may not be alive in two days. You are not neutral about them, Monsignor. I know you're not."

"We are not talking about me, David. If it were up to me, I'd be in that truck with Miss d'Erasmo. I'd give anything to help those people myself. Like you would. Are you going?"

Warburg answered, simply, "No."

After a short silence, the American priest said, "So what are you telling me? The whole thing rides on a papal halo hovering over Fossoli? That's what the Air Corps commander needs?"

"So I'm told."

"I can't offer him the Pope, David. Forget it."

Warburg's eyes narrowed. "What else is there?"

Deane shifted in his chair to look out into the Vatican gardens below. He steepled his hands at his lips. He said, "*Acta Diurna.*"

"Which is?"

"In *L'Osservatore Romano,* the Vatican newspaper. *Acta Diurna,* 'Daily Acts.' It's the list of public notices, everything from statements of the Holy See's profound concern, to intentions of the day's pontifical liturgies, to agenda items of the bureaucracy." Deane hesitated. Was he really proposing this? But then he thought, what the hell. He said, "Do you think your Catholic air wing commander would be reassured by a monsignor's guarantee that Fossoli would be featured in the Pope's own *Acta Diurna* the day after the bridge drops? You could tell him — page one, *L'Osservatore Romano.*" When Warburg did not react, Deane added, "You wouldn't have to mention it's in small print, near the bottom."

Warburg smiled. "I'm under the impression that all the colonel needs is a little Catholic mumbo-jumbo."

Deane smiled, too. "That I can deliver. Here" — he turned to his desk — "wait'll you see my stationery."

A few moments later, as the woman and Warburg were about to leave, he turned back to Deane. "Monsignor, about the Haganah and the Delegation. If it's true, that's news to me. How do you know that?"

"*Ad limina,*" Deane said. "Periodic accounts rendered to the Pope —

from everywhere. The nuncios enunciate. From London *and* Jerusalem. Information mingles with the incense around here."

"I need that incense, Kevin," he said. Then added, "Do you have a nuncio in Budapest?"

In the jeep, Warburg had ridden in front with the driver, leaving the bench behind to her. They had careened across Rome, at last screeching down the Via Veneto to the Palazzo Margherita, which the Americans were already calling Clark's headquarters, although to her it remained the magical palace in which her namesake queen had lived until her death. Marguerite remembered how, as a girl of seven or eight, she had seen the great arched windows draped in black, bunting that seemed all the more austere in contrast with the pink stone of the monumental edifice. That Her Majesty the Queen Mother was dead had been, for Marguerite, an opening into the mystery of mortality. If Her Majesty could die, so could her son, King Victor Emmanuel. If kings and queens could die — Marguerite shuddered to remember this exact moment of recognition — so could her own mother and father.

Warburg had ordered the driver to keep the jeep's engine running, leaving her to wait while he hurried in to deliver the monsignor's letter. Then, coming out, he had dismissed the driver and gestured Marguerite into the front. He did this without imperiousness, but nonetheless with an authority to which, despite her by now habitual wariness, she immediately yielded. With Warburg at the wheel, and her providing directions, they had hurried to the Jewish neighborhood on the banks of the Tiber — the ghetto — where the first meeting with Lionni had taken place. They found him in the same rooms, and he leapt with joy at their report. The bridge would be attacked, probably in the morning, at first light. Now the Jewish leader and Marguerite had their plan. They would set out as soon as the store of medicine and food could be loaded onto the truck, noon at the latest. With luck, they would make Carpi before dark.

Lionni had drawn Marguerite aside, away from Warburg. In a corner of the room, he opened a drawer. Without comment, she looked at what it held—bundled currency. They turned back to Warburg.

"And so, tonight is for sleeping," Lionni said with a clap, dismissing them. "Every minute matters." So it was that the American had insisted on driving her to Trastevere, even though it was not far to walk.

Now they were sitting side by side in the jeep in front of the shabby rooming house where Marguerite lived. The glow of twilight lent the façade of the scarred and shuttered building a golden hue. The approach of midsummer meant it was late, even if darkness had not quite fallen. The nearby streets were deserted, as if the German curfew still held. Warburg said good night and wished her luck. When she did not move, he pushed the ignition button, shutting the engine off.

He said, "Tell me about your father."

She said with quiet detachment, "My mother and father were killed when their automobile was forced off the Ponte Alto on the road to Trento."

"Forced by whom?"

"Fascists. Nine years ago. When Il Duce seemed invincible. Not a rabbit, running scared."

Her own incidental use of the word "rabbit" startled Marguerite, calling to mind as it did the harelip of the Franciscan in Croatia. His white handkerchief catching saliva, falling as a starter's flag. She blocked the thought, resuming, "As the colonel said, my father was director general of the Red Cross. My father told the truth about Italian mustard gas in Ethiopia. Il Duce was *arrabbiato*—enraged."

"So the Red Cross is your . . . patrimony."

Marguerite nodded. She did not know why she was finding it difficult to leave this man's company. What was it about him? She allowed herself to fix her stare on his slender fingers, resting on the steering wheel. He wore no jewelry. His nails were clean. He had turned in the seat, inclined toward her, and she was aware of his eyes on her face. A gentle gaze.

He said, "Monsignor Deane asked if I was going to Fossoli with you. I answered no. I wish I could."

After a moment, Marguerite laughed. "At the sentry points you could show your *repoussé* Washington card—the card, you say 'embossed'? You could answer for us in your fine Italian. The Gestapo would salute and let us through."

He laughed, too. Then, somber again, he said, "It will be dangerous."

"Jocko Lionni is wise, very practical."

"Is he Zionist? Haganah?"

"The monsignor asked that."

Warburg said, "I noticed when Jocko pulled you aside. He opened a drawer full of money, showing you. I just saw that. Where did the money come from?"

"I do not know."

"It's for bribes."

"We say *dono*," she said. "Donation. Every barrier on every road lifts at *dono*. And I have my passport." She flicked at her Red Cross hat.

"If the Haganah's involved, it will be even more dangerous."

She said, "This will be nothing. I was in Croatia."

"How?"

"With Partisans. Not Palestinians. Communists."

"When?"

"Until a few days ago."

"Is that where you received the bruises? There, on your face?"

If she could not tell Père Antoine, how could she tell this stranger? Yet she found herself unknotting the red kerchief at her throat. As he took in the sight of her mangled neck, she waited. When he asked at last "What happened?" it was so softly she was not sure he'd spoken.

"This cloth," she said, twisting the kerchief around her fingers, "you see it in the north, in the hills. The Garibaldi Brigade. I was with them for more than three months. Before that, when the Nazis came to Rome, I had to flee. I was making my way to Switzerland, but I—"

"You joined the Partisans?"

"Not joined. I was one of the women. Our work was knitting the *calze*, the stockings—"

"The socks."

"— for the men. In the winter especially, the socks are essential. To keep men in socks is important work. Blistered feet become infected."

"But what happened?"

Marguerite shook her head. She had gone as far with this as she could. She looked Warburg in the eye. "I was not there when my father's auto plunged into the river. But I see it every day, the black Lancia driving away on the bridge above. White tires. A silver panther bibelot on the front. Two men, black shirts, one black-gloved hand made into a fist, raised outside the driver's window. Pumping in triumph as my mother's body washed away in the river current, as my father was trapped in the car, where he drowned or died of head injuries. They never said. And I never speak of it."

"Except now. You are speaking of it now."

"My mother's body was not recovered for four days. Two miles downriver, partly eaten by eels."

Warburg said nothing to this.

After a long silence, Marguerite said, "And *your* parents?"

Warburg's head drew back just enough to show that the question startled him. He said softly, "My father was a butcher. A small city. Both my parents are deceased. Heart attack. Pneumonia. Natural. My life has been quite different from yours."

"American."

"Yes. Therefore privileged."

"But the deaths of parents is never privilege."

"No."

"And they were Jews."

"Yes."

"It is bad for Jews here. Very bad."

"Worse in the north," he said. "If Fossoli were across the Alps, the prisoners would be dead already."

"I do not understand why Jews should be so contempted."

"Hated."

"Why?"

"You're asking me?"

"Yes."

Contempt. The word pushed into Warburg's mind his unwelcome memory. "Once," he said, "I took a *tallit,* my father's *tallit* . . . You know the word?"

"Yes. The Jewish prayer covering."

"Shawl. My father offered it to me, but I refused to wear it. He was asking me to be a Jew. I said no. Instead, I let the *tallit* sink beneath the surface of a lake, like a drowning."

"You say that with sadness."

"Thinking of Fossoli, it is sad. It bothers me. Would it not bother you to have done such a thing?"

Marguerite said, "So, Budapest. You spoke to the monsignor of Budapest?"

"I am here in Rome because this is as close as I can be to Hungary. Thousands of Jews are being taken each day. Each day. Budapest is the last place we can stop it."

"How?"

"Swedes. Neutrality. My group is sponsoring a Swedish diplomat in Budapest. Tomorrow, perhaps the next day, I will know if Stockholm has agreed. Then the Swedish official will provide Jews with the *Schutz-Pass.* He will offer Jews a Swedish refuge. Hungarian officials will be paid to believe it, a fiction, a lie."

"You have money for bribes, as we do. *Dona nobis doni.*"

"I saw what Lionni showed you, the banknotes were tinted red. That means reichsmarks, no? In denominations of one thousand? Where does Lionni get such currency?"

Marguerite said only, "To Germans at the checkpoints, lire would be worthless."

"So is it the Haganah? Who else could get such reichsmarks? Is what the monsignor said true? Is Lionni a Zionist?"

"Who would *not* be a Zionist? What Jew would not want Palestine?"

"America is a better place for Jews. I will be taking Jews to America. It's why I came."

"You said Budapest is why you came."

"From Budapest to America. Through Rome. I am hoping you can help me. After Fossoli."

Marguerite faced him, smiling suddenly. "So you think we will return?"

"Of course I do. Otherwise I wouldn't let you go."

She laughed at the outrageous presumption of his statement, and then so did he. "What I mean to say . . ." Warburg blushed.

But she teased him. "Do you claim this authority over me because you are American? Or because you are a man?" For a moment there was nothing uncertain in her.

"Perhaps because you were a girl without a father," he answered. "Your father—that is where we began our conversation." He paused again, then looked directly at her. "Your father's death."

"After that, I wanted to become a religious woman. A nun. It was impossible. I became a convent student instead. Père Antoine, in the beginning, was like my second father. Eventually I realized he was like my God. Then, what I understood was—I have no God. That was what the death of my parents did to me. I do not believe in God. I still say my prayer, but only for magic. Not for faith. My prayer is called Remember, but I have forgotten. *Memorare.* Do you understand?"

"I think so. I have no God either."

"But for a Jew, that perhaps is easier."

"Why?"

"Jews . . . the death of one's parents is nothing compared to what Jews suffer . . . not just now, but always. If God abandons Jews, then Jews have a right . . . What Jews suffer is unjust."

"I do not suffer," Warburg said.

"Not true," she replied. "You suffer with Jews. I see it in your face. If you do not believe in God, you believe in . . . Jews."

Warburg forced a laugh. "I think we Jews call that idolatry."

She shook her head. "If there were a God, he would be Jewish. Today, in Italy, in Croatia, Poland, Europe, God is a Jew, that's all. That is what I believe. It is not idolatry. Instead of actually praying, I believe in helping where I can."

"Red Cross."

She nodded decisively. "A cross without a god."

"And in helping, you have been . . . bruised."

She drew the kerchief back around her throat. "It was not in helping that I was hurt."

"What do you mean?"

She knotted the kerchief, too tightly. With no awareness of doing so, she closed her eyes.

And for an instant she was in Trieste once more, in its farthest, foulest alley. The red-bearded monster had choked the air from her lungs, and she was about to lose consciousness. But instead, as if channeling the writhing of her death throes, she began to fight again, clawing at his face with her nails. Carlo would not be stopped. He banged her head against the pavement. Once more, she felt close to losing consciousness, even as the clearest thought she'd ever had took over her mind: He is murdering me!

It was true. But his furious passion was then her great advantage. Her hand, on instincts of its own, went to the holster at his hip. She found the pistol handle, grasped it, her finger sliding into the trigger notch as if she had handled such a thing before. She had the snout of the Luger against his shoulder, then his cheek, then his lust-distorted eye. Just before passing out from lack of oxygen, she closed her finger.

"A man," she said now. "A man I thought a friend . . . attacked me."

Warburg knew to wait.

"And I killed him."

There. At last she had said it to someone. And of course it had to be to a stranger, a man she would not see again. She threw her right leg over the lip of the jeep door, but before she could step out, Warburg took her arm. She stopped and drilled him with a look. How could he possibly have heard her absolute declaration as an opening, when it was termination, pure and simple?

But all he said, repeating himself, was "Good luck."

FIVE

A Jew's Fantasy

WARBURG AND MATES were seated at a sidewalk table in late-afternoon sunshine, but clouds had darkened the western sky and a breeze had kicked up. A summer thunderstorm was coming. The café was on the edge of the plaza in front of the Pantheon, with its massive dome. Each man had his demitasse and cigarette. If the rain came, Warburg thought, they could retreat into the great building's becolumned portico.

The large open square before them was a mechanized scrum of olive-colored traffic, knotted around a multitiered fountain. Rome's cascading water displays were resolutely festive, but to the newly arrived drivers of trucks, half-tracks, and jeeps, they seemed little more than roadblocks. The Yanks leaned on their horns — insistent, blaring, useless. Horses stood in their harnesses with mulish indifference.

Threading among the vehicles were the Eternal City's newest survivors, and Warburg tracked them: a trio of giggling clerics tugging at their skirts, a cook in checkered pants and wooden clogs, a hammer-toting blacksmith in a leather apron, a pair of blatantly entitled drinkers. And the pigeons were back, signaling with a synchronized swoop that the danger of being snared, roasted, and eaten had passed. The city was dizzy with life that only days before, upon Warburg's arrival, had been nowhere in evidence.

"Peter, thank you." Warburg spoke loudly because of the traffic, but that same noise guaranteed that no one would overhear them. He waited for Mates to meet his gaze, but the colonel was eyeing a pair of young Italian women who, with linked arms, were walking past in step, a knowing stride. Finally Mates looked over, and Warburg said, "I appreciate it."

"I'm glad it went well," Mates replied. "One pass, Colonel Killian said. Apparently the bridge was timbers, not steel. The pilot reported that it crumbled back to both banks, like dominoes falling away from a center. Now let's hope your gang gets to that camp in time to do some good. Jesus"—Mates squinted, shielding his eyes—"I hope it doesn't rain."

Once again Warburg wondered, What's with this guy? He himself had been unable to get Marguerite out of his mind, her lame partner, Fossoli. That the camp's prisoners had just been given a reprieve by some unnamed flyboy seemed the first specific triumph of his time in Rome. All else till now had been plans, groundwork, preparation. Finally the needle of fate had been nudged, perhaps a degree or two, away from death. Yet here was Mates, caring only about the weather.

Or was that counterfeit? The colonel's exquisite detachment seemed studied. Warburg decided to match it. "How goes Civil Affairs?"

Mates smiled. "Very well, my good T-man. Very well indeed. We have a mostly constituted City Council now, and they are primed to give us a suitable mayor—Andrea Doria Pamphili."

"A woman?"

Mates laughed. "Don't be deceived by these Wop appellations. The man's given name is Filippo, but forget that. He's from an old patrician family. 'Andrea Doria' has the ring of Thomas Jefferson here." Mates threw his hand toward the Pantheon. "Speaking of whom, did you know that's the model for Monticello? You've been carrying that building in your pocket on the tail side of a nickel. Think of it: from Rome to Charlottesville. This city takes the cake."

"And its new mayor?"

"The Pamphilis are descended from Virgil *and* Alexander VI, the Borgia Pope who sponsored Michelangelo. Our man is anti-Fascist to the core, started out the war in one of Mussolini's concentration camps. The main thing, though—he's no Red, and the unions won't control him. He gives a good speech, but what he really cares about is getting the family princedom restored. He claims vast Doria estates between here and Genoa."

"And vindicating the claim depends now on—?"

"Right. On the Allied powers. Me. We expect him to cooperate." Mates grinned. "As I say, CAD affairs have been going very well indeed."

"And tomorrow you get your star. You're on the promotion list for brigadier general."

"My, my, David, you impress me. How do you know that?"

Warburg offered his hand, and Mates took it. "Congratulations, General." Warburg grinned as they shook, flaunting his inside knowledge. "Less than one percent of commissioned officers make it to BG."

"Jesus, you Treasury men *are* accountants, aren't you?"

In fact, Warburg had heard about Mates's promotion from Sergeant Rossini, having already learned that in the Army, NCOs are the real source of inside dope.

At that moment a clap of thunder sounded, and the pace of pedestrian movement quickened in the piazza while engines gunned. Mates studied the sky, but Warburg finished his thought. "Point is, I'm delighted for you."

"And for yourself?" Mates laughed. "Since you think you have me eating from the palm of your hand."

"Isn't that what you want me to think? And in return, I'm to keep you posted on Communist agitation among the refugees. It's a box step we have going here."

"Since you bring it up—"

"Communist agitation and Zionist plotting. Those are your two interests, no?"

"Why would I care about Zionists?"

"For your British friends."

Mates did not answer.

"Or do they amount to the same thing?" Warburg said. "Reds and Hebes." He stubbed out his cigarette in the tin ashtray.

"You're a fool, David, to pretend the Brits aren't right to worry over

Palestine. It's the sharp end of the wedge. If they lose Jerusalem, they lose the empire. But you're also a fool if you picture any other destination for the Jews you're helping *than* Palestine. There's the rub, for the Brits at least. Your fantasy about sending them stateside on empty troopships is just that—fantasy."

"Oh? Do you know what else is happening tomorrow, besides your promotion to brigadier general?" Warburg paused, but at that moment the darkened skies opened, thunder cracked again, and rain poured down. People in the piazza began to run. Mates and Warburg scurried away from the table and into the shelter of the nearby Pantheon portico. A crush of others followed, forcing the two Americans into the rotunda proper, the expansive open space under the largest free-standing dome in the world. In its center was a circular opening to the sky, and the downpour had found it. A beaded column of water was falling right into the heart of the shadowy cavern, splashing the stone floor in the center. Mates and Warburg took up dry positions near the wall, below one of numerous vacant niches. The classical statues in the place were long gone, although here and there stood Baroque figures of the Virgin Mary and her defeated husband.

"Damn," Mates said, as he used his golden silk handkerchief to brush water from his jacket shoulders. "Good move, though. In here. Fantastic in the rain with that." Mates indicated the hole in the ceiling. "I used to pick up girls in this place on rainy days when I was a teenager."

"Teenager?"

"My old man ran the Roman office for a New York bank. Girls think it's mystical, rain indoors. Never failed." Mates himself seemed entranced, watching the water. "Tears from the very eye of God—the oculus. That's the line I used." His voice fell into a slightly self-mocking rhythm of recitation. "They built this temple as part of the divinity cult for Caesar Augustus, the emperor who took on the baby Jesus—both of them divine, imagine! Gods were cheap in those days." Mates laughed. "I'm not much for gods myself."

The Americans were in deep shadow now, and the damp air between them, as Warburg sensed it, was suddenly more clandestine than before.

"But David," Mates said, "you were interrupted. 'Be sure of it.'" With a flourish of his handkerchief, Mates grandly swept the space. "'Give me the ocular proof.'"

"Othello to Iago," Warburg said, laughing despite himself. "The 'ocular proof' was Desdemona's handkerchief. No wonder the girls swooned for you."

"But you were speaking of tomorrow. Of your Jews."

No banter now. Warburg said, "President Roosevelt is holding a press conference at the White House. He will announce the opening of the Emergency Refugee Shelter at a decommissioned Army post named Fort Ontario, in Oswego, New York. It will be the first 'free port' in the United States, a center where displaced persons will be admitted without visas as guests of the United States. Their immigration status to be determined at a later date."

"And you know this because . . . ?"

"I'm the one who found Fort Ontario, Peter, months ago. I wrote the statement the President will read. And now with my small garret crew I am compiling the names of the first of these guests — refugees from liberated Italy, at present housed in a dozen camps within an hour's drive of Rome. The current count approaches two thousand souls."

"And you are *selecting* from among them?"

Warburg heard the implication in the loaded verb: First the Nazis select them, now you do. "Priority to family groups," Warburg said. "No one suffering from communicable diseases. People with useful professions and skills, because in Oswego they will be mainly self-sufficient. So yes. Selection. Bound for upstate New York as soon as a returning troopship is assigned and a convoy is set."

"So — as soon as your ship comes in."

"And with luck, and a little more help from you, a long line of other 'guests' will follow." Warburg smiled — a genuine display of hope.

"But what *about* the Reds?" Mates asked. "I need to know who among these people decline the invitation to go to New York. The ones who prefer to stay in Italy, doing mischief." Mates faced the center of the rotunda, where the streaming rain was letting up, the downpour now a steady drizzle. He put his silk square back into its pocket. "You're compiling names. I need to know who the camp leaders are. They're the ones I'm interested in." Mates seemed to be looking around to see if they were being approached.

"You? Or the Brits?"

"I could care less about Zionists. If your refugee camps hold Jews, they hold Partisans, too. It's the Communists I'm tracking. Wops. Agitators. I can't have labor strikes here like they had in Naples." Mates turned back to Warburg.

"My information," Warburg said, "is that the Nazis pretty successfully weeded the Partisans out. There are labor leaders and anti-Fascists in the camps. And plain deserters. That doesn't make them Reds. The Nazis killed the Reds."

"Or drove them underground. I have to smoke them out. You need to tell me who refuses your invite to New York."

Warburg shook his head. "For an intelligence chief, Peter, you're pretty dumb. Most Italians who fled the fighting or the bombing have homes to return to. Why would they go to New York? *My* people are Jews who fled to Italy from elsewhere: Poland, Ukraine. Or, if they are Italians, they're Jews who were driven out by their neighbors. My people have nowhere to go. You have no idea, Peter, how desperate the refugees are. OSS has no idea."

"Let's leave OSS out of this. Reds equal strikes, strikes equal civil unrest. Civil Affairs, get it? It's CAD that has the interest."

"I don't care what initials you use."

"Good. Because I want CAD interrogators teamed with your staff in the processing. I want the camp leaders identified and interviewed separately by my people. You soothe, we sort. My people will have the final say on who goes where."

"The hell with that. These poor souls are entrusted to me, not the Army. Not you. You saw Clark's orders. The final say stays with me."

"But the interviews?"

Warburg was shaking his head, but at last he saw that he could be more than supplicant. "I'll give you interviews in camps on one condition, speaking of ocular proof."

"What?"

"Doesn't OSS have a man in Bern?"

"Why are you asking me if you already know?"

"I need him to get to the Swedish embassy there. You heard what I laid out for Ambassador Sundberg here. I need your man to second the motion with the Swedes in Switzerland. Stockholm has yet to approve the nomination of Wallenberg as special envoy. They're stalling. I need turns of the screw. U.S. Treasury has prepared charges against Sweden for neutrality violations, criminal charges. Your man in Bern gives them the way to get the charges dropped, makes clear what happens if they don't cooperate. Jews. Tell your guy to say 'Jews.' Put it together with the word 'Budapest.' Tell him 'Jews in Budapest' is Swedish for 'Open sesame!'"

Mates again turned away, taking in the crowd. The rain was no more than a trickle. He began, with studied casualness, "Beg your pardon, David, but isn't Stockholm the State Department's—"

"Peter, it's Budapest I care about." Warburg drew closer, grasping Mates's arm. "Budapest, you hear me? I want Wallenberg appointed by Monday. That's four days from now. Four days equals twenty thousand Jews in cattle cars."

"You're hurting my arm, David."

When Warburg released Mates, the officer raised his arm to look at his watch. "Jesus, I'm late." He squinted up at the oculus. "And the rain has stopped."

"I need your help, Peter."

"You should have Secretary Morgenthau call General Donovan. He's the intelligence chief, not me. The OSS in Bern, if there is such an outfit, does not take orders from Civil Affairs in Rome. I can put in a word with an air courier I know, but that's it."

"What schedule is your courier on? What clock?"

Mates began to back away. "Think calendar, David, not clock. You're dealing with the Army. Which is why I myself am late. Very late." Mates saluted, turned on his heel, pushed through the shelter seekers, and left. Warburg followed him to the outer curb of the portico, watching. As Mates passed the café table, he threw a handful of lire notes down and plunged into the resuming chaos of the now glistening piazza.

Warburg knew that Mates was toying with him. "Air courier"—a hedged way of saying yes. "Calendar, not clock"—a way of saying no. Warburg was suddenly aware of his clenched fists, his fingernails cutting into the flesh of his palms. Lies and obfuscation came so naturally to Mates that he probably believed most of what he said. From Virgil to Andrea Doria. Girls in the temple of rain. Built by Caesar Augustus, the emperor divine. What bullshit.

Warburg knew that the Pantheon was built by Hadrian a century and a half *after* Augustus, a monument to transcendence, not vanity. And transcendence still defined the place. Warburg looked up at the oculus—the eye of God, why not? As for girls, his thoughts went again to Marguerite d'Erasmo. Where was she?

As if he would find her there, he faced the piazza and went up on his toes. She was, of course, nowhere to be seen, but Mates was. Warburg glimpsed the man rushing away. Marguerite was a confounding mystery, but so was this American—and he was the mystery at hand. Mates was late, but late for what? All right, Warburg thought, let's find out. Warburg set off to follow him. The ocular proof.

As a young priest, Kevin Deane had misunderstood the first words said to him in the sacred forum of the confessional. "Bless me, Father, for I have sinned," the young male penitent had begun. Then he added, "I kissed myself off." A litany of other sins followed that one, mundane offenses against charity or the rules of fasting, white lies. But Deane was stuck on the penitent's having—what?—kissed himself off? What in God's holy mercy was that? A sexual sin, certainly. Masturbation, probably. But it embarrassed Deane never to have heard of it, not in the seminary's careful run-up to ordination, and not in his prior life as a college jock. When another penitent, coming soon after, a woman whom he took to be older, began her confession, also with the same abject admission, he interrupted her. "You what?"

"I kiss myself off, Father."

"You kiss what?"

A long silence. The confessional booth was dark, but the close air on both sides of the screen was filled with the red heat of blushing. Finally the woman whispered, "Not kiss, Father. Accuse. 'I accuse myself of.' These are my sins."

When Deane related this story, which he did only to fellow priests over highballs in the rectory, they roared with laughter and relief, rattling ice cubes in their barely diluted Scotch. Then Deane would offer the punch line, "Kissing myself off. Something else I thought I was missing"—a crack to goose the slightly uneasy celibate laughter, make it raucous.

But the joke, in fact, was always on him, and the real power of the story was the reminder of what a prurient-minded fool he could be. The priest's side of the confessional screen is no place to sit if you imagine you are better, and that lesson was in Deane's mind now, sitting in the most sacred confessional of all, St. Peter's Basilica, by God. Administering the sacrament in the Eternal City: not even Deane was immune to the inbuilt awe.

Awe was the point, for with the arrival in Rome of Clark's legions, off-duty GIs, bearing names like Mulligan, Triozzi, and Dudziak, made a beeline to the Vatican. Entering the embrace of the Bernini colonnade, every one of them was entranced by the indelibly maternal greatness of the Roman Catholic Church. And then, after crossing the piazza, on into the harmonic vastness of the great basilica itself, each one automatically removed his peaked service cap. There, on the mammoth threshold of the largest church in the world, each one waited for his pupils to dilate, for his heart to slow down. Jesus, Mary, and Joseph! More than twice the size of St. Patrick's Cathedral in New York!

Stepping inside, each GI dipped his fingers in the huge amber water basin and signed himself. He looked for a place to kneel, but there

were no pews. Sixty thousand people could fit in here! His untethered
gaze floated around the vast space that held not only the Chair of Peter
himself, but a sense of connection to everything that mattered to him.
Back home, this Catholic kid was accustomed to a Protestant culture's
condescension, but here he could see for himself the world-historic
glories of Catholicism, centered in Michelangelo's masterpiece, the
greatest work of the greatest artist who ever lived. Jaw-dropping awe —
you're damn right.

On the lintel of the confessional booth in which Deane sat was a
sign that said *English*. As an American priest, he had been conscripted
by the papal master of ceremonies to take his turn here, for GIs by the
hundreds were lining up nonstop to confess their sins in this place,
whether for the tourist thrill, or because forgiveness seemed more certain here, or because the ubiquitous unease of war made it necessary.
Even the foulmouthed, the schemers, the condom carriers felt the tug
of conscience. A dozen booths, positioned at intervals, marked the
length of each of the basilica's side aisles. Indicating the makeup of
the Allied forces, a few were labeled *Polska*, a few *Français*, but most,
like Deane's, said *English*. In an exceptional accommodation, said to
have been ordered by the Pope himself, the sacrament was on offer
through the daylight hours indefinitely. The lines of uniformed young
men snaked around the statues of saints and the marble cenotaphs
of emperor popes. It would have given the lads the willies if they'd
known the monuments they brushed up against were tombs.

"God bless you, my son," Deane said once more. Again and again
he had turned from one side to the other, sliding the screens open and
shut, a punctuation. In New York in recent years, Monsignor Deane
had rarely been in a position to administer the sacrament of penance,
and in truth he didn't much miss it. But now he was profoundly moved
to hear the whispers of these boys.

Deane himself routinely went onto his knees to confess his sins to
a fellow priest, but compared to this, his admissions were studied abstractions addressing tendencies to arrogance, impatience — or, when
he was really honest, doubt. He found it possible not to mention his

overweening zeal for sly self-promotion, the unstated longing to be made a bishop.

Nor did he confess sins of the flesh, for the simple reason that he was not guilty of them. He had never been with a woman in his life, and it would never have occurred to him to think sexually of men. For decades now, he had stifled carnal feelings as a matter of discipline and will. Yet to listen to the subdued or even trembling GIs, one would think sex — if more fantasized than real — was at the center of every army's mission. What the hell, maybe it was.

And his mission? The troubling image that lately came unbidden into Deane's mind was of that old peasant woman sitting on the edge of a cot in the crypt beneath Santa Marta, her fingers entwined with rosary beads. Convert Jews in the caves of the Vatican had become his proximate occasion of sin, the storm of self-righteous indignation that had taken him to Tardini. Yet, Deane asked himself, who am I to think myself better than these others? Or was it that fellow from the airplane asking? David Warburg often came to mind — or was it conscience?

But *his* conscience was not the point now, not here on this side of the screen.

Occasionally some poor kid would struggle to make a wrenching admission that drew Deane closer. He heard what burp guns did to bodies, and grenades to huts, and flamethrowers to the faces of men. Or he heard — most abject of all — self-accusations of cowardice. To the utterances of one scorched conscience after another, Deane whispered, "You know what war does to us, my son." With these kids, his compassion came in a rush. "What happens during the unwilled course of combat in a just war is not sinful. And this is a just war if ever there was one."

"Thank you, Father," the boy would whisper, sometimes with the telltale sound of snuffling.

In the face of such compunction, Deane would feel an overpowering sense of gratitude and respect. "No, son, it is I who thank you. Now say the act of contrition while I pronounce the words of absolution on behalf of your Lord and Savior." And when, at the end, Deane said, "Go in peace," the lad would.

But this time, Deane having opened with the ritual benediction, the person on the other side of the screen said nothing. In the shadows the man was immobile, yet Deane whiffed his cologne, and that told him. Deane let his head rest back against the wood, where across centuries confessors had found relief from the burden of human fallibility. He waited.

Finally Mates said quietly, "I'm a little late. I had to wait in line to get in here, but I was already late. I hate being late."

Deane moved his head close to the screen, his ear only inches from Mates's lips. "We'll call that your confession, Colonel," Deane whispered.

"Glad to get it over with, Monsignor. Now for the litany. Do you have it?"

"Yes. You'll find a folded sheet of paper under the pad on your kneeler."

After a moment Mates said, "I can't read this in the dark."

"It's the names of contact clergy in Vienna. In each parish there's a Catholic Action group, and the priests will serve as the coordinators. They are listed. But I—"

"Vienna *and Zagreb!* Yugoslavia is the firebreak, the first place to hold Stalin off. First Croatia, *then* Austria. You have to get me the Croats!"

"Sorting out the Croatians is complicated."

"The Croats are key, Monsignor. The clergy in Zagreb have been leading the charge against the Reds. Those are the names I need."

"Some of them are a little too *gemütlich* with the Nazis. I'm still working on it. But there's something else."

"What?"

"German Catholics are ahead of us on this thing. Archbishop Graz got to the Pope."

"Who the hell is that?"

"Rector of the German national church here in Rome. They've come up with something called the Danube Federation."

"A Habsburg restoration? Same idea?"

"Yes."

"This can't be seen as a German plan," Mates said.

"The Pope has already agreed that Graz will be the archduke's sponsor when he's named to the Order of Malta."

"Where'd this come from?"

"Von Weizsäcker. He plays Graz like a puppet. They're using the Danube Federation as a wedge, aiming to pry open 'unconditional surrender.' If Washington will buy the Habsburg restoration to stop the Russians, the anti-Hitler generals in Berlin want to be selling it. It's the green light they need to assassinate the Führer. The Pope is with them."

"Fuck!"

"We keep our voices down in here, especially in French."

"Sorry, Monsignor."

"And the conferring of the papal knighthood on Otto is step one. It's to be announced next week. Ceremony to follow. He's already been told."

"That's too soon! We're nowhere near ready." Mates could barely rein in his agitation. "You don't turn the deposed archduke into the Holy Roman Emperor from on high. There have to be pleas from the people first. The archduke *answering* the pleas. We're just getting that going. I told you: first Zagreb, then Vienna."

Deane said, "But the anti-Hitler group needs terms from Washington now, not later."

"If you do it now," Mates hissed, "the Soviets will see the Habsburg ploy for what it is. And this just can't be German-sponsored. It's got to be the Pope."

"It *is* the Pope. Unfortunately, it is *also* German. German Catholics."

Mates asked, "How did the Krauts get wise?"

"Obviously the Vatican faucets leak. Have you heard of Roberto Lehmann?"

"Who?"

"The priest who's behind Graz. See if you have a file on him. He claims to be from Mainz."

"Spell 'Lehmann.'"

Deane did.

Then Mates asked, "Roberto?"

"Born in Argentina. Something fake about him. The Nazis must have left records behind. Who would have had him on their list? The Gestapo?"

"No, the Abwehr. Military intelligence—my counterpart."

"If you can find him on a Nazi list, I may be able to head him off."

"The Abwehr headquarters is a half-burned mess. We've just begun sorting through their records."

"Check for Roberto Lehmann. The Abwehr had to be using him while they were here. Certainly von Weizsäcker is using him now."

"We have the ambassador under surveillance. If he meets with a priest, we'll know it."

"You're meeting with a priest."

"We're better than they are, Monsignor."

"I wouldn't be so sure, Colonel. Check out Santa Maria dell'Anima, the German church near the Piazza Navona. It's where Lehmann has an office. He lives in a fancy apartment house across the piazza, with his mother. Lehmann is the key to this. If you can give me proof he was working with the Abwehr, I can force the issue with Cardinal Maglione. They'd have to cut him off. Archbishop Graz, too. Check on Graz."

Deane heard the faint rattle of paper as Mates folded the sheet and stuffed it into his blouse.

"But I still need your priestly ward heelers," Mates said. "Priests and monks to stir up parishioners for a new Holy Roman Empire. Assuming this Habsburg crate can still fly. Zagreb. Get me Zagreb."

Deane drew closer to the screen. "And Budapest? Do you know what's happening in Budapest, Colonel?"

"The Jews, you mean? Yes. I know." Neither man spoke for a long time. Finally Mates said, "The Jews of Budapest will be finished with before anyone can do anything about it. Keep your eye on the ball, Monsignor. The ball is Stalin, not Hitler. Catholics, not Jews. It's too late for Jews. We're playing for central Europe, but for now the game that matters is here in Rome."

"Some game," Deane answered. He forced a shrug into his voice, but there was no shrug in what he felt. He thought of those people in Fossoli, the notice he'd put in *L'Osservatore Romano*, running tomorrow — the least he could do. Then it occurred to him: No wonder they hate us, if all we come up with is impotent resignation ahead of their murders, or guilt afterward — or both. *It's too late for Jews.* He deflected all this with a brusque dismissal of Mates. "We both have work to do. I'll make a point to be here same time tomorrow. Try not to be late, Colonel."

"So now what?" Mates asked. "Do I just pull the curtain back and leave?"

"Bow your head, Colonel. Hunch your shoulders. Act like you've just met a merciful God."

And Mates did, although not to the extent of trailing the other forgiven sinners to the kneelers that banked candle displays and side altars. Instead, having walked out of the booth like an actor entering from backstage, he moved into an open space and stood still for a few moments, as if talking to someone in his head. Then he drifted to the center of the huge church, where a flummoxed GI, surprised to see a man of rank, saluted, despite being indoors. Instead of rebuking the breach of regulations, the merciful Mates nodded.

From beside a stout marble pillar a few dozen yards away, Warburg stood watching. While waiting for Mates, he had found himself numbly resisting the spell of the church. He was aware of it when, through the great open doors, gusting wind blew in, a signal that the rains had begun to fall again, now in earnest. Severe weather outside only enhanced the mystical aura of this soaring interior. The closest he'd ever come to standing in such a place had been at the High Victorian Gothic chapel at Yale, where he'd gone occasionally to hear music, but this massive basilica was in a category of its own. Unaccountably, he thought of the synagogue in Burlington, a measly place — and he'd never been inside.

Now Colonel Mates had emerged from the confessional as if from behind a magician's curtain. "I'm not much for gods myself," he'd said. Yet here he was. Ocular proof, Warburg thought, but of what?

Some instinct told him that the better object of his attention was no longer the Army officer but his putative confessor. And so Warburg remained where he was, even as Mates left St. Peter's, having made his way first to the *Pietà,* where he doubtless noticed that, in Michelangelo's rendition, the mother of the dead Jesus was an exquisite girl of no more than sixteen, with a perfectly turned ankle showing from beneath her robes — the most alluring virgin ever made of stone. Perhaps it was the sight of her that put the bounce in Mates's step as he turned up his collar, paratrooper-like, and plunged out into the storm.

It was not long before the priest came out of his sacramental closet, and for some odd reason Warburg was not surprised to see who it was. Monsignor Deane set out into the vast church like a man with a purpose, walking swiftly. He carried his breviary. His eyes were downcast. As it happened, his path took him directly toward Warburg, who had merely to take one step away from the pillar to intercept him. "What the hell, Kevin," Warburg said, an impropriety, but a quiet one.

Deane, startled, jolted back. Before he could speak, Warburg poked him in the chest. "You came to Rome for refugees? You're here to feed the starving and rescue the displaced? What bullshit." Warburg was speaking softly, but the heat in his words carried.

Deane lifted his hand. "Hold it there, David. Hold it right there."

"I will not. I demand to know what you're up to. Mates on his knees? That man a penitent? What gives?"

"I can't discuss it."

"But using refugees as a cover for Vatican intrigue. You *pretend* to care about the —"

"Not pretend. Not cover. Get down off your high horse. I'm responsible for more than one thing, David. That's all. Not everything is as simple as you think."

"The Pope and the OSS are in cahoots, and you're the go-between? All Mates cares about is the Soviets. What? The Holy See brokers a deal with the Germans. What?"

Deane's face went blank. He said nothing, which Warburg took as a sure admission. But of what?

"It *is* the Germans," Warburg said. "German Catholics? Austrian? A separate peace?"

"No. You know that's impossible. Unconditional surrender. Washington has spoken."

"But the Pope's circling some kind of deal. He hates Stalin more than he hates Hitler. So does Mates. And the Pope wants to save Germany from utter defeat, that's obvious. What's he up to? If you won't tell me, I have to draw conclusions from what I see."

"All you see, David, is a man coming from confession."

"Two men, Kevin. I knew that one was a liar. I didn't know that both were."

By the time Marguerite and Lionni drew near the place at dawn, a fierce rainstorm had begun, drumming the ash and charred flesh so that a general wet stench, stinging nostrils and souring the tongue, forecast what they would find. They had rendezvoused in Carpi with two dozen locals — men once vaguely associated with Partisan bands, perhaps, but by now a timid, poorly armed bunch. Once the Gestapo took Fossoli the year before, stuffing the camp with the true Partisans, the mere threat of the place had efficiently emasculated them. Even now, the prospect of approaching the doomed enclosure cast its pall. Inside the truck bed's firmly shut canvas, the men had clung to the side slats as far as the crossroads half a mile back, where, under the last bottom of darkness, they were glad to offload.

In the barn where they had gathered earlier, Lionni had immediately imposed the force of his determination on the men. Marguerite had taken note of the relief with which they'd deferred to him. Across a bale of straw, he had unfolded a sketched diagram of the camp, and, taking into account the true character of the sorry band in front of him, he had improvised a plan. The dozen men with rifles were to position themselves, in squads of three, at the broad flanks of the camp entrance. Half a dozen others, carrying wire cutters, jerry cans of gasoline, and sticks wrapped at one end in paraffin-soaked rags, were to set up on the side of the camp where the canvas-and-board lean-tos stood, ready to break through the wire and torch the guard shacks. The rest, with handguns, were to follow the truck on foot, at a distance, ready to rush forward—which would, of course, be suicidal if the Germans were still there to resist. In that case, everything would depend on Marguerite and Lionni successfully presenting themselves as Red Cross relief workers, arriving with food and medicine—which, with luck, was all they were. So it was that she and he were first to behold the drenched ruins. The ongoing downpour had doused the fire, but thick, rolling clouds of steam and smoke still rose skyward.

The gate of the camp was wide open, which confirmed the locals' report, given in the barn, that the Germans, once rail transport was stymied by the bridge collapse the day before, had been ordered to abandon the camp. Word was, they had left the remaining prisoners behind. Upon hearing that, tears of relief had come into Lionni's eyes, but he had not allowed them to spill. His emotions were at home in the vise of his will. Now Marguerite downshifted and slowed the truck almost to a standstill. The one working windshield wiper slapped loudly at the rain, but because of the foul-smelling cloud, neither she nor Lionni could at first make out what they were seeing. They edged through the gate.

"Marguerite," Lionni said. He and the tall woman were alone by now under the sheltering overhang of one of the only buildings not to have fully collapsed. He was soaked to the skin, face streaked with ash, body reeking—and so was she. Their hands were bloodied and scorched. The ferocious rainstorm continued to rage. Dawn had given way to a morning only somewhat brighter. What they had found was clear to see. A dozen naked chimneys stood in a row, each in its cone of rubble, the remains of torched ramshackle wooden walls and roofs that had housed inmates. Here and there, blackened upright beams and skeletal staircases smoldered, smoke still rising even in the rain.

An accidental pile of corpses, with others strewn around it, stood in a lane between the tall barbed-wire fence and the line of chimneys. Onto that pile Marguerite had launched herself, desperately clawing through the bodies, looking for life, not finding it. By the time Lionni pulled her away, she was whimpering with the effort to lift the dead, one off the other, as if untwisting limbs and disentangling bones would quicken breath. When she recognized Lionni, she said only, "Please, please."

By that time, Lionni and others had, with cold efficiency, raked through the burned-out buildings, a similarly futile search for survivors. The rain had doused the fires enough to stall the general cremation—an interruption that, given the condition of the cadavers, was less reprieve than further insult. In the stupor of his willed detachment, Lionni had taken refuge in the act, yes, of counting. Enumeration had defined his entire last year, and once again he was counting Jews.

Lionni was certain to have come across some of these people before, but there was no question of recognition. Within the boundaries of the former buildings, he had made a rough estimate of the human remains able to be identified as such—more than a hundred. Then, in the lane, he had quickly surveyed the corpses piled and strewn there—somewhere between seventy and a hundred people, apparently killed with bullets. Many seemed to have been shot in the neck and head at close range.

By now Lionni and Marguerite were a long time standing in their sheltered corner, not speaking. Most of their failed rescue party had drifted away from the charnel camp, theoretically to alert Carpi and to retrieve the carts, tools, and tarps necessary, once the lashing rain eased up, to dignify the grotesque remains of the dead. All dead. Unless some had been able to flee into the surrounding woods, which seemed unlikely. Every prisoner had been burned or shot; every woman, every child, each of the few males. Dead.

"Marguerite . . . ," Lionni repeated. She seemed hardly aware of his presence.

"Yes?" she finally said, but from the underworld into which she'd first fallen from that hilltop overlooking Sisak. When she moved her head to look at Lionni now, it seemed to her that his upper lip was misshapen, and she expected him to wipe it with a handkerchief.

Lionni said, "I cannot think how to speak of this . . ."

"Then don't," she said.

"But we must. If we don't speak of it, the evil here will swamp us, too." He paused, then said, "I found bodies of Germans, Wehrmacht uniforms. There were Germans killed here also."

"By whom?"

"Other Germans. They fired into the crowd, but from both sides. Stupidly. They shot each other. Their bodies fell on both sides of the penned-in prisoners. I see that the Germans themselves are young, very young. Almost children. The left-behind German guards were boys."

"Not Gestapo? Not SS?"

"No. Youths. Not *Oberführers* — not one. The fools shot each other because they had no idea what they were doing or how to do it. They had guns. That was all. And hatred, of course. The frenzy of hatred. Guns against half-dead weaklings with no way to resist. Who knows if the soldiers were even ordered to do this?"

"Then why would they?"

"Because these people were Jews."

The rain drummed.

After some moments Marguerite said, "You were wrong about the bridge. If the train could have gone, these people would still be living."

"On the way to certain death. Probably they were already dying. Typhus. If I was wrong, it was only in expecting that normal German soldiers would not behave as beasts. So yes, I was wrong."

"Normal Germans?" Marguerite repeated, but she was thinking — Croatians. The Sava River. The laughing guards racing their trucks in the great oval. The presiding priest, Vukas. "Normal? What is normal?" she asked dully, not expecting Lionni to answer. Nor did he.

Instead, Lionni led Marguerite out, thinking they should go to the truck now. As they crossed back into the narrow lane where the dead were strewn, he saw a figure in black stooped over one of the corpses, a man wearing a cape and an odd hat. Lionni approached the man, slowly at first. When he realized what the man was doing, Lionni, with his limping gait, began to run. He was screaming, "*Fermo! Fermo!*

Stop! Stop!" It was a biretta the man wore, and under his cape was a cassock. A purple stole draped from his neck. A priest. In the rain and mud he was kneeling in prayer, performing last rites. "Stop!" Lionni screamed again.

The priest had barely come to his feet when Lionni crashed into him, knocking him back, almost making him fall. As it was, the priest dropped the small black case he was carrying, and vials spilled to the ground — the sacramental oils, holy water.

"How dare you! How dare you!" Lionni screamed. "Get your filthy prayers away from here! Get out! Get out!"

The priest backed away, terrified of the lunatic who'd attacked him. The priest clutched a crucifix in one hand and held his biretta down on his head with the other. One of the Partisans appeared and stepped between the priest and Lionni. "What's wrong with you?" the man asked Lionni. "Prayers for the dead. What's wrong with that?"

"Not *these* dead! Not *Christian* prayers! Leave them be." Lionni lunged at the priest. The Partisan, a much bigger fellow, held him back. "If you want to pray," Lionni shouted, "pray for the Germans. Go to the corpses in uniform. Kiss your cursed cross to *their* lips. *They* are yours. *They* are the ones who did this! *They* are Christ's! Not the Jews. Don't you dare go near the Jews!"

Marguerite was stunned. Only moments before he was comforting her. Now he was mad.

Lionni struggled to get free, apparently to attack the priest. The Partisan threw him roughly back. Lionni accidentally stepped on one of the sacramental vials, and when he saw what it was, he stomped on it again, and on the case, the candles, the sacred cloths. He jammed his heel down on the second vial, crushing it all. He stomped and stomped, kicking up rainwater in a frenzy of curses and sobs. Then he slowly sank to his knees, to all fours, banging the soggy earth with his fists, splashing the mud so that it bounced up into his face. "*Cristo!*" he muttered. "*Cristo! Cristo!*"

Marguerite stooped to him, cloaked his shoulders with her arm. In Lionni this hatred was ancient, but it was entirely new to Marguerite. Christ! Diabolical Christ! Christ had done this! That once unthinkable recognition was new to her, yet she also realized that at some point in the past she had felt this. But when? She closed her eyes against the question.

But the answer came anyway, in the form of his face — the brilliantly red-bearded Carlo Capra, his irresistible toothy smile. *Amore!* A Partisan hero. An anti-Nazi. The one who'd plunged her into the abyss to which now she had found the bottom, the absolute ground of her great split — the two distinct women who would live on as bedeviling ghosts of the girl she was: Marguerite before and after, outward and inward, alive and dead. The pressure in her right forefinger came back to her, her body's memory more than hers. In her tensing finger was the answer.

"Normal? What is normal?" she had asked Lionni. Even holding Lionni now, Marguerite curled that finger again — the slight movement of knuckle and muscle required to pull the trigger of a gun. She herself was normal. She saw it. A normal beast.

The Pontifical North American College was established by the Vatican as a counterbalance to the slyly undermining influences of Protestant — and democratic — dominance in the United States. Since the turn of the century, nearly all of America's bishops had been alumni of the elite Roman theologate, and they had shown their gratitude to their alma mater by lavishly funding it. That was why the college, with its palatial main building and elaborately tended gardens and fields, was so beautifully set on the crest of the Janiculum, the second-highest hill in Rome. A view of the city spread to the east, across the Tiber, a panorama of bell towers and domes. In the late-afternoon sun, shadows emphasized the dominating ocher of the ancient clay from which so many of the visible structures had taken form.

Since the outbreak of the war, the American seminarians' sojourn in Rome had been suspended, and the place had essentially been empty for three years. But it had been maintained by its faithful Roman staff as if the boys were coming back tomorrow. The broad playing field nestled between the two wings of the building was a carpet of closely mowed grass, and to one side was a paved basketball court—a tip-off to the American character of the institution, since that sport was played almost nowhere else in Rome. But now, on that court, a pair of grown men in undershirts were engaged in a fierce competition, the one-on-one adaptation that distilled team basketball into a kind of hand-to-hand combat.

Deane and Warburg had not come up to the Janiculum intending to play ball. Little more than an hour before, Deane had shown up at Warburg's office. "I want to show you something, David," he said. "That I *am* serious about refugees. Will you come?"

Warburg did not answer at first. Then he said, "Yes."

Deane led the way out to his car. It had the same papal flags on the bumper and the same black-uniformed driver beyond the glass screen. Deane started to explain, but Warburg interrupted him. "I saw this morning's *L'Osservatore Romano*. I don't read Latin, and my Italian, as you know, leaves something to be desired, but I didn't see any mention of Fossoli. The bridge was dropped yesterday. You said the notice would run the day after."

"It will run. I told you. One of the Holy See's 'Daily Acts.' Patience, David. You must wait and trust."

Warburg ignored the hint of condescension. The Vatican newspaper ploy was aimed at the Army Air Corps commander, who had already done his part. Warburg wasn't sure what else to make of it.

"Fossoli is why I wanted to see you, in fact," Deane said. "Hoping those people make it, I want to show you where they can go." As the car purred through the bustling streets of the city, he told Warburg about the unused North American College—its dozens of outfitted bedrooms, spacious halls, fully equipped dining facilities. "A true refuge," he said, "for the Fossoli survivors."

Warburg was surprised. "But it's been vacant all this time?" he asked. "Why would the Pope let refugees use the college now?"

"First of all, David, don't believe what you hear about His Holiness. He cares for beleaguered Jews." Deane stifled the contradicting *converso* memory of the cellars beneath the Santa Marta hospice. "Second, the Holy See credentials the college, but it's owned by the organization of American bishops. That means Spellman, which means me. I control it."

"Really?"

"You'll see," he said. "The college is the perfect place. And the first guests can be the Jews from Fossoli."

"We haven't heard yet—"

"I mean, with any luck," Deane said.

"But what about Budapest, Father? I told you what's happening in Budapest."

"That's five hundred miles from here. What did you think I could do there?"

"You were going to see about the Vatican's nuncio in Budapest."

"His name is Archbishop Angelo Rotta. I know that he has sent descriptions of the impositions on Budapest Jews to the Holy See. I've asked to read his dispatches, but so far—"

"You don't need to read dispatches. We know what's happening."

"Nuncio reports are closely held, David." In fact, His Most Reverend Monsignor Tardini had taken offense even at Deane's inquiries. Tardini's assistant, that Dominican nun, had simply walked away from him without speaking. "I'm working on it," he said now.

"Last week," Warburg said, "the Germans ordered parish priests throughout Hungary to open baptismal records, to establish who is and isn't Jewish. Four thousand mother churches. Four hundred dependent churches. Two hundred abbeys. Twenty-one cathedral chapters. That's a lot of baptismal registers."

"Abbeys don't baptize. Otherwise, you are well informed."

"I'm told the priests are doing it, helping the Gestapo compile lists. Couldn't the Pope forbid that?"

"Forbid the Germans?"

"No. The Hungarian priests. Couldn't he order them to refuse to cooperate? Couldn't the Pope command them to destroy all baptismal records? Just burn the damn stuff. That way, no one could be identified as anything. Apparently the civil birth registries depend on the Church."

"For Catholics."

"Right. And the Protestant and Orthodox have their records, too."

"And they cooperate."

"So far. But they couldn't possibly continue if the Pope spoke. This isn't about neutrality. Helping with Nazi identification according to race makes the Church actively complicit. Don't you see that?"

Deane had no answer.

Warburg pressed, "If you shut down all the birth records, two hundred thousand Jews are safe. Like that."

"Don't kid yourself, David."

Large wrought-iron double gates suddenly loomed before them. Hung from a pair of Tuscan pillars, the gates opened at their approach, an invisible pulley handled by an equally unseen attendant. The two men fell silent, the air between them curdled. A long serpentine driveway took the car up the hill, winding among perfectly trimmed hedges and sprawling lawns.

Finally, in the voice of a man revealing himself, Deane spoke. "I loved being a student here, a one-toilet Irish boy from the Bronx. A long way from the cracked sidewalks of the Grand Concourse. Opened my eyes, wide." Almost self-mockingly, Deane shot the French cuff out of his jacket sleeve, tugged on the gold cufflink. "Never looked back."

When the car pulled up at the entrance, Warburg got out while Deane gave instructions to the driver in Italian. As the two Americans ascended the grand entrance staircase, the car drove away.

"Janiculum," Deane said as they turned to take in the view. "For Janus."

"The two-faced god," Warburg said.

Deane stared at him for a moment, then shook his head and laughed.

A few minutes later, having crossed through the echoing marble of the palatial public rooms of the first floor, they found themselves on the rear terrace overlooking the park-like expanse of lawn. But it was the basketball court toward which they both looked. The one-on-one began as a passing joke, then became a dare, a pair of aging hotshots egging each other on. The gardener had come up with the basketball.

They had stripped to their undershirts—Deane laying aside his red-marked rabat and collarless white shirt with the sleeves folded back to protect the cufflinks, Warburg taking off his shirt and tie. In street shoes, they gave themselves less to pivots and lay-ups than to long set shots and hooks. Neither man had lost the touch, and they immediately recognized it in each other.

Warburg was junior by fifteen years, and Deane was heftier; he could be seen to carry a bit of a paunch. But Deane had clearly kept up his game, one advantage of being a member of a sports-obsessed and sublimating fraternity of celibates. In New York, he'd been out to the gym at Dunwoodie every week for pickup games with younger priests and seminarians, who'd dubbed him Antiquus, the old one. Behind his back, they'd called him Auntie.

Here, the game shifted when Warburg faked going up for a shot, and Deane was fooled. Warburg put the ball down hard, just past Deane's hip. He protected the ball with his body and with abrupt quickness took a first long step toward the hoop. Deane responded with quickness of his own and slapped at the ball, nicking it, but not enough. Warburg drove past, into the open, and scored easily.

Deane's ball. He smiled thinly. Warburg's eyes were locked on his. What a relief to be channeling all thought and feeling into bodily movement. Adrenaline and a peak of concentration moved the pair into the zone for which, long before, each had lived. But now Warburg was lulled into overplaying to his right, and at Deane's next jab step, Warburg bit. Deane took the long cross to the outside of Warburg's left foot, then—bang! He swung the ball away, showing for the first time that he could dribble equally well with either hand. He drilled past the flat-footed Warburg and made his lay-up.

They traded basket for basket—and elbow for elbow. On defense, Warburg took to making himself bigger, spreading his feet wider than his shoulders, flaring his elbows, hands up. Deane began to bump, using his weight. Sweat dripped from their faces. What began as a low-key exercise in nostalgia had become a true contest.

"Foul!" called Deane as the ball bounced off the rim.

"Says who?" Warburg challenged.

"You pushed into me as I was shooting. My points!"

"You're kidding yourself, Father," Warburg said, and waited for Deane's signal that he heard the rebuke. Deane's already red face reddened more. Then Warburg said, "You were charging. My feet were planted."

"What rules do you Elis play by?"

Warburg froze. "'You Elis'?"

For a long second, the two men stared at each other. Sweat fell in droplets from each man's chin. "Elis?" Warburg repeated. As in Eli, the Israelite judge? As in Eli, the Hebrew name for God? As in Hebe? What was he being called?

"Eli," Deane said, with a hint of perplexity, "from Elihu."

"Elihu?" Warburg was flummoxed.

"Elihu Yale. Didn't you play at Yale?"

"Yale?" Warburg was still confused, then it hit him. Undergraduates at Yale went by that nickname, tied to, yes, the seventeenth-century founder. "No. No. I played ball at Middlebury. Went to Yale for law school. No Elis at the law school."

"I played at Fordham. Different league."

"Fordham. No wonder."

"No wonder what?" Was Deane, too, set to take offense?

"Fordham's Division One," Warburg said. "No wonder you're good." Warburg flipped the ball to Deane. "Take it out."

They resumed play, but something unfriendly had seeped into the game. Deane showed himself to be the better player, but Warburg's edge in speed and agility was enough to let him begin to dominate. And yes, Warburg's aggressiveness was lashed by his vexation at the priest's double game with Mates. Janus indeed.

If fate—or street shoes—required one of them to get hurt, it was going to be Antiquus, and so it happened. Fighting hard for a rebound, Deane went up at an impossibly twisted angle, which was aggravated by a bump from Warburg's hip. Deane snagged the ball but landed hard and off balance on the side of his right foot, which snapped under, crushing all his weight onto the lower end of the tibia where the long leg bone joined his ankle. "Oh, Jesus!" he gasped, and went down clutching his leg. The pain, nested in adrenaline, prompted him to move, and he bounced up off the pavement. Before Warburg could stoop to him, Deane had drawn himself up onto his good knee — the posture of prayer. He left the injured leg loose and to the side, dropping his head into his right hand. "Jesus," he said again.

"Oh, man, I'm sorry," Warburg said. "Are you all right?"

"Give me a minute."

"Your ankle?"

"My shin, my lower shin. Jeesuss!"

"I am so sorry, Father."

Deane let the younger man hoist him up, draw his arm across his shoulders, and take most of his weight. Their sweaty upper bodies fit together. Each had an athlete's unselfconsciousness. "Can you hop?" was Warburg's only question, and Deane answered with several one-legged leaps, across the basketball court to where their clothing was folded. Warburg helped Deane into his shirt and put on his own, making a bundle of their two jackets, the rabat and collar, and his necktie. With Warburg taking Deane's weight again, they slowly made their way to the circular driveway in front. There was no sign of the priest's car, nor of any other vehicle they might commandeer. They zeroed in on a stone bench, and Warburg eased Deane down. Acute pain was showing in his face. Blood had drained away, leaving him pale.

Once seated, Deane reached for the rabat. "I'd better get this damn thing on if I'm going into a Roman emergency room."

Warburg helped him fasten his cufflinks and put his arms into the garment's slings. "Like a shoulder holster," Warburg offered, thinking of the firearms instruction he'd received in the weeks before leaving Washington. He'd protested at first: *I'm not that kind of Treasury man.* But he was headed for the war zone. He'd been issued a pistol with shoulder holster, which, ever since, he kept under his bed. At that, he thought of the Red Cross woman, her frigid declaration: *And I killed him.*

After Deane was dressed, Warburg tucked in his own clammy shirt and put on his tie and coat.

Deane pulled his wristwatch out of his coat pocket and, fastening the strap, said, "Oh, brother. I'm supposed to hear confessions at St. Peter's."

"You can forget that."

"No. I have to get there."

"Why? With all the priests in Rome?" Warburg eyed Deane carefully, knowing he'd used the confessional as a rendezvous.

"English-speaking priests — at a premium," Deane said, "because of GIs streaming in."

Warburg felt that they were back on the basketball court, with Deane faking him. Warburg's counterfake consisted in letting it go. He knelt before Deane to check his leg. He untied the priest's shoe. "Your foot is swelling, and above your ankle the skin is already purple. You may have bleeding in there. No protrusion, though. That's good. But I think you're better off without this." He slipped the shoe off.

The long black car appeared then, swiftly rounding the corner from behind a string of tall poplar trees. The tires squealed when it stopped. The driver hopped out, saluting. He quickly got the picture and joined Warburg in helping Deane up, across to the car, and into the back seat. "*Buon Pastore,*" the driver said. Behind the wheel, he popped the gear and headed off, all at once a man of authority.

"Good Shepherd Hospital," Deane announced. "The good sisters. Good God. Oh, Jesus, give me a smoke, will you."

Cupping his hands against the in-draft from the open windows, Warburg lit cigarettes for both of them, then handed one over. Only then did Deane notice, between them on the seat, the folded *L'Osservatore Romano* — an early copy of the next day's edition.

"I sent the driver to fetch this," he said, picking the paper up. Clipped to it was a brown envelope about six inches square. Deane put the envelope aside, unfolded the newspaper, and scanned it. "Front page," he said. "As promised. Patience pays off. *Acta Diurna.*" He held it for Warburg, who saw, near the bottom, the one word "Fossoli" leap out of the small print.

"What's it say exactly?"

Deane held the newspaper at arm's length, to sharpen his focus. Translating was a welcome diversion, and he slipped into his preacher's voice: "'For the Church prays that God, the Father of mercies, hears the prayers of His children in the village of Fossoli, in the commune of Carpi, in the province of Modena. If Job's sons were purified by their father's sacrifice'"— Deane paused to look at Warburg, who showed him nothing, and Deane resumed reading—"'why should the Church not believe that this prayer to the Father of Lights, from whom comes every good endowment, will not also be heard? For she prays in union with Christ her head, who takes up this plea and joins it to His own redemptive sacrifice.'" Deane lowered the paper.

"Job's sons," Warburg said.

"Euphemism for Jews. Not that Job was Jewish, strictly speaking. Not that he existed, for that matter."

"I wouldn't know."

"The point is, the Catholic air commander will be pleased. Here it is, what he needed, in the Pope's own newspaper. The two key points: Jews, Fossoli. I know the text sounds — what? — liturgical, but that's the house style."

Deane handed the paper to Warburg, who fixed his eyes on the lower corner of the front page. Deane turned his attention to the brown envelope, which was closed with a red wax seal and ribbon, stamped with an unfamiliar crest. He leaned forward toward the driver. "*Che cosa è questo?*"

"*Dall'editore.*"

Deane tore at the envelope, cracking the seal, so that soft bits of the blood-red wax fell on his suit. He removed a piece of paper that held a few lines of tidy script. He read. "Jesus," Deane muttered, then crushed the paper and let his head fall back.

"What?"

"It's bad. Very bad."

"What?"

"The editor says they have reports coming in, a terrible fire at Carpi . . . many deaths . . . The local priest was at the camp. The editor says that Cardinal Maglione is demanding to know why tomorrow's paper mentions Fossoli. Maglione has told the editor to kill the edition."

"I don't get it."

"I'm afraid it's obvious. Your friends took a chance. The chance was, if the Krauts couldn't move those people, they would kill them. That seems to be what happened."

"Good God."

Deane winced. Mostly he was angry at himself—what a fool he'd been to accept this scheme. But he fixed his anger on Warburg, the first fool. "Surely you saw that. It was the *likelihood*. The Germans set fire to the camp. Who knows what else they did. Surely you aren't surprised."

"I am surprised. I am constantly surprised."

"Surprise like yours is a luxury. You're on the wrong side of the ocean for surprise. And for now, those friends of yours, the woman included, are in German territory. Dealing with God knows what. This is what happens in amateur hour. And I got sucked into it. You and I are why those people are dead, don't you see that? *We* started the fire — with this Latin tabloid as kindling."

"If you'd put Fossoli in the Pope's paper *this morning*, like you said you would, maybe the Germans wouldn't have dared—"

"Don't be ridiculous. You have a Jew's fantasy about the papacy's influence. The Germans could care less about papal proclamations."

"What proclamation? You're saying, even though it's after the fact and useless, the Vatican is taking the prayer for Fossoli back? Who is? Who's doing that?"

"Cardinal Maglione. The secretary of state."

"Can they do that?"

Deane snorted. "It's Maglione's newspaper. Of course they can do that. Simple as printing a new front page. Easy. In the presses right now."

"But why?"

"Fossoli is on fire! Fossoli is a battle scene!" Deane lifted the letter. "An 'instance of active belligerence'! You can't have the Vatican anticipating German offensives."

Warburg started to speak, then stopped. Deane sensed how thrown he was, with guilt, remorse—or was it panic? But then Warburg pushed the feelings back. When he spoke now, it was more quietly, with a hint of supplication.

"But if Fossoli is on the front page of the Pope's paper *tomorrow*, people will take notice. Now more than ever, Father. If those people *are* dead, the least the Pope can do is offer that prayer. Draw attention. Killing this edition of the newspaper is like killing those poor people again."

But Deane wasn't buying it. "No," he said. "Let it go. Bombing that bridge was a half-baked connivance to begin with. I can't believe I let you rope me into it." Deane's leg was really hurting. How was he going to get back to St. Peter's in time? And sure as hell, tacked to his door would be a *citazione* from Tardini, summoning him to explain how he had dragged Fossoli into St. Peter's Square. Jesus! He flicked his cigarette out the car window.

Warburg was silent. The car screeched along, carried by momentum gained on the lower slopes of the Janiculum. Visible ahead was the bridge across the Tiber. The driver was blasting his horn, swerving around other vehicles, making horses rear. Deane gripped his left knee with both hands, bracing the leg. He was unable to deflect any longer the real truth of what had just happened. This Jew had not roped him into anything. He had gone along with the cockeyed scheme for the sake of his own vainglorious ambition, thinking he himself could rescue the Church's tattered reputation. Yes, helping some desperate Jews, but along the way gaining praise for himself when the camp inmates were rescued, pleasing Spellman and greasing the upward promotion chute for both of them. He felt ashamed. Using those people. He felt disgusted with himself. He deserved this goddamned pain.

Finally Warburg said, "What did you call them? Sons of Job? Why not just say 'Jews,' Father? What's so hard about the word 'Jews'? And if that pathetic prayer is a violation of Vatican neutrality, your Church has already been taken captive."

"The prayer wasn't pathetic. It was heartfelt. I wrote it. And I meant it." At least that.

"But without the word 'Jews.'"

"Why does that matter?"

After a long silence Warburg said, "I can't explain it to you, Father."

"Just as well," Deane said. "I can't deal with this now. My leg is killing me."

"I'm sorry, but I have another question for you." Warburg paused to give Deane a chance to look at him, but he didn't. "How did you know I went to Yale?"

Now Deane met Warburg's eyes: "What?"

"Eli. Yale. I never mentioned that to you. How do you know?"

"You thought I'd slurred you or something."

"Never mind that. How do you know? You have Vatican intelligence *on me?*"

Before Deane could answer, the car screeched to a halt and the driver called, "*Arrivati!*" The papal flags did their trick. Attendants and nurses swarmed the car, and in short order Deane was on a wheeled stretcher being pushed away. He called back to Warburg, "Find out what happened in Fossoli. Have the driver take you." And to the driver, "*Accompagnalo! Accompagnalo!*"

Warburg instructed the driver to take him to the Jewish enclave on the banks of the Tiber, to the building to which Giacomo Lionni first summoned them. Warburg was better informed now than he had been three days before. Jews had lived on those blocks by the river since before Christ was born. But since the Reformation, which sparked a brutalizing insecurity in the Catholic Church, the district had been a kind of open-air prison, the ghetto. Walls were built, and the gates were closed at dusk. For more than three hundred years, until only eighty years ago, Roman Jews were the Pope's prisoners — here.

The building in which Warburg, Lionni, Mates, and Marguerite d'Erasmo had met was adjacent to the synagogue, a kind of library and community center, and it was there that Warburg left Deane's car. The driver was clearly anxious to get back to the hospital. Warburg watched the limousine gun away behind its fluttering yellow flags.

The sun was still high in the sky, but the heat had eased off, and here the riverside boulevard was in the shadow of rangy, high-canopied pine trees. Warburg looked up and picked out the second-floor window of the room in which Lionni had gathered them. The blinds were drawn. The door to the building was locked, but it was double-sided and poorly latched. Warburg banged it loudly, and the frame shook. He had no real reason to expect that Lionni was back in Rome already, or that he would have returned here. He stepped back and saw that the windows on the *third* floor were roughly nailed over with boards.

Warburg crossed the nearby side street and entered the small piazza that fronted the looming synagogue. Built after emancipation as a kind of declaration, the synagogue was one of the largest buildings in Rome. Its Moorish, squared-off dome rose as a majestic counterpoint to the cupola of St. Peter's, across the river. As he approached the entrance, he sensed a chill on his neck, the same brief discomfort he'd felt years before, walking up to Beth Israel in Burlington, hoping to hand his father's *tallit* to the rabbi. He blanked that memory. Here, a high, spiked fence surrounded the synagogue. The iron gate was slightly ajar, and Warburg saw that its square lock was broken, the metal plate jimmied back. When he tugged the gate it swung open but unevenly on the hinges. A few steps took him to the oversized door, made of oak into which was carved a triptych of filigreed arches above Hebrew letters he did not understand.

The door lock, too, was broken. He went inside. What he beheld took his breath away — not the grandeur of the soaring space, though once it had been grand, but the wreckage of it. Enough light filtered in through the high, arched yellow-paned windows for him to see that benches were upended, haphazardly piled front and back. Wooden slats protruded from the nearest pile, jagged rods, broken chairs, charred cardboard boxes — the remnants of an interrupted fire, a squatter's fire perhaps. *Fires at Fossoli.* He thought of Marguerite d'Erasmo. Where was she?

Rows of columns supported the roof. On the high ceiling, he could make out a ribbon swirl of several bright colors, and he thought of his father, whose rare biblical reference, on rainy days, was to the rainbow: *Lookie there, Davy! Sign of God's promise to Noah. No more floods!* But a flood of hatred had swamped this place. So much for promises, including the One God's.

On walls and columns, wires hung loosely from places where light fixtures had been ripped away. Tapestries had been half torn from the walls, and fell in tatters from the railings of a three-sided balcony. The great sanctuary, on the wall opposite the entrance, designed to house the Torah ark, a pulpit, and a reader's stand, was wrecked beneath the collapse of a massive wooden canopy. All was still. *A Jew's fantasy. One God. Marguerite.* Filtered shafts of twilight wedged through the air, with motes of dust floating before Warburg like souls. And then he saw, crumbled in a corner on the floor, a white cloth with black stripes, a *tallit* like his father's, although this one was soiled with what could have been blood.

SIX

Cleopatra's Needle

OBERTO LEHMANN PULLED the bell rope at the broad
entrance to the Casa dello Spirito Santo. Though the nondescript, multistory façade showed nothing of the monastic
enclosure it concealed, he could picture the scene within: stone tower,
arched portico, colonnades of the cloister walk. He had begun his religious life as a boy in a Rhineland version of such a place, a dozen years
before. How he had loved the aroma of incense, the stone-cooled air,
the silence infused with the lilting echoes of chant. The monastery was
his first taste of heaven.

He pulled on the bell rope again, with impatience. Finally the small
portal within the much larger gate creaked slowly open. A hunch-
backed gargoyle of a man, in the ubiquitous blue smock of a manual
laborer, stepped to the threshold as if to block it. *"Che cosa volete?"* he
asked brusquely. Only then did he look up from his stoop to see that
the visitor was a soutaned cleric. He stepped back with an apologetic
drop into near prostration. *"Entrate, Padre. Entrate."*

Knowing full well there was no point in approaching the mother
abbess, Lehmann instructed the man to take him to the priest. Moments later, he was standing in the rear shadows of the small chapel. A
figure was bent in prayer, kneeling at a bench halfway to the sanctuary,
from which the one permanent candle sent its red flickers around the
darkened space. Lehmann heard something, then realized the sound
was swallowed sobs. He slowly walked forward, aware of the alerting

patter of his footsteps, and stood beside the white-robed priest, who responded by drawing himself up from his knees to sit. Otherwise the man made no move, and there was no acknowledgment.

"Padre Antonio," Lehmann said.

"*Sì*."

"Or should we speak in French?"

The old priest looked up. "Italian is good."

"But you are from France."

"*Sì*. And you?" But the old priest seemed to know. Lehmann liked to think his own Italian was accentless, but it wasn't true.

"May we speak, Padre?" Lehmann assumed the priest would lead him out of the chapel, but he did not move. Lehmann sat on the bench, separated from the priest by several feet. "I know your history. You came to Rome in disgrace."

"What is that to you?"

"How old is your child by now? A child no more."

Padre Antonio said nothing.

"Does Mother Abbess know who her chaplain has been all these years? A renegade priest?"

Still Padre Antonio was silent, impossible to read.

"I have come from the Vicariate of the Holy See. I speak for the cardinal vicar. I am providing official notice of an apostolic visitation, pending a canonical reclassification of Casa dello Spirito Santo."

"Official notice must go to Mother," the French priest said.

"Mother has received such notices before," Lehmann said, "but this one will be enforced. You are commanded by the cardinal vicar to inform her. The Congregation of Apostolic Visitation acts with solemn authority. The French Cistercians are to be transferred to the Convent of Santa Maria della Vittoria. Mother Abbess must prepare herself and her sisters. This monastery is to be restored to the Order of the Friars Minor."

"German Franciscans?"

"Why do you say German?"

"You are German."

"I am here on behalf of the Vicariate. Not Germany. The friars had canonical residence here for more than one hundred years."

"Italian friars."

"What province is of no matter. This is a simple restoration of canonical order. Franciscans do the Church's work of charity."

"And they need a Vatican dependency—exempt from searches by the police?"

"That is of no concern to you. This monastery will be a center of caring for refugees."

"What refugees?"

"Those who turn to the Church. The contemplative sisters have no need of this place. In any case, they are French sisters who were received here, as you know, in an act of charity during the expulsions of the Third Republic. Anticlericalism in France is finished. If they choose, the sisters may return."

"Anticlericalism is finished, yes," Padre Antonio snorted, "because the Church embraces Vichy."

"You are to facilitate Mother's compliance."

The old priest laughed. "The cardinal vicar does not know Mother."

"The cardinal vicar knows the abbot primate. Mother will be dealt with by Sant'Anselmo. You tell her. You, too, are under obedience."

"My vow is to the Lord."

"To whom was your vow when you broke it in order to marry? What of your secret wife? And what of the matrimonial vow you took to her, a lie in the moment of love? You did not answer me before. Does Mother Abbess know your history?"

"She knows enough."

"Ah, but does she know what became of your 'wife'? Her suicide when she learned of your deceitful double life? You then resigned as a priest of the diocese of Marseille to join your penitential order, Cistercians of the Strict Observance. Hah! No observance, no matter how strict, atones for sin like yours. And what of your daughter, the child born of your illicit love? Your daughter remains in Marseille, your sin made flesh, an aging *cocotte* by now, having spent her life swallowing the smoke of sailors." Lehmann paused, then turned the blade. "Your daughter never answered your letters."

"My file in the Apostolic Congregation is under sacramental seal. How did you get it?"

Lehmann shrugged. "Under certain pressure, seals are known to break. Like vows, Father. I would expect you, of all people, to understand this. You will speak to Mother Abbess. Prepare her for the congregational visitation. And for solemn submission."

Lehmann stood. He felt the crisp satisfaction of a duty successfully fulfilled, and that welcome sensation brought the monastery of his youth to mind once more — Mariae Mons. That first summer, as young Brother Roberto, he had come upon the monastery's secret — that the mayor of nearby Mainz had refused to allow the swastika to be flown anywhere in the city, and had boycotted Chancellor Hitler's visit during his triumphant tour of the Rhineland. Naturally, that made the mayor a fugitive, and, relying on boyhood friendships with certain of the monks, he had come to Mariae Mons to hide. This was done without the monastic vicar general's knowledge.

Brother Roberto, as part of his duties as a kitchen helper, was one of those who'd brought the visitor bread and soup, without knowing who he was. One night, the frightened mayor had entrusted Lehmann with his story, making him promise not to tell the vicar general. The secret proved too heavy a load to carry. But, given his promise, whom could he tell? Just then, the monastery hosted a celebration of the treaty between the Church and the newly empowered Third Reich. German dignitaries attended, including Herr Hitler's vice chancellor, Franz von Papen, the Catholic who had negotiated the treaty, and the vicar general's friend.

So it was that, after the glorious Mass of celebration, the young Brother Roberto had approached the black-uniformed officer hovering at von Papen's side. Lehmann did not know Heinrich Himmler — who he was or who he would become. The earnest lad knew only that this stern-looking man of authority was the one to whom he would unburden himself. Lehmann told Himmler the monastery's secret.

The fugitive in the attic soon disappeared. After that, the grateful

vicar general knew Roberto's name. Lehmann was promoted ahead
of his mates, from postulant to novice and on through the orders. At
the ceremony attending each advance, climaxing in ordination to the
priesthood, his dear mother was present, letting him see her bliss.
He had then been specially commissioned to serve as an aide to the
archbishop of Mainz. When the war broke out, his assignment shifted,
bringing him to Rome. Here, blending in with the clerics of the Curia,
he had left his gray robes and monastic identity behind for something
far better — especially once his mother joined him. And *Obergruppen-
führer* Himmler had stayed in touch.

Now, when Lehmann left Casa dello Spirito Santo, he stepped into
the thick traffic of Via Sicilia, dodging trucks and pushcarts. The street
was swarming with early-morning bustle, all Rome desperate to re-
discover rhythms of the old routine. A man confident of his ability
to maneuver through the clandestine chutes of catacombs and looted
tombs, where the true pulse of the ancient city could be felt, the German priest was unaware of the street worker dressed in a peaked cap
and soiled smock, like so many others, but who was following him.

For the sake of perspective when beheld from below, the Renaissance
master Bernini had designed the grand staircase of the Apostolic Palace with each white marble step a slightly different height from every
other. Monsignor Deane had never noticed that minuscule gradation
before, but then he had never made the climb on crutches before. The
cast on his leg had made it impossible to put on the black trousers that
he always wore under his red-trimmed cassock, and he hated being
turned out like one of those effete Italians — pantless wonders. Not to
mention the draft on his bare legs beneath the skirt.

The stairs were such slow going that he was sure he would be late
for his appointment. Vatican functionaries passed him, ascending and
descending, all avoiding a direct look at him, as if crutches in this holy
place were a sin against faith. *Get up. Pick up your mat and walk!* But
the Lord had not yet healed Deane's fracture. In truth, it still hurt like
hell.

And so did his head, since he'd over-anesthetized himself with

Chianti the night before. With both crutches under his right arm, left hand on the railing, he'd found the rhythm: step up with good leg, push down on crutches, up with broken leg, pause, then up with crutches — repeat. His nightmare had been that he would have to mount the stairs on his buttocks, but not so. Easy does it. One step at a time. There.

The message from Cardinal Maglione's apostolic administrator had said 10:15, *punto*. Deane had been angling for a one-on-one meeting with the papal secretary of state since arriving in Rome, and if it took what the prelate regarded as an infraction to get it, well, *Benedicamus Domino*. From infraction to fracture, he was on a roll. Step. Crutch. Balance. There.

At the top of the stairs, standing in the shadow of a larger-than-life statue of Peter clutching keys, was a blue-uniformed papal gendarme, a revolver holstered at his side. Maglione's bodyguard. It startled Deane to come upon the sinister-looking character, and because of the crutches he felt liable to be accused of some malfeasance. He nodded, but the Italian ignored him. Deane hobbled by, aware of being watched the entire stretch of the long, long corridor.

Compared to the cardinal's residential apartment where the weekly lunches for resident diplomats were held, Maglione's working offices were spartan. In the windowless outer room, a black-veiled nun sat at a desk. He thought of the nun he'd seen at Monsignor Tardini's elbow. Nuns in offices, not just in laundries: Was this an effect of Mother Pascalina's status as the Pope's exec? Or was it just the war — women here, as everywhere, moving into the jobs of men?

Deane had a bit of trouble handling the large wooden door, and the woman stood up. Only then did he recognize her: she *was* the nun he'd glimpsed in Tardini's office. He remembered how she'd taken custody of a sheaf of documents, as if she had more than a clerk's authority over Vatican diplomacy.

"May I help you, Monsignor?" she said in brisk English, moving out from behind the desk and taking the weight of the door as he hopped into the room. He caught a quick look at the papers spread on her desk, sheets covered with rows and columns of numerals. Was she an accountant?

"Thank you, Sister." He found it possible to grin at her. It had never occurred to him she wasn't Italian, but: "Do I detect a touch of the Thames in your voice?"

She immediately faced away from him, returning to her desk, where she quickly turned the papers over one after the other, a repeat of what he'd seen her do in Tardini's office. She said, "If you mean am I British, the answer is yes." Once all of the pages were hidden, she looked up. "What happened to you?"

Deane let the grin overspread his face. "War wound." He tugged on his cassock to display the cast. The toes of his foot were covered with a black sock. "The war was with my own three feet. I lost. A rout."

"I saw you at Monsignor Tardini's office not three days ago, and your leg was fine."

"I broke it yesterday."

"Storming into some apostolic office?"

"That was rude of me. I apologized to the Most Reverend Sir, and now I apologize to you. I could see that the business I interrupted was important." He paused, as if to give her a chance to explain what her business was. She said nothing. "But it never occurred to me you were English."

"English Dominican."

"How do you come to be here — in the Secretariat, I mean. The inner sanctum of the Curia. A sister, a Brit."

She did not reply, a pointed signal of no interest in the personal. As before, he was struck by her appearance, but now, looking more directly, he could see why. Amid the cloaking, only her face registered, hence its impact. The starched white linen at her forehead and temples framed an aquiline nose, sparkling blue eyes, a mouth made for what it had renounced. On any other woman, such fine features would be alluring, but on her they gave paradoxical emphasis to chaste unavailability. Guessing her age, he could not have come within a decade. Maybe fifty. Maybe thirty.

Deane remained standing, leaning on the crutches in front of a pair of swan chairs with frayed red velvet upholstery. Between the chairs was an oval leather-topped table. As if she'd offered him one of the chairs, he said, "I'll just stand. It's easier."

"It won't be long," she said. "His Eminence is eager to see you." She pulled a watch on a cord out from beneath the folds of her habit. "Indeed. It's time." She stood, turned, and opened the door, then stepped back so that Deane would have the space needed to enter. Passing her, he picked up the whiff of that certain aroma, the scent of a nun — plain soap, a hint of incense. Once behind him, she returned to her desk, removed a stenographer's pad from a drawer, and followed him into the office. She took a seat in the corner by the door, adjusted the rosary beads hanging from her cincture, and crossed her legs under her habit, a pencil poised above the pad. The discreet record keeper.

This was another unadorned room, but its large window opened onto the broad vista of St. Peter's Square, centered on Cleopatra's Needle. Deane knew the Egyptian obelisk's match in Central Park, behind the Met, but this one was different, he also knew, because Bernini had shaved its pointed cap so that a golden reliquary containing a piece of the True Cross could be affixed. The window, framing such a masterpiece and its surround, was enough to make the simple office magnificent.

At the outsized desk, bathed in morning light, sat the crimson-robed Cardinal Maglione, fountain pen in hand, bent over a document. The red zucchetto drew attention to the slight tremor in the prelate's bald head — or skull, actually, since bone showed through the tissue-like flesh. The yellow pallor of his cheeks was made more pronounced by the contrasting red silk of his getup. El Greco's *Saint Jerome*, yes, but without the beard. Even seated, he looked frail and gaunt. His breathing was a wheeze. He neither looked up nor visibly registered Deane's entrance.

On the wall opposite the window was the room's only adornment, an ornately framed photograph of the present Pope. The famously ascetic pontiff's stern expression was a Catholic cliché. The gold-leaf filigree of the frame was out of sync with the cheaply produced black-and-white picture; the frame had no doubt held the portraits of numerous popes. Across the centuries, Vatican secretaries of state, in effect prime ministers to a monarch, had wielded enormous power from this room, and Deane sensed its aura.

Finally the cardinal slammed down his pen. He brought his head up, equally sharply. If the sight of Deane's crutches surprised Maglione, he didn't show it. All at once there was nothing frail about him. "*Come osate!*" he said fiercely. How dare you!

Deane infused his voice with a deference not quite evident in his choice of words: "Your Eminence, the poor souls at Fossoli were worthy of our prayers."

"Our prayers. Not our apostolic proclamation. By drawing attention to the camp, you encouraged the Waffen-SS to destroy it."

"Not true, Your Eminence. The *Acta Diurna* mentioning Fossoli was never published. At your order. And if it had been published, it would have been after the fact. The Germans never knew of the Holy See's interest. Which, in light of what happened, seems regrettable."

"The Holy See had no interest there."

Deane pointedly made no reply to that.

The cardinal sat back in his chair, a strategic adjustment. Deane knew from his reputation as a wily diplomat how rarely Maglione led with openly expressed anger. "Monsignor Deane, I know that your work with the Pontifical Assistance Commission is already exemplary. Please be seated. You have become injured?"

Deane would have preferred to remain upright, but he carefully lowered himself onto the straight-backed wooden chair opposite the desk, the supplicant's chair. The cardinal's question required no answer. As he laid the crutches on the floor, he glanced over at the nun, but she was intent upon her pad.

Maglione said, "Monsignor Tardini tells me that you are already fulfilling the promise of our great work. Our urgent work, bringing the succor of Our Lord to so many victims of the terrible war."

"Thank you, Your Eminence." Deane saw the implication of an

opening, and he promptly pushed through it. "And I welcome this op-
portunity to bring warm and personal greetings to you from Archbishop Spellman."

At the mention of Spellman, Maglione nodded, but barely.

Deane went on, "As you know, His Excellency is leading an emergency fund drive in America through the National Catholic Welfare
Council, and we expect within weeks to put additional substantial
benefactions at your disposal."

"Not mine."

"The Holy Father's."

The cardinal shook his head. "The Pontifical Assistance Commission." A stern correction.

"Of course." Deane hesitated. Could he speak openly in front of the
nun? He resisted the impulse to look again in her direction. He began
slowly, obliquely, thinking that if Maglione wanted to cut him off, he
could. "And as you saw in the report I submitted about Archbishop
Spellman's initiatives at the direction of the Holy Father . . ." The nun
was scribbling away, shorthand, taking down his every word. *Okay.*
". . . the archbishop has successfully engaged high-level figures in the
Roosevelt administration . . ." Again he paused, awaiting the prelate's
interruption. None came. ". . . in discussions about an Anglo-American recognition of a central European Habsburg restoration."

"What high-level figures?"

"General Donovan, a Catholic."

"A bad Catholic. Married outside the Church."

"But he is head of the OSS, Your Eminence. He is close to Roosevelt."

Maglione answered with a dismissive wave of the hand.

Deane pushed on. "Archbishop Spellman has seen to it that both
the President and Donovan get the point of the Catholic anti-Soviet
bulwark in Europe, and they understand the Holy See's role. They welcome it. Both favor the Habsburg initiative." Deane paused, thinking
briefly of Mates in the confessional, how he had pressed the issue of
timing. "But Washington can only entertain this plan for a Catholic

monarchy as applying *after* the German surrender. Unconditional surrender, as you know."

"Unconditional surrender is an obstacle to peace."

"Nevertheless, it remains Roosevelt's firm policy."

Maglione slapped a hand down on his desk. "A firm policy that helps Hitler stay in power. We have conveyed that. We have been ignored. Spellman was supposed to make it clear — unconditional surrender helps Hitler. It hurts the Germans, many Germans who oppose Hitler. Germans oppose Hitler, Father. Many Germans."

"The slaughter at Fossoli, Your Eminence. That was not the work of the Waffen-SS. It was common German soldiers. Wehrmacht infantry, not storm troopers. Germans did that, not the SS. We see few signs that common Germans oppose —"

"Unconditional surrender is immoral!" Maglione said, his voice rising in volume and pitch, his face flushing red.

Deane waited. As he expected, Maglione calmed down, knowing his outburst had cost him control of the exchange.

Deane took advantage of that, shifting. "If I may speak directly, Your Eminence."

Maglione did not move, which was answer enough. Deane said, "For the Church to advance the Habsburg restoration prematurely, especially in conjunction with figures associated with the Third Reich — this will kill it. Moscow will kill it, but so will London and Washington."

Maglione glared at the American monsignor as if daring him to elaborate. Here is where Deane could have usefully announced that Archbishop Graz, through his factotum Lehmann, was attempting to preempt the Holy Father, making the plan seem like the proposal of a German cabal instead of that of the Holy See. An Abwehr plan, he wanted to say. *The loyalties of Graz and Lehmann are to Berlin, not to His Holiness!* But Deane's suspicions were not knowledge.

Colonel Mates had come through with nothing about the German priest — indeed, had simply not shown up for their confessional rendezvous the evening before, though Deane himself had moved mountains to get there, straight from the emergency room. But what the hell, he thought, why not puncture Lehmann's balloon in any case. "For example," he said to Maglione, "if the Holy Father were to consecrate Archduke Otto in the Order of St. John of Malta this month, that would alert the Soviets to his dynasty's fresh importance. Moscow would spark an immediate Allied repudiation of His Grace's legitimacy. No House of Austria. No Catholic restoration."

"There has been no promulgation about the archduke." Maglione's meaning was clear: How do you know about his elevation to Malta?

"As a simple matter of speculation, Your Eminence. So it occurred to me. I am under the impression that Archbishop Graz would like to be the archduke's consecrating sponsor, if indeed the archduke is so honored."

Maglione stared at him for such a long time and with such utter immobility that Deane suspected some sort of catatonia. No such luck. Maglione spoke at last, backtracking in their exchange to say with measured contempt, "I expected Archbishop Spellman to exert his influence in Washington in this matter. If your report is accurate, he has failed me."

Deane now sensed that Maglione might be dying. His desperate hope was to offer the last drops of his life's blood, like melted wax, as the seal on a new alliance built around Catholic Austria. A legacy of peace and a blow against Moscow. But time had run out. He had Germans willing to work with him. Where were the Americans? Germans were good. Americans were bad. Unconditional surrender was the locked door. Maglione would rather blame Spellman than face the fact that he, the Vatican lord of *realpolitik,* had been living in a self-serving dream world. In the name of that dream, he had, moments before, been frantic that a nearly meaningless — and never published — prayer for desperate Jews in a death camp only hours from here might have compromised the ferocious political detachment on which Maglione's fantasy depended. Or was the fantasy a mere excuse for that detachment? The desperate Jews were dead now. No longer a problem. Which is why Maglione had so abruptly conquered his anger about Fossoli.

The whole repugnant truth of the Vatican's futile policy of neutrality was suddenly manifest to Deane—a policy he himself had defended to Warburg. Was it Maglione's policy, or did it in fact originate with His Holiness? Maglione's influence mattered, because if the Pope took his view from the sitting secretary of state, Spellman's only chance at being named to Maglione's chair had just gone up the chimney like papal smoke. And getting Spellman's ass into that chair was job one for Deane in Rome. *Jesus.*

The cardinal reached forward and picked up his pen. He adjusted the papers on his desk, readying a new document for his signature. He wrote his name with a flourish, then rolled a green and bronze curved blotter over it. As far as Maglione was concerned, the supplicant nobody was dismissed. Audience over.

The rudeness was astonishing, and Deane thought back to the exuberant charm of Cardinal Maglione's arrival in his formal apartment the other day. Here was the man in his naked boorishness. Deane looked over at the nun. She had closed her steno pad and, while standing up, gestured toward Deane, indicating the door.

Deane pulled his crutches up and hoisted himself from the chair. Once again he towered over the stooped prelate. "And one other matter, Eminence, if I may. You should know this, and so should the Holy Father. I would be derelict not to report it. President Roosevelt has sent a personal emissary here to Rome. He was on the military plane that brought me. The local chief of the War Refugee Board. Roosevelt's intervention for the Jews."

"Morgenthau," Maglione said without looking up from the next document. He continued to read with his pen poised, but said absently, "The Jew among Roosevelt's ministers."

"Yes, Secretary Morgenthau is the head of the board, but it is decidedly Roosevelt's initiative. The President gave a speech in Washington about it yesterday. One thousand Jewish refugees, he said, will be exempt from normal quota limits. *Jewish* refugees. Being promptly brought to America. Washington is speaking up about the Jews, and doing something."

"What is one thousand? We have one thousand just in our Roman convents." He signed his name.

"One thousand is just the beginning, Your Eminence. Many Jews will be rescued to America. But the larger point is that it's public. A *public* initiative on behalf of the Jews, Your Eminence."

"Too late. You know that. Too late."

"Are you aware of Budapest? Roosevelt's man is moving to help Jews in Budapest."

Maglione looked up. "Moving publicly?"

"No. But he is taking direct —"

"*Not* public!" The cardinal banged the blotter down on the paper, his point proven. The Holy Father's point. Public initiatives — condemnations, protests, denunciations — only get people killed. Maglione rolled the blotter over his signature, rocking the device back and forth. If Maglione could have flattened Deane with that blotter, he would have.

In the outer office, with the door to the cardinal's office closed, the nun stood at her desk, staring down at it. Deane sensed some turmoil, saw a person struggling to make a decision. He said quietly, in English, "May I read your mind, Sister?"

She looked up sharply, conveying her dislike of his recourse to forced whimsy.

He made his guess: "Archbishop Angelo Rotta, the Budapest nuncio."

She stared at him. In her eyes he saw the cloud of uncertainty. Perhaps fear.

Deane said, "You are the Holy See's cipher clerk. Am I right? Twice I've seen you with sheets covered with numbers. I thought accountant at first. But no. Code. Cryptograms. I saw you instructing Tardini. And here you brief the cardinal. He depends on you. You manage the communications with the papal nuncios."

The nun only stared at him.

"So you have read what Archbishop Rotta, in his secret dispatches, is saying about Budapest. Thousands of Jews being taken."

She said, "Do you know the Sala dei Chiaroscuri?"

"The chapel of Nicholas the Fifth. One floor down."

"Wait for me in its sacristy."

In 1937, Jane Storrow earned her DPhil in applied mathematics at the Mathematical Institute at Oxford, one of only a handful of women ever to do so. But throughout the last two of her seven years there, she had attended Mass each morning at Blackfriars Hall, the Dominican college. For her, the plunge into the cold abstractions of geometric logic had involved an unexpected confrontation with transcendent mystery, especially once she fell under the spell of Blaise Pascal, who was as much her spiritual master as her philosophical mentor. The limits of the axiomatic method, and the ultimate impossibility of mathematical certainty, were, for both of them, channels into the mind of God. Yet formal religion was at first repugnant to her, as if devotedness betrayed intelligence. But at Blackfriars the simplicities of sacramental language — bread, wine, gestures of kneeling and bowing, aromas of incense, the touch of water, silence — came to seem as elegant as the solved formulas of theorems, though with far surpassing significance.

Even as her faith quickened, she continued to understand herself in secular terms, like the layman Pascal. Thus she welcomed it when, upon receiving her degree, she was recruited to Bletchley Park, the just established security service enterprise on the Varsity Line, a short train ride from Oxford. That only the top four in her class were invited to join this vaguely defined project made it irresistible. Soon enough, she understood that the red brick Victorian manor house, amid its white-trimmed complex of buildings surrounded by two hundred acres of pasture, was the center of a war-spawned crash program in cryptanalysis, and she fervently embraced the work. For a year she remained there, living in the eaves below the copper roofs; applying the factoring of large composite integers to protocols of code-making and -breaking; and falling in love with Philip Barnes Morton, a Cambridge mathematician for whom her attraction to God was the only indication that she was not perfect. His imperfection lay in his being married to the doe-eyed Edith.

Jane might have been capable of illicit lovemaking, but she was not remotely able to join Philip in a betrayal of his wife. Because of that, she'd found it impossible to stay at Bletchley. On an impulse that at the time had seemed mad, but would later come to seem to have been inspired, she'd bolted. A breakdown? Perhaps. She went straight to Blackfriars, asked to see the novice mistress, and requested admission to the order as a postulant nun. To the Dominicans she was a catch. No one pressed her on the motives behind her flight to God.

Upon her solemn profession three years later, a ceremony centered on her being vested with the white habit — *Clothe me, O Lord, in the nuptial robe of chastity* — she was singly honored with the name of the order's greatest mind, Thomas Aquinas, a rare approbation, especially for a woman. From now on, braced by the vows and the monastic hours, simplicity was to define her. Simplicity, she'd learned from Pascal, was the surest mark of truth. She was in no way prepared for it when, a short time later, the Dominican master general summoned her to the Angelicum in Rome. Stunned and a bit frightened, she obeyed, of course. Soon enough, it made sense that her postulancy had been uniquely shaped by intense schooling in Virgil's Latin and Dante's Italian.

When Deane, before leaving Cardinal Maglione's office, asked her her name, she replied, "Sister Thomas."

At the head of the center aisle of the papal chapel, Deane bowed to the Blessed Sacrament, since genuflection was out of the question. He realized that the melody of the hymn *Pange Lingua* was floating through his mind, and he recalled being one of several dozen seminarians lined up in these very choir stalls, tiered like bleachers in a gym. Now, he stood still. His gaze floated, once more drawn to the chapel's brilliant adornments — frescoes, statues, carvings. Like many of the sacred rooms in the Vatican, it seemed more a place to be visited in wonder than in devotion, yet a prayer came unbidden into Deane's mind. *Into your hands, O Lord, I commend their spirits.* Whose spirits? But he knew. The poor souls at Fossoli, who had not been far from his thoughts since he'd heard their fate.

He blessed himself and resumed his gimpy lunging across the soap-smooth marble floor.

So also the sacristy—vacant. The room behind the sanctuary was surprisingly small and undecorated, low-ceilinged and dark. Through a small window poured a narrow wash of morning light that emphasized shadows in the corners. Beneath the angled beams, Deane waited, alone.

When Sister Thomas arrived, it was through a door obscured by the molding of the walnut paneling—not a hidden entrance, precisely, but surprise enough to, literally, throw Deane off balance. She carried a leather satchel. On the tabletop of the vestments case, she laid out its contents. "These are the dispatches from Archbishop Rotta. Also here are messages from Archbishop Roncalli, the nuncio in Istanbul, who joins in urging action for Budapest. Roncalli has traveled there. Roncalli is even more insistent than Rotta. Terrible things are happening. I am violating my solemn oath to show these cables to you."

"Sister," he began, as if to reassure her, but she brusquely cut him off, moving on to what mattered.

"Hundreds of Jews have crowded into the papal nunciature. Rotta and Roncalli are urgently asking for instructions. Jews are crowding into churches. Nazis are dragging them out. Lower clergy are confused. Hungary is mainly Catholic. Small minorities support the Arrow Cross and Nazis on one side, or the Communists on the other. The vast population is numb, thinking only of their own survival. They must be addressed. Here, in this dispatch . . ." She picked up a yellow page. Deane saw the careful handwriting, recognized a word or two of Latin. ". . . Archbishop Roncalli is asking that Vatican Radio broadcast a decree that helping Jews is an act of mercy approved by the Church."

"Doesn't that go without saying by now?"

Sister Thomas lifted her face toward Deane's. "The Hungarian people are frightened. And many of their leaders — priests, bishops — welcome the removal of Jews. Roncalli wants the Holy See to overrule them."

"What does Maglione say about a broadcast?"

"He waves his hand. 'Unthinkable. The first principle holds.'"

"What's that?"

"*Ad maiora mala vitanda.* Do nothing to make things worse. That principle. A Vatican broadcast would make everything worse. Defend Jews, and the Nazis round up Catholics."

"Catholic *Jews*," Deane said. "I'm told Maglione has repeatedly sent discreet messages about *conversos*. Defending the rights of the baptized Jews. As if other Jews are of no concern to the Church. Is that true?"

"I composed such statements for him myself. It is the most I could get him to do. Now Rotta and Roncalli are trapped by that." She seized another page. "Roncalli asks if he must restrict assistance to the baptized. But clearly he seeks to do more. He and Rotta want to be *told* to do more."

"Well, let's tell them, then." Deane waited for her to look at him. When she did, he said, "When they defend the baptized Jews, what do they do?"

"Roncalli arrived in Budapest with specially made sacramental certificates to give to baptized Jews. The Germans apparently are respecting them."

"Well, why not supply certificates for everybody?"

"Roncalli proposed it. Cardinal Maglione misunderstood. He thought Roncalli wanted to begin *baptizing* Jews, to save them. '*Falso!*' the cardinal said. Angrily. You saw what he is like. When I explained that the nuncio only wants to provide baptismal *certificates,* the cardinal repeated, '*Ad maiora mala vitanda.*' A profane misuse of the sacrament. And furthermore, the issuing of false certificates is deceit. A sin."

"What about His Holiness?"

Sister Thomas answered calmly, "His Holiness knows what is happening. He knows it all. He stays above. He has no response."

"There's a first principle embedded there, too. *Qui tacet consentire videtur.* Silence is consent, Sister. His Holiness may see himself as constrained, unable to act openly. But has he ordered anyone to stop? Rotta and Roncalli aren't stopping, and neither are you. The Pope wants the Jews helped, doesn't he?"

"Yes. Yes."

"And if baptismal certificates are off limits, what about Vatican visas? *Political* documents."

"To go where? How would we get visas to Budapest?"

"I know of someone here in Rome who can help with that. Sister, you have to encourage these nuncios. You control the communications. You can give them what they're asking for. They want to do something! You can help them!"

"Monsignor, I cannot issue instruction in the name of the Secretariat."

"Not instruction. Example. What if, say, you sent out a routine reiteration of the procedures involved in issuing Vatican employment visas? Persons carrying out the business of a neutral state are privileged with the exemptions appropriate to neutrality. It is up to the state to define its employment. Isn't that another first principle? If Germans are respecting baptism, they will respect state assertions of neutrality." Deane paused, adjusted his crutches. He realized that, for the first time since the basketball game, he'd forgotten the pain in his leg. "You could simply quote already promulgated procedures — no authorizing signature necessary. *Here* it is. What if you just replied to these Nuncio cables with citations from the Lateran Treaty, defining terms for the issuing of Vatican safe-conduct passes? Don't you think those inclined to do so would take the point?"

"Employment visas are specific diplomas," Sister Thomas said. "If you expect German recognition, documentation must be official. That requires the authenticating seal of the papal chancellery, embossed over the signatures upon issuance."

"Do you know where such forms are kept? The accreditation stamp?"

"I know the sister who administers the employment office." Sister

Thomas hesitated. "But we could never send such material in the diplomatic pouch of the Holy See. Cardinal Maglione himself seals the
pouch. There is no way to get the visa forms from here to Budapest."

"Yes there is. I have a way."

"The American you spoke of."

"Yes."

David Warburg had never seen a more beautiful sight: a dozen American Navy vessels, all at anchor across the great horseshoe bay, rhythmically keeping time with its tidal undulations, bows alike in nosing
westward in the wind. The ships were already forming the line that
would define their convoy, warships posted between troop and cargo
ships, all strung out like knots in a rope. So aligned, and with luck,
they would traverse the Mediterranean, slip through Gibraltar, and
cross the Atlantic.

The sight was beautiful for being framed by Mount Vesuvius to the
east and the cliff-hung peninsula of Sorrento to the south. A dozen
mammoth cranes defined the harbor foreground, structures of re-
newal. Naples, formerly the site of an Axis submarine base, had been
the most heavily bombed city in Italy, perhaps Europe. But that was
months ago, and now the port was the active center of Allied supply and reinforcement. In addition to the forming-up convoy out in
the bay, dozens of other ships, closer in, vied for channels and pier
space. On shore, trucks and personnel carriers lined up for their brief
shots at the quayside, to take on crates and squads of freshly arrived,
gawking yardbirds. Sacks of grain, cartons of canned goods, pallets
loaded with K rations, as well as machinery, weapons, racks of shells,
raw materials, supplies of every kind — a cornucopia of American
production. And, in the faces of its fresh legions of boys, a display
of American determination, disciplined by fear. The meaning of such
undefeated resolve was more apparent than ever at this crowded place
of debarkation: the port of Naples was a snapshot of the coming vic-
tory.

But most pointedly, there was beauty in what Warburg beheld because one of those distant convoy vessels soon to weigh anchor was

the USS *Henry Gibbons*, a troopship carrying, in its aft holds, a thousand wounded GIs and, forward, 982 guests of President Franklin D. Roosevelt, most of whom, before the ship had left the pier three hours before, Warburg had personally welcomed on board.

The refugees were brought to the port of Naples by Army trucks from four different camps in the environs of Rome. Before their arrival, Warburg had boarded the ship to inspect the cramped quarters — low-ceilinged, divided by rows of multitiered bunks — where they would spend the next three weeks. There was almost no space for stowing personal possessions, but, alas, that lack would burden few of these passengers.

With Sergeant Rossini and others of his operation, Warburg had taped to the bulkheads translated copies of President Roosevelt's message to Congress dated June 12, 1944:

> As the hour of the final defeat of the Hitlerite forces draws closer, the fury of their insane desire to wipe out the Jewish race in Europe continues undiminished.
>
> Therefore, I wish to report to you today that arrangements have been made to bring immediately to this country approximately 1,000 refugees who have fled from their homelands to southern Italy. These refugees are predominantly women and children. They will be placed on their arrival in a vacated Army camp on the Atlantic Coast. The War Refugee Board is charged with over-all responsibility for this project.

When the refugees began to board the ship, Warburg had positioned himself at the head of one of the two gangplanks, with Lieutenant Benny Cogan at his elbow, a Flatbush boy who'd been raised in a Yiddish-speaking home. No matter their place of origin, most of the refugees seemed to know Yiddish, and their faces registered Cogan's greeting, "*Shalom aleichem!*" Warburg took each one's hand and said, "On behalf of the United States of America, I welcome you aboard and wish you a safe journey." Cogan translated.

Most of the Jews were too exhausted or too wary to respond with more than a nod, but sometimes a man or woman would break into sobs as Cogan finished. For over an hour Warburg greeted them. As aware as he was of feeling gratitude to these people just for their being alive, he also experienced a kind of inner dislocation as the line moved slowly past.

If these were Jews, what was he? And who was he to have presumed a life that set him apart not only from this desperation, but from the unbroken bond of peoplehood that had so inflamed the enemies of Judaism, down the centuries to Hitler? And in what was that people-hood rooted if not in the unbroken bond with the One God? The taste of ashes was on Warburg's tongue. He felt ashamed of himself. For what? For not believing in that God.

When the last of the refugees was aboard, Lieutenant Cogan briskly saluted Warburg. All at once Warburg's gratitude flowed to this one man, as if the snap of that martial gesture bestowed forgiveness. War-burg put his hand out. "Thank you, Lieutenant. Good luck."

When Warburg had descended the gangplank and stepped ashore, ahead of the ship's lumbering move away from the pier, the last of his team to do so, he'd felt numb. Three shrill blasts of the vessel's whistle had given perfect expression to all that was buried beneath his calm demeanor.

Now, most of an hour later, with the *Henry Gibbons* in its proper column behind the convoy leader, far out in the bay, he was calm. He was finding it impossible to leave the pier until the ships were actually under way, and he assumed he would watch the departure until the ship of refugees dropped below the horizon. But he was interrupted.

"Well done, David." It was Mates, having drawn up quietly beside him. He offered Warburg a cigarette, and Warburg took it. Mates was wearing dark aviator sunglasses. His crisp uniform jacket was snugly buttoned at his waist. A silver star gleamed from each of its epaulets. He'd been wearing the star for only a week, yet carried himself as if he'd been born to the rank. He asked, "You had the trucks where and when you needed them?"

"Yes. Thanks for that," Warburg replied. "And the escort squads you assigned were impressive. They were kind."

"Christ, if anyone deserves a little kindness . . ."

"Right. Christ."

"What's needling you? And where the hell have you been? It's been a week since you slept at the Barberini."

"I have a cot in my office. I've been busy."

"I thought you might be avoiding me."

"Why would I do that?" The note of innocence Warburg struck was deliberately false. He had yet to confront Mates with what he knew— that Mates had business with the American monsignor, something besides the sacrament of confession.

"Because you're keeping my interrogators away from the camps, that's why." Mates was pissed off and let it show. "You're claiming authority you don't have. We have a deal, and you're not keeping it."

"We've been through that, General. My authority, in its sphere, is total. Your interrogators have to wait."

"You owe me, Warburg."

"What? What do I owe you?"

"In addition to this, you mean?" Mates tossed his head toward the *Henry Gibbons.*

"It's Roosevelt I owe for that."

"Then your man in Budapest, Swedish minister plenipotentiary— what's his name?"

"Wallenberg."

"You owe me that. Without the OSS turning the screws at the Swedish embassy in Bern, Stockholm would never have bought your plan. And now Wallenberg's hard at it. I hear that Jews are rushing to him."

Warburg hesitated, then yielded the point. "It's true. I do owe you that. Who knew that the Swedish ambassador in Bern is the king's nephew?"

"I did."

"You know everything. I forgot."

"Not quite. What happens now? In Budapest, I mean. Wallenberg buys up properties, declares sovereignty, takes Jews in. Then what? How do they get out of Hungary?"

"Not clear yet, but the Church is helping. Baptismal certificates. Vatican visas."

"The Church! Good God, the Church could care less about Jews."

"Not so, General. Priests and nuns. Parishes and convents. Across the Alps, the papal nuncios are crucial. With luck, we'll have a lot more refugees coming through Rome. Some Catholic will have helped every one of them."

"But the Pope. The Pope could care less."

"Perhaps. But perhaps not. Maybe it's just that His Holiness is more worried about Communists. In that case, not so different from you. Which makes me wonder if you and the Holy See are doing business."

"What sort of business?"

"You tell me."

Mates's declining to speak was answer enough.

Warburg shrugged. "I say let's finish off Hitler. Worry about Stalin later."

Mates countered, "Hitler became Hitler because we weren't worried about him soon enough."

Warburg turned to stare out at the convoy. "What I'm worried about, General, is my next ship. That's all. Believe it or not, the Navy claims all upcoming transport billets are spoken for, looking ahead for weeks. No space for refugees, despite FDR. All returning troopships are scheduled over to transporting German POWs back to the States. *Nazis!* Headed to Nebraska! While my refugees are told to wait."

"Clark wants the captured Krauts off his hands. There's just no way to deal with POWs here."

"Meanwhile, Roosevelt's getting hell in Congress for singling out Jews. I was ordered at the last minute to round up some Catholics for inclusion today. Out there on that ship — seventy-four Catholics, twenty-eight Greek Orthodox, seven Protestants, just so the President can deny he's helping only Jews. The Swedes are doing more at this point than we are."

"The Gestapo in Budapest will never let that guy — what's his name again?"

"Wallenberg."

"Never let him get away with it."

Yes, the convoy was setting sail. A plume of smoke burst from the funnel of the *Henry Gibbons*. Warburg welcomed the distraction, and its silencing of Mates. A bevy of small planes had taken off from the escort carrier, the start of the free-roaming air patrols that from now on would buzz around the ships like mosquitoes, looking out for enemy subs. General Mates was like a sub, Warburg thought, running silent below the surface of his own easy, slick manner.

Mates pulled the golden silk square from his breast pocket, and Warburg thought of the girl he'd seen leaving Mates's bedroom that first morning. A child. Now Mates removed his sunglasses and began to polish the lenses. With his eyes now visible, he looked weary, somehow vulnerable. Lines creased the skin at his brows, a delta of wrinkles at each eye, a bruise-like shadow in its hollow. The burdens of time, if not of this war, were leaving marks on the general's face. Or maybe it was the strain of hiding the truth of what he was up to.

Something caught Warburg's eye, a flash of brown movement on the quayside. He looked again. Not brown, but nearly lost within the buff field of a canvas tarp stretched over the bed of a rolling truck was a faded red smirch—the shape of a cross. The Red Cross truck. Her. "I'll be back," he said, then began to move quickly along the quay, dodging stacked cartons and huge pieces of off-loaded machinery, pumps, oil tanks, bulging burlap sacks. His eyes were fixed on that red mark as he moved, waiting for the angle to shift so that he could see the driver. The truck, though, was also moving, and Warburg started to run, fearing that he would lose it.

He had lost her once already. On the day after learning, with Monsignor Deane, of the massacre at Fossoli, he had returned again to the Jewish library near the synagogue. He pounded on the door until someone finally answered. An old woman stood inside, back somewhat from the barely cracked opening. She spoke no English, and he was not able to make himself understood. He'd repeated the name "Lionni . . . Lionni!" And "*Delegazione!*" Her muttering response was as unintelligible as it was alarmed, and it horrified him to think that he was frightening her. When she firmly closed the door, he did not press further.

Since coming to Rome, he'd been introduced to perhaps a dozen men described as leaders of the Italian Jewish community, and over

several days he'd asked among them for news of Lionni. They'd offered none, whether because they genuinely knew nothing or because
they did not trust Warburg, he could not say. And then, the last time
he was in the ghetto, Warburg had seen two British Army trucks
pulled up in front of the library—the vehicles' muddy brown color,
the crown insignia on the doors. The sight stopped him until he saw
a knot of six or seven uniformed soldiers exiting the synagogue. They
wore the webbed harnesses and flat-brimmed, netted helmets distinctive to tommies, but two had removed their helmets, and each of them
was wearing a yarmulke. Strange, he thought, then forgot about it.

He had to find her. He returned to the derelict rooming house in
Trastevere where he'd dropped her off that night, but now he brought
along Sergeant Rossini to translate. The old lady who answered there
said that Signorina d'Erasmo had indeed come back to her flat two
days before, but she had gone away again, without explanation—
which was, the woman said, what she always did.

"Gee, Mr. Warburg, if you don't mind my asking," Rossini had said
from his place at the wheel, "who is this dame?"

Indeed. Now Warburg was running hard, his tie flying, his stare
fixed upon that cross without a god. Every night for the past week,
Marguerite's face was the last image in his mind as he went to sleep,
and more than once he'd awakened with her name on his lips. He almost called it now, and was certain by the time he caught up with the
truck that she was at the wheel. It was moving steadily as he leapt onto
the passenger-side running board, reaching through the window. The
driver was startled and immediately hit the brakes, almost throwing
Warburg off.

The driver was a corpulent man, his forehead streaked with sweat,
his cheeks bristling with an untrimmed growth of beard. Warburg
brushed past the disappointment of not seeing her, and asked, "*Per
favore. Signorina d'Erasmo, sapere?* Do you know?"

"*Vada! Vada!*" the man said with a wave of his fist. His eyes flashed
angrily—crazily. But if there was madness here, Warburg realized, it
was all his own. He jumped away from the rolling truck, and he landed
hard.

PART TWO

Postwar

SEVEN

Road Out

I T WAS EVENING. The lilting chapel plainsong was disturbed by the suddenly stirred-up air, a summer wind that blew open the heavy oak door. It caught pages of the psalters, hems of the friars' robes, flames licking candles. The golden light of the lowering sun washed in. One of the brothers got up from his knees and crossed quickly to close the door, but not before Roberto Lehmann felt the intrusion of weather as an omen. Which of the robed visitors had drawn the displeasure of nature? Or was it him? Lehmann thought back to how he'd finally come to be here, beginning with his onetime and ever discreet mentor, Heinrich Himmler.

By March, four months ago now, Himmler knew that all was lost. Claiming to be deathly ill, he abandoned the Führer by cabling his resignation to Berlin, not daring to face the man himself. He stripped his uniform of insignia, shaved his mustache, donned a disguising eye patch, and set out on foot for the border with Denmark. British soldiers caught him. Before they could begin an interrogation, he swallowed the cyanide capsule he had been carrying for two years.

Suicide had not begun as Himmler's chosen mode of escape. Earlier, without informing the Führer, he had devised a better plan — *Aussenweg*, the Road Out. He had hoped to take it himself, but prepared it, in any case, for his most trusted brothers: a mythic road through Rome, where the gatekeeper would be the dependable Argentine-German priest, whose transfer from Mainz to Rome Himmler had arranged in the first place. Then, a year ago, Himmler had ordered Lehmann to see to the confiscation of the monastery on Via Sicilia — yes, for its diplomatic privilege.

Events since then had traumatized the priest, but also purified his purpose. Lehmann felt Himmler's end as a personal loss, yet it changed nothing. Subsequent news of Hitler's suicide and the abject surrender — no, destruction — of German forces changed nothing. The Catholic war against Bolshevism continued, more urgently than ever. And he, Father Roberto Lehmann, commissioned by the noble Himmler himself, was central to it. The Road Out stretched from Vienna to the Plaza de Mayo in Buenos Aires. It would rescue the most stalwart enemies of the Kremlin atheists and set them up to continue the great crusade. At each point, from Vienna to Zagreb to Rome, Franciscans and other clerics stood ready and willing to shore up the passage. Thus, only months after the end of the war in Europe, the choir stalls of Casa dello Spirito Santo were crowded at Vespers with gray- or brown-robed men. Of the twenty-seven men in habits, only fourteen were actual monks.

The Croatians among them were true Franciscans and true fugitives, both. While Croatians were a lesser race, even if Himmler had declared them free of Slavic blood, Lehmann knew them as invaluable allies. Having survived the old war, they were ready for the new one. Indeed, the Croatian Catholic network was proving pivotal to his entire enterprise.

Casting his eyes about now, Lehmann could distinguish the impostor friars by the unpracticed diligence with which they moved their lips around the Latin syllables. Most wore spectacles, which were probably fake. Some had monkishly small beards. In addition to the Croatians, the company included Frenchmen, Germans, and Hungarians — men in flight from Allied search teams but also from vengeance-seeking mobs who knew them as Gestapo, Ustashe leaders, or Vichy officials. Lehmann did not know who they were or what their roles had been, nor did he care to know.

The chief *Aussenweg* tollkeeper operated from Vienna, a German whom Lehmann had met once, in the archbishop's palace in Mainz. His rank of *Reichsleiter* had been clear to Lehmann from his distinctive gold lapel insignia. Now the *Reichsleiter,* presumably no longer in uniform, launched men on the secret pilgrimage, equipped with the necessary passwords and gold coins for bribes and with the understanding that everyone would be using a false name. Everyone but Lehmann, a fact in which he took due pride.

After Vespers and a light collation in the refectory, Lehmann went walking alone in the outer courtyard. Soon the friars would be at Compline, and then the great silence would fall. They would retire to their cells. The wind was howling and carried the damp odor of the fetid Tiber a few blocks distant. Above, the swifts of dusk soared like one creature in a great wheel.

At the monastery, Lehmann held the office of procurator, and he demonstrated that he stood apart from the friars, and above them, by this habitual opting out of the day's final communal service. His postprandial walk kept him in the shadows of the cloister at one end and of the high blank wall at the other. In this way, like a lord surveying his demesne, he circled the sheds, the carts, the chicken coop, the automobile with its Vatican license plates, and the priest's cottage, which he had taken for himself the year before.

Being removed from the monastic discipline in 1941, upon his assignment to the cathedral in Mainz, had meant Lehmann could care for his widowed mother. His father, a successful importer, had recently died of tuberculosis, but since then, *Madre* carried herself like a highborn war widow, her satins black. With Lehmann's transfer, he brought her to Rome, rescuing her from the incessant Mainz bombing raids, but also ushering her into the social whirl of the papal court.

At the Casa, he might have been expected to resume his hemmed-in life as a Franciscan. If he declined, it was not mainly because of his mother — although he used her as an excuse. More important, he had to maintain his status as a priest of pontifical right, diplomatically credentialed in the Holy See, and he could not do that as a friar. He continued to keep his room in his mother's apartment near the Pi-

azza Navona, but he also valued the Casa's distance from her. He spent
three or four nights a week in his cottage here, a secret pleasure to be
on his own, belonging neither to *Madre* nor to the cloister.

As he strolled along the arcade now, he preferred his polished shoes
to common sandals, his fine black cassock and white linen shirt to a
coarse brown habit stinking of body odor. He liked his cologne, his
shirt's double cuffs, his gold cufflinks, his gold signet ring stamped
with the seal of the House of Habsburg.

Because his walk had taken him into the outer courtyard, he heard
the knock on the main gate—a sound that, at such an hour, should
have been heard by the watchman alone, but where was he? A watchman who sleeps! Lehmann again had the thought that he should not
have kept the dolt on after the Cistercian sisters had at last evacuated
the place. The knock was repeated. He went to the gate himself and
pulled open the small, eye-level hatch. On the other side he saw a
veiled figure, and at first he thought it was a religious sister. But then
he recognized the black lace mantilla cloaking a woman's head, a Roman lady—the look his mother had mastered. Though her face was
obscure in the shadow, Lehmann sensed how fiercely her eyes were
fixed upon him.

"*Buona sera,*" she said softly.

"*Che cosa?*" Lehmann asked.

"*Il sacerdote.*" The priest.

Lehmann hesitated, suddenly alert.

"Padre Antonio," she said then. "I have come to see Padre Antonio.
Père Antoine."

"He is not here."

"*Per favore. Il mio confessore.*" He is my confessor.

Lehmann's first impulse was to close the hatch, the simplest and
most truthful answer to the woman. Yet it seemed cruel. He opened
the gate.

When she saw his cassock and collar, she said, "*Buona sera, Padre.*"

Lehmann shook his head. "I am sorry, Signora, Father Antonio is
not here. He is gone."

"I don't understand."

"More than a year, he is gone." The shawl obscured her face somewhat, and she was still in shadows, but Lehmann sensed something
familiar. She was tall. Her hair was dark, a cascade to her shoulders
in line with the mantilla. She wore a cape, closed at her throat. Her
left hand was at her cheek. He said, "Are you all right?" He nervously
fingered his ring.

"I came to see Father Antonio. He is my friend. I was his student.
Here, with the sisters."

"The sisters are gone. This is a friary now. Religious men. Franciscans."

"What?"

"You should not be here at this hour. *Magnum silentium* is soon to
begin."

"I am sorry, Father."

"I know you. We've met. Where have we met?" Lehmann pulled the
door wide. "Come in."

"No, Father. No. I am sorry. I did not mean to intrude." She lowered
her eyes, demurely hugging herself. "I thought—"

"It's all right." Lehmann felt the pull of her predicament. And he
caught the scent of her perfume, which underscored her allure. It hit
him then, how beguiling she was. "Come in," he said. "You can see the
courtyard. It is as it was. You say you were a student? Would you like
to see the courtyard?"

"But where can I find Father Antonio?"

"I do not know. The sisters were moved to the Convent of Santa
Maria della Vittoria. Perhaps with them." Lehmann knew very well
that the sisters had jettisoned the old priest.

"But why are they gone?" she asked.

"Who are you?"

"I am Marguerite d'Erasmo."

"I remember," he said. "We met in the Vatican. An office in the Apostolic Palace. Briefly. Some time ago."

"I do not recall. I was with Rome Red Cross. So perhaps the Pontifical Relief office."

"Yes, that's it. You wore a Red Cross cap."

She said shyly, as if making an admission, "I have been away from Rome, in Geneva — the Red Cross Committee International. But I am returned now. Only as of today. I came here first."

"Seeking your priest."

"Yes. I should go now. Thank you, Father."

But he stepped toward her, touching her arm, which was still wrapped around her body, just below her breasts. "No, Signorina, one moment. You will be with the Red Cross in Rome — once more?"

"Yes."

"That is good. I myself work with refugees, also for Vatican offices. Rome is more filled with lost ones than before. You will see. I consult the Red Cross. No doubt we will work together now that you are returned."

"You have refugees here, in the Casa?" she asked.

"In a way. This is a place of prayer. A house for holy men. You know that the friars are an international order, and here have come monks driven into exile, enemies of Bolsheviks and Mensheviks and Chetniks. The Church once again has martyrs."

"Chetniks from Croatia?"

"No, *enemies* of Chetniks."

"I was in Croatia," she said. "I knew Franciscans." Vukas. She knew better than to say his name. "Are you Franciscan?"

Lehmann opened his arms wide, indicating his soutane, the getup of a secular priest. He bowed and, with a hint of self-mockery, said, "I am a delegate of the Sacred Congregation for Extraordinary Ecclesiastical Affairs. I am Father Lehmann."

"You are German."

"Yes. From the Rhineland, seat of resistance to the National Socialists. But I spent most of the war here in Rome, attached to the Vatican, working for peace. Now, instructed by the Holy Father, I minister to German-speaking prisoners held in camps throughout Italy. I am their poor priest. There are tens of thousands."

"Yes. I know. Also hundreds of thousands of others."

"Indeed. All children of the one merciful God. Do come in. See the courtyard. That, at least."

At his gesture, she stepped over the portal frame and preceded him into the courtyard. Her heels gave her calves an arresting turn. She was wearing silk stockings with a perfectly aligned hem slicing up the back of each leg. She took a dozen steps, then stopped. In the half-light of evening, the roof lines were defined, and lights shone from several windows in the main building. Lehmann saw a movement in one of them, a dark form, a flash of white — someone watching. Only a few seconds passed, but the German priest took note of the woman's hesitation, her focus. She had seen the dark form, too. The white glint flickered again, a handkerchief dabbing at a mouth. She turned away.

Because the priest's cottage door was ajar, the wash of its interior light spilled out onto the packed dirt. Indicating the cottage, she said, without turning back to him, "This was where I took my lessons with *mon père.*"

"This is my house now."

"Père Antoine is an old man," she said. "He was frail. Is he all right, do you know?"

"I am sure he is fine." Lehmann remained behind her. In the wind, the point of the mantilla fluttered at the small of her back. Had she worn that shawl, like a Roman noblewoman, as the feminine vestment for the sacrament of penance? "Signorina," he said quietly, "did you want the priest for confession?" He spoke the words without breathing, a proposition.

She turned to face him. "Yes," she said with surprising frankness. "I need a priest."

"I am a priest."

The silence hung between them.

Then Lehmann gestured with one upraised arm, pointing the way to the chapel.

But she turned toward the cottage. "Since this is where I met with Père Antoine . . ." She stepped toward the open door, with Lehmann following. She ducked her head slightly as she crossed into the small house. An oil lamp sat on the table, casting its flickering light around the space. As Lehmann followed her in, he pulled the door closed behind, conscious of the illicit air. If that watchman had awakened, he might be seeing this. The friars, though, were at Compline by now.

The woman drew one of the chairs away from the table and knelt before it, resting her elbows on the rough twine seat, her knees on the broad-planked wooden floor. Adjusting the mantilla forward, she lowered her head onto her hands. Lehmann moved the second chair and sat facing her shoulder, so that she had his profile.

"*Benedicite, Signorina,*" Lehmann said softly. The words came to his lips naturally, but otherwise he felt cut loose from his mooring. He was at the mercy less of this woman than of a threatening sexual arousal, which made him more conscious of himself, in fact, than of her.

Lehmann was a man with little intimate experience of women, but also one who lived to impress women whenever he encountered them. He was the favorite of every female circle to which his mother belonged, and even if those women were always older, that made them, if anything, more susceptible to his charms. Erotic implication with erotic unavailability — the lethal mix of his magnetism. His Latin good looks, his studied congeniality, the heat of his own affection for himself, these were dark stars in his personal night sky, and all at once they had been pulled into stunning alignment. Tonight.

She began to whisper, and though her words were barely audible, Lehmann recognized at once the act of contrition: "O my God, I am heartily sorry for having offended Thee . . ." She recited the formula slowly but precisely, right to its conclusion: ". . . with the help of Thy grace, nevermore to offend Thee, and to amend my life. Amen."

When she fell silent, Lehmann was nonplussed. "But Signorina — your sins. You did not confess your sins."

She said nothing.

"Signorina, Christ in His mercy requires the confession of sins. You must confess," he said, intending to be stern.

But instead of enumerating her sins, she whispered, "Please forgive me, Father."

Lehmann felt something like panic rising in his chest. "I cannot forgive what I do not know. The manifestation of conscience is required. You must tell me."

"I have sinned. That is enough."

"No. You must tell me."

"Then I will go." She shifted her weight and began to rise to her feet.

"Wait." Lehmann turned in his chair to look directly at her. She met his gaze with naked plainness, and at once he was lost in the green depths of her eyes. But canon law makes it plain: if the sacramental norms are not observed, the guilt of the sinner is compounded by the guilt of the minister. She was asking him to join her in sin. And, as if she had exposed herself physically before him, he could not find it in himself to refuse. The norms be damned. He raised his hand, nearly touching her forehead with his fingertips. *"Dominus noster Jesus Christus te absolvat et ego auctoritate ipsius te absolvo . . ."*

No sooner had he completed the rote recitation, stirring the air above her head with the sign of the cross, than she seized his hand and pulled his fingers to her lips as if she were a peasant woman. She kissed him. He remembered that he, too, had once kissed her — in exactly the same place, her hand. Had she come here to reciprocate, this woman, so unlike the fawning Legionaries of Mary? The touch of her mouth to his flesh, even there, ignited an impulse on which, despite a lifetime's sublimation, he might have acted. But before he could move, she was up from her knees, through the door, out into the black wind, and gone.

"Jesus H. Christ," Deane said when Warburg told him that the War Refugee Board was being shut down.

They were sitting on a bench beneath the canopy of an artfully pruned pine tree, on the edge of what had once been the playing field of the Pontifical North American College. Now the grassy plain atop the Janiculum Hill was a crowded tent city, the college building and grounds, including the basketball court, having been given over to displaced persons months before.

As camps went, this one achieved a relative luxury, anchored by three large canvas structures braced by ropes stretched from towering cypress trees on either side of the field. Centered on those olive-drab behemoths were orderly rows of smaller brown tents supplied by the U.S. Army. Wood-framed structures were set aside for hygiene, medical services, a school, and cooking, and at all corners of the compound were sentry-manned checkpoints to keep bandits out. But the American pair were focused on neither the near scene nor the far. Instead, Warburg explained what had happened.

He did not know whether things would have been different, he said, had Roosevelt lived. After all, the promises of the year before had been left unfulfilled, even for as long as FDR survived. Astonishingly, there had been no repeat of the *Henry Gibbons*. That first thousand refugees setting sail from Naples had been the last. At Fort Ontario, in upstate New York, they had been denied immigrant status, and remained in guarded barracks to this day, prisoners.

The WRB had succeeded in slowing deportations out of Budapest, with about twenty thousand Hungarian Jews successfully evacuated to the south and nearly two hundred thousand others provided safe haven in place long enough to live out the war. But an untold number were lost, and the Swedish diplomat Raoul Wallenberg had disappeared in the storm of the Soviet conquest of Budapest. From an appallingly safe distance, Warburg had done his part to preside over too little, too late, and he knew it.

And the horror was far from over. As the war had wound down in paroxysms of destruction, including the Allies' springtime bombing of German cities, the floodgates of desperation had broken fully open, with millions of "dehoused" people driven out into the countryside, clogging the roads, having nothing to eat but weeds plucked from gullies. Across the continent, almost no one had clean water. Plague stalked the streets of Europe again.

Italy continued to be a destination for migrating Jews, and by now Jews from beyond the Alps made up the vast majority of those held in Italian camps. More arrived every day. Warburg's charges had been made not only homeless but stateless, with no hope — or, for the most part, desire — of returning to former shtetls, towns, or neighborhoods. Therefore they were at the bottom of every relocation list — the Army's, the Red Cross's, and the UN's. Relocate? Where? And what nation would sponsor what visa? The undocumented and undocumentable were condemned to a self-perpetuating limbo.

Warburg, together with WRB officials operating from Turkey, Portugal, and, lately, from Germany itself, had been blocked at every turn in their attempts to bring more displaced persons to the United States. And "DPs" was how Warburg's workers had taken to speaking of their refugees, since they had learned not to draw Washington's attention to the overwhelmingly Jewish character of those in need.

The British, meanwhile, had effectively shut off the only other avenue of Jewish escape. Within weeks of the European war's end, Churchill had shockingly been ousted as Prime Minister in a snap election, and Clement Attlee's new Labour government showed signs of sticking to the anti-Jewish restrictions of the 1939 White Paper. The Royal Navy had clamped the flow of immigration to Palestine by seizing the Jewish-sponsored ships that had managed to sail from Mediterranean ports. The British were interning intercepted passengers in camps on Cyprus. Jews making it to Palestine were counted in the hundreds.

Thus the WRB, along with other relief agencies, had been reduced to the static management of tin-and-canvas asylums in Europe and North Africa. Most infuriating to Warburg, though, was being required by an utter absence of alternatives to maintain most of the German concentration camps, even if rechristened as temporary "transit" points. But not temporary enough. Nearly four months after the end of the war in Europe, Jews were still living behind barbed wire that the Nazis had strung, still wearing rags, and, in all too many cases, still starving. And Warburg was one of those in charge of this disgrace.

But with Roosevelt's death, the truly unthinkable had happened. Before President Truman had set off for the July summit meeting of Allied leaders in Potsdam — last week — murmurs had rumbled through Washington about presidential succession. Since the newly appointed secretary of state, James F. Byrnes, was to travel with Truman, the next-in-line official was the secretary of the treasury. If something happened to Truman and Byrnes, flying into the still hot war zone on the same airplane, the new President of the United States would be a Jew.

Was it coincidence, then, that just before departing for Berlin, Truman had startled the nation, to say nothing of an unsuspecting Henry Morgenthau, by abruptly announcing the appointment of a new treasury secretary? Snap: Truman's poker pal from Kentucky, Fred Vinson, was in; Morgenthau was out. If the presidential plane went down, no Jew would succeed to the White House.

Soon enough, Morgenthau's personal project, the War Refugee Board, more needed than ever, was abolished by executive order.

The sun was high in the sky, and the canvas sprawl behind Warburg and Deane was quiet, siesta hour, with most of the refugees having sought out the shade of trees or tent flaps. In this heat, even the children were quiet, except for the inevitable knot of boys huddled around a soccer ball on a patch of open grass.

The two bareheaded Americans were dressed as always, the priest in his red-trimmed cassock and collar, the Treasury official in his gray suit and tie. *Former* Treasury official, actually, since Warburg had cabled his resignation to Washington that morning. Their bench faced a sea of weathered red clay roof tiles. Between the men on the bench lay Deane's breviary. He had been at prayer when Warburg interrupted him. Knowing that the monsignor was habitually in the camp at this hour to help serve the midday meal, Warburg had come up here directly. Deane was the first with whom Warburg had to share the news.

"Jesus *H.* Christ, Monsignor?" Warburg asked.

"For *How* the *Hell* can Washington shut you down?" Deane was red-faced. "I don't get it."

"The ease with which the hatred comes, that is what astonishes me," Warburg said. "And the universality. Not to equate this with Hitler, but in the beginning I thought his anti-Semitism was unique."

"Hitler was unique, David. No point in mitigating that."

"But in this one regard he was the world's instrument. Your Church's. Our country's. My government's. Why are Jews still behind barbed wire? Why haven't the Jews in this camp been taken to the States? *Welcomed* to the States! You know why. Don't we owe it to what you and I have seen this year to face the fact of it?"

"Facts. Not fact. Don't reduce it to one thing."

"It is one thing."

"The Jews in this camp, David, are children of God. You see that. So do I."

"The Vatican begrudges their being here. You see that, too. These Jews wouldn't be here if it weren't for you."

"I am the Vatican, David. Don't reduce *us* to one thing, either. For every Tardini there are a dozen Sister Thomases. As for what you and I have seen this year"—Deane paused and touched Warburg's forearm, lightly resting his fingers there, a gesture of such fraternal tenderness that the agitated Warburg was able to take it in—"remember that line from Dostoyevsky? 'Men love the downfall of the righteous.' I think that's it in a nutshell, the source of anti-Semitism, why Washington could do this."

"Jews are righteous?" Warburg said. "I thought 'perfidious' was the word in the Catholic prayer book."

"Yeah, well, some of us omit that adjective. I prefer 'righteous.'"

"Why not 'human'?" Warburg asked. "Let it go at that?"

Out of nowhere, the soccer ball flew toward their bench with two or three boys in pursuit. Deane jumped to his feet, hiked the skirts of his cassock, and deftly kicked it back to them. "*Andiamo, scimmie!*" he cried, and they threw him familiar waves. He sat down, laughing.

Warburg said, "With your bad leg, no less."

"Right. Bad thanks to you." In fact, Deane's leg had fully healed. He had welcomed the ball's interruption. For some moments the two men sat watching the scramble of monkeys. Then the priest said, "What will you do, David?"

"Morgenthau and I exchanged cables back and forth," Warburg said. "When the announcement was made that he'd been fired as secretary, he immediately heard from Jewish leaders in New York. He was asked to take over the top job at the JDC."

"Jewish Distribution Committee."

"*Joint* Distribution Committee. The American Jewish Joint Distribution Committee. Boils down to Jewish fundraising. Morgenthau told me that, if he took the job, he'd love to be able to drop the name Warburg in his *shnorring*." Warburg laughed. "I said fine with me. That used to drive me nuts, being taken as Sutton Place. No more. Whatever's necessary, I say now. I told him, if he took the job, I'd work for him. He did, and I will."

"Where?"

"Here. Relief in the short term, resettlement in the long. I'm not quitting Rome. The JDC needs to be here."

"The JDC in Tel Aviv is pure Zionist. What will it be in Rome?" Deane had to speak carefully. They rarely touched on this subject anymore, it was so loaded. "You say 'resettlement.' To the JDC that means Palestine. You know that. It's their main thrust. JDC funds illegal Jewish immigration."

"Illegal according to whom? I'm a lawyer, Kevin. Everyone needs an advocate."

"Isn't that what lawyers say when their clients are guilty?"

"Guilty of what?"

"All I'm saying is that the JDC represents a shift for you."

"Food, clothing, medicine, *here*. That's still got to be the priority. But resettlement has to feature, too. Shift, Kevin? What, Jews should just stay behind wire in Bavaria? Die there? The hell with that. And what the hell, maybe London will shift, too — make the *aliyah* legal."

"Someday, over the rainbow."

"No, think about it. A newly elected Prime Minister has scope for maneuver. We have a legion of homeless Jews, and there *is* a Jewish homeland."

"There are Arabs in Palestine, David. The British have to think of Arabs, too."

"Like the Vatican has to think of Christians? The Arabs supported Hitler, Kevin. Including Christian Arabs. Palestinian Jews joined the British Army."

"And now they assassinate British officers in Jerusalem."

"You're quick to see the Brit point of view," Warburg said. "I still don't get it — why the Vatican is deadly hostile to the Jewish return?"

"You just half said it. The Vatican has to protect the Christian holy places in Palestine. Not for Arabs, but for the whole Christian world. It's that simple." Deane's face had reddened, but there was more sadness in his voice than anger.

Warburg asked, "Where else do you propose they go? 'Next year in Jerusalem,' Kevin. Maybe it was for this moment that we kept saying that."

"My friend, you're referring to Jews both ways, as 'they' and as 'we.' You're all over the place."

"No, I'm not. For the first time in a year, I know right where I am. Look, it never occurred to me to want Jews back in Jerusalem. But guess what? America's golden door has been closing in their faces. My orders from the Treasury Department were to slam the door shut once and for all. 'Give me your huddled masses yearning to breathe free . . .' What bullshit! Well, the hell with that. So I quit."

"You haven't quit, not by a long shot."

"But I am at a new door, and I am jumping at the chance to help pry it open." Warburg stood, turned to face the tent city behind them. He threw his arms out as if to embrace the people on the plain. "A door to life, Kevin. Food. Shelter. Basic decency. The continent of Europe tried to kill these folks, and *still* has no place for them. Goddammit, would you notice that, please!"

Warburg whipped back to face Deane, who now was staring at his hands. Warburg lowered his voice, slowed down. "You're a good man, Kevin, and you've given these Jews a few precious acres on this lovely hilltop, a real gift. And I can tell you that I have loved you for it. But even here the clock is running. The U.S. seminarians are coming back to North American College. This door, too, is closing. Tell me I'm wrong."

"You aren't wrong," Deane said, chastened. He remained seated, with Warburg towering over him. Deane added, "I do notice."

Warburg went on, unaware that his voice was growing louder. "Do you know what it means to me that I never got another boatload of Jewish refugees to the States? Not one! Nazi POWs shipped across the ocean by the fleet. Thousands already! Goddamn Nazis! But not one more boat for Jews! Can you hear me?"

"Yes," Deane said. "They hear you across the Tiber."

"And now the War Refugee Board abolished. So — the JDC. That's it. I have no other moves to make."

"I see that," Deane said.

Warburg was silent a moment, then said, "I know this isn't your game and I don't expect it to be. But I need you for this. I need you more than ever."

"Visas."

"Exactly." Warburg's tone had shifted. He was a lawyer now, reviewing his brief. "What makes British interventions legal is Jews arriving at Jaffa or Caesarea without passports. Stateless, they have no rights. With passports, they have landing rights, and they must be given due process. In other words, no unadjudicated internment on Cyprus. Vatican visas mean Red Cross DP passports. Which mean, at least, a hearing before a Mandate magistrate, rules set by the United Nations."

"And Vatican complicity in Jewish immigration to Palestine adds to the pressure on Clement Attlee."

"Also exactly."

"But you still say 'they' more than 'we.' I'm thinking of your own refusal to be a bar mitzvah. To be a Jew."

What was this, Deane's way of deflecting the obvious problem — the Vatican's legendary opposition to Jews in Jerusalem? Warburg said, "I've discussed it with you, and I've continued to attend synagogue."

Warburg flashed back to the winter night when, having donned a yarmulke for the first time in his life, he'd found himself urgently wanting to talk with Deane, of all people. They'd met in a café and sat over coffee and cigarettes until midnight. Warburg had described both his impulses to embrace the religion of his ancestors and the feelings of hesitation that made him distrust those impulses. Deane had listened with an air of quiet kindness, good confessor that he was. But in truth Warburg had been left feeling that the priest, so certain in his own faith, had not really understood.

Now Warburg said, "I thought speaking Italian was my big challenge." He laughed. "It's been Hebrew."

"You told me that you're not so sure about God," Deane said. "Not even about God's existence."

"Yes. And you seemed, that night, to think that was disqualifying. I thought so, too. But now I see that being unsure is also a way of being Jewish. A year ago, all the reason I needed was that Hitler said I was a Jew. But no longer. I started out thinking of Jews as victims, pure and simple. No more. Not 'perfidious.' Not 'righteous.' Not victims, either. We Jews are human beings, Kevin. That's enough. It saddens me that not even you see that."

"I do see victims, that's true."

"As long as that's all we are, Hitler wins."

"Jews are like everybody else only more so? Like that? A continent strewn with victims, but Jews only more so?"

"You are missing something, Kevin. Jewish refusal over the centuries has been refusal to be reduced like that. Don't sentimentalize the survivors. Victims, yes. But maybe they're victimizers, too." Warburg fell silent, looking out across the tents. Then he said quietly, "To survive the camps, who knows what some Jews had to do?"

Warburg waited for Deane to comment. Deane said nothing. So Warburg continued, "This camp here, and a hundred others like it, are telling the story. Jews can't wait for someone else to rescue them — rescue *us*. Kevin, the British are unrolling barbed wire for *new* concentration camps."

"Don't confuse Attlee with Stalin."

"Don't worry, I don't," Warburg said. "Stalin is why a lot of Jews are still running. He makes my point." Warburg looked down at his friend and, trying a shift toward levity, said, "Too bad you guys didn't pull off that Habsburg ploy last year. A way to stop the bastard."

Deane shrugged. "Not even close." Warburg sensed a hint of the priest's defensiveness, as if he, too, knew how cracked the Habsburg idea had been. And sure enough, with an air of *This is going nowhere,* Deane stood. He faced Warburg and said, "I'll see what I can do about refugee documentation. I agree with you about the camps. Intolerable. We have to find another way."

"Get in touch with Archbishop Roncalli."

"The legate in Istanbul? Why?"

"He's helping us. I went to Turkey and met with him. But the Holy See's put a quota on visas he can supply. He's hit the limit."

"If Roncalli is enabling Palestinian immigration," Deane said carefully, "he's acting on his own."

"Shows it can be done, Kevin. Get the quota lifted. Start there."

It took a moment, but Deane nodded.

Warburg said, "Oh, and get word to Archbishop Spellman in New York that Secretary Morgenthau is going to be calling on him."

"The archbishop no doubt expects as much. You can tell Mr. Morgenthau, on the QT, that a consistory is about to be announced, and the archbishop is going to be named a cardinal."

Warburg slapped Deane's shoulder. "That's good for you, right?"

Deane looked away.

Warburg said, "And then Spellman's up for Vatican secretary of state?"

"Not so far," Deane replied. "Gossip is that the late Cardinal Maglione won't be replaced."

"Oh. Too bad. *Not* good for you."

Deane returned the shoulder slap. "Not good for *you,* you mean. You thought Spellman, riding high here, with me at his elbow, would get these folks to Tel Aviv, if not Jerusalem." Deane let his gaze linger on the sprawling tent city.

"Yes," Warburg said, as he, too, took in the scene before them. "Spellman would help, if only to clear the Jews off his college football field. What's college without football?"

Deane looked at Warburg deadpan. "There's basketball," he said.

An hour later, Warburg was back at the large, nondescript building that had housed the WRB headquarters. In the beginning, he'd had just three garret rooms, but over the past fourteen months he had taken over the entire top floor. Now, of the two dozen people who had worked for him — half were Americans assigned by the Army and half were Italians — only the Italians were there, packing up files, camp surveys, records of names, lists of the missing — material he would still need. None of the workers made eye contact with him, a measure of their disappointment. He didn't know yet which of them he could take along. Warburg went to his office, where he found Sergeant Rossini bent over the cabinet drawer he was emptying.

"Hi, Sarge," Warburg said. "Surprised to see you still here."

Rossini straightened up, grinning. "I spoke to the general. Good news. He said he could pull strings. I can stay with you."

"You mean General Mates?"

"Yes. On loan, he said. The jeep, too. I can still be your driver. Not that you need me for translating anymore."

"I don't know, Sarge. This is outside General Mates's chain of command. He doesn't have the authority to cut your orders. My orders are crystal clear. No U.S. government support. As of yesterday."

"But Civil Affairs," the sergeant said, "that's General Mates, right? You'll be really civilian now, outside the Army altogether."

"Which is why he needs you at my side, I guess, eh? More than ever?"

"What do you mean?"

"Look, Sarge. We're friends, so we can level with each other." Warburg moved to his desk, opened the top drawer, and pulled out a flask and two shot glasses. He poured a finger of bourbon into each, then picked them up. "Here you go."

Rossini took the glass uneasily.

Warburg toasted him. "You've been great. Thanks." They clinked and each threw his shot. Then Warburg said, "Now Mates will have to find some other way of keeping track of me."

"Jeez, Mr. Warburg . . ."

"Don't worry about it, Sarge. I know you had no choice. And it never hurt us that Mates knew what we were up to. But that's over."

"But you're still at it, right? Your new gig? Still the refugees."

"And it's a long way from finished, no matter what Washington says."

"Where will you go?"

Warburg grinned, pouring two more shots. "Your last tidbit for the general? Tell him how much I appreciated you." Clink. And they drank. Then Warburg said, "And my new office is at the Villa Arezzo on the Aventine Hill."

"Rome Red Cross?"

"Right."

The Aurelian Wall had been constructed with brick-faced cement in the third century. The fortification set a world standard, yet was breached again and again, by sacking Visigoths in the fifth century, Normans in the eleventh, and the berserking forces of the Holy Roman Emperor at the Reformation. Marguerite d'Erasmo wondered if Queen Victoria had been aware of this history when, for her embassy in the Eternal City, she had purchased this palace long nestled against the wall's stoutest rampart. It would not protect the British, either.

She mounted the grand staircase of the embassy. The British had shuttered the building during the war, but Fascist hooligans had repeatedly broken into the place, doing their ransacking worst. Now its marble floors, its Venetian mirrors, its stucco works, and its frescoed halls had been almost completely restored to a high polish, and Marguerite felt she was being ushered into the private quarters of royalty. But no, she was simply being shown to yet another set of offices where functionaries worked on the problem of refugees.

Her escorts were Sir Noel Charles, the ambassador, and his wife, Lady Charles, who had been abruptly summoned when Sir Noel realized that the Red Cross delegate from Geneva was a woman. Representing the International Committee under the mandate of the 1929 Geneva Convention, Signorina d'Erasmo was there to set up liaison procedures between Geneva and Britain's recently expanded internment camps on Cyprus, which were being administered from the British office in Rome—here.

Marguerite had sensed the ambassador's unease at her arrival. His

job was to make plain that in all relevant matters — sanitation, nutri-
tion, health, and so on — conditions maintained by Mandate Immigration Services on the balmy Mediterranean island of Cyprus would be
humane. There was nothing intimidating in the way Marguerite had
presented herself, a harmless woman whose uniform hung inelegantly
on her sylph-like frame, who handled her briefcase without panache,
and who'd blushed when, on impulse, the ambassador had kissed her
hand.

On the way up the grand stairs, addressing herself mostly to the
chatterbox Lady Charles, Marguerite asked polite questions about
the palazzo. Amid all the home decor trivia that cluttered the replies,
she learned that, owing to slovenly Italian building-trade practices
and strike-driven interruptions of supply, the renovations had been
hopelessly delayed; only these, the public spaces and offices, had been
properly restored to this point. The living quarters in the east wing,
where the ambassador and his senior staff would take up residence,
were not expected to be habitable for some months yet.

The innocuously named Migrant Relocation Office was on the
third floor, where the ceilings were lower, the floor tiles less opulent,
and the walls decorated with hung artworks instead of murals. There
Marguerite was introduced to the four men and two women whose
desks and tables were covered with what to her were the familiar odds
and ends of refugee accounting: lists of names, documents carrying
the distinctive United Nations relief stamp, "safe and well" sheets,
commodity aid forms. In clipped English, while the ambassador and
his wife stood awkwardly at the office threshold, she asked the staff
about record keeping, medical staffing, agricultural markets, child nu-
trition, and the plight of the aged. Her expertise was on full display.
She withdrew from her briefcase several sets of Red Cross forms and
officiously explained that weekly census reports and camp condition
evaluations would be required to be filed with the Rome Red Cross
office for forwarding to Geneva. International Red Cross would be
establishing its own on-site station in Cyprus as soon as possible, but
in the meantime the Migrant Office here in the embassy would be
regarded as the responsible point of contact. Was that clear?

The ambassador was relieved at the woman's efficiency. She refused Lady Charles's offer of tea.

In descending the grand staircase, Marguerite was again able to make casual chat with the ambassador's wife, and she confirmed her impression that, as of now, no one lived in the villa, which was empty at night and only occasionally patrolled by passing policemen. The advantage of a truly great house, Lady Charles pronounced, is that petty pilferers are incapable of imagining it as penetrable. As with the Aurelian Wall, she said, gesturing behind her and ignoring ancient and recent history of sacking, the impression of security is the best security.

In short order, the English aristocrats, ignoring the butler, had shown the Geneva official out of the embassy, and closed the door behind her with just enough alacrity to suggest relief. Within moments of that, Marguerite had accomplished her rendezvous with Jocko Lionni.

David Warburg looked up from his desk, his eyes snagged by a form passing on the other side of the frosted glass of his office door. He put his pen down, snuffed his cigarette, checked himself momentarily, then pushed the swivel chair back on its wheels. Again he told himself to stop. He was all at once at the mercy of an impulse he had not felt in many months, a visceral intuition tied to the barest of glimpses.

How many times had he retraced his steps in a narrow street, returned to a corner, crossed a restaurant dining room, dashed along the Tiber embankment, haunted the small piazzas of Trastevere? But none of that since winter. He had, meanwhile, at intervals of months, lain in the arms of three — no, four — women, none of them repeated. In their eyes he had seen only hers.

What a fool it had all made him. He was in no hurry to return to that untethered state of mind — to feel, again, like such a sap. So for the longest minute he just sat there looking up at the angled ceiling. The marmoreal plaster was sagging as if about to collapse — a doom that had no doubt threatened here for centuries.

His office was in the eaves of the ancient building, with slanted low ceilings and narrow windows that overlooked the masts of cypress trees. The dozen or so WRB workers whom Warburg had brought with him to the JDC were scattered elsewhere in the building. They were Italians for whom loss of status as employees of the American liberators was a jolt, and he regretted that their offices were even more ad hoc than his.

Dozens of silhouettes regularly passed his door-panel window, characters in a shadow parade to which, normally, he was indifferent. But this time — something. What? The feminine form, exceptionally tall; the neck of an Egyptian princess; the posture of one carrying a tray of crystal; a stride of pure purposefulness. When, the year before, she had disappeared after Fossoli, Warburg had come here to the Red Cross offices more than once. The report of those who knew her was that she had abruptly resigned and departed Rome, which had left her colleagues mystified. Their puzzlement was later redoubled when they learned from *Il Tempo* that Andrea Doria Pamphili, the Allied-appointed mayor, had included her family villa on the list of Fascist requisitions to be reversed. This meant the release to her, as the daughter and only heir of Angelo d'Erasmo, not only of the walled Parioli mansion in which she'd spent her childhood, but of the Bank of Rome's d'Erasmo accounts that had been impounded on Mussolini's personal order. Warburg had subsequently learned that, at the turn of the year, a priest had claimed the property in her name, but Marguerite herself had never reappeared.

He got up, crossed to the door, opened it. Again he hesitated. But what the hell. He went into the corridor, which, as usual, was bustling. Displaced persons were only one emergency among many here. Staff and volunteers, organized by *corpo* and *comitato*, addressed problems of water purity, blood supply, rodent removal, prosthetics, nurses' training, hospital equipment, mobile clinics, POW packages, missing person searches — on and on, the detritus of war.

At the end of the corridor, Warburg entered the canteen, an open garret space that had wall racks suggesting ancient storage uses. Now the staff refreshment room was all card tables and folding chairs. At either end of a long counter stood, sentry-like, an oscillating floor fan that drew summer air in through the open windows. A dozen people stood or sat in clusters of two or three. On the far side of the room, at a table holding a large coffee percolator, she stood with her back to him, stirring milk and sugar into a cup.

"*Buongiorno, Signorina,*" he said as he drew up behind her, ready to have the woman show herself to be someone else. But no. When she turned, the first thing that struck him was how unblemished her face was. He put his hand out. "*Sono David Warburg.*"

"I remember," she said in English. She seemed entirely unsurprised. She took his hand, the briefest of shakes. She was wearing a dark blue four-pocket tunic and matching skirt. A white patch with the red Geneva cross marked her left shoulder. The silver buttons of her tunic also bore the cross. Her black hair was knotted into a bun on the back of her head, exposing her Nefertiti neck. Inside the open collar of her tunic, a notch emphasized the hollow at the base of her throat, an allurement he'd not seen before because, a year ago, she'd never been without that red kerchief. She wore no makeup. A thin line of perspiration rode her upper lip. And, yes, her eyes were dark green.

The buzz of talk in the room gave their encounter a kind of insulation, as if they were alone. They stood in silence for a moment, but the gaze of neither fell. Finally he gestured toward a pair of chairs on opposite sides of an adjacent card table. "*Ci sediamo?*"

She smiled. "You have Italian now."

"I'm a slow learner, but I've had time," Warburg said. "It's been a year. More than a year."

"Has it?" Seated now, she sipped her coffee, then gestured toward it. "This is very bad."

Warburg held out his pack of cigarettes. She declined. He took one and lit it. Waving out the match, he startled himself by asking, point-blank, "What are you doing here, if I may inquire?"

She shrugged. "What do you mean? This is my place. I should ask you." She crossed her legs. The sheen of silk. And, he noted, her legs were cleanly shaven.

He pretended to study the tip of his cigarette. "DPs still. I've moved over here to coordinate my work with the Society. I am still organizing relief, refugees, searches, repatriation, transit, all of it. Although not for my government."

"Who then?"

"American Jewish organizations. A joint committee."

"The Joint Distribution Committee. Of course, I know of it. There is an office in Geneva."

"You went to Switzerland?"

"Yes." She looked away.

Warburg said, "But I was told you had left the Red Cross. No one here knew anything about you."

Still not meeting his eyes, she said, "In Geneva they needed someone with languages."

"Giacomo Lionni also disappeared. I know the Roman Jewish community well by now, and Lionni, too, has been gone all this time. One might have thought you'd both been killed at Fossoli, but you were seen in Rome a day or two later. I spoke with the *portiere* at your building in Trastevere. You returned there and collected your things. Lionni, too, was seen. Then disappeared."

Marguerite was watching the cloud swirl in her coffee. "I heard from Signora Paoli, later, that you had been asking. You returned many times, she said."

"I thought you might have gone to Geneva. I made inquiries there as well. You were not at Red Cross headquarters. Not as of September. Nor January, when I checked again."

She shrugged. "Nevertheless, I am there now. I am coordinating among national societies. I make supervising visits to camps, transit points, and offices. Seven countries. One of them Italy, which is why I am here. Updating card index systems. The record keeping is falling far behind. To save the people, we must save the records. Many, many more people keep arriving from the East."

"Fleeing the Reds."

"Yes." After a pointed silence, she added, "And fleeing from Catholics."

"So you are speaking of Jews."

"There is much to flee, even now," she said. "Even without the war.

In France, half a million dwellings are reduced to rubble. In Greece, a thousand villages and towns simply disappeared. In Holland this past winter, many thousands of elderly froze to death. In Germany, what they call 'Russian babies' are being born. We conclude that between seventy and a hundred thousand German women are pregnant from rape. In Berlin, women tell each other that when the water gush comes from between their legs, they should get on the tram, because the seats are clean and the ticket taker will help. Naturally, he does not help. Here in Italy, too, where it seemed less like rape, perhaps—a plague of pregnancy. War babies everywhere. And where is the milk for these infants? Clean water? The death rate for babies under the age of one year—across Europe!—is nearing half. The Dark Ages have returned."

This litany of catastrophe was as familiar to Warburg as to her. Relief workers were accustomed to pronouncing such lists, not to inform one another but as a way to keep from going mad. Warburg said, "At the WRB, we were reduced to pleading with the Allied authorities for separate concentration camps for Jews so they wouldn't have to go to the latrine ditch side by side with Nazis, who are now prisoners in the same camps. Our pleas were ignored. What is Jewish suffering amid so much? Our pleas became demands. The result? Instead of separating Nazis from Jews in Germany, we have the abolition of the War Refugee Board."

"I am told your work has been good, very good."

"You know better than I how far short we fell of doing what was needed." He took a drag, exhaled.

She said, "Hungary. Budapest. Who did as much? And much of it from here in Rome."

Warburg's demons put an outrageous question to him, and he asked it. "Are you talking about me?"

"Not you," she said. "I mean the War Refugee Board."

"Now defunct."

"So America declares the war refugee question—what? Answered? Finished?"

"Not the refugee question. The Jewish question. Done with. The WRB is dispersed, whatever is left of it folded into the UN 'Relief and

Rehabilitation,' such pretty words. Like repatriation and resettlement."
Warburg put out his cigarette on a tin plate. "Alas, there can be no rehabilitation without habitat, no repatriating without a *patria*. Are you
aware of that particular problem?"

"You mean Palestine."

The word hung between them, a stopper.

Finally she said, "I am surprised the Croce Rossa would allow you
offices in this building. In Geneva they keep their distance from Zionism."

"But not from Jewish philanthropy. The JDC contributes to the Red
Cross, too. As for the office here, in the past year Signor Nucci and I
have worked closely together. He trusts me. I understand what the Red
Cross requires and will respect it."

"Neutrality."

"Yes. But neutrality is not indifference. Postwar definitions have
room to expand, including Signor Nucci's. If I can trust you with a
secret—" he risked a small smile—"that is why I sought out offices
here. Not the grand vision of Zionism, about which I could care less,
just the picayune details of immigration policy. When it comes to formally stateless persons, I aim to loosen up Red Cross visa restrictions,
which, whether they like it or not, loosens up British restrictions."

"The British?" Marguerite said, surprising him with her deadly
tone of voice. "The British are hopeless."

"Hopeless?" Warburg asked. He waited for her to look at him again.
When she did, he said quietly, aware of making the shift to the personal, "That's how I came to feel about you. I worried that you were
hurt. It troubled me that I would not see you again. More than it should
have."

"And now you see me. I am not hurt. After Fossoli, I was rebuked by
Geneva for unduly acting on my own authority, risking the organization's neutrality."

"You were bringing medicine and food to Fossoli."

"I allowed Partisans inside a truck bearing the Geneva cross. Therefore it became a combat vehicle. Obviously forbidden. As punishment,
I was made probationary. You say that?"

"On probation."

"Not to be reinstated until the end of the war. Since then . . . May I?" She reached for his cigarette pack. He held a match for her. She said, "I will be in Rome only for as long as it requires to regulate procedures at this office here. I am a clerk. A traveling clerk."

"But a clerk has to eat, no? Even a traveling clerk." For a year, passing a certain restaurant, Warburg would think, Is this a place she would like? "Would you have dinner with me?"

She abruptly put out her cigarette in the tin plate and stood. "I am late for a meeting." In one deliberate move through the crowded canteen, she was gone.

Antonio Dubois no longer referred to himself as Père or Padre. He dressed in the loose clothing of a laborer, including the undyed linen wagoner's smock that fell to his thighs. None of his charges would be intimidated by his dress. For shoes he wore wooden clogs, a primitive version of the sabots of his Brittany youth, but common footwear now, when leather enough even for sandals was still in short supply for everyone but soldiers and priests. The thudding of his clogs nicely served to let the girls know when he was approaching. There were always about two dozen women living in the house, most in the late stages of pregnancy, which was when, typically, they admitted to needing help.

But one day, because the grass in the garden muffled his footsteps as he approached the far bench, where he aimed to take his silence, he surprised a girl, coming upon her in a heap in the corner behind the hedge. She had been weeping, and when she looked up startled, she pulled at her dress, trying to get up. But, like the others, her belly was huge and she could not get her balance. Instead of automatically reaching to take her arm, as he once would have, he asked, "May I help you, Signorina?"

Only when she nodded did he reach down to offer a hand. She took it and pulled herself up. Tears continued to course down her cheeks, and, taking a place on the bench, she wiped at them as if they were the cause of her shame. She sat as if she'd been offered just a few inches on a ledge high above the street.

When she lifted her eyes to Antonio, he saw the telltale flood beyond tears that, in combination with her evident sweats and the flush of her skin, made clear she was in the savage grip of withdrawal. He would have to get her to the brain doctor, who came twice a week to treat the heroin addicts by injecting them with cocaine.

The girl grasped his hand as if to keep from falling off that ledge. Antonio sat with her. Soon, in her weariness, she leaned against him, letting her head fall against his large shoulder. When he put his arm around her, she snuggled in. She fell asleep. They remained like that for the better part of an hour, slow-passing moments for him during which, again, he could lie back in the feeling that at last he had found his daughter. The living Christ had nothing to do with it.

He remembered sitting in the public garden in Arles, watching a worker bent over her plants. As it happened, she had been surreptitiously watching him. She wore the green canvas apron of the town's crew that maintained the lanes and pools, not to mention the camellias, lilacs, and bearded irises that Van Gogh had immortalized. That it was a garden made their coming together seem both foreordained and good. Very good, as God observed of the garden primeval.

Her name was Marie. She showed him how the silvery blue-gray of dwarf junipers emphasized the apricot tones of the peonies. She showed him the satin lime undersides of water lilies. His eyes were opened. That first time — who was leading whom? — they went from the garden to a seamen's hotel. After all the nudes he had seen in paintings and in marble, he had begun by wanting only to see her in that way. Once she showed herself to him, though, the cosmic creation itself was reduced to her breasts, the well between her thighs, the invitation her legs made — and the purity of his own responsive ardor. To call this lust, he understood at once, *there* was the sacrilege. Adam was right.

Yet Marie had made him feel torn in two, as if, against Genesis, another *man* were being ripped out of his ribs. He became a second person, even while the first stood by, a witness. Ecstasy: from the Greek, to stand outside oneself.

And according to her own report, something like that happened to Marie. Sin had nothing to do with it, nor did vows, nor even Christ. Their double life began in a double moment. When she became pregnant, it seemed less wrong to marry, with all the lies that made necessary, than to part. Later, he was accused of having deceived her, but it was not true. She knew from the start that he was a priest, and she agreed to share him with his parish in Marseille, a two-hour drive away in his old Citroën. Back and forth he went, celibate priest here, family man there. The secret was safe from everyone but her. Marie lived it, too.

That acids from this arrangement were all along devouring the very core of her came as a complete surprise to him. Sin. Sacrilege. Remorse. Regret. Self-condemnation. Marie hanged herself from a beam in the shed behind the house in Arles. Their daughter, Sophie, found her corpse. Sophie was fourteen. Antoine had then found it impossible to keep from her the truth of his other life, which, when she learned of it, seemed to Sophie another death. She disappeared. His sin, he saw for certain, was unforgivable.

Did Marguerite d'Erasmo know of his disgrace before she'd had the solicitor dispatch the letter? He could not be sure. Mother Abbess had come to him after Matins that winter morning months before, informing him both that the Cistercian foundation would be removed from Casa dello Spirito Santo to the sister convent attached to Santa Maria della Vittoria, and that his services as chaplain would no longer be required. So the German priest had succeeded in his Vatican manipulations, in acquiring the extraterritorial monastery on Via Sicilia and in punishing Antonio for refusing to help him do so. That Mother had learned of her chaplain's canonical status as an excardinated priest of restricted faculties seemed clear from the brusqueness of her dismissal. He didn't blame the woman for resenting the fact that, without her knowledge, her community had been a wayward priest's place of penance — the Casa his own personal penitentiary. Their years on opposite sides of the one communion rail apparently counted for noth-

ing. Mother informed him that she had been in contact about his status with the Vicarius Urbis, the office of the cardinal vicar, to whom,
she announced, he was solemnly obligated to report at once.

Whether it was only her tone of voice, or the accumulation of insult from across the Tiber, or a final verdict on his own unworthiness,
he went over an edge, silencing for good his own ferocious argument
with himself. He had already resolved to have nothing further to do
with the cardinal vicar when the solicitor's letter arrived.

Marguerite had, in absentia, signed over the leasehold of her father's
house in Parioli to him, on the condition that he put it at the service
of Roman women and children. Funds for the provision of services
would be supplied. There was no need for those services to be defined,
nor any reason for Antonio — what redeeming joy he felt just to know
that his princess was alive somewhere! — to do anything but agree.
Working with a matron retired from the Bambino Gesù Hospital, Antonio needed only a matter of weeks to outfit the house with obstet-
rical instruments, birthing beds, cradles, scales and weights, linens,
stainless steel vats, and kitchen equipment. Midwives who had been
working for devalued lire in ill-equipped clinics were happy to accept
his offer of room and board, and payment in cartons of American
cigarettes. Any pregnant woman who presented herself was welcome.
Word spread among Rome's prostitutes that the d'Erasmo house was
safe. To the once elegant neighborhood came the humblest women in
Rome.

By now, seventy-four children had been born there, and from the
looks of the girl on the bench next to him, it would soon be seventy-
five. If she could hold on, perhaps this wraith's misery would be transformed — as was his own when, only days ago, Marguerite herself had
at last appeared. She had come to the door and pulled the bell as if she
were one from the streets. But in her blue uniform, the high color of
her face, the poise with which she held herself, and the soft smile with
which she greeted him, her ownership of all that she beheld was implicit. The one room in the house that had not been given over to the
women and babies, besides his own cell in the attic, was her father's
study, which, according to the lawyer's instructions, had been kept as

it was. No surprise, then, when Marguerite claimed it for herself, pronouncing the divan suitable to sleep on. In the study they sat together
that first night, surrounded by books and family photographs.

It was soon apparent that, for reasons of her own, Marguerite could
not explain where she had been or what she had been doing. He understood that, rather than lie to him, she would tell him nothing. So it
was that their lifetime habit was reversed, and it was she who did the
sympathetic listening, he the confessing.

Her only pointed questions, when she finally put them, were about
Roberto Lehmann.

EIGHT

Reds

THE EXPLOSION CAME in the middle of the night, and though General Peter Mates was hard asleep almost three blocks away, it woke him up. Reds, he thought, fucking Reds. He knew a bomb when he heard one, and his first assumption was — headquarters. His cognac-induced bleariness was instantly replaced by a concentration of senses. He threw the satin sheets aside and, stark naked, went to the half-open floor-to-ceiling window, where filigreed curtains wafted in the warm night air. Behind him, his pretend contessa snatched at the sheets as if they offered cover from whatever was about to fall.

The sky to the south, above the Quirinal Hill, was red, and Mates thought at once, Not headquarters, but the palace of the king. He threw the window wide and leaned out over the railing without a thought for his nudity. He could make out the dark forms of structures and landscape high above. The Quirinal was the tallest of Rome's hills, the site of the greatest patrician palazzos, including Victor Emmanuel's. Before the kings, popes had lived there for three hundred years. Yes, the royal residence, Mates thought, that's what the Reds would hit.

Then a second, equally violent detonation clapped — a boom to rival the first, followed by a low fading roar. The red in the sky brightened, pure color projected onto the screen of the clouds. Seconds later, Mates felt a blast of air against his face, chest, balls. Only then did he realize that he was unclothed. He backed away from the window. When had he felt this knot in his chest before?

Slovenia. The bomb-bay plunge into the night abyss; the heart of existence caring nothing for him or for anything he valued—not even his own fleeting pleasure inside the faceless woman behind him. Here it was: the coarse fact not just of his coming extinction but of the Eternal City's, too; all of life coming and going—like *that!*

Within minutes, Mates was dressed in khaki trousers and an olive-green T-shirt and was out into the night, running toward the Quirinal Palace. With no awareness of having snatched it from his bedside drawer, he was carrying his service pistol. When he reached the boulevard, he saw that, instead of toward the left, the explosion had occurred to the right. Not the Royal Palace. What then? Fuck. He was already breathing hard. Sirens were sounding, and the red glow of the low sky told him that the detonating fire had caught. He could feel its warm wind against his face. Ahead on the broad sidewalk, he saw a group of people silhouetted against the roaring flames of a burning building. What building? And whose bomb?

As he ran, he calculated, grinding through possibilities: the CLN, the Action Party, the PCI, the Green Flames. The power of the two detonations suggested serious military ordnance. The Garibaldi Brigade, resistance veterans. Palmiro Togliatti, Luigi Longo. Reds.

Drawing close, approaching as the first fire truck came screeching onto the scene, Mates realized where he was—the British embassy. Fuck. He stopped.

Flames were licking at the topmost cornices of the four-story structure. Half of the façade had crumbled into a pile, and room interiors were exposed, ornate furniture and frames on walls illuminated by the glowing fire. Just then a groan went up, trumping the low roar of combustion, and before he felt yet another force-blast on his face, he sensed the coming down-pressure. Sure enough, *pop . . . pop . . . pop,* the exposed second floor gave way and collapsed. Heat rolled out in a billowing puff of dust, debris, eye-stinging cinders. The British embassy. The gears of his mind were jammed. It made no sense.

• • •

"Jews," the Englishman said. It was moments later. Mates had joined about a dozen bystanders, two of whom were Brits, quickly on the scene from their nearby quarters. A second fire truck had arrived, and the firemen were uncoiling hoses, deploying ladders. Three or four police vehicles had stormed onto the scene. Somehow the police had already erected sawhorse street barriers. The night was alive with the chaos: whistles, further sirens, the ferocious barking of an unseen dog.

"What did you say?" Mates asked.

"Bloody Jews," the man repeated. "Has to be."

"The Yids have an air force?" the other Englishman said, looking skyward as if he expected to see an Avro Lancaster with a white Star of David painted on the fuselage.

"You stupid arsehole," his companion sneered. "That blast took out the wall, not the roof. It came from the street."

From what Mates could see of the worst damage—the first floor cratered at the entrance—the man was right, though the fire had clearly picked up fuel inside the building and would reach the roof soon enough. Haganah, he thought, his inbred calculator clicking on again. Irgun. Palmach. Stern Gang. High-powered ordnance pilfered by the king's own Jewish Brigade Group. But the underground Zionist war was being fought in Palestine, not here. British Mandate police stations were being bombed, tax offices, rail yards. Palestine, he thought again, not Rome. Mandate officials targeted, Cairo perhaps. An attack here made no sense.

Mates realized that one of the British bystanders was staring at his pistol, and only then did he see what they saw—a lout in his undershirt, nothing but dog tags on his chest. He pulled the shirt out from his belt, into which he then tucked the gun, and covered it with the shirt. "Who's in charge?" he asked.

The Brit nearest him pointed to a black Rolls just then weaving through the sawhorses and being waved by Italian police into the chaotic circle. "That would be His Excellency."

"The ambassador?" Mates asked. "But why isn't he inside?"

"He doesn't live there yet. Engineers are still posting girders in the residence wing. Construction. No one lives in the embassy yet, thank fuck. Not tonight."

The second Englishman grimaced. "Cipher clerks?"

"Christ," the other said.

Mates had met the ambassador at a glittering party in the Palazzo Venezia, and he approached him now as if he, Mates, were in uniform. Hand extended, he said, "Hello, Sir Noel. It's General Mates. My quarters are nearby. I heard the bombs."

The ambassador, dressed in shirtsleeves and open collar, was clearly startled by Mates, but his dazed expression suggested that he was startled by this entire disastrous affair. Before he could respond, his attention was snagged by a fire official, a hulking figure in black canvas overalls and helmet, who strode up, hammering away with a barrage of questions. Seeing the Brit's confusion, Mates began to translate. "He needs to know where to look for people. What floor? How many are inside? Where are they?"

At first the ambassador seemed to understand Mates no more than the Italian, but then his face went bright with recognition and relief. "No one," he declared. "No one is in there at this hour. The building is unoccupied at night."

Mates translated. The fireman turned to head off, but Mates grabbed one of his belts. "*Aspetti!*"

And to Sir Noel he said, "What about cipher clerks?"

"No. No. Our code rooms moved. Division HQ, not here. Not yet."

Mates released the fireman, who rushed away, happy to have no further need of these fools. The ambassador turned to his aide, a bright young major who had somehow managed the complete uniform — peaked hat, braided shoulder aiguillettes, swagger stick. Like a steam trap blowing, Sir Noel exploded at this underling: "Goddammit! I told London this was no place for the Cyprus operation! Goddammit, I told them. Cyprus should be managed from Athens, Istanbul, not here."

The major muttered his "indeed so"s as the ambassador slumped, facing the inferno, watching the destruction of his dear-bought personal dominion. The Brits had no further use for the Yank in his undershirt.

Just then, across the street, Mates saw the familiar form of an open American jeep. Up, and with an arm draped over the windshield, the driver was Rossini. Mates went to him. Rossini wore a properly solemn expression, but he cut it with a self-satisfied toss of his head. "I thought you might need me, General."

Mates hopped in. "Back to the Barberini," he said. "I'll get dressed. Then take me to Warburg. You know where he's billeted?"

"Yes, Sir."

At Warburg's apartment, near the Piazza del Popolo, neither sound nor fury had carried over from the distant Quirinal Hill. The plaza was deserted, the night was still. It was not yet four a.m. From the curb, Rossini pointed to a window, saying, "Second floor, left." Mates, now in a pressed khaki shirt with a star on each collar, took the stairs two at a time. Banging on the door, he wondered if he'd find Warburg in bed with a woman — a little night baseball, why not? Maybe that was the real reason he'd bailed out of the Barberini, which, in the end, had been fine with Mates. When he had just returned to that suite, reeking of smoke from the embassy fire, Veronica was gone, thank God. Night baseball? Sex with Veronica was like striking out the pitcher.

Warburg came to the door in his underwear. "Peter. What the hell?"

"Sorry, Warburg. But something's happened. You'll want to let me in."

While Warburg dressed in the other room, Mates paced a small oval in the main digs. The place was minimally furnished. File cartons were stacked in four distinct columns. Scrawl-ridden graph paper was tacked to one wall, and taped to another was a map of Europe, stuck all over with colored pins. Papers littered both a field desk and a dinner table. The space had more the feel of a sales office than a living room. Not a place to entertain. So, no woman. Not a chance. Should have known.

Warburg reappeared in his gray flannels and a second-day white dress shirt, sleeves rolled up. He removed papers from a chair for

Mates, then crossed toward the kitchenette. "I'll put the coffeepot on."

A few minutes later they were seated opposite each other, a cleared corner of the table between them. On the corner were their cups and an ashtray. As soon as Warburg had waved out the match they'd both lit from, Mates said, "Your friends bombed the British embassy tonight."

Warburg was too surprised to react.

Mates continued, "A major detonation. Two blasts. Brought the front exterior wall down, four stories' worth. Ignited a fire that's roaring away right now. I've just come from there. The whole building will fall."

"My friends?"

"Jews. Zionists. Palestine."

"Here? In Rome? Impossible."

"Shall we step outside? You can see the glow from the street. Shows all over the city."

"How do you know — Jews? Zionists? What about —?"

"Anarchists? Revolutionaries? Reds? Syndicalists?" Mates forced a smile. "We'd still be talking Jews, right?"

Warburg did not respond, not a muscle.

Mates said, "The embassy was the organizing center for Cyprus internment camps."

"How the hell do you know that?"

"Makes sense, doesn't it? I just heard the Brit ambassador ranting about Athens or Istanbul being places to run Cyprus from, but Italy is where Jewish refugees still muster, no? Like a glacier from the Alps sliding south, plunking down in Rome if they can, awaiting their chance for the great *aliyah*. Isn't that what you call it? And isn't that your work now? Sneaking Jews onto tin cans bound for Jaffa?"

"Sneaking?"

"No insult, Warburg. You can hardly do it openly. Like planting a bomb. Secrecy of the essence, but the motive is obvious. Your Jews blew up the embassy because Clement Attlee just expanded the holding pens on Cyprus, and he put the embassy in charge."

"My Jews?"

"Palestinians. Zionists. The groups the JDC is funding. Don't play dumb with me."

"It's Attlee who's dumb. He has made a big mistake. Europe is saying *Juden raus!* Okay. But *raus* to where? Attlee needs to get the message."

"And that justifies an attack on civilians?"

"How many were killed?"

"By a miracle, maybe none. No one was in the embassy. Damn lucky."

"Why lucky? Why miracle? Perhaps it was planning."

"Fuck."

"No, really. Whoever did this, they could have attacked at noon. They could have taken out a hundred people, two hundred. If they attacked in the middle of the night, it was deliberately *not* to kill."

"Double fuck."

"And if you're right about the embassy as HQ for the Cyprus internments, then that matters, too. It was Cyprus being attacked, not Rome. British concentration camps, not an embassy."

"Sure looked like an embassy. Face it, Warburg, your friends are ruthless killers. Obviously they've come through hell, but it's brutalized them."

Warburg reined in his feelings. "Why are you here?"

"Because you know these people — whether you know you do or not. And I need to know who they are."

"This is not an American fight, General."

"If the U.S. embassy was bombed, London would regard it as a British fight. Maybe if you wore the uniform you'd understand that."

Warburg was not so stupid as to rise to that, but neither was he swift enough to grasp, quite, what Mates was up to.

Mates met Warburg's rigid self-possession with a studied sangfroid. "If an embassy's not immune, my friend, what is? A basic note of civilized behavior — not attacking embassies. I'd pull these bastards back if I were you. Or are they just out for blood at this point? Anybody's blood."

Warburg slammed his hand down on the table. The cups jumped. "What are you saying? Jews *want* blood?"

"I wasn't—"

"No, blood is your point. We want Christian blood. Pure, High-Church English blood. For what? To mix in with our unleavened bread?"

"Warburg—"

"No! What are you saying, you with your 'Fuck. Double fuck.' With your anarchists, Reds, syndicalists—all Jews, right! Listen to yourself. You sound like Father Coughlin, and you're not even Catholic."

"Calm down, David."

"You're here for your next report on me, is that it? I know what you've been doing."

"What?"

"'OSS Reports—Station Rome.' Cited by Washington in shutting me down. OSS said the WRB singled out Jews as if they were the only ones suffering. 'The WRB singles out Jews.' That was you."

"Well, it's true, for Christ's sake! The Krauts mauled the whole fucking continent. What's with the focus on Jews?"

"Jews were Hitler's focus. Only then were they mine." Warburg leaned toward Mates. "Look, General, if 'OSS—Station Rome' had a criticism to make about my approach, why didn't you make it to me?"

Mates shrugged. Fuck it.

The general's blithe indifference pushed Warburg to the line. He said, "I've watched you set your dogs on my DPs for a year, looking for Bolsheviks among those poor, desperate people. Looking for Stalin's spies, labor organizers, Partisans—looking for goddamn Trotskyites. Why? Because my DPs are Jews. You set Rossini on me, turned the poor bastard into a snitch. I played along because I like the kid. But why turn Rossini? Because I'm a Jew!"

"You're sure as hell acting like one now."

"How does a Jew act?"

"Sniveling moneygrubbing shysters, parasites! Is that what you want me to say? Okay. Fine. I'll ask you a question you hear at the officers' club. Why did it fall to the U.S. *Treasury* to do something about

Jews in Europe? Not the War Department. Not the State Department. The fucking *Treasury*. Don't you find that amazing?"

Without thinking and in one motion, Warburg came to his feet, pivoted, cocked his arm, and threw a downward shovel hook, landing squarely on Mates's right cheekbone. Mates fell from his chair, but he quickly got up and bulled into Warburg's midsection, pushing him halfway across the room. Butting upward, he banged the crown of his head into Warburg's chin. Mates was over fifty, but he'd trained. The two exchanged blows, punching and counterpunching. Warburg—younger, stronger, taller—would have had the advantage in any case, but he was attacking in Mates so much more than Mates, whose mistake then was to stay on his feet.

Warburg pushed him out into the corridor and, gripping him at each of his silver stars, pounded him backward down the stairs. Warburg felt it in his fists as Mates's spine registered each jolt.

Oddly, perhaps because of the cloth at the general's throat, the white and black *tallit*, sinking into the waters of the lake, came momentarily to Warburg's mind, but otherwise he was focused on Mates. He slugged him one last time, sending him through the door and out into the street.

Rossini was waiting at the curb. Mates fell in a heap at his feet, but it was Warburg at whom he was agape. "What the hell, Mr. Warburg?"

"Take care of him, Sarge," Warburg said. "A little iodine, a little bourbon, he'll be fine."

Mates struggled up. "I'll see you court-martialed!" the general said, barely more than a groan.

Warburg, adding to the ruefulness he would feel later, laughed. "I'm not military, General. I'm not even a government employee. No question of court-martial. If you want the law, you'll have to call the Carabinieri. They won't give a shit—unless, of course, you tell them you were ambushed by a Jew."

If they had been lovers, the Nicholas V sacristy would have been their trysting place. But no.

They had met there roughly every other week, poring over maps spread out on the vesting case, as Sister Thomas brought Monsignor Deane the latest from cables crossing her desk in the Vatican cipher room and from Tardini's briefings for which she was note taker. Always, she tracked the lava-like westbound flow of refugees, lately speeding up, with hundreds of thousands risking what little was left them to escape the closing vise of the Red Army.

Sister Thomas was one of the first outsiders to know of secret agreements among the British, French, and Americans that shut the Soviets out of Western occupation zones. She reported on the reprisal killings of collaborators across the continent. From Vienna came reports of a surviving Nazi cell called Die Spinne, or The Spider; other reports spoke of Italy's own Gladio, clandestine Fascist military units secretly supported by the Allies. From Vilna came rumors of failed anti-Soviet efforts — meetings of Lithuanian, Ukrainian, and Polish conspirators, aborted because of disputes over what language would be used in the meetings.

But yesterday, something much closer to home had prompted Sister Thomas to leave a single rose at the feet of the Virgin in the grotto of the Vatican gardens, the signal for Deane. Now she was kneeling alone in the Sala dei Chiaroscuri, and though her face was buried in her hands, she kept seeing the images of martyred saints painted on the frescoed walls around her — arrows into blissful Sebastian, the amputated breasts of Agatha, the sword at the throat of Agnes, Stephen eternally being stoned. All such figures, in the Catholic imagination, went unclothed to God, a quite lovely nakedness that clashed with the Puritan impulse to cloak the flesh, as Sister Thomas's own was cloaked. As always, she wore the white Dominican habit with its black veil flowing over her shoulders.

Each morning before dawn, she nimbly removed her coarse nightgown, naked as any martyr. She welcomed the chill on her body — the physical sensation — for the few moments required to bathe. No question of gazing upon her nakedness in a mirror, since there was no mirror. But she was often aware of the turn at her hip, the slight protrusion at her abdomen, the bristle below. When she stretched, with her arms high, her small breasts flattened and her skin lost its wrinkles.

Oddly, vanity about her body had not reared itself until she'd turned forty, when it dawned on her that the ripeness of youth had not yet wholly withered. As for her hair, she'd been wearing it clipped close to her scalp for ten years now, and she had no idea what that looked like on her. How amused she'd been in recent months when modish girls began appearing in the streets of Rome with hair like hers—a style named for Julius Caesar, she'd been told. Those girls would be appalled to know they looked like nuns at bedtime.

Someone entered the shadowy chapel behind her. Through her fingers, she watched. Monsignor Deane strode up the side aisle, his leanness emphasized by the black, red-trimmed cassock swirling at his knees. At the head of the aisle, holding his upright martial posture, he executed a crisp genuflection with one hand lightly on the communion rail. Usually his movements struck her as gracefully unselfconscious, but this morning she sensed their performance aspect. Having apparently ignored her, he disappeared through the innocuous door into the sacristy. A few moments later, she rose, blessed herself, and followed him. No satchel today.

He stood leaning at the vesting case, arms folded easily across his chest. He smiled when he saw her. She was aware of the lift he felt in her company, because she felt it, too. But not today.

"Good morning, Sister," he said quietly, standing up straight, a gentleman.

She nodded. "Monsignor."

Normally they would turn away from the slight flare in their greeting, sublimating what sparked it in the business of file folders, maps, and cable ledgers. But today they stood face to face, separated by the width of a prie-dieu. Between them, a wedge of sunlight from the small window emphasized the shadow in which they stood. Neither was able to discern what was written in the other's expression.

"I've learned something you should know," Sister Thomas said at last. "A shipment of hand-rolled beeswax altar candles arrived by truck from Zagreb this week, an order sent to the Holy See as a gift from the Confraternity of San Girolamo. Twenty-five cartons, each weighing about two stone."

"Beeswax candles?"

"Laced with frankincense and myrrh."

"I don't follow."

"A PCA truck on a return run, having brought grain and flour to Trieste. Exempt from searches." PCA — Pontificia Commissione di Assistenza. Deane's shop.

Sister Thomas continued, "The cartons were offloaded two nights ago, the candles stored in the crypt of Santa Marta. The operation was personally supervised by a bishop of the Curia."

"Marini? The papal master of ceremonies?"

"No. Antonio Caggiano."

"The Argentine? The Catholic Action fellow?"

"Yes."

"Candles? That's the liturgy office, ceremonies. What does Catholic Action have to do with candles?"

"That was my question when I learned of it. I went to Santa Marta yesterday. Sister Portress told me that Caggiano removed the key to the storage room from the key cabinet and kept it, no further entrance except through him. She assumed I was acting on Tardini's authority, up the pyramid from Caggiano. As I expected, she had a master key. She averted her eyes as she handed it to me, as if to be able later to deny knowing how I got it. I entered the crypt alone, examined the cartons of candles, several of which had been recently unsealed, presumably by the good bishop."

"Not candles."

"No."

"What?"

"Gold, smelted into bars. By my calculation, twenty-five cartons, each holding twelve bars, each bar at one kilogram — something like three hundred kilograms. Value, twenty-five million pounds sterling."

Deane pursed his lips as if to whistle. Only after some seconds did he say, "A hundred million dollars."

"Approximately."

"In the crypts at Santa Marta? Not the bank vaults?"

"Correct. As far as I can tell, not recorded anywhere."

"From Zagreb."

"Yes."

"A gift from San Girolamo? That's Franciscans."

"Peter's Pence, then?" Her face fell into what he thought of as her all-knowing smile, but she snapped it off with an abrupt wag of her head. "The bars are stamped with a U — Ustashe. Almost certainly this gold is from the Croatian state treasury. The Croatian state that ceased to exist in May. From the looks of the carton I opened, two bars have been removed. Nearly eight hundred thousand dollars."

"Does Tardini know?"

"Perhaps. There's more."

"What?"

"Tardini is preparing to ask British and American authorities to release Croatian prisoners of war from Allied custody. I've seen a draft of the letter: '. . . unjustly oppressed children of the Faith.'"

"Probably," Deane said, "if Eisenhower freed Croatian POWs, they would sign up to fight Communists." He thought a moment, then added, "Ante Pavelic is the Croatian leader, but he's on the Allied war criminal list, and no one knows where he is."

"Tardini does. I'm sure of it. There are cables coming in that are kept from me."

"Who handles them?"

"That German."

"Lehmann?"

"Yes. He has met privately with Tardini six times that I know of. And he brings others with him. German speakers, but they may be Austrian — or Croats."

"Clerics?"

"They wear clericals."

"But—?"

She shrugged. "Franciscans wear sandals. These blokes wear brogans. I don't talk with them. But there is something off . . ."

Deane was quiet. When Sister Thomas met his pensiveness with her own, the silence built. Finally he said, "Lehmann was born in Argentina."

"Like Bishop Caggiano."

"Can you find out what Lehmann is up to?"

Sister Thomas did not answer. She had dropped her eyes, fixing them on her hands, which were fiercely clasped, pulling against each other.

"What?" he asked.

"Something else. I have no idea how to speak of it."

He waited. Then he said, "You can speak of it with me."

"I had a visitor. An Englishman. A man I knew in Bletchley Park."

She paused, then continued, "I went, as usual, to the Wednesday general audience for the Holy Father's blessing. As the crowd was leaving the auditorium, I was making my way toward the cloister and he appeared before me. I thought at first I was hallucinating."

"A man you knew well?"

She nodded. "Because of him I fled to Blackfriars. Because of him I took my vows. I expected never to see him again. He asked to meet with me. I agreed. We met in the Belvedere Courtyard, chatting on a bench, to all appearances — cousins." She stopped again.

Deane prodded, "What did he want?"

"He asked me to work for him."

"Return to Bletchley?"

"Not precisely."

"They brought him from Bletchley to Rome to ask you."

"Yes. He was rather direct about it all. They have assigned him here, assuming I would be responsive to him. Military Intelligence, Group Six. Rome." She stopped, palpably deciding whether she, too, should be direct. She plunged forward with, "He told me that his wife has died." She laughed abruptly, bitterly. "Once I dreamed of Philip coming to me like that, with just such news. Think of it! Wishing a woman dead! The dream, of course, was that then he would insist upon my leaving the order to be with him, our love allowed at last. Married life, cottage in the Cotswolds, all of that."

"Philip."

"Philip Barnes Morton. He *did* propose, but what he proposed is for me to remain in my consecration, good Sister Thomas. Not his wife, but an agent inside the Holy See."

Deane was lost. She had never spoken so personally to him before, never of a man or the dream of love. And now—had she said MI6? Deane sensed how thrown off she was, but still, it made no sense that he was the one she turned to with this anguish. "What did you say?"

"I said no, of course. Out of the question. How dare he? That was when the real surprise came." Sister Thomas turned away, bracing herself against the vesting case. "He replied that the Crown has urgent need of an independent source in the Vatican, to balance what it learns from the Americans."

"Learns from the Americans about the Vatican?"

"About *everything*, from what comes *through* the Vatican. During the war, London had need of nothing more than Bletchley, because German ciphers were being read. But now, against Moscow, they are scrambling. It's what the Church knows that is of interest, especially of activities in the Catholic countries, Poland, Czechoslovakia, Hungary, Croatia—the 'captive nations.'" She turned her head toward Deane. "Philip told me to ask you about 'Operation Captive Nations.'"

"Me?"

"You are the American source. He said you were sent to Rome last year as an OSS agent. He said that if you are working for the OSS, I should do as much for MI6, since most of what you know comes from me. What is 'Captive Nations'?"

"I have no idea."

"It's the OSS project of undermining the Soviets in Eastern Europe, using the Church."

"That's ridiculous. What can the Church do?"

"You just said it: Croatians fighting Communists, a leading role for the archbishop of Zagreb. Croatia is the wedge, and Tardini is pushing on it. Hence the letter about freeing Croatian prisoners. Philip made it crystal clear how very much MI6 needs this. Are you working for OSS?"

"No. I am working for the Church. If I report to anyone, it's Archbishop Spellman. You know that. His palace on Madison Avenue is called the Powerhouse, but the only real power he has, with Washington *and* with the Third Floor here, is information. Which is my role. Spellman's intrigue is with the Communists, sure. But it's also with the Curia. Especially your boss, Tardini. If I'm an agent, I'm Spellman's agent."

"Not OSS? Not even indirectly?"

"Only that fantasy last year about restoring the Habsburgs, a Catholic empire to stop Moscow. Cardinal Maglione's fantasy, the Pope's probably. Spellman's for sure. Yes, OSS had a hand in that, and yes, I played the hand as long as the cards lasted. That's what brought me to Lehmann. The Germans wanted the new Holy Roman Empire more than we did, which is what nixed it. Kaput. But you know all that. It was Irish mist and the Red Army stormed right through it. I've had nothing to do with OSS since."

He slowed down. A new experience for him: a man making an explanation to a dubious woman can both tell the truth and realize that the truth is impossibly more complicated. "Sister, I would never betray your confidence. Except for Spellman, refugees are my only work now. And yes, I have been sharing information about the displaced, but with Warburg. You remember that — it was Budapest that first brought me to you. The WRB, not the OSS."

"And now the WRB is gone."

"Warburg is working with Zionists now, and obviously I'm wary. He's making a big mistake. Is that what British intelligence is after? The Jews? Palestine? Was it the embassy bombing that sent them to you? They want to know what the Holy See hears from Jerusalem?"

"I'm sure they do."

"Sister . . ." Deane touched her sleeve. Not her arm, just her ample white sleeve. ". . . our friendship is important to me. Very important."

"I admit that what Philip said to me was upsetting. What he said about you. And, speaking of Irish mist, he did refer to your Irishness."

Deane grinned. "Which is worse, my being Irish or being American?"

Sister Thomas laughed, but briefly. "That what he said about you bothered me so much—there is the surprise."

"That I would be duplicitous with you."

"Yes."

"It bothered you because our partnership has become friendship."

"Yes."

"Sister . . . Jerusalem, Zagreb, Vienna, Budapest, Vatican cables galore—none of it matters to me like you do."

Sister Thomas straightened her posture. "I suppose, Monsignor, that is what I needed to hear from you. Now we should resume as before."

Deane accepted her brisk shift away from feeling, welcomed it. He matched her new tone of voice. "But what about MI6?"

"I told you. I said out of the question."

"Sister, we began by discussing a hundred million dollars in gold. If it's Ustashe gold, that makes it loot. Unregistered. Coins smelted into bars, but also jewelry and—we should acknowledge this—teeth. Held here, in the Vatican. Perhaps already being dispensed. You are at the center of something with this. Who knows what? There may come a time when you can influence British thinking about such matters, and perhaps British policy. If you acted as a source . . . must you burn the bridge—?"

"Monsignor, that bridge was a conflagration, burned long ago. Gold has come to the Holy See, and so, obviously, has some malign intrigue. I have no choice but to be responsible in handling this knowledge. But no gold for me. And as little intrigue as possible. I will have only one co-conspirator here. And, for better or worse, that is you."

Deane heard the echo in "better or worse," and he recognized as inappropriate the happiness he felt at her declared preference.

At night, the summer heat brought the Romans outdoors: old men on stoops sucking briar pipes, clustered women snapping church fans to the beat of gossip, families bedding down on sidewalks, shirtless lads dancing in fountains. Father Lehmann observed the passing scene as if it had nothing to do with him, such was his mood.

He occupied the right rear seat of the big Mercedes limousine, the dignitary's place, where he belonged. Earlier, he'd been forced to ride in front, beside the driver, like a footman. He still felt the overweening presence of the three men who had made the trip out. They had been dressed, as he was, in the black suit and clerical collar of priests at large in the world. None was present now, just Lehmann and the driver, winding up the long day's journey to and from Genoa, where Lehmann's companions had boarded the liner *Fernando Ruiz*, bound for Buenos Aires. Everything had gone smoothly, from roadblocks to seaport checkpoints to the customhouse to the gangplank. At each stop, the men had presented credentials and visas to the Carabinieri or the American military police. Addressed deferentially in Italian and English, they had mumbled their replies, with Lehmann standing by to step in at any question. But there had been no questions, not one. The Vatican license plates, the clerical dress, the papers stamped with the seal of the Holy See, and, at the pier, the collar-wearing ship's chaplain waiting to greet them as Church dignitaries — all successful.

As the three black-clad figures made their way up the gangplank, the chaplain turned to Lehmann and addressed him *sotto voce* in Spanish. "You are the Argentine priest from Rome."

"I am German," Lehmann replied coldly, but in the unaccented Spanish he had learned at home. "*You* are the Argentine priest." He was not pleased to think of himself as the object of talk. Indeed, there was much about the day that had not pleased him, beginning, as they were first leaving Rome, with the tone of voice with which the unnamed German seated directly behind him had whispered in his ear. The man had leaned forward and grasped his shoulder, squeezing it painfully. "We know your mother," he'd said. "She favors her mantilla. If there is a problem today, your dear mother will be made to know of it."

At that moment, the man had ceased being merely a fugitive with whom to empathize and had become a menace whose history included the slaughter of mothers. Lehmann had found it possible to sit rigidly for a long moment before offering the barest nod, his only reply. In truth, he had wanted to turn, grasp the man's hand, and plead,

"Not my mother! Leave my poor mother alone!" But now, hours later, came the rush of words he wished he'd said: *How dare you—you who shamed the fatherland! You dare to threaten an old woman, whose only son is even now saving your pathetic skin!*

What a fool he'd been to think himself central. The magnificent Himmler would have prepared an entire syndicate of escape, roads out everywhere. Thousands of senior figures of the Reich were fugitives now—Gestapo chiefs, Nazi Party magistrates, SS *Gruppenführers*, ghetto administrators, Wehrmacht generals, racial policy officers, killing center commandants. Legions of Allied investigators were out to get them, and escape hatches would be popping open from Lisbon to Amsterdam. Who knew how many dolts like Lehmann there were? To the men he was rescuing, he was a mere bag handler, a nobody. And, in truth, was that not exactly the case?

Had the war gone another way, these men would have been heroes worthy of Wagner, but instead they were base criminals. Lehmann could acknowledge, if only to himself, how failure had transformed the Führer's entire project like that—gold into lead, conquerors into cowards, demigods into beasts. *So yes, run, you bastards! And if along the road you find a mongrel dog, then kick it. And be sure to kick also the dog's bitch of a mother. Or, better, just kill her. Madre!*

The Piazza della Rotonda, in front of the Pantheon, was choked with a crowd of young Romans, men and women. A midnight festival, raucous laughter, glad shouts, bottles of Chianti being passed, cigarette smoke wafting in the air like incense. A mundane fact of the city's overcrowding, youngsters escaping the confines of tiny apartments shared with siblings, parents, and grandparents. Only in public spaces centered on fountains could romance bloom. Indeed, gushing fountains could seem the promise.

The crush around this fountain had ensnared automobile traffic, and Lehmann's driver joined others to lean on the horn, pointlessly adding to the cacophony. Outside Lehmann's window, close enough to reach out and touch, a young man and woman were passionately kissing, the hands of each one kneading the other's buttocks. Lehmann looked away.

He felt as if he had stumbled into *Primavera,* Botticelli's celebration of sensuality, dancing girls, flying cherubs, one of the women draped in diaphanous white, her naked form fully apparent, being seized at her breasts by a winged male. *You, I want you.*

Without a word to the driver, Lehmann opened the door and got out of the car.

Hours later, he was still walking the streets of Rome, aimlessly in motion. Somewhere, he had unfastened his rabat and collar and, together with his black suit coat, discarded it all, leaving him in shirtsleeves, a man with no collar whatsoever. For all he knew, he'd been grinning madly the whole time, thinking: This is what a life comes to, a life for God, for Germany, for the Church, a life for *Madre* — how dare that bastard threaten her!

Breathe, he commanded himself again and again, recalling the long-lost contemplative discipline of his monastic youth. Breathe the Jesus Prayer: *Lord Jesus Christ, have mercy on me, a sinner. Lord Jesus Christ, have mercy on me, a sinner.*

But instead of calming, his mind raced. Was it only now hitting him that the war had been lost? Germany humiliated once again. His nation's humiliation identical with his own. Lehmann clung to his postwar distinctions: Hitler wicked, Deutschland virtuous. Nazism flawed, Bolshevism irredeemable. If grotesque crimes were committed, that was the effect of war itself. Hadn't the now self-righteous Allies given themselves over to nihilistic destruction, and didn't the selfsame sanctimonious Allies include the devil Stalin? And if anything was to be faulted for the last catastrophic year, wasn't it Washington's diabolical demand for unconditional surrender, which gave sane Germans no alternative to insanity? Bolshevism was the war's truest victor.

As he walked, these mantras rolled unbidden off the prayer wheel of his mind: *This is what a life comes to, a life for sad-eyed prisoners of war, for Archbishop Graz, for* Aussenweg, *for Himmler, a life for vowed poverty, obedience, chastity. Chastity! Where is my nymph in white?* With no knowledge of how he came to be there, Lehmann greeted the dawn on Via Sicilia, at the gate of Casa dello Spirito Santo.

His hangover, as if produced by an alcoholic binge, lasted for days, but eventually Lehmann regained control of himself. He satisfactorily fulfilled his duties as the Vatican's delegate to the Allied Control Commission for Italy, responsible for administration of POW camps, which still held hundreds of thousands of German prisoners. Three days a week, traveling in his limousine, Lehmann visited "disarmed enemy forces" in open-air camps and improvised prisons in half-bombed factories in Viterbo, Pisa, Villa Marina, Vercelli.

His access was complete because, as a priest of pontifical right, he was the Vatican's delegate, not Germany's. Yet he grew tired of hearing that Germany had openly repudiated the Geneva Conventions, and that therefore punitive policies were acceptable. The poor men he saw were emaciated, suffering from infected wounds, unset fractures. Mess tents were as unsanitary as latrines. Wehrmacht officers were as ill treated as men of low rank. Barbed-wire cages were open to the rain. Cholera and typhus were epidemic.

It was Lehmann's place to register Vatican protests against such abuses, which he did with self-righteous passion. His Holy See superiors regularly backed him in his high-level complaints.

Of all of this he spoke to his mother. Two or three nights a week, he stayed in her opulent apartment. She was proud of him, his work for the Church, his work for the unfairly maligned heroes of the fatherland. Of what he did in secret for the other heroes, though, he never spoke. Not to her. Not to anyone.

One warm evening shortly before dusk, as he returned from his Vatican office to the Casa dello Spirito Santo, his driver made the usual turn onto Via Sicilia, and he saw her. She was sitting at a sidewalk table at the corner café. He stifled the impulse to order his driver to stop. Moments later, inside the Casa's courtyard, he got out of the car, went straight into his small house, and removed his cassock. He donned the one civilian shirt he owned, rolled the sleeves to his elbows, and went out again, not caring who in the monastic enclosure saw him leave. Only as he approached the café did he slow his pace, relieved to find that he had not imagined her.

"Buona sera, Signorina."

She looked up at him, an unabashed docking of his gaze. Otherwise, she did not respond.

Was she expecting him? He said, "I am Father Lehmann."

"I know who you are."

She was wearing a light brown sleeveless dress, open at the throat, so that he could trace the line from its hollow down to her breasts, the valley there just hinted at. Her upper arms were bare. Her lips were pale. She wore a thin gold chain around her neck. Between the two long fingers of her left hand was a smoldering cigarette. In her right hand was a small book, which she held as if about to resume reading. To her he was a moment's distraction, nothing more. With a lurch in his stomach, he realized he had nothing to say to her.

She said, with a flick of her head toward the Casa, "You are at leisure?"

Lehmann felt himself blushing. To be on the street without his clericals was like being in his underwear. Leisure was the last word he'd have used — *licere,* the Latin for being allowed. "I was coming out for air, yes. A leisurely walk about." He forced a grin. "About the streets of Rome." How different this was from their first meeting in that Vatican office, when he had found it possible to lean over and kiss her hand. But he was a different man then. Born to impress. The war was not yet lost. And — how did he know this? — she was a different woman. Capable of being impressed.

She closed the book and placed it beside her glass, which seemed an invitation. He touched the empty chair opposite her and raised an eyebrow. "May I?"

"As you please."

He sat. The waiter appeared at once. Lehmann nodded at her glass and said, "Cinzano?" A moment later, a small tulip glass had been placed on the table before him. He picked it up and held it toward her, as if to toast. He said, "Vermouth. From the German *Wermut.* Do you know the meaning of that word?"

"No."

"Wormwood. From the Book of Revelation. A star that falls upon Earth and poisons a third part of the waters." He sipped his drink and grimaced.

"'And many people died of the waters,'" she recited, "'because they were made bitter.'"

He laughed. "I thought, among laity, only Protestants knew the Bible."

Marguerite gestured down the street, toward the Casa dello Spirito Santo. "A convent girl," she said. "Complete instruction. The Book of Revelation speaks of Satan's reign of a thousand years. The original Thousand-Year Reich."

In reply to this, Lehmann only stared at her.

She smiled and said, "I come to this café occasionally because, as a girl, this was where we came for gelato. Because of those happy memories, I am at leisure here." She looked straight at him with her dark eyes. She was that girl again. Innocent. Direct. Then her glance flitted away.

He was certain the woman had just seen him afresh, but how? Had seen him as someone of interest, but for what? As if in answer to these questions, her eyes returned to his face, but now stared openly with a question of their own.

His questions rolled on: Am I a mystery to her? What does she want me for? He had no idea, but the skin on his neck tingled. All he knew was that he had never been gazed upon so nakedly before.

He straightened his posture and touched a finger to the curl at his forehead, to remind himself of his handsomeness. "Did you find your priest?" he asked, hardly breathing. When she did not answer, he went on, "You came to the Casa that night looking for your priest from the convent days."

"No. I did not find him." She ashed her cigarette and put it to her mouth.

He was aware of her lips, the barest sight of her tongue. He said, "I thought I might meet you when I visit the Red Cross offices, but I did not."

"What brings you to the Red Cross?"

"To register protests, how German prisoners are mistreated in the camps. The Red Cross ignores us."

"Mistreatment should not happen to anyone."

"Germans are especially mistreated."

"For example?"

"The massacre by Americans."

"What massacre?"

"At the very end, German soldiers were attempting only to surrender, but the Americans shot them. Twenty. Thirty. Shot dead while trying to surrender. This is well known. Only one example. There are others."

"Where did that happen?"

"In Bavaria."

"Where?"

"Near Munich."

"A place called Dachau?"

"Perhaps."

"The German soldiers were guards at Dachau?"

"Perhaps."

"The Americans saw what the German guards had done there. Is that why the guards were shot?"

"It is not for the Red Cross to judge. Geneva requires the respect of soldiers who surrender. The Red Cross refused to condemn the massacre."

Marguerite nodded slowly. "If there was a massacre, it should be condemned. Of course, you are right about that."

"I know of my own experience . . . My uncle was taken prisoner on the eastern front. He was a regimental officer. His captors simply shot him dead. Bolsheviks."

"How terrible for you."

"Terrible for *mia madre*. He was her only relative." Lehmann felt himself blushing.

"You are her relative," she said quietly, "no?"

"Yes. I meant others. Now there is only me."

"And the loss of your uncle was painful for you as well." She said this with a quality of sympathy that had rarely been directed toward him. Always toward his mother, rarely him.

She sipped her Cinzano, and he did likewise. Above the rims of the tulip glasses, their eyes met. She said, "You have a difficult position, Father. A man in between, no?"

"Very much so. You speak more accurately than you know."

"And sometimes the difficulty of your position becomes more than you can manage. And you remove your soutane, put on your tired white shirt with rolled sleeves, and come out into Rome looking for the night. What are you looking for, Father?"

"I saw you. I was passing in my car. I saw you sitting here. Do you sit here often?"

"Sometimes. Only sometimes."

"Because of gelato."

She gestured with her glass. "Vermouth now. Wormwood." She quaffed her drink, then threw her head back, laughing. "Waiter!" she cried. "More wormwood. More bitters." She laughed again, and he joined her. Both their faces were happily transformed, but only for a moment. After the waiter put a fresh Cinzano in front of her, she raised it. "To the Book of Revelation." She took a large swallow, then said gravely, "And the many people dying of the poisoned waters."

"I sensed that in you when you confessed to me."

"You sensed it because neither of us was made to be alone with bitterness."

He waited for her to lower her eyes, but she did not. He was not breathing.

"Am I wrong?" she asked.

"No. But when you confessed that night, you did not specify your sin. I was wrong to absolve you. It has troubled me since. The sacrament requires specificity. You refused. And I yielded." He looked away from her, made a quick survey of the others in the café, of figures passing on the street. Who was watching them? *Madre,* he thought. But no, *Madre* was across the city. *Madre* was asleep. He brought his eyes back to the woman and said, "I was wrong to do that."

"Is this your confession, Father?"

"I, too, am a sinner."

"But neither do *you* specify."

He found it possible to say, but quietly, "I am here with you."

Still holding his eyes, she put her glass down, retrieved a few lire notes from the side pocket of her dress, threw them on the table, and stood. As she turned and walked away, Lehmann understood that she expected him to follow, and so he did.

Less than ten minutes later, after moving through a maze of narrow streets and small, crowded piazzas — the sweet life of Rome at night — she entered a small hotel, ignored the desk clerk, crossed to the staircase, and went up. In the cramped lobby Lehmann hesitated, but the clerk took no more notice of him than of her. Lehmann went to the stairs, and as he took them, he unconsciously reached to lift the folds of his cassock, only to realize again that he was a man without vestments, a man like any other.

Marguerite had sensed at once that Lehmann was even less sexually experienced than she. Her advantage in what followed was in acting out of the numb core of dissociation.

Lehmann's *dis*advantage, the result of having hesitated slightly at the door he'd found ajar in the dark corridor, consisted in finding her already naked, stretched out on the bed. Her arms opened to him, but it was her inner thighs he saw, her breasts, nipples pink, the offering of Eve. The further arousal of his fully erect penis fulfilled an exquisite longing, yet the sensation alarmed him. Knowing nothing else, he knew to go slower, yet the pulse of blood was leaving him behind. *No. No.*

He danced on alternate legs to remove his trousers. He pulled at his shoes, but snagged the laces. Because his eyes never left the unclothed woman before him, he stumbled. This, the most intense erotic sensation of his life, gave way, as he realized what was happening, to dread. Then dread gave way to humiliation, the dead opposite of pleasure, when his untimely ejaculation overrode his ferocious will. Will had nothing to do with it. *Oh. Oh.*

He fell gracelessly upon her as sperm pumped itself out of his penis, soiling the woman's leg. In truth the priest had rarely even masturbated. Those climaxes, quick as they were, had reliably left him briefly elated, but this was instant ignominy. He groaned — *No, no* — and rolled away, awash in shame amid the stench of his own mean emission.

As he lay immobile beside her, the question came *vox Dei: Have you eaten from the tree of which I commanded you not to eat?* He would have laughed — I tried to eat, I tried, and what a tree! — but in fact he was weeping. Sobs broke out of him in spurts, just as unwilled as the ejaculation had been. In control of almost nothing, he was yet able to choke back the unwilled words rising in his throat, *Madre, mia madre,* aware that such infantile pleading would obliterate the last vestige of his dignity. Debased and wretched. Craven. He loathed himself.

Only gradually did Lehmann become aware of the finger tenderly brushing his cheek, blotting the tears. He had his back to her, and so had not seen it when she turned toward him. She enfolded his body in the curve of her own. Her mouth was by his ear. "Be still," she whispered. "Be still."

As if she were the mistress of nature, he obeyed. Stillness soon came, and he entered it as a sacred space. His sobbing quieted, his heaving chest settled, his fists unclenched themselves. All the while she moved her forefinger lightly on his cheek. Nestled against him, she pressed her legs into the hollow of his bent knees. He sensed a moist warmth against his buttocks, the faint scratch of her pubic hair. She enclosed him with her arm around his chest and drew him fully into the bow of her flesh.

Slowly, he became aware that the soft pushing against his back was pressure from her breasts. Her tranquility engulfed him. He'd been schooled in mystic contemplation, yet here was an unprecedented coherence between his relaxing body and his quiet interiority, a vacancy of the mind combined with acute awareness of every sensation.

Time meant nothing. At some point — minutes? an hour? longer? — he felt the stirring in his loins. She seemed to sense it too, for her hand moved slowly to his penis, and with her caress the stiffness came back.

Growing erect, he turned to her and she welcomed him. When he
moved to kiss her, he found her lips parted, and she fondled his tongue
with hers. All the while she continued to hold his erection, pressing
it, then guiding it. He was in her, pumping as quickly as before, but
now in sync with the bouncing of her hips. He sensed the detached
willfulness with which she moved, but mistook it for expertise. The
surprise to Lehmann was in the way the physical communion about
which he'd read, and dreamed, and offered spiritual counsel — ecstatic
communion, a mode of transcendence — boiled down to fucking.

After, the word that spilled from his lips, pressed into the hollow of
her shoulder, was "*Gracias.*"

As if his speaking even that word broke the spell, she came up onto
her elbow, stared hard at his face, waited for his eyes to find their focus
on her, and said, "Bless me, Father."

"What?" He craned back, away. "What?"

She pulled the sheet free, wrapped herself with it, rolled off the
bed, and fell to her knees in the posture of a child at bedtime prayers.
Wrapped in white, not diaphanous, a vestal virgin. She crossed herself
and bowed her head. "Bless me, Father, for I have sinned." She buried
her face in her hands, just when he was most desperate to see her eyes,
to read what madness was glowing there.

Lehmann did not move. Like Adam, aware in the instant of being unclothed, exposed. *Vox Dei: Who told thee that thou wast naked?*
Paralyzed, he waited.

Instead of God's, her voice came, a whisper he could barely understand. "I have sinned against chastity, Father."

Lehmann sat bolt upright, reaching to the foot of the bed for the
tattered blanket. He covered himself, draping his shoulders as if with
the amice, the first of the vestments donned for Mass. "No, Signorina,
no."

"I engaged in sexual relations with one to whom I was not married. For this and all my sins, I am heartily sorry. Please forgive me."
She raised her face to him, a wretched display of rebuke, yet aimed at
herself. Now it was she whose face was streaked with tears. And, given
how tenderly she had rescued him from the pit of self-loathing, and

given, equally, that he was in possession of the means of her relief, it was all at once unthinkable that he should refuse her. Surreal, bizarre, baffling — but yes, unthinkable.

He knew the canon law: "*Latae sententiae . . . de delictis gravioribus . . . anathema sit.*" A priest who attempts to absolve a partner in a sin against the Sixth Commandment is himself *ipso facto* excommunicated. But all of that was in a realm apart, a realm that held no meaning for him then. Lehmann realized that he had been at this point with her before, as if she'd tested him, or prepared him — her request for absolution when she had refused to specify her sin. He had granted it, a sin of his own. Rehearsal. But now her sin was as specific as it could be, and who knew better than he? Her sin, his sin.

But sin pales before sacrilege — this sacrilege. It would belong to him alone, absolute and permanent, pure blasphemy. The sullying of his holy orders, the debasement of his vow. Yet already he had chosen her above all virtue, above all faith, above all hope. He had chosen love. And now he was choosing love again.

He reached to her, his lover, and placed his left hand upon her head. His right he held above her. If he could do this, it was because she wanted him to. He would do anything for her, and how, given the purity of his love, could that be wrong? "May Our Lord Jesus Christ absolve thee, and I by His authority do absolve thee from every bond of excommunication, or interdict, as far as I am able and thou art needful. I absolve thee from thy sins . . ." And here he made the sign of the cross, warding off all demons except the one alive in him. ". . . in the name of the Father, and of the Son, and of the Holy Ghost."

"Amen," she said in a clear, firm voice — certain. She blessed herself again, then came back up onto the bed, letting the sheet fall away, once again caring nothing for her nakedness. She leaned toward him. They went into each other's arms and reclined. She kissed his brow and pulled him close. She arranged the sheet to cover them both, and, after all of that, they found an unexpected repose, and, lo and behold, it was chaste. She was his Madonna. He was her Child. Lehmann heard nothing but the beating of her heart until, out of their astonishing serenity, she said, "Tell me about the Casa."

NINE

Obbedienza

I T WAS MORE than a year since he'd first entered the Great Synagogue of Rome. The place had made a better recovery than the people who worshiped there. For this Friday-night service, Warburg sat in his accustomed bench toward the rear, where, unobserved, his focus could shift from the text to the soaring space and back. He was dressed, as usual, in gray, but in here he wore the black yarmulke he'd first worn some months earlier. He had yet to don the *tallit*, however.

Moorish windows rose above him in three tiers, but after sundown the light came from the repaired wall fixtures and electrified candelabra that once again decked the columns and balconies. The sanctuary could hold about a thousand, but for this, the weekly ushering in of the Sabbath, perhaps a hundred men were scattered in the main space in front of Warburg, with a few dozen women in the balcony above. The tapestries had been restored to the walls, and the painted ceiling rainbow had been brightened, but the prayers were being recited in disjointed murmurs, and the rabbi, with his back to the congregation, rocked gently toward the ark as if he were praying alone.

Warburg liked the way the service called participants only loosely together, leaving him to wrestle with the text at his own pace, to brood. The recovered beauty of the synagogue contrasted with figments of those he'd met in the camps, whose funerals he'd attended, whose names he'd upheld while reciting the Mourner's Kaddish. In Warburg's mind, the roll call had never ceased: Simone Luzatto, Bettina Chiara, Isaac Samuel Reggio. Here in the synagogue his people hovered in the air above him, witnesses to all that he had failed to do in their behalf. Giuseppe Nathan. Fiorella Coco. And always, still missing but never far from his mind—Wallenberg. Reciting their names to himself was as close as he could come to prayer for the living and the dead.

The others in attendance included elderly and middle-aged Romans, a number of ill-clad refugees who were housed in the city, and a smattering of uniformed American GIs, present more out of homesickness than devotion. For tomorrow morning's service, at which the Torah would be brought out, there would be twice this many in attendance, and the prayers would be recited more robustly. Warburg, though, preferred this quieter ritual. And tonight it was a harbinger of what was coming in an hour.

He himself had insisted on what was sure to be an awkward confrontation with the leaders of these people. No longer badgered by inquisitors or popes, now their nemesis was the British government. Hence the bombing of the embassy.

Some Jews had rejoiced: the British were the new tribunes of an eternal Jew-hatred, and retaliation was overdue. But other Jews still saw the British as valiant conquerors of the Nazis: to attack London was cowardly and treasonous.

Warburg surveyed such arguments within himself. If the violence of the embassy bombing had shocked him—and he had gone at once to see the wreckage for himself—his own violence in response to Mates that same night had been even more unsettling. What a dawn had broken then. As if by controlling a group he could control himself, Warburg had demanded a meeting of the leaders of the Delegation to Assist Hebrews, his main Roman counterparts in getting aid to the camps.

The meeting convened immediately after the service, in the Jewish library across the square. Warburg had been in the second-floor room dozens of times since that first meeting, when the issue was Fossoli. The glass-enclosed shelves held the same books. Sepia landscapes of a dream Jerusalem still decorated the brown walls. The cone-shaped light fixture hung over the same table, but now a dozen chairs were pulled up to it. In each chair sat a man — bespectacled or sharp-eyed; bearded or clean-shaven; between the ages of about twenty-five and sixty; jackets open, neckties; several wearing yarmulkes, making a Sabbath exception to conduct business. At Warburg's entry, they had all stood.

Once they were seated, Warburg came right to the point. "I bring a message from Mr. Morgenthau in New York. I can tell you that the telexes nearly caught fire with his anger. Joint Distribution Committee funds are not to go to the killing of Englishmen. I must know how your groups are tied to the so-called Hebrew Rebellion Movement. If the Irgun war against the British has moved from Palestine to Europe, the cutoff of JDC funds will be complete." Warburg's statement was met with silence.

Finally Lorenzo Anselmo, the Delegation chairman, spoke. He was a white-haired man, formerly the prosperous manufacturer of porcelain ware who had lost his company in the Fascist requisition of Jewish property. The courtly Anselmo had spent the war years in Switzerland, but because of the force of his personality and the memory of his open defiance of Mussolini, he had resumed his role as a leader of Rome's Jews. "You know, Mr. Warburg, that we are not the ones to whom you should be conveying this message. No one here is associated with the Haganah. And the Haganah would be foolish to associate with us. Is that not obvious?"

Another man spoke, Stanislaw Monash, the head of the new Central Committee of Liberated Jews. This coordinating body of DPs in various camps had, in fact, been formed at Warburg's insistence, and with his help. Monash, a survivor of Warsaw, was a Dante scholar and fluent in Italian. "The British secret service watches all of us," he said. "They are watching this meeting. To them, one Jew is like another."

"To Morgenthau also," a man whom Warburg did not know put in. He was glaring at Warburg. "The JDC will punish those still languishing in the camps because of the actions of Jewish resisters? That is collective punishment, a Nazi tactic."

"The JDC will do no such thing," Warburg said firmly. "You think *I* will abandon those in camps? Do you know me, Sir?" Warburg returned the man's unfriendly stare.

"Yes, I know you," he said, but with sudden sheepishness. "You said the support will be cut off—"

"Yes, from expressly Jewish groups. From *your* groups. Bricha, the Delegation, Merkaz, Aliyah Bet, even Comunità Ebraica di Roma. That is the message the Hebrew rebels need to hear, whoever they are. Jewish *groups* will be cut off, not Jews. The JDC is under pressure from Washington now, because Washington is under pressure from London."

"Truman already bars Jews from America."

"Yes," Warburg said. "That is why he supports Jews in Israel. Israel solves his problem. That works for us so long as we do not defy him. The JDC cannot sponsor war, period. JDC support of refugees will continue through other channels. The International Relief Committee, the Red Cross, our own medical centers. JDC's work will not flag. But nothing will go to *groups* associated with attacks on the British."

"Every group with Zionist sympathies will be associated," another said.

"We all have Zionist sympathies," Warburg said. "But we are not killers."

"No one died at the embassy. Whoever did that put up police barricades ahead of time, to keep innocent people away."

Warburg himself had made that point to Mates that night, even before knowing about the barricades. But now he was making a different point. "We all want the British to open up immigration. Hell, Truman wants it. He's leaning on Attlee right now. But American support, both financial and political—and support from American Jews themselves—depends on the widespread sympathy for the plight of refugees. If refugees become a pawn in the war, justifying terror and assassination, then the sympathy disappears. Disappears from the White House. Disappears from American synagogues. Disappears! Who here does not understand that?"

Warburg cast his eyes slowly around the table, inviting dissent, ready to snuff it out. He placed his hands together, leaning forward. "The Jewish war must not come to Rome. Palestine is another matter. The Jewish war must be kept separate from the Jewish refugees. I am delivering the message to you because I assume some at this table can carry the message further. Leave morality out of it. Violence against the English will only stiffen their refusal to open immigration."

No one disputed Warburg's declaration. After another interval of silence, they began to turn toward each other, speaking in twos and threes, in Italian and Yiddish, stepping on one another's statements, preferring contention among themselves to confrontation with the American. Voices were raised, a release of the tension that had built in the room, a resumption of the arguments Rome's Jews had been having with themselves since the bombing. Catching snatches of what was said, Warburg listened as if the "he" referred to were not himself.

"How dare he leave morality out of it!"

"Morality requires resistance!"

"The Jewish Agency has denounced the bombing. Ben-Gurion denounced it."

"No one knows who did it. Who said it was Jews?"

"Jews are being scapegoated. An old story."

"Lionni did it."

"At the Bagnoli camp, the inmates cheered the news of the bombing."

"Bagnoli is full of Ukrainians and Hungarians. What do you expect?"

"They cheered because they know what's happening on Cyprus."

"Attlee is not Churchill. He can be reasoned with. But no Englishman will—"

"Cyprus is the issue. New camps in Cyprus. There's the violence!"

"And Jews are being attacked again in Poland."

The stew of complaint was familiar to Warburg, and he ignored the roil, except for the young man who had dropped Lionni's name into the cauldron.

The young man's face was vaguely familiar. Thick black hair crowded his forehead. He was sitting next to Anselmo, and now Warburg noticed that the older man was gripping the younger by the forearm, a quiet gesture of pressure: *Say no more!*

Then Warburg saw that the young man's face — thin lips, wolf's jaw, deep-set dark eyes beneath hairy brows bridged above the sharp nose — was a version of Anselmo's. His son? Warburg had heard of Anselmo's son. The young man was staring at his clenched hands. His father was staring at Warburg, worried, as if to ask, *Did you hear?*

The argument was going full bore, and it was clear that several in the room were prepared to take the battle to the British. Enough of Jewish passivity! But why bombs against Englishmen and nothing but surrender to Nazis? Where was the great Irgun before? And so on.

Warburg stood and left the room. At the end of the corridor was an open window. He went there, lit a cigarette, tossed the match out into the night air, and waited. A few minutes later the men began to leave. As he expected, when Anselmo appeared at the threshold, his eyes found Warburg's. Anselmo nodded when Warburg lifted his finger. Anselmo was not a man to avoid what he knew was inevitable. He walked down the corridor to Warburg, with his left hand stretched behind, firmly gripping his son's arm, pulling him along.

Warburg had his cigarette pack ready, and each man took one. Then each took his light from Warburg's match.

"This is my son Enzo," Anselmo said, adding with a smile, "He takes his name from the *end* of Lorenzo." He nudged the young man forward. "He is the end of me." An old joke between them.

"I'm David," Warburg said. They shook hands. Enzo's grip was firm.

"My son was in the mountains," Anselmo said, a euphemism for service with the Partisans.

"I've heard that," Warburg said. "So you know about resistance."

Enzo nodded.

"Are you with Jocko?"

"No. Lionni works alone. Almost alone. A small group from Palestine. You know him?"

"When he was with the Delegation, I knew him, yes. Seems long ago. He left Rome. Are you saying he's back?"

Enzo did not reply. His father poked him. With eyes downcast,

Enzo said, "They say he was in Palestine. Italian kibbutz. Training with the Irgun. He returned to Rome last month."

"Where is he?"

Enzo did not reply. His father nudged him. Enzo raised his face, with a miserable look that Warburg immediately understood.

"Enzo," Warburg said, "you are sworn to secrecy. Is that right?"

The young man nodded.

"I am not asking you to betray Lionni. But do this for me, would you? Get this to him." Warburg produced a card, the contact card he handed out to the desperate and bereft, if judiciously—not wanting to promise what he could not deliver. "Pass the word that I need to see him."

Where had Lionni disappeared to the year before? He answered with a rambling account. Kibbutz Lavi, in Galilee, near Tiberias, was a collective founded in the late twenties. Lionni had liked Galilee for its rolling hills and familiar weather, the wet, dank winter. Umbrian grape growers had been among the first to make *aliyah* at Lavi. Once the war broke out, the vines were neglected, as the young men of the kibbutz divided between those who joined the British Army and those who went underground with the Haganah. By 1943, Lavi, because of its still lively ties to Italy, had been a training center for Jews joining the Partisans there. At the onset of the Irgun's open revolt against the Mandate authority in 1944, the kibbutz had become a training center for the underground. Jewish Partisans with whom Lionni conspired during his time as a fugitive from the Nazis had brought him there.

Warburg interrupted Lionni. "So it was Fossoli?" He let the question elaborate itself in silence. *So it was Fossoli that sent you away and brought you back, armed?* In the nearly thirty minutes he'd been speaking, Lionni had not mentioned the death camp. The two were seated at a corner table in the deep, isolated interior of a Trastevere café. Warburg had found a note under his door the night before, instructing him to come here. It was late afternoon. Lionni was haggard-looking, coughing, obviously ill. That had not stopped him from talking. He seemed eager to explain himself to Warburg.

"Of course. Conscription. I was conscripted at Fossoli."

"But into an army too late to kill Germans."

"Perhaps not." Lionni coughed, a hollow rattling from deep in his chest. He wore a soiled shirt under a tattered serge coat, what was left of a suit. Under his clothes the skin hung on his bones. His fingers *were* bones. His flesh was gristle.

"But it's the British you attack now."

"We made our point. It remains to be seen if the point must be made again."

Warburg shook his head. "From reports out of London, Attlee has just ordered a doubling of the Cyprus garrison, which presumably means a doubling of internment capacity. There are plans being laid for a camp in British-controlled Port Said. The Admiralty has ordered two fresh destroyer squadrons deployed to the Mediterranean, one to Piraeus and one to Malta. The JDC was preparing to buy ships for emigration, but to run a Royal Navy blockade? Never. So much for the point you made. Incredibly stupid, Jocko."

"The embassy was the center of operations for Cyprus. A new Fossoli."

"No. Don't confuse the two."

"You think we Jews should simply wait until the world decides to be nice to us? The British will never yield the Mandate without force being applied. Some Jews are uneasy about force. A habit of passivity. If Attlee is doubling the Cyprus garrison, that is good. It means he heard us. And he must not be able to unroll fresh wire there without the world knowing it. A bomb in Rome — and the eyes of the world go to Cyprus."

"We want the eyes of the world on the camps in Germany, Jocko. In Hungary, Romania, Italy. There's the outrage — Jews still in those camps. Some in the same striped uniforms."

"Jewish victims. To the world, not so different from Jewish vermin. Meanwhile, the Nazis escape. Speaking of outrage."

"What do you mean?"

"That's why I returned to Rome. Nazis escaping *here*. Rome is a sewer of Nazis, fat turds washing along its tunnels, spilling out into the sea, away from Europe. Jews can't leave, Nazi criminals can. So don't speak to me of outrage."

Warburg was accustomed to layering over his uneasiness with the business of cigarettes, and he did that now. Lionni declined his offer with a snap of his head. Waving away the match, Warburg said, "How?"

Lionni snorted. "*Afifyor.*"

Warburg waited.

Lionni said, "The Pope."

"The Pope helps Nazis escape?"

"Of course. He is a Nazi himself."

"That's not true, Jocko."

"A friend of Nazis. There are German criminals on Vatican premises all across Rome. Places exempt from being searched. The Germans approach the Red Cross for displaced person visas with identity papers stamped by the Pontifical Commission." Lionni produced a sheaf of papers from his coat and spread the sheets on the table, smoothing creases with the same deliberation that had marked his display of the railroad map at their first meeting. Warburg had been brought here, he realized, to be shown this. He leaned forward. Lionni's nubby fingers poked the papers as he spoke — here, here, here. What Warburg saw was a list:

> Jesuit Academy, Via Borgia 6, Slovenian
> Franciscan Monastery of the Holy Spirit, Via Sicilia
> Illirici Foundation: Collegium Illiricum, Croatian
> Collegium Orientale, Via Carlo Alberto 7, Slovenian
> Pontificio Collegio Croato di San Girolamo, Croatian
> Santa Maria dell'Anima, Piazza Navona, Austro-German

Another page held a list of names:

> Ante Vujovic, Minister of Defense, Croatia
> Lazar Socic, Police Chief, Zagreb
> Dr. Stefan Pujak, Director, Krajina Institute
> Eng Valiljevic, Commerce Minister, Croatia
> Marislav Petrovic, SS Formation, Croatia

Dr. Boris Miladic, Chief of Police, Sarajevo
Jusuf Kosovac, Ustashe assassin
Rev. Slobodan Vukas, Sisak
Isa Noljetinac, Chief of Police, Pristina
Dr. Dimitrije Najdanovic, University of Dubrovnik
Dr. Hefer, Deputy to Ante Pavelic
Rev. Krunoslav Draganovic, Director of Resettlement

Warburg looked up at Lionni. "These are Slavic names."

"Known criminals from Yugoslavia. All at present guests of the Holy See in Rome. Here in Rome. Now."

"You said Germans."

"I said Germans receive false identities from the Vatican. We are working on the German identities. They forgo the name Hans."

"You said the Pontifical Commission. Which commission?"

"Pontificia Commissione di Assistenza."

Warburg reined in the rhythm of his own breathing: Kevin Deane's commission. "Why would the Pontifical Commission help Nazi war criminals to escape?"

"They are not war criminals. They are 'anti-Communist heroes.' And not all of them seek to escape. Some are waiting to return. Waiting in Rome to be restored, in Croatia, for example. No need as yet for new identities. Proud men. The Pope believes a Catholic regime is coming soon to Zagreb. The Pope makes it come. To defeat the Bolshevik Tito. So Croatian heroes sit quietly, for example"—Lionni poked the page—"here in the Monastery of the Holy Spirit. Headquarters of a new Catholic Croatia."

"Holy Spirit, on Via Sicilia? Wasn't that Padre Antonio? Your friend?"

"Yes. It was from him we began to learn what was happening. He was forced out of Holy Spirit. The French nuns were replaced by Croatian friars." Lionni slapped the table, the pages jumped. "Do you know what happened to Jews in Croatia?"

"I know it was bad. The death camp at Jasenovac. But we see few refugees from Croatia."

"You know why."

Warburg did know, although not until that moment.

Lionni coughed brutally. "There were forty-five thousand Jews in Croatia in 1940. Now, none. Forty thousand murdered—by ratio, the worst toll in all of Europe. Why is that? Croatia is the most Catholic nation of them all. That is why. Jasenovac was run by priests. Finished with Jews, they murdered Orthodox. Roma. The Ustashe makes the Nazis seem good. The Pope met personally with Pavelic in the Vatican. Pavelic is to be head of the new Croatian state. The Vatican is protecting him."

"You know this? You know where Pavelic is?"

"No. But we will learn. He is here in Rome. The Pope protects him. The Pope has convinced the Allies to release Croatian prisoners. The Americans are arming them."

"How do you know all this?"

Lionni shrugged. "I have a hairdresser on the Via Veneto."

"You said the Red Cross. The Red Cross is issuing DP visas to war criminals?"

"Yes. The Red Cross does not refuse the Pope."

"You have a source in the Red Cross?"

Lionni shrugged again. "We have many sources."

Warburg toyed with his cigarette, tracing the edge of the ashtray with its tip. He thought of the Villa Arezzo on the Aventine Hill, where he had his offices; the crammed corridors, walls marked proudly with the Geneva cross; the once grand stairways now lined with cartons. He thought of the rooms lined with file cabinets into which he himself had plunged, desperate to match names, uncover histories that might qualify this DP or that DP for the prized visa. The Red Cross was a final arbiter of legitimacy—no, of life itself. Until the Red Cross said otherwise, stateless refugees simply did not exist.

For most of the past year, neither had she existed. Yet only weeks ago, Warburg saw her, in her blue uniform, in the canteen. He had not seen her since. "Did she go with you?" he asked now.

When Lionni did not acknowledge the question, Warburg added,

"To Galilee." He gave Lionni a chance to answer. When still he said nothing, Warburg went on, "She disappeared from Rome when you did. Now she is back, same as you. Same schedule."

"Kibbutz Lavi is for Jews only," Lionni said with ice in his voice, a match to his dark-hued skeletal body that could have been cold with death already.

So Lionni knew of whom he was speaking, and Lionni's answer told Warburg more than he had asked. "She converted," Warburg said, as if testing the outlandish idea by speaking it aloud. "After Fossoli." Lionni did not respond. It was true. "She became a Jew."

Warburg's heart hammered. Still, Lionni said nothing.

"Am I right?" Warburg asked. "How would that work?"

"She was instructed by a rabbi."

"But to become a Jew out of pity? Is that—"

"She is one of us," Lionni said. "Becoming one of us saved her."

Warburg recalled how she had fled from him in the canteen. Was this what she could not talk about? But he realized that the caring woman's embrace of a devastated people was not unlike his own.

Lionni gave way to another fit of coughing. When he had collected himself, he said again, "The Red Cross cannot refuse the Pope, even if they know the identities presented are false. Identities presented to the Vatican are false, too, of course. But the Vatican Secretariat requires photographs."

"If the Red Cross required photographs, no one would cross a border in Europe."

"That is why our source in the Red Cross is insufficient," Lionni said. "The Vatican has the means of checking photographs, determining who the fugitives are, which no doubt it does. The Vatican only pretends not to know whom they are dealing with. You have an American friend in the Pontifical Commission, no? The sealed signatures below the Latin rescripts we see are Perugino, Filipepi, Bugiardini. We do not see the signature of your friend Deane. What does he know of this? There are dozens of officials on that commission operating all over Europe. Does he know what they are doing in its name? Making documents that certify good German Catholics."

"And you know that these Germans are not good?" Warburg was off balance, having Deane brought into this.

"If they are good, why are they not dead?"

"But you don't know who they are."

"They are SS. They are senior Gestapo. Their real names are on the Allied war criminal lists. They are being hunted. That is why they need Vatican documents in other names. That they have come here, or soon will, proves they are important Nazis. Otherwise they would not be making it as far as Rome. They follow a map drawn for them by Himmler. He called it *Aussenweg*, the Road Out."

"How do you know that?"

Lionni tossed his head sideways, as if Himmler's posthumous mischief was obvious. "The map points them to Argentina. But from Vienna to Zagreb to Trieste to Rome, they are using the Croatian underground, based here. The Croatians are protected by the Vatican. The Croatians are creating a Catholic state-in-exile in Buenos Aires, in the event they do not push Tito back to Serbia soon. For now, Rome remains the Croatian foothold. Hence Pavelic here, somewhere, awaiting his chance at Zagreb again. The escaping Germans care nothing for Zagreb. To them the Croatians are the sheep of the Cyclops. German Nazis riding out of Europe clinging to the Croatian underside the way Odysseus and his men rode out under the sheep of Polyphemus. The Croatians are happy to be used in this way, but they are prevented from knowing whom they are dealing with."

"Only the document providers in the Vatican know that."

Lionni coughed. Warburg sensed how much less than everything he was being told. If the Jewish fighters knew senior Nazis were at large and making their escape, why not just kill them? But then the escape route would detour away from Rome, to Istanbul or Barcelona. Lionni and his comrades wanted Rome to remain the *Aussenweg* crossroads.

"You said important Nazis. How important?"

"So far — how shall I say? — *Gruppenführer, Oberführer*, not *Reichsführer*. Himmler's escape route is being tested before the top Nazis try it. We know the most infamous criminals are waiting — in Vienna, in

Trieste, in Marseille, in Basel. Waiting to run, waiting until the route is proved safe."

"Who?"

Lionni raised his hand, ticked his fingers: "Klaus Barbie, Gestapo chief in Lyons; Franz Stangl, commandant of Treblinka; Alois Brunner, commandant of Drancy; Adolf Eichmann, the deportation chief in Hungary; Gustav Wagner, commandant of Sobibor; Hans Stendahl, Stangl's deputy; Klaus Hillmann, Gestapo chief in Paris—"

Warburg interrupted, indicating the list on the table between them. "But the men on this list—"

"Croatians, Slovenians, resident in Rome. Monasteries, churches, living as priests, monks. We know where they are. We are watching them. The *Germans* are on Himmler's list, men he promised passage on the *Aussenweg*. For now, most are waiting, but they are expected in Rome. They will be greeted with large automobiles bearing the SCV plates of Vatican City."

"And when they come—"

"We are waiting also."

"So the Germans are ushered into the monasteries with the Jesuits and Franciscans, robes ready for them," Warburg said, understanding. "And you cannot target underlings or mere Croatians, however despicable, because it would set off alarms."

Lionni nodded.

"Himmler is dead."

"Yes. His cyanide *Götterdämmerung*. Typical coward's end."

"Yet you have the list of those he promised *Aussenweg*? How is that?"

Now Lionni was immobile.

"And no source in the Vatican?"

"Your friend the monsignor will be our source. You."

Warburg stared at Lionni, having come to a final recognition. "So, Jocko, you have killer teams here in Rome, but for Germans, not the British. The British embassy bombing was a diversion."

"Such things can have more than one purpose."

"But the bombing *was* to deceive Stangl and Eichmann."

"And also the Pope. We want him to bring his German favorites to Rome. Or do you believe the Pope is blind, like Polyphemus?"

The gathering of the scarlet-robed prelates, along with hundreds of violet-cloaked bishops and black-and-red *monsignori,* in the apse of St. Peter's Basilica was one of the world's great spectacles. Behind them, the mammoth nave was jammed with tens of thousands of the faithful, and the loggias on both aisles were crowded with diplomats in white tie and tails, sashes and medals. Fur-capped soldiers, pike-bearing Swiss Guards, candle carriers, censer-waving thurifers, ribbon-bedecked members of the black aristocracy, the females covered with lace mantillas—no circus parade more colorful, no menagerie stocked with more exotic creatures. At this consistory, the wartime decline of the College of Cardinals—normally numbering seventy but now down to thirty-seven—was being reversed, the forces of the Vicar of Christ on Earth being rallied. And, with Joseph Stalin clawing at Europe, just in time. The Church militant was on the march!

A roar went up from the far reaches of the basilica as a dozen papal footmen in red, maneuvering their shoulder poles, carried the Pope in on his *sedia gestatoria.* Deane, because of his height, had no trouble seeing. From the gilded, silk-upholstered armchair, His Holiness rhythmically waved the sign of the cross while the throng cried "*Viva il Papa!*" Trumpets blared, massive organ pipes bellowed, and the papal choir intoned the polyphonic Bruckner rendition of *Ecce sacerdos magnus,* but resounding above all else, *Papa! Papa! Papa!*

Slowly and somewhat unsteadily, the Pope glided up the center aisle. Light flashed off the lenses of his rimless spectacles. His visage was, as always, organized around a stern, unsmiling mouth. Perhaps he had dallied in his velvet rooms while Hitler stalked Europe, but Deane knew it was not from cowardice. This Pope was showing himself now, grimly determined before what lay ahead: the apocalyptic battle with the one whose name meant steel.

The ceremony began with the *obbedienza*—a procession of the existing cardinals, who, one by one, presented themselves at the papal throne, each with his crimson *cappa magna* flowing behind, which attendants carried as if every cardinal were an aged bride. Each prelate threw himself to the ground to kiss the Pope's extended foot, and each was then hoisted to kiss the air beside the Pope's sallow cheeks. *I obey.*

The new cardinals, thirty-two of them, were posted in a large semicircle before the throne, and their contrast in youth and vigor with the older prelates was dramatic. As the choir chanted the *Te Deum,* they prostrated themselves with a certain practiced grace, hoods alike in being pulled over their heads. These were the field marshals in the coming conflict, men chosen more for the strategic significance of their seats than for their individual brilliance, much less holiness. China, Latin America, the heart of Europe, London, New York, Berlin. Stalin's archenemy Adamo Stefano Sapieha of Kraków was here to be elevated, despite being nearly eighty, and so was Thomas Tienchen-sing, archbishop of Peking, despite his pastoral charge over fewer than ten thousand Catholics amid a pagan population of five million. The one pagan on whom Pius had fixed his sights was Mao Tse-tung.

The Right Reverend Monsignor Kevin Deane was here, as supernumerary privy chamberlain, standing behind the red-cloaked prostrate form of Francis Spellman, the fifty-six-year-old archbishop of New York, the Boss. As Spellman's chaplain, Deane's job was to ensure that the faceless attendants properly swished Spellman's skirts as he took his turns in the sacred choreography, getting up from the floor once the litany was finished and mounting the stairs to receive his ring, zucchetto, and biretta. To all appearances, Deane was a stoic courtier, but his mind had been cut loose.

For most observers, the high drama of the consistory came from the Pope's appointment of the men from Eastern Europe and China, the front lines of the war against the atheistic Communists, but what struck Deane was Argentina. One of those on the floor before him was Antonio Caggiano, the fifty-seven-year-old archbishop who, until recently, was the Vatican chief of Catholic Action, a tool for jacking up the Church's political influence everywhere. But Caggiano had just been named archbishop of Rosario, a second-rate city of about half a million, nearly two hundred miles northwest of Buenos Aires. What the hell? Deane eyed the prostrate form of the Argentine prelate, blanketed in red, impossible to read—but not to guess. He was the man who'd seen to the stashing of the Croatian gold in the crypt below Santa Marta—gold that had mysteriously and entirely disappeared right after Deane had dutifully reported it to Tardini. What the hell indeed.

Only two things suggested why such a minor city as Rosario might have been sent the Red Hat. Rosario was the center of the junta leader Juan Perón's strength, the place from which the anti-Communist colonel was poised to solidify control of Argentina. And, nicely positioned on the Parana River, inland from the Atlantic, it was a harbor that passenger vessels favored over the grimy industrial port at Buenos Aires—the debarkation point, therefore, of many travelers arriving from Europe. The Rosario–Vatican Express.

> V. *Agnus Dei, qui tollis peccata mundi.*
> R. *Parce nobis, Domine.*

The choir had rounded the last curve and was heading into the litany's home stretch. Deane picked up the chant himself.

> V. *Agnus Dei, qui tollis peccata mundi.*
> R. *Exaudi nos, Domine.*
> V. *Agnus Dei, qui tollis peccata mundi.*
> R. *Miserere nobis.*
> V. *Christe, audi nos*
> R. *Christe, exaudi nos.*
> V. *Kyrie eleison.*
> R. *Christe eleison. Kyrie eleison . . .*

The new cardinals rose to their knees, then to their feet, as the choir prayed the souls of the faithful departed into peace. Amen.

Deane watched closely. The Boss did well, moving with an agile grace that bespoke his happiness. Acolytes fluttered among the prelates, arranging capes. When Spellman turned briefly to beam back at Deane, Deane nodded. The Boss had not been named the Vatican secretary of state, but neither had anyone else, and it had become clear that the Pope was reserving the office to himself. So if Spellman had not moved ahead, neither had he fallen behind. Indeed, he was arguably the most powerful figure on the sanctuary floor today, surely the most powerful non-Italian. With Europe in ruins, only the American Church could carry the costs of the Vatican's administration now: Spellman was the Vatican's new banker. But the diminutive new cardinal was certain that his bond with His Holiness went deeper than such worldly ties. Spellman believed that there was a personal intimacy between them, an absolute sense of trust — enhanced, from his side, by a reverence that approached veneration.

But Deane knew that, in some way, Spellman was kidding himself. The Pope's refusal to name him or anyone else as secretary of state was more than a simple reservation of the diplomatic portfolio to Ourselves. It was a way of making sure the Vatican bureaucracy lacked a center, which in practice meant that from now on the fiefdoms would compete, keeping secrets from one another, guaranteeing that no one would behold Church power whole. It was obvious to Deane why such scattering served the purposes of the supremely wily Pius XII. The Pope and his court had been bested by Hitler, despite postwar Vatican triumphalism. Not just bested — humiliated. Pius was determined not to repeat that failure with his archnemesis, Stalin. If Russia was a riddle wrapped in a mystery inside an enigma, then the Holy See, under its genius pontiff, and he alone, would be more so.

When the cardinal archbishop of New York now kissed the Pope's foot, he was not fooling. Deane chastised himself for wincing at the sight of the ritual obeisance, which in any other context would have been seen as groveling pure and simple. He reminded himself that there was a cross embroidered on the Pope's velvet slipper, and it was that sign of Christ, so they said, that was being kissed. But really.

Deane backed away from his disdain. This ritual of allegiance had been enacted by the predecessors of these men for a thousand years. Foppery and vanity, all part of the picture. Yet this pinnacle of the sacramental pyramid topped off not just Catholicism but Western civilization, which over the past six years had very nearly succeeded in suicide. Even museums were laid waste across the continent, yet the Church was no museum. What but dissolution was left to Europe except the last vestiges of Christendom? This.

"Somewhat to my surprise," Deane said later, "I was moved by it. The flowing crimson cloaks and all."

"Reminded me of Westminster Abbey," Sister Thomas said. "Especially the ermine shoulder capes. You lads do like your regalia, don't you. Put us nuns to shame." With a flick of her head she made her black veil swirl. "At Westminster, of course, the peers carry sandwiches in their coronets."

Deane laughed. Yet then he said, "Why shouldn't we be moved, though, to find our deepest fear — the near triumph of nihilism just yesterday, the thunder of its approach again tomorrow — addressed directly by the glories of that place and its rituals?"

Sister Thomas did not reply.

Deane pressed, "No?"

Outdoing him in earnestness, she asked, "What would those rituals mean in Cinecittà, Bergen-Belsen, or Föhrenwald? What's the purpose of all this" — she gestured toward the crowded room — "if not somehow to help the poor people still awaiting succor after all these months?"

Her question silenced them, and they turned. Monsignor Deane and Sister Thomas were standing near the great frescoed wall in the Sala Regia, the broad antechamber to the Sistine Chapel, which had long been used as the hall for receiving princes and royal ambassadors. Today it was serving a more mundane function, as the site of the celebratory collation for curial officials, senior Vatican functionaries, and VIP guests, including the Duke of Savoy, the Prince of Naples, the various contessas in their mantillas, the bedecked diplomatic corps. The cardinals were gathered in the Sala Clementina, the grander hall at the entrance to the papal apartments — the Third Floor. His Holiness would not deign to present himself even there, but he could no doubt hear the happy chatter of men whose day had come. Here in the Sala Regia, their hangers-on could celebrate more robustly, flapping streamers on the kites that had just climbed in the only wind that mattered. Breath of God.

Deane and Sister Thomas fell into separate reveries, each taking in the festive scene. In a nearby corner, a string quartet, decked out in tails, was chirping away at Vivaldi. Of all before him, it was the women whom Deane noticed—the patrician beauties in gowns and lace head coverings; the dozen or so nuns, like Thomas. Not long ago, having women at such a gathering would be unthinkable. Chalk up another to Mother Pascalina, running the Pope's office. It was said that she rather liked bubbly functions like this.

Deane was holding a crystal cup with fruit punch laced with Asti Spumante. Sister Thomas had let the drink tray pass. She was looking at the nearby fresco, the scene, from five hundred years before, of Pope Gregory XI's return from Avignon to Rome. The painting was cluttered with figures, not one of whom was female. Sister Thomas indicated it. "Who's missing?" she asked.

Deane looked. "What?"

"Catherine of Siena. She should be in there somewhere. It was she who badgered the Pope into returning to Rome. Shamed him, really. Don't you think Catherine should be there, perhaps on that little ledge with the fellow in feathers?"

"She was a Dominican sister of yours, as I recall." Deane grinned. He gestured at the crowd. "But the women are present here, and so"— he pointed at a Maltese knight—"are the fellows in feathers." His eye then fell on a familiar figure, the swarthy, lean priest in his well-tailored cassock, standing beside a faded beauty twice his age, a woman whose long black dress nevertheless displayed her well-preserved figure, whose mantilla did not so much cloak her hair and face as showcase them. With one of her long-gloved hands she coquettishly fluttered a fan at her cheek. The other she had through the priest's arm, with high-court formality.

"It's Lehmann," Deane said. Given the din of talk around them, he and the nun could have been alone. Still, his voice was barely more than a whisper. "That must be his mother."

"Lady of Spain," Sister Thomas said.

With a closer look, the woman's pallor outweighed her elegance — a hint of the pathetic in the way she'd forced herself into her presentation gown, as if this were her cotillion. Even from across the room, the coal black of her hair had a bottled dullness. "Her ladyship," Deane said, "is not getting the message that time is sending."

"The lad keeps her young," Sister Thomas said.

A fancy older couple presented themselves to Lehmann and his mother with familiarity. The priest bowed and took the woman's hand, thrilling her with his kiss. Deane thought, Not Casanova, but a mama's boy. Lehmann's mother now held the fan at her décolletage.

"Did you notice where he stood in the ceremony?" Deane asked.

"From where I was sitting? Are you serious?"

"He was supernumerary privy chamberlain, same as me. Standing behind his cardinal-designate."

"Berlin?"

"Rosario."

"Argentina? Caggiano?"

"Sí."

"That's a bit blatant, don't you think?"

"Or a signal. A very public signal, declaring that Lehmann is a man to trust, if you are a man with reason to distrust. An imprimatur, stamped for those with an interest in Argentina. Have you learned anything?"

"Yes. Did you not see the rose?" The question was her way of saying, Not here. "I put it there this morning."

"This morning I was laying out Spellman's new buskins and mozzetta. You laugh, Sister. But when they depend on you for the small things, the big things come naturally."

"I don't laugh, Monsignor. I've been known to sew a button on His Eminence Cardinal Tisserant's mozzetta. And Tisserant is part of what I need to tell you about. But now you should be mingling, listening to the gossip so you'll have something to tell your cardinal." Sister Thomas excused herself with the barest of nods, then glided away.

A waiter drifted by, white tie and tails, white gloves. Deane placed his cup on the tray, which never stopped moving. The happily reconstituted College of Cardinals would be adjourning soon from the Sala Clementina, each of the newly consecrated prelates to hustle off to his own private festivities for the family and friends he had brought from home. By Deane's arrangement—a coup—Spellman's party would convene in one of the spectacular rooms of the Vatican Museum, the Sala Rotonda, modeled after the Pantheon, centered on a massive bust of Zeus and a gilt bronze statue of Hercules. When Deane had escorted His Excellency there the day before, to show him, Spellman had clapped his hands with pleasure, saying, "Wait'll Henry Luce gets a load of this." Feet bouncing under his cassock, Spellman had danced a little jig, and, not for the first time, the short, stout archbishop had reminded Deane of the comic strip character the Little King. But then Spellman noted the sculptures of the gods. "Who are these fellows?"

Deane grinned. "For Henry Luce? *Time* magazine? Let's just say Abraham and Moses."

"Right," Spellman had chirped. "Jew boys."

Once, Deane would have thought nothing of such a crack, but now it unsettled him—an unfortunate moment to feel a spike of dislike, since Spellman then said, "And by the way, Kevin, now that I have the Red Hat, I'll be passing along a miter."

"Your Eminence?"

"My new auxiliary bishop in New York. Any ideas?"

"I can draw up a list for you, suggest some candidates."

"No need for that, my friend. None at all." Spellman winked and said, "Coming soon to a theater near you." The cardinal gave Deane's shoulder a congratulatory slap, as if his episcopal consecration had just happened. Deane blushed. This news was not unexpected, yet it filled him almost completely with pleasure. Almost—but for the sour taste in his throat. *Jew boys.*

The next morning, Deane celebrated an early Mass for the cardinal's New York entourage. Henry Luce was there with his wife, Clare Boothe Luce, the most famous convert in America and one of the few women in the U.S. Congress. She had only recently turned to the Church, devastated after the death in an auto accident of her nineteen-

year-old daughter. As Deane placed the sacred wafer on the congress-
woman's tongue, he saw tears coursing down her cheeks. For her, this
entire religion was an exercise in grief and always would be. Deane
realized that, after the past year, that's what it should have been for
him, too. The feeling shook him.

An hour later, he was in the sacristy, waiting. Sister Thomas soon
arrived, satchel in hand. She plunked it on the vestment case next
to the briefcase Deane had already placed there. She unbuckled her
satchel and began pulling folders out of it. "You were right," she said. "I
found cables in the file, mislabeled, perhaps deliberately. The Americans arrested Ante Pavelic two months ago. He had been hiding in a
monastery in Salzburg, disguised as a monk. Someone tipped off the
Americans and they snagged him. They were about to transfer him to
Frankfurt, where senior Nazis are being held pending the war crimes
trials. The archbishop intervened, by his own report."

"The archbishop?"

"Of Salzburg. Grubner. He protested the violation of cloister in the
arrest. He indicated the Holy Father's interest. Pavelic was mysteriously released. The cables are dated as of weeks ago."

Deane scanned the yellow cable forms she had spread on the case.
"Can we know if the rumors are true," he asked, "about his being
here?"

"Not likely in Vatican City itself. Croatians seem to be ensconced
in the extraterritorial dependencies. They got to Rome first, snapped
those places up. Have you discussed with Spellman what Warburg told
you?"

"*Aussenweg*? His Eminence waved it off as Tito's propaganda. Croatia is Catholic to the core, and Tito is a Catholic-hating Bolshevik—
period. And if there are Germans being credentialed by the Pontifical
Commission, it's because German Catholics, like Adenauer, *resisted*
Hitler, and they should be supported now—also period. Besides, Germans, too, need compassion, and the vast majority of them were as
much victims of the Nazi cabal as anyone."

"Do you believe that?"

"Look," Deane said, "if I was German, believing what Germans believed, would I have behaved so differently?"

"The SS?"

"Not the SS, no. I would not have behaved like that."

"So why the compassion?"

"The Church judges and forgives. And then it helps. Sanctuary, Sister, is for the guilty. We may not like it, but there it is. The Vatican's ancient instinct is to offer sanctuary. Is that bad?"

"It depends, Monsignor. Wouldn't you say it depends?"

"Sister, Spellman is proud of the fact that it was he who insisted with General Marshall that Vatican visas not be overly scrutinized. Guards at American checkpoints don't look twice if they see the seal with crossed keys. Visas are the new sanctuary. This whole thing depends on the Allies' being loath to antagonize the Pope. Spellman spent all of Thursday afternoon with Tardini. And the next morning, all morning long, with Tisserant. Tisserant is pushing the innocent-Catholic line, too."

"Tisserant approved Vichy," the nun said. "In his mind, the French criminals deserve protection, which he offers by protecting the Germans. Tisserant's ties to Vichy are well known on the Third Floor. And he was just promoted to cardinal bishop. What does that tell you, Monsignor?"

"Tells me the train is leaving the station, get aboard. Commies are the problem, not Nazis." Deane took a small key from within the folds of his cassock and unlocked his briefcase. He withdrew a large manila envelope, unfastened the figure-eight tie, and spilled out its contents: photographs. "Take these," he said.

"The Germans?"

"Yes. These are the big-fish candidates for *Aussenweg*, the photos to match with what you find in the visa application pool. These characters send in faked baptismal certificates — Catholics! — looking to get new names validated."

Sister Thomas flipped through the pictures, official Wehrmacht portraits for the most part, stern faces, sharply peaked hats with leather visors, the telltale eagle badges. Three or four wore the Waffen-SS hat with its skull. "Grim lookers," she said. "The inner circle?"

"Treblinka, Sobibor, Drancy. Like that."

"That's what I meant—when you sang of sanctuary—by 'it depends.'"

"Yes."

"But I can promise you, Monsignor, no one wears hats with skull badges in the photographs that come across the visa desk."

"The photos they submit to the Holy See will be doctored to make them look like S-Bahn ticket takers," Deane said. "But these eyes, these noses, these faces—same men."

Sister Thomas fingered the photos soberly. Then she asked, "Where does Mr. Warburg get these?"

"From Jews," Deane answered. "Not sure who. There may be Haganah units after these Nazis. Maybe Jewish renegades from the British Army. Polish fighters. Warburg won't tell me."

She took in the photos for a moment, then said coldly, "Let's assume the Nazis who've gone to ground *are* looking to get out. Safe assumption. If they expect to help one another, then yes, their names *could* have been compiled. At some organizing center. Vienna, you say? And interested Jewish groups might have gotten hold of the list. Plausible. It would be a simple matter to match names with German file photos. These. But not addresses. Traceable addresses would come into play only here at the Vatican, when the Germans submit false papers for authentication. They supply addresses because we have to be able to respond to them."

"That's what the Jews want. Contact points. And they want advance notice of German plans to come through Rome. Rome, according to Warburg, is halfway between Vienna and Buenos Aires." Deane fell silent for a beat, then said, "This all assumes that the Holy See has put itself at the service of men like these. Do you believe that?"

Sister Thomas lifted one of the photos, a man with the face of a vulture. Slowly, she shook her head. "No. Not the Holy See. Lehmann, yes. Maybe the low-level clerics who sign off on the applications. Who

knows what that Croatian gold is buying by now? But Tardini? Mon-
tini? They would never allow such a thing without His Holiness knowing about it."

"But Argentina," Deane said. "Someone senior advanced the Red
Hat for Caggiano. And where *did* that gold go? And why did it disappear right after I told Tardini about it? Meanwhile, shady people are
going to Argentina. You yourself have seen those phony monks."

Deane's agitation might have sparked hers. But the nun's mind was
stuck on something else. She said, "So if Warburg's source *is* Haganah
. . . what? I find a photo match for one of these Nazis, give you the
monster's new identity and an address, you pass it on to Warburg, and
. . . then what? We become party to Jewish revenge? Assassination? Is
that what you're asking me to do?"

Deane did not answer her.

She said, "Isn't that what makes us different, that we bring the criminals to trial? Isn't vengeance a mark of the Jewish God, not ours? Don't
we have the law instead of revenge?"

"The law, Sister," Deane said, "that comes to us from the Jews."

"But these Jews blew up my nation's embassy!" Sister Thomas's
cheeks had suddenly become as white as her wimple, the starched
linen frame of her face. Her mouth was drawn thin with feeling. Her
eyes were flint. "My brother was killed in the Blitz! And now the Jews
blow *us* up! England's embassy! These Jews are imitating Nazis."

Deane touched her arm. "Hold on. Hold on, Sister."

She checked herself and whispered, "I just need to know what you're
asking me to do."

He pressed her arm through the multilayered folds of her sleeve.
Don't compare them to Nazis, he wanted to say, they just want to prevent the bastards from escaping. But of course she was right. What,
Warburg's people would arrest the Nazis and send them off to the tribunal at Frankfurt? Not likely. Deane had allowed Warburg to steam-
roll him.

He maintained his grip on her arm, and she did not resist it. He
felt bone through the folds of her garment. Now he saw how thin her

face was, thinner than before. "No," he said, forcing himself to focus. "I'm not asking you to join in lawless revenge. I have another thought. Warburg is in over his head here. I've promised him nothing. What he laid out—significant and senior Vatican complicity with Nazis—I did not believe, and said so. It's only now that I see what's happened."

"So parse it for me."

"*Aussenweg*—that's all Warburg and his friends care about. The Germans. But that means Croatians, which means Catholics, which means us. There is a needle's eye here, Sister, and we have to thread it. You said the Americans had Ante Pavelic in custody in Salzburg. Did the cable say what Americans? What unit?"

Sister Thomas turned to the stack of cables, removing her arm from his grip. The nun flipped through the stack until she found it. She read, then held it up. "'CIC,' the cable says. What's that?"

"Counter-Intelligence Corps," Deane said. "It's what replaced the OSS after Truman canned Donovan. The head of CIC in Rome is General Mates."

"The man you worked for."

"You could just as readily say he was working for me."

"But isn't Mates the one who told you Lehmann was harmless? He investigated Lehmann and said he was free of German intrigue, but we know Lehmann is the linchpin of this entire bloody affair. And are we to believe your General Mates does not know what Lehmann is up to?"

"Sister, he is not *my* General Mates. But if CIC is involved here—"

"That means you will go back to him."

"Going to Mates instead of proceeding through the rogue Jews Warburg may be dealing with—that's the point."

Sister Thomas said nothing.

Deane said, "Which is complicated between us."

"Indeed so, since my own government's Secret Intel Service is still waiting to connect with me."

"Your Philip."

"No. His Majesty the King. My country."

"But your contact would be Philip? He's stayed in touch with you?"

"Monsignor, if I'd heard from Philip, wouldn't I have told you? Wasn't that our agreement?"

"Our agreement is why I am telling you about Mates, that I have to bring him into this. Our agreement matters to me, too."

Now it was Sister Thomas who put her hand on Deane's arm. He did not move. Pathetic celibate gesture, he thought. Yet for them erotically charged. That's what made it pathetic, of course.

After a moment, Deane said, "But you do know how to contact him. Philip."

"Yes."

"Maybe you should. There are things happening here that should be stopped. Treblinka, Sobibor, Drancy, the skulls on their hats! Sister, these men are high on the Allied war criminal list. It's Allied authorities who should be dealing with this, not assassins from Palestine. And not the Swiss Guard."

"But the Americans?" She removed her hand, began to pull the cables together, stacking them beside the photos. "Ante Pavelic in custody in Salzburg, then 'mysteriously released.' Doesn't that suggest the CIC let him go?"

"All the more reason for me to approach Mates. He'd be enraged to know that. Obviously the Americans in Austria had no idea who Pavelic was. But Mates ran the OSS Balkans operation. He knows the Ustashe. His operation supported Tito *against* Pavelic. If Pavelic *is* here, or in one of the Holy See dependencies, Mates would stop at nothing to get him."

"Nothing?"

"That's the problem, isn't it?" Deane said. "Where is the morality in all of this? You and I have to protect the morality."

"Monsignor, perhaps first we should try to find it." With this rebuke, she filled her satchel, buckled it, and made ready to go.

How ridiculous he felt. A pompous, self-important cleric, knowing nothing: *I kissed myself off.* All at once he realized that he'd failed to take in the most pressing fact of the encounter that was about to end.

The woman before him looked gaunt, almost sickly. Her arm was not bone, it was rope.

"Sister?"

"Monsignor?"

"I have to ask. You seem . . . are you losing weight? Are you unwell?"

She shook her head. "A fast, Monsignor. Fast and abstinence. This is a penitential season, wouldn't you say?"

TEN

Nakam *Means Revenge*

A S SOON AS Lehmann had left their small hotel room, Marguerite hurriedly douched herself, grimacing as always. She dressed, went downstairs, and, as always, paid the bill. But this time, she went as quickly as she could to a street off the Piazza Mattei, a narrow lane whose four- and five-story buildings kept it perpetually in shadow. The old buildings had been subdivided into lodging rooms and dormitories; no shops. The flats were transient hovels for indigents, Rome's riffraff. Nothing done there but sleep and fornicate.

Climbing up two grimy flights in a spiraling dark stairwell that reeked of urine, she came to a door, rapped softly, and waited. Moments later, the bolt of a lock was thrown, the door cracked. "It's me," she said, but even those two words carried a note of apology. She was not supposed to come here.

Lionni pulled the door fully open. He wore trousers and a sleeveless undershirt that drooped, leaving most of his chest exposed. He held his cane but was not leaning on it, and she realized he'd readied it for use as a club. Exposed, his chest was hollow, his scant flesh hanging loose. He was stooped and looked old. His face was etched with disapproval.

"I must talk." She brushed by him and entered the room, which was cluttered with a cot on one wall and a small table by another. Clothes were piled in a corner. Papers and file-card boxes covered the table.

Before Lionni could protest, Marguerite said, "I've just come from Lehmann. He told me there is a meeting of the Crusaders' high council today at a monastery somewhere outside Rome. Pavelic will be there. Harelip is going. It's the first time he will have left Spirito Santo. He is taking the Vatican car. We can follow him. He'll lead us to Pavelic."

Lionni registered what she'd said, looked calmly at her for a moment, then slowly shook his head. "Not 'we,' *cara*."

"What do you mean?"

"This is what Abel has been waiting for. He won't permit you to come."

"You've discussed this?"

Lionni fell into a fit of coughing, made his way to a pack of cigarettes, lit one, and inhaled deeply, an antidote. The cough was silenced. Finally he said, "Abel is the commander. And of course we have discussed this. Pavelic is a prize. He's not one we simply watch, hoping for someone bigger. No one is bigger. You know that."

"So they will kill him."

"Of course."

"But Abel needs us," she insisted. "He does not know these men, what they are capable of."

"He knows the type. Knows it well."

"He thinks these monks are women. They wear long skirts. Therefore they threaten nothing."

"You yourself have reported on the German priest, his hollow core, his weakness."

"The Croatians are different. These monks especially so."

Lionni shrugged.

"So you and I are left out?"

Lionni did not answer her.

"Only I am left out," she said, not with surprise.

"Not a woman's task, *cara*."

"Vukas is my task, Jocko," she declared. The image of the hare-lipped, brown-robed priest holding his handkerchief aloft, the starter's flag, had never left Marguerite's mind. Indeed, when she was with the German priest, but hiding from him in the space behind her closed eyes, she deliberately called it up: the scene at Sisak, the Franciscan with his hand over the heads of children, the ferocious dog, the trucks gunning around the track. She had regularly conjured the Croatian priest to avoid the German one, even as she went naked into the German's arms.

"We have left Vukas be, waiting for this," Lionni said. "We will leave him be today. The job of Vukas is to lead us to the behemoths. Pavelic is one. Abel would never permit you to come."

"There is my point. Abel is a fool if Vukas, too, is not counted as a behemoth, a monster!" She drew closer to Lionni. "At Lavi I was trained to fight. No one in Galilee spoke of what was a woman's task. Am I to take it now that a woman's task is to open her legs? That's all?"

Lionni's sad eyes were his unspoken response — that and the simple act of extending his arms. She went into his embrace, she who towered over him. He held her as she sobbed. The torrent broke through a year's worth of steely numbness. He did not insult her with the obvious: *We would be nowhere without what you bring us.* She entrusted him with her self-lacerating shame, unburdening her soul not in the least. From Trieste to Fossoli to Galilee to the shabby hotel room. *Yes, my open legs.*

Three hours later, Lionni was in the back seat of an innocuous black automobile, purring along the Via Cassia, the winding road that had carried travelers through the rough country north of Rome since the time of the caesars. Tombs hewn out of craggy rock, a ruined amphitheater, scrub pines clinging to an escarpment, a running precipice. On either side of Lionni sat a stolid, quiet man, each with a shortstock automatic rifle discreetly at his feet. In front were the driver and, in the passenger's seat, the only man whom Lionni knew, Abel, the commander.

Not that Lionni knew him, really — Abel certainly not being his actual name. These were hard men from Palestine. They depended on Lionni for his contacts, his knowledge of Rome, and the weight of his local authority, but there was no pretense that he was one of them. Lionni had his eyes fixed on a target ahead, into and out of which the car they were following came and went, according to the curves of the winding mountain road. Intermittently, he could see the license plate, the defining SCV.

From behind, it had been impossible to tell which of the four brown-robed friars was Vukas. Lionni's car had simply fallen in after the larger, fancier one when those Vatican plates had appeared, coming out of the gate at the Casa dello Spirito Santo. The Franciscans' driver was dressed in chauffeur's black, and judging by the speed with which he was taking the coils of the snaky, cliff-hugging road, he had earned the uniform. To keep their pursuit from being obvious, Abel's driver was staying back enough so that the car behind them pressed occasionally, its engine loud. More than once, whipping around a curve, the car behind had to brake. Mostly the road was too narrow for passing, which apparently made the following driver impatient. Lionni's throat was dry. Something was not right.

Perhaps the mistake was a function of the team's having thought of its prey as religious men. Lionni recalled Marguerite's warning: *Abel is a fool if*. . . If the Vatican limousine had been a military vehicle, would Abel have made a different calculation? A more discreet surveillance? Used a second trailing car? That Abel had rushed the matter, assuming the softness of a monastic convocation, was apparent to Lionni as soon as the first bump came from behind. Marguerite's words had, in fact, never left his mind: . . . *if Vukas, too, is not counted as a behemoth, a monster!*

The Jews' car was jolted sideways, toward the roadside, where a flimsy, low guardrail stood at the cliff's edge. The driver oversteered, sending them into a skid away from the cliff, and Lionni felt his center of gravity drop from the hollow behind his throat to the cavity of his lungs. The rear of the car slammed into the rock wall on the other side of the road. Before the driver could react, there was another bump from behind, a sharper one, and the car began to spin. From his place in the front seat, the commander turned to look back at who had done this to them, and Lionni took in the sight of Abel's face with acute precision, the mouth agape, the dark eyes wide. Abel had drawn his pistol. Lionni's mind was clear enough to know that Abel was intending to shoot at the car behind them, their unexpected enemy. But Lionni also understood that if Abel fired, he, Lionni, would take the bullet. Before that happened, their car slammed through the guardrail. Abel was thrown through the passenger window and out as the car went over the cliff's edge. Lionni hurtled forward, his face crushing first into the crown of the front seat, then against the rearview mirror, as his body plunged with the car and its men into the ravine.

The car came to rest upside down. Lionni alone was alive. He lay face-up where the door had sprung open. He was able to move only his eyes. The driver beside him had the steering wheel in a death grip. Abel's corpse, having been thrown clear, was caught on a jagged outcropping of rock about thirty feet above. The wheels of the car were still spinning. Lionni saw a robed figure making his way down into the ravine. He had a snarling dog on a short leash. The figure craned over the smoking tangle of wreckage, and his eyes met Lionni's. Lionni saw the misshapen mouth. The cold steel barrel of the man's Luger pressed hard against Lionni's upper lip, the last sensation he felt.

Giacomo Lionni had not been a religious Jew, but he'd have expected the prayers to be said, and they were. More than a thousand people crowded into the Great Synagogue the next day. Tradition called for members of the bereaved family to rend their garments, but as the pine box holding Lionni's body was carried into the sacred space, hundreds tore fabric, men and women both — some using the symbolic ribbon, most ripping their shirts or blouses. Though Lionni had disappeared from their midst more than a year before, Rome's Jews had not forgotten him. That he died in an automobile accident on the Via Cassia, along which he was said to have been driving alone, was as much a mystery as his disappearance had been, since Lionni was famous for his bicycle. It was news that he could drive a car.

"*Baruch atah Adonai Eloheinu . . . ,*" the rabbi intoned. David Warburg couldn't help wondering about the impulse to praise God's name in the thick of loss. But he knew so little. He was one of only a handful present who had cause to imagine that Lionni had not died the way the rabbi said, but the Delegation members with whom he'd spoken, including Lorenzo Anselmo, claimed to know no more than he. Through Legal Affairs at the U.S. embassy, Warburg had obtained the police report, and the matter was explicit: Lionni had driven a car through the guardrail on a mountain road near Sutri on the route to Ravenna. No other vehicles were involved, and he was alone. He had died instantly when the car slammed into the ravine floor, fifty feet below the road.

Warburg was hemmed in by the mourners around him, the packed pews a far cry from the regular Sabbath services. Jews all, yet it was clear from their wandering sorrow that few understood the Hebrew of the rabbi's recitations, or could follow the cantor's somber melodies. Men and women were not separated but mixed together in the sanctuary. Almost all of the women's heads were covered no matter where they sat, mainly by shawls. The heads of perhaps half the men were covered, and of those, most coverings were street hats. Warburg was among the minority who wore yarmulkes. He took in such details of the grieving congregation's appearance as if they were the reason for his observations.

When it came time to intone a psalm as the coffin was carried out, an inarticulate rumble rose from the mass of bowed heads. Lionni's box rode unevenly on the shoulders of Lorenzo Anselmo, his son Enzo, Stanislaw Monash, and other leaders of Comunità Ebraica di Roma. As the coffin approached the doors of the synagogue, the crowd stirred uncertainly, for tradition required their hesitation, to allow the immediate family of the deceased to lead the way out. At first no one moved. Lionni was a man without relatives. His family had been the Delegation, and now the inner core of that organization, perhaps a dozen men, crowded into the aisle, some holding each other by the elbow. They fell solemnly behind the coffin, and no one stepped into the aisle ahead of them.

Warburg had expected to see her there, perhaps leading the procession behind the coffin. But from what he had observed, Marguerite was not present. For an instant, when the congregation stood, his glance had risen to a woman in the balcony. She was dressed modestly, her head covered in a black kerchief, tied at the nape of her neck. She was turned slightly away, so he could not see her features, but, at her exceptional height, he felt a momentary rush of recognition. But she was wearing spectacles, and with a second glance he saw that it was not she. He rebuked himself for this slavish habit of mind, this constant looking.

A cortege of automobiles assembled in the cobblestone plaza, circling the synagogue. The crush of mourners made for a chaotic scene. Again Warburg caught sight of the tall, covered woman, but from behind. Her long sleeves came to her wrists. The hem of her dress was at her ankles. He would not have given her a further thought, but then he saw the man who was holding the door of a rounded Fiat two-seater with bulging fenders and bug-eyed headlights. The man was wearing a tattered suit jacket and an off-kilter necktie. He was bareheaded, gray-haired, somewhat stooped — and Warburg was sure he knew him. But from where? The woman disappeared into the car, and the man got in beside her, to drive.

The cortege followed the hearse at a good clip, running north on the Tiber's broad embankment boulevard, through the Villa Borghese, where Lionni had huddled under bushes during the occupation, past the Termini and the Transport Ministry he had burgled just after liberation, and out along the Via Tiburtina to the Campo Verano cemetery, which, since the early nineteenth century, had included a section set aside for Jewish burials.

Lionni was laid to rest in a grave not far from a colonnaded walkway. After his coffin had been lowered into its hole, mourners lined up to gently shovel dirt onto the lid, and it was then that Warburg saw the woman again. The gray-haired man was beside her. Then Warburg realized who he was: the priest who'd come to his office the year before, Padre Antonio. Why should the priest have been dressed like a layman? Warburg let that question go in order to concentrate on Marguerite.

And, of course, he understood, if only then, that appearing at Lionni's funeral involved some risk for her. Her need for obsequies had trumped caution, but caution explained why she had worn the modest clothes of an observant married woman. After dropping dirt on

Lionni's coffin, she stepped back into the crowd, aiming to lose herself, but Warburg never took his eyes from her.

Back beside the Fiat, she reached in for a black bag, which she slung on her shoulder. She said goodbye to Padre Antonio, kissing both his cheeks. He climbed into the car as she made her way, against the flow of mourners, out into the open field of the cemetery, heading off alone, nothing but tombstones around her, all awash in bright morning sun. Her loosely fitting black skirt rippled as she walked. The long tail of her head covering fell down her back, lifting like filament behind her. The black bag swung, a counterpulse pendulum. Even from a distance, her grace registered, and the modesty of her clothes oddly emphasized the feminine rhythm of her movement. Warburg followed.

Through the rolling terrain, past the obelisks and urns, he trailed her, not attempting to close the distance. At one point, and though strictly speaking the cemetery required it, he removed and pocketed his yarmulke. When at last she stopped to sit on a stone bench within a circle of hedges, in the shade of a towering cypress, he continued to walk toward her. There would be no pretense of accident, and no denying that his arrival was not intrusion.

As he drew near, she looked up at him. She removed the spectacles, and he saw that her impassive face was devoid of surprise. He hesitated before her. A fabric fastener on her blouse, a black flap below her breasts, was hanging loose. She had torn it, the ritual garment-rending, but with a conservative woman's modest care to expose nothing, not even a hint of undergarment. Warburg's own shirt, beneath his tie, was torn. He had channeled more feeling than he'd known, leaving a jagged flap of broadcloth at his chest, showing his undershirt.

When she said nothing, he chose to take that as permission, and he moved to the bench and sat down next to her. The bench was narrow, and their hips nearly touched. They sat in silence for a time, staring out at the same scene, the tombstones, the rough grass, the protruding granite markers. No crosses in this part of the cemetery, no carved angels.

"It is difficult to talk," she said finally.

"But necessary," he answered. "Talking is what keeps us alive."

She firmly contradicted him, shaking her head. She busied herself with her bag, withdrawing a cigarette pack and gold lighter. She took a cigarette, awkwardly held the pack for him. French cigarettes. He took the pack, removed a cigarette. After she had lit her own, he bent to the gold lighter she held for him.

Exhaling, he said, "Nice lighter."

She looked at it. "A friend," she said. When she realized he was staring at it, she slipped it back into her bag, but not before he'd seen what was engraved on it.

"That's the sign for Christ," he said.

"I carry the lighter . . . to please my friend. He does not know I am a Jew."

"Who does know that?"

"You know it. Jocko told me that you'd guessed about the *mikveh,* my immersion."

"I couldn't picture you in a *mikveh.* I found the idea of your conversion hard to fathom. But it moves me, what you did. You once told me you did not believe in God, but you also said, If there is a God, He is Jewish."

"Even Jesus was Jewish. That he was Jewish is enough. As for God . . ." She shrugged. "For me, the people are enough."

"I have some idea what you are involved in. Jocko trusted me."

"I know. I told him he could."

"He even told me he had a source in the Red Cross. I knew it was you."

"Your Red Cross lady." She smiled thinly.

"So who was he on to?"

"Pavelic."

"The Croatian."

"Yes. Jocko was following a group of Croatian priests."

"Jocko did not drive."

She let out the briefest of sounds, yet it connoted both a laugh at the thought of Lionni driving and anguish. "Of course he did not drive. He was not alone. He was with a unit, a team of five. They all died. The Croatian priests had guards, apparently. Protectors. It was my fault for not insisting on that danger firmly enough. Their mistake: to imagine that those with Vatican protection — priests — would not also have had Ustashe protection — killers. I had been watching the Croatian priests —"

"At the Convent of the Holy Spirit."

"Yes. There were never signs of armed protection. I reported that, but the unit leader made too much of it, making him careless. I wanted to go with them. The leader would not permit it." She fell silent.

"I am glad you were not permitted," Warburg said. When, instead of replying, she drew on her cigarette, he said, "Croatia was where your story began."

"Almost. My story began before that, on the road to Trento."

"Where your parents died."

"Yes."

"And now Jocko died the way they died," Warburg said. "A supposed accident, but it was murder."

"With Mama and Papa, it was murder. With Jocko . . . it was combat." She said this calmly — not coldly, but with a matter-of-fact assumption that the combat continued. That's how it differed from murder. Without looking at Warburg she said, "Your shirt. It will need mending. Is that how you felt, to make such a tear in your shirt?"

"Jocko was what brought me here to Rome last year. Because of the Delegation, the WRB had a way to begin. When I arrived here, he was all I had."

"By now he was all I had, too. I know who killed him."

Her benumbed voice chilled him. He remembered that night, sitting in the jeep: *A man I thought a friend attacked me . . . and I killed him.*

"Who killed him?" Warburg asked.

"A man with a deformed upper lip. The car wreck did not kill Jocko, a bullet did. The back of Jocko's head was exploded, but where the bullet entered was intact. An up-close shot. An execution, precisely through his upper lip. A signature. The priest's name is Vukas."

"A priest?"

"He was a 'relocation official' in Zagreb. 'Relocating' Jews and Serbs.

Serbs could convert and be spared the 'relocation.' Jews could not." She looked directly at Warburg. "I saw Vukas tormenting children with a snarling dog. The flesh on Jocko's arm was half eaten away — the teeth of a Doberman pinscher. That is Vukas. The worst of them are priests." She stopped. What else was there to say? Priests. But then she resumed, "When my parents died, I turned to the Church —"

"Padre Antonio."

"Yes. Père Antoine to me. With him, I prayed, 'Remember, O most gracious Virgin Mary,' but the Virgin forgot. In the Church now, across the Tiber, Père Antoine is anathema, Vukas is protected. Vukas! Jocko said, Leave Vukas be. But I will see to his being killed. His death is my purpose now. Does that surprise you?"

"I don't blame you."

"Blame? It would not occur to me — blame. You have an American innocence. You came from the New World to the Old World to save the innocent. It was beautiful, watching you. Watching you make them give me the milk for the starving children. Watching what you did for Budapest. Only in Budapest did an action for Jews succeed. Watching what you are still doing for Jews in camps. You think I have avoided you, but no. I have been watching you. All this time. Your beautiful work. Saving the innocent from the guilty. But David . . . may I call you David?"

He was as calm as she was. "Of course you may."

"David, innocence has nothing to do with it. None of us here is innocent. My 'friend' — the gold lighter from Christ? He also is a priest. He is one of them, a German. Also one of the worst. Himmler's priest. I trick him. He trusts me. He tells me their secrets. I tell their secrets to the Haganah."

"But Marguerite, I know all this. Jocko laid it out for me, what you are doing. He asked me to join you, and I did. The thought of Nazi criminals escaping is intolerable to me. Why do you think I came after you just now?"

"Not because of Nazis, David. You came because I lured you — to tell you I am not innocent."

"I knew you lured me. I came anyway."

"Yes. Because, imagining me innocent — your Red Cross blue angel — you think you want to be with me."

How bold she was. How right. "I do think I want to be with you, that's true," he said. "As for innocence, put it this way: if you want Vukas killed, I will help you."

She laughed, a burst of breath through her nose. "You are innocent, but naive as well. What could you do?"

"We'll see," he answered, taking no offense.

She tossed her cigarette. "No. That would be wrong for you. I am beyond what is wrong. The innocent and the guilty — for me, that difference no longer exists. You must still uphold it. You are American."

"I am a Jew."

"Not all Jews are alike. The Church says we Jews are damned. In my case, it is true."

Warburg said nothing to that.

She added, "Besides, no help is needed with Vukas." She stood.

"Haven't you noticed something, Marguerite? I refuse to be left behind by you. How many times have you walked away from me? You can walk away now, but you are not rid of me." He remained sitting, looking up at her.

"Because you are innocent, David, I must say the thing more clearly. I am the German priest's woman. His mistress. His lover. What pleasures he wants from me I give. Also pleasures he does not know he wants until I give them. He, too, is damned, but too foolish to know it. And Jocko — Jocko was my *protettore*. My pimp." There. She had sealed herself against him for good. She added, cruelly, "*Now,* you are surprised?"

And, in truth, he was. How could he have allowed himself not to see this? He had pictured this woman naked, in the throes of lovemaking, in the arms of a man. Blue angel? No. He had never imagined her as untouched. But the dream presumed, of course, that the man in whose arms she peaked was him.

For a long time she returned his sad gaze, waiting for him to drop his eyes. He did not drop them. She found it in herself to say, "If it were otherwise, David, I would return your feeling with feeling of my own — for you. Only you. But as it is, I feel nothing. I am damned."

Warburg slowly stood up. "That is not true," he said. "I don't believe it. You are the farthest thing from damned." And with that he gently closed his hands around her covered head, brought his mouth to hers, waited an instant, and kissed her. She who was beyond surprise was surprised by his move toward her, but more by his having seen before she did what made her instantly responsive. She opened her mouth to his tongue, pressed her breasts flat against his chest, circled his body with her arms, felt the press of his erection. Her response was total, emotional, carnal — and chosen.

They kissed. She pulled back. "Oh," she said, but meant, I am still alive. *Alive!* And then, more fiercely, she kissed him again. A moment later, Warburg was the one to pull back. "I love you," he said, words that had never passed his lips. "Marguerite, I love you!" They fell back toward the hedge, behind it, and once again — in grief and its opposite — set about the rending of garments.

They made their way to his place, where they spent the rest of the day, into the night. At one point she waited in the bed while, still naked, he went into the other room. When he returned, he was wearing a bathrobe and carrying two tumblers, each with a couple of inches of amber liquid.

Rising to lean against the headboard, she pulled the sheet to her shoulders.

"Bourbon," he said.

Taking the glass, she asked, "Do you drink too much?"

"No," he replied. "I don't do anything too much." He joined her on the bed again, although still robed, and on top of the sheets.

"Too bad," she said.

"I've always thought so. What about you?"

"I walk alone too much."

"Perhaps I can help with that."

She sipped the bourbon.

He sensed her allergy to the future tense, and understood it. He, too, had allowed himself to think of his small room as confining time, the brackets on a present moment that would last forever. The silence that came over them now carried implications that were new, and unwelcome. Was the spell broken?

Perhaps he had been the one to crack the enchantment by leaving the room, if only to fetch the booze. In the bathroom, seeing his robe on the hook, he had donned it without thinking, just as, at the sight of him wrapped in the robe when he reappeared, she had automatically pulled the bedclothes up to cover herself.

"You can walk with me to the river," she said at last. She placed the glass on the bedside table.

"You can stay here," he said. "We can sleep."

"I could never sleep, David."

"I was wrong before. That's what I do too much of . . . sleeping alone."

"Going to bed with someone is one thing," she said with forced levity. "But staying through the night, that is something else. As you know, I have been with a man, but I have never slept with one."

"In that case, may I be your first?"

"You ask politely. It doesn't bother you . . . ?"

"The other man?"

"Yes."

"I trust you. I trust the choices you must make."

Marguerite shook her head. "I don't."

"I understand that," he said. "But you should."

She stared at him, and a kind of wonder showed on her face as she registered afresh his simple goodness. Oddly, that worked against him. She shook her head slowly. "There is just a wide, deep . . . something between us. You say 'void'?"

"Gulf? Chasm?"

"Yes. Far too much separating us. You are good. This was very good of you, receiving me."

"But it's impossible?"

"Yes."

"Why?"

"I told you."

"Because you are damned."

"Yes."

"But didn't you hear what I told you?"

"You told me that you love me, and I answered you with all that I have to give. But it is not enough."

"I told you that you are the farthest thing from damned. We came together as lovers, caught up in each other, finally, without really choosing it. Perhaps the emotion of having said farewell to Jocko . . . It was chosen for us. Isn't that how it felt?"

"Yes, which makes the point."

"But now, Marguerite, in this aftermath . . . you French have a word for it . . ."

"*Tristesse.*"

"Yes. Exactly. Between a man and a woman, this is the most important time. Not passion, but calm. If you allowed yourself to know me, you would see a man incapable of giving himself to what is damned."

"You have given yourself to the death camps."

"The death camps, for all their horror, are what make you and me know that we are alive. That first day, your passionate demand for what life requires. You would not be refused. You wanted milk for children. You demanded it. Why? *L'chaim!* You know that word?"

She nodded and whispered, "Life."

"Marguerite, it's what I saw in you. And what I love in you. Your deep, unquenched life. Out of which you act so bravely."

"I am a killer."

"For life. If you killed, Marguerite, it was for life."

"But I told you also . . . I am not finished with killing. *There* is the chasm."

Warburg said quietly, "'For wheresoever you go, I will go. Wheresoever you stay, I will stay.'"

When Marguerite turned her face to him, her eyes spilled over. She attempted a smile, but it would not come. "I thought that was what the woman said."

"But she said it to a woman, so perhaps I am half permitted . . ."

Warburg reached across her to set his whiskey down on the table. Then, as he had in the cemetery, he put his two hands at her face and looked directly at her. Tears were coursing down her cheeks, but she found it possible to return his unrelenting gaze. "I meant everything I said to you before," he said. "But when I say it this time, it is different. What I am expressing to you is not longing or the fulfillment of a dream. You are not the figment of my desire. I am not your haunting stranger. This is the harsh moment of our difficulty. You are the real woman beside me, and I hear what you are telling me. We know that we are different. We know that obstacles remain. Obstacles that perhaps for others would be impossible. A chasm, too far, too deep. But not for us. Do *you* hear? Not for us. I love you, Marguerite. And I say that understanding very well that you cannot say it in return to me."

"If I could . . ." She was sobbing.

He put his finger gently to her lips. "I will wait for you. Do you hear me?"

She nodded and fell against him, clinging to him.

She was correct about not sleeping. And she was right about his walking her to the river. It was deep into the night, and the streets were deserted. Walking along, they held hands, as if they were young. When they came to the bridge that would take her across the Tiber, she stopped him. He wanted to continue with her, but she put her hand firmly on his chest. He nodded and said, "But remember, 'Wheresoever you go . . .'"

She replied, "'And your people will be my people.'" She kissed him good night. And he let her go.

Clutching his robes, Father Lehmann ran up to the third-floor apartment, desperate to find his mother, to see that she was all right. When he burst in on her, she was seated at her embroidery table, the floor-to-ceiling window open behind, the soft breeze wafting the gauzy curtain at her side. She was garbed, as usual in the morning, in her plain black silk kimono, formal wear in Japan, but for Lehmann's mother, with its ample sleeves and loose fit, a lounging dress. That she began her days covered from neck to foot in black had become a joke between them, as if she, too, had given herself to the Church. As always, though, she was wearing typical Argentine footwear, rope and canvas espadrilles, and there was nothing nun-like in the long black braid of hair that curled on her shoulder like a pet, nor in the yellow dahlia pinned by her ear. At the sight of her agitated son, anxiety came instantly into her face. She was a woman ever on the lookout for unhappy news.

The news had come to Lehmann from the woman with whom, as he would now forever think of her, he had fallen from grace. Even in just having confronted the great deceiver, what had amazed him most was that, in some unplumbed depth, he was not surprised. If he had foolishly trusted her, he had never trusted the situation they created together. He'd known from the start that it would somehow end badly. How badly he never imagined.

He had arrived at their hotel room that morning exquisitely on edge with anticipation — he loved their early trysts. The tension of the previous days at the Casa dello Spirito Santo had jangled his nerves, and he was longing to unburden himself to her, ask her advice — but mostly to climb inside her, to fuck. She had been fully clothed, though, sitting at the round, scarred table, smoking a cigarette. She was wearing her blue uniform and the beret with its cross. On the table was a pack of cigarettes. One hand held her cigarette, the other was in her lap, hidden.

"Sit with me, *mein Bonbon,*" she said.

It took a moment for him to adjust; this was something new. Dressed. Normally whoever was first to arrive waited under the sheets. He took the second chair, opposite. "Even covered, you are beautiful. I had forgotten that." He smiled, trusting that she would as well. But her expression did not change.

She leaned toward him. "I have been concerned for you," she said. "It has been days. Why haven't I seen you?"

"There has been trouble. The enemies of Croatia have shown themselves. There are Chetniks here in Rome, agents of the Bolsheviks. They are after Pavelic. So far they have been thwarted."

"But Vukas has not returned to Spirito Santo. The SVC limousine returned, but he was not in it."

Lehmann stared at her. "How do you know this?"

"I know it," she said, the totality of her answer.

Lehmann could not think what to say. She was frightening him.

"My darling," she said finally, "I want you to tell me where Vukas is."

"How do you know his name?" There was fear in him, yes, but also urgency.

"I know it." Once more, her abrupt, unprecedented authority. "Where is he?"

Instead of answering, Lehmann stood. He knew at once what this change in her meant. This week's mystery at the Casa had been: Who is the traitor? He saw: *The traitor is me, myself!* Seized by the threat she posed, he lunged, to shake her, to choke her. The deceitful bitch.

But she stopped him by slapping the table, *bang!* With a swift movement she had brought her hidden hand up from her lap, and though the sharp noise had been of metal hitting wood, he saw that her hand was concealed inside a black drawstring bag. The bag was just large enough, he realized, to contain a weapon, a Beretta pistol around which her fingers would be closed. She could kill him on the spot. He all but collapsed, shrank back, stifled a whimper.

It was the reaction she knew would come. In so many ways he had exposed his perfect cowardice to her. "You will tell me where Vukas is, or you can be certain that the *Aussenweg* fraternity will learn that you have been their enemy. And you know what they will do."

"My mother. They will harm my mother."

"No. They will kill her. Where is Vukas?"

Lehmann did not hesitate. "In one of the other Croatian or Franciscan foundations, a monastery, a college, here in Rome."

"Which one?"

"I do not know. Why would I know?"

"I believe you. But I want you to learn where he is. Tell the Croatians that you are under orders from the *Aussenweg* operators in Vienna — *Germans* who must know of Vukas, his condition, his whereabouts, where his authority stands with the Crusade. You explain: for the Germans to continue trusting the Croatian network after the debacle on Via Cassia, they must know. The Croatians will tell you. Write it down—where Vukas is! Leave the message for me in the donation box at the Church of Santa Maria della Vittoria. You will do this by dusk tonight. Do you understand?"

"Tonight, impossible. I must visit each foundation personally, to make the inquiry seem normal."

Marguerite saw that. "Tomorrow night, then. The donation box at Santa Maria. Dusk."

Across Lehmann's face fell an expression of such pathetic helplessness that she almost pitied him. "Vukas is nothing to you," she said. "He is important to me."

"You are Chetnik."

Without hesitating, Marguerite said, "Yes. I am Chetnik. Get me Vukas and I will spare you. Do you understand?"

"Yes."

"I do not expect you to do this for me. Do it for your mother."

Marguerite stood. Only now did she withdraw her hand from her bag. He shrank halfway back again, but then he saw that her hand held not the Beretta pistol he'd imagined but a small object, which she placed on the table. His gold lighter. She had no weapon.

Before she closed the door, she looked back. "Goodbye, Father."

After a moment, Lehmann reached for the lighter, picked it up, traced the Christ symbol with his finger. From now on, this golden object would be a relic of his humiliation.

His mother, with her embroidery hook suspended in midair, was waiting for him to speak. He crossed the room and closed the tall windows beside her, as if for privacy. He spoke in Spanish. "Mother, you must instruct Maria to ready your bags. And her own. We are traveling tomorrow." From his inside pocket he withdrew a pair of leather passport folders and placed them on her table. "One for you, one for Maria."

She opened the top folder and found a passport stamped with a coat of arms — an eagle atop an open crown, flanked by columns, the Pillars of Hercules. She recognized the seal and the words beneath, *Estado Español.* "Spain?"

"Yes. It's where we are going."

"But our plans have always been for Mainz, to return home, our beautiful villa overlooking the Rhine."

We can't go to Mainz! he wanted to scream. *Mainz is ruined for us! Germany is ruined for us!* Germans were now his enemy. Any number of Germans would slice his throat open for what he had done, his mortal sin. *I have betrayed the sacred trust, Mother. I have betrayed you.* The very thought of declaring himself to her was enough to make him nearly vomit. He covered his mouth. *Never, never must you know!*

His mother flipped the passport open and saw a photo of herself, familiar if not particularly fetching. But the name on the page opposite — Carmela del Socorro. She looked up at her son. "What is this?"

"Mother, you know the situation. The time has come for us to move."

"But the Holy See protects us. The Holy Father safeguards us. Archbishop Graz shields us."

"No more. We are exposed here." *The Holy Father now protects those who would kill us. Graz would hand us over.*

"Who is this Carmela —?"

"She is you, Mother!" Lehmann banged his hand on her table, knocking the embroidery hoop and its taut fabric to the floor. He had so raised his voice that the servant, Maria, appeared at the door. His mother burst into tears.

She put her hand out, and Maria was immediately there to supply a silk square, with which the Señora covered her face, yet amplifying her sobs instead of stifling them. Lehmann backed away from his mother, horrified. He had not caused her to cry since being a headstrong adolescent. One impulse was to get on his knees and plead for forgiveness, but another, the stronger — because rooted in terror, not guilt — was to move forward with the plan. He turned to the intimidated servant. "Maria, we are traveling tomorrow. You must prepare things. I will come back later. Mother —" Lehmann approached to kiss her, but she faced away, wailing.

Lehmann descended the villa's wide staircase more rapidly than he'd come up. He dashed into the street, where his car and driver were waiting. He threw himself into the right rear seat. "*Vada! Vada!*" he said. For a terrible instant he thought that he, too, would break down in sobs, completing his humiliation, exposing him to the peasant contempt of the Italian chauffeur.

Lehmann looked at the back of the man's head as he shifted gears, pulling the stately auto smoothly into the flow of traffic. How long did Lehmann stare — the considerable tilt of the chauffeur's hat, the hair too short at his collar, the broader shoulders, the ears flat to the head instead of protruding — before realizing that the man was not his driver? Lehmann's eyes went to the rearview mirror, where the man's were waiting. "Good day, Father," the man said in English, then smiled.

The clean, white American teeth. The trimmed mustache. The bright blue eyes.

"Good God," Lehmann said, "General Mates." The priest looked wildly around. "Here?" Coming up on the right was Santa Maria dell'Anima, the German church — Archbishop Graz!

"Relax, Father. No one will take notice. We chauffeurs are invisible. The windows are sealed. We could be in one of your confessional booths." They whizzed by the church, yet Lehmann remained pressed back into the corner of his seat.

The car broke free of the congestion, turning onto the broad Via della Vetrina, heading north, gunning it, taking full advantage of the car's legal immunity. Even at speed, the American's eyes were as much on Lehmann, through the mirror, as on the road.

"Look at me."

Lehmann met the eyes of his handler.

Mates said, "Your having it both ways is over. From now on you are taking orders only from me. What happened on the Via Cassia was too close. What if they had reached the Crusader meeting at Regina Angelorum? You think we snatched Pavelic out of the brig in Salzburg to lose him in Rome? Lose him to bumbling assassins? You think I'm risking the others we've lined up?"

"The others are Himmler's men, of no interest to the assassins," Lehmann explained. "The assassins on the Via Cassia were Chetniks. The Yugoslavs. They wanted Pavelic. They wanted Vukas. They care nothing for Germans. It was Tito's Bolsheviks on the Via Cassia."

"You are stupider than you look, Father. They were Jews."

"*Juden!*"

"And the Jews know all about you, you dumb shit." The general's eyes bounced back and forth, from the traffic to Lehmann in the mirror. "They have the names of the Croatian sheep you are shepherding. They have the names of the *Aussenweg* bigshots you are expecting. They know the Road Out runs through the Vatican. They know about the gold. They know about Argentina. Our entire scheme is at risk. And all of this Jew knowledge has to have come through you. You're the only one besides me with the whole picture."

"Do they know about you?" Lehmann asked desperately. "If the Jews knew that Americans are partners in this, perhaps they would—"

"You think the Jews want to join me in saving Krauts we can use against Reds? Hell, Jews *are* Reds." Mates downshifted to take a curve, like a Grand Prix racer. He had bombed up an incline, into the verdant isolation of Monteverde, a neglected hillside park. "As for your American partners, you dumb prick, my government is on record as wanting these bastards at the war crimes tribunal. You and I are *off* the record, Padre. *Capiche?*"

Lehmann thought back to the woman. *Yes. I am Chetnik.* Her being Jewish was impossible. He would have known. "You are wrong," he dared to say.

Mates stared at him through the mirror. He said, "Jewish teams have already killed dozens of SS and Gestapo officers in Austria and Germany—in POW camps and in hideouts. They call themselves Nakam, which means revenge. An eye for an eye. Now they are in Rome, setting the trap for our crew. And you are their bait, you stupid asshole."

Lehmann pressed himself back, back into the corner, finally facing the truth of what he had done. Sprawled on their tangled, damp sheets, he had thrilled his *Liebchen* with the saga of *Aussenweg*, his heroic role, the first real blow in the new war against the transcendent enemy. Not merely Germany's enemy, although that, too — but God's. Yet filled with the grandeur of his narration, the danger of his sacred mission, and the unmistakable admiration in her eyes — now he knew: he had missed the only thing that mattered. His convent girl, somehow, was a Jew. A Jew who fooled him. A Jew to whom he had revealed everything.

With one last rocking swing of the car, Mates pulled off the road into a gravelly parking area, the kind of place to which whores brought Giovannis in the old days. Mates slammed the gearshift into reverse and ran the car backward into the overhanging foliage, so that the feathery claws of an ancient olive tree clutched at Lehmann's window. Mates shut the engine and faced backward, throwing his elbow. "Listen to me, Lehmann. I haven't wasted a year's coddling to have you go all weak in the knees at this point. We're making this thing work. You get *your* people out. I get *my* people out. We're just getting this thing up and running. I'd toss you aside in a flash, but I need you at the visa desk in Vatican City."

"The Nazis have threatened my mother. I cannot stay here."

"I know about your mother. I'm taking her under my protection. From now on, she'll be safe, because I will have her." Mates paused before adding, "I am taking her home."

"What?"

"To Mainz. Mainz, right across the Rhine from U.S. headquarters in Frankfurt, where the war crimes trials are about to start. It's the last place fugitive Nazis would hang around. Safest place in Europe. Wouldn't your mother like to return there? I have colleagues standing by to escort her on my personal aircraft. She could resume her role on the Ladies' Altar Guild at the Mainz Cathedral. She'd have status as a special dignitary of the German-American Friendship League. Wouldn't she like that? I've already seen to the requisitioning of your family *Landhaus* on the river. I'm having it repaired and staffed, just waiting for her. She could sponsor teas for the wives of American brass. Wouldn't she like that?"

"Yes. Actually, she would."

"Father, I solve your biggest problem, Mama, so you can focus on what you have to do in Rome. Once things are running smoothly here, you can visit Mainz on my aircraft."

"And if I defy you, my mother is at your mercy. Your hostage."

"You're not dealing with Nazis here, Father." Mates let a beat fall, and another. "Not hostage, but collateral. A reason for me to trust you from today on."

"And my reason to trust you?"

Mates laughed. "Let me remind you of something, you Kraut bastard. You fuckers lost the war. You have no choice here. You defy me now and I let out the word that you're working for the Jews, that you sent the Nakam team after Pavelic. Down here in the loosey-goosey Med, the Nazis can track you *and* your mother. They can do it in Barcelona, too."

"Barcelona!"

"Isn't that where you're headed? Isn't that the point of the *Estado Español* passports — for Señora Carmela del Socorro and her maidservant?"

"How—?"

"You forget, Father, I am the connoisseur of passport forgery in Rome. Your master counterfeiter also works for me. But he works for others, too, like the *Aussenweg* operators. You think the Nazis aren't wise to your plans for Barcelona?"

Lehmann silently took this in. Then, quietly, he asked, "And if something were to happen to me . . . what would become of my mother?"

"I would take care of her. I would see to it that she had what she needed."

Lehmann said, "When can this happen? When can my mother be in your airplane?"

"When can she be ready?"

"Tomorrow. By dusk."

"All right. Tomorrow. Have her — and her Maria? — at the American flight line at Ciampino at eight." He faced away, turning back to the wheel.

"General, wait," Lehmann said. "May I have your word of honor?"

"For —?" Their eyes locked again through the rearview mirror.

"Protecting my mother. If something befell me."

"Yes, Father. My solemn word." He pressed the ignition. "We'd better get back. Your driver is waiting for us at the Campo dei Fiori, beside the statue of Giordano Bruno, whom you Catholics burned at the stake for thinking."

He was like one of those cramped priests railing against the vices of the poor banished children of Eve, bitter refutation of every hope, the frenzied legacy of flesh, the lash of an unforgiving purity. But the object of his final negation was himself.

Drums sounded in Lehmann's ears as he drove. Unusually, he was at the wheel of the SVC automobile, and he was alone. The slim white body of the Via Cassia stretched out in the headlights. The road was his lean lover whose curves beckoned, urging him to drive ever faster. The way ahead was hard to see because the bilge of his self-loathing had flooded into his eyes.

Less than an hour before, he had left the airport with the screeches of his mother ringing in his ears. Only when she had made her way up the aluminum stairs and into the American plane, her bags and Maria ahead of her, did he tell her the truth. She had been overjoyed at his news about Mainz — going home after all, to resume the Rhineland life she loved. But when he then said that he was to remain in Rome without her, she collapsed on him, clung to him, a kind of animal embrace that shocked him with its indecency.

He'd explained nothing, said only that he would follow her, forced her arms from his neck and pushed her back more roughly than he'd intended. The stewards on the plane helped her take a seat in the posh cabin, one man holding a tray bearing a tulip glass and a bottle of Henkell champagne, which, coming from Mainz, should have delighted her. But she never noticed. Lehmann's accidental roughness was the last thing she took from him, and her last look at him was scrubbed clean of tenderness, leaving only the desert of hurt from which he knew he would never escape, no matter how long he lived.

From the airport, he'd driven back to the center of Rome, to the Church of Santa Maria della Vittoria near the Via Veneto. By then it was completely dark. The woman whom he had so foolishly thought of as his had commanded him to be there by dusk, and he was late, but he did not care. The Jew. The lying Jew.

He'd left the car purring at the curb. He pushed through the leather curtain that defined the narthex of the church and stood for a moment while his eyes adjusted to the dark interior, settling on the two banks of votive lights, one red, one blue. He'd been in this church dozens of times, always to stand transfixed before its side chapel sculpture, the *Ecstasy of Saint Teresa*. Lehmann had treated those sojourns with pious devotion, pilgrimages with the saint's autobiography in hand, to read again the words that Bernini had so outrageously rendered in stone: the Carmelite's transported face, her eyelids fluttering closed, her lips barely parted, a hint of her tongue, the suggestion of lewd color in her cheeks despite the marble. She was in the throes of female ecstasy, yet Teresa was holy.

Lehmann spied the donation box near the door, but before depositing his envelope, he made his way through the shadows to the statue, beside the raft of blue candles. The saint's words came automatically to mind: "The pain was so great that it made me moan . . . and yet I could not wish to be rid of it." As always before, Lehmann went missing for a moment. And, as always, he came to with a chill on his neck, with the urge to look quickly, guiltily around to see who had witnessed his standing there.

He moved away, down the aisle to the box. He deposited his envelope and then went out into the night, away.

Now, the savage wind from the open window at his elbow tore at his sleeve. He was miles from Rome, well along the ancient road, a solitary intruder on the rough and hilly terrain. Far ahead in the black sky, well above the cone of headlights, was a single brittle star that mocked him with its beauty. Stars burn out, eternally unremembered, with their one huge advantage of knowing nothing of their fate. Lehmann knew his.

The road's next curve came more sharply than he expected, and he was driving much too fast. He hit the brakes, sending the car's rear wheels into a sideways movement, an uncontrolled drift into the guardrail. The guardrail held, hurtling him back across the road. The collision caused his head to bang against the door frame, a blow above his ear, jolting his teeth onto his tongue, the taste of blood. Not here, he thought, not yet!

He was able to correct and bring the car back to center, onto the naked female form of the road ahead. Her naked form, faithless and deadly. Of course, he had known from the instant of his sacrilegious absolution of her that first night in the priest's cottage in the Casa that he was being seduced, willingly seduced. Yet his mortal sin was not fornication but treason.

Instead of slowing, he pushed the pedal down, but the blow to his head had sharpened his perception, and now he was focused on the guardrail, looking for the break. Because he knew it was close, he opened the palm of his right hand and put the gelatin capsule into his mouth, a flashing thought of Herr Himmler.

He saw it, an open gash in the rail where the Jews' car had gone through. He aimed for it, and the powerful engine of the Vatican automobile roared as he pushed the pedal to the limit. When the wheels left the road and the car soared out into the inscrutable air, he bit down on the capsule. *Madre! Madre!*

ELEVEN

Ratline

THE PRIEST SPEAKS, and lo! Christ the eternal and omnipotent God bows His head in humble obedience to the priest's command." Where had he read that? *Our Sunday Visitor* or some such. In Deane's mind, the self-mocking shorthand had become, "The priest speaks and lo!"

He bent over the altar with the round white disk of bread between his thumbs and forefingers. He brought his mouth close to the bread as he'd done every day of his life since ordination. And the priest spoke.

As the rubrics required, he pronounced the transcendent phrase with exquisite precision: *Hoc est enim corpus meum.* "This is truly my body," words uttered by Jesus at the Last Supper. But as Deane placed the host on the gold paten, closed his eyes, and genuflected, he always continued with what, according to Saint Paul, Jesus had gone on to say then: *quod pro vobis tradetur,* "which will be broken for you."

The body of Christ is broken. Deane paused with his knee on the floor, his head bent so that it nearly touched the altar, his mind mobbed by the truly broken figures with whom he had become obsessed. At this moment of the Mass, across the past year and a half, he had increasingly been seized, paralyzed in the attempt to make an oblation of the sons and daughters of the camps, the living and dead, the bags of bones, the breathing skeletons—the Jews. But again and again, something stopped him. This: if Jesus were present in those camps, Deane had finally to acknowledge, it would not have been as the eternal and omnipotent God, but as yet another anonymous figure in the selection line. Lo! Jesus was a Jew. He never spoke in Latin. And, heresy of heresies, some burnt offerings are not redemptive.

There. He'd said it. At last. The suffering of Treblinka, Fossoli, Sobibor, and places yet unknown had redeemed nothing. In no way was that suffering willed by God. The priest speaks, and lo! His consolations of salvation through sacrifice are lies.

Only moments later, Deane had the wafer between his fingers again, and, obeying the ritual, he snapped it in half. Broken for whom? This time, his mind went to the body of his fellow priest, the German, whose broken corpse had been found yesterday in a wrecked car at the bottom of a steep ravine below the cliff road en route to Ravenna.

Even if Deane had yet to figure the math, Roberto Lehmann embodied the Church's deadly entanglement in the nihilism that had swamped Europe — nihilism the war's true victor. Now the metaphoric brokenness of Christ implied the Church's own quite literal brokenness — how, in the Pope's very household, robed men routinely passed one another with slyly averted glances, as if what bound the papal court at last was fear of the evil eye.

For all his supernumerary prestige as a privy chamberlain, Deane had been privy only to the shadows of Vatican secrets — with the shadows themselves casting shadows: savage Croatian fascism tied to the Franciscans; the Holy See plotting to castle Tito with Pavelic; Church congregations, tribunals, and commissions at the service of Nazi fugitives; powerful figures of the Roman Curia, beginning with Tardini and Tisserant, sponsoring criminal escape in the name of mercy. Always, there was the missing gold. Meanwhile, an ethereal figure hovered above these blatant corruptions, whether with detachment, ignorance, or rank approval: Pope Pius XII himself.

But what the hell — privy chamberlain means private bed maker, nothing more. In truth, Deane was a lowly nobody, an American outsider who had been fed only what the Italians wanted him to know, crumbs.

Still, crumbs can mark the way through the forest, and Deane had just come to a clearing at last, seeing—lo!—Jesus with a number tattooed on his arm.

The priest speaks and gets it wrong. So why shouldn't the rubrics command a triple striking of the breast, as Deane, bowing low, enacted it then? *Domine, non sum dignus! Domine, non sum dignus! Domine, non sum dignus!* "Lord, I am not worthy that Thou shouldst enter under my roof." Until lately, this confession had been a rote formula, signifying little. But today Deane brought his fist against his chest as if he meant it. Not worthy. No kidding. Monsignor Obvious.

Thomas Aquinas, he thought then. Not the saint.

Again he genuflected, chiding himself for these rampant distractions. And anyway, there was no impropriety in a passing thought of Sister Thomas. She and he were friends. Nothing wrong with that. He made the sign of the cross over the chalice and the ciborium, swept his arms heavenward, then said, "*Oremus . . . audemus dicere . . . Pater Noster.*" We are bold to say, Our Father.

Bold. Sister Thomas had boldly come to his confessional the day before, the sacred booth in which, several afternoons a week, he continued to put himself at the service of repentant GIs. When he'd slid the screen open, she'd said at once, "It's Sister Thomas, Monsignor," but he'd known already—her scent, soap overlaying sandalwood incense. She apologized for presenting herself there, but it was the only way she could promptly see him, having just learned of Lehmann's death.

Stalking Curia offices, the nun had already compiled a partial list of Germans to whom pontifical credentials of various kinds had been issued in recent months, including certificates of appointment as Vatican delegates to international bodies, confirmations of membership in the Order of Malta, and general letters of recommendation. Again and again, she'd found the signature or scrawled initials of the Very Most Reverend Roberto Lehmann.

On the other side of the screen, she had quietly wept, not confessing sin but drowning in it. Deane sensed how, for her, Lehmann had come to represent a grotesque suspicion of moral degradation, and how, with his death, the suspicion was confirmed. In this matter of Nazis, her beloved Holy Mother the Church was on the cusp of becoming the Whore of Babylon. Deane knew this.

He wanted to reach through the screen and touch her, wipe the tears from her cheek with the knuckle of his forefinger. All he could do was sit in silence, watch her dark form, and wait for her face to lift. When it did, he said only, "Sister, I know what you are feeling. I feel it with you."

"But Monsignor, what do we do now? To whom —?"

"I'm waiting to hear back from General Mates," he said.

"Monsignor, when I learned about Father Lehmann, I acted impulsively." Her confession, after all. "I called the number that Philip gave me."

"Because of Lehmann's death?"

"Surely it was no accident. Was it murder? Lehmann was swimming with piranhas. So are we. Monsignor, how can such wickedness have intruded upon the Church? I haven't felt such turmoil since I fled Bletchley Park."

"What did Philip say?"

"Someone else answered the phone. He told me Philip has been reassigned. Apparently they gave up on hearing from me. I told the man I would speak only to Philip. He said Philip is in service in Palestine. They are contacting him. He will come to Rome. He will be in touch with me." She fell silent. Then she said, a whisper, "Is that all right, Monsignor?"

"Of course it is," he answered, cloaking the sudden distress he felt. "This thing is a runaway train, Sister. General Mates swore me to secrecy. When I spoke to him, he could not have been more alarmed. He said fugitive Nazis have riddled Rome. And now they are killing people." *There* was reason for distress. Of course. But, perversely, Deane knew that what also distressed him was the nun's having turned back to the man whose love had driven her into the convent. Her Philip. Deane leaned closer, the odd physical intimacy of his lips only an inch or two from hers, but in semidarkness and with the chaste mesh between. Neither of them moved for a long time.

He whispered, "What was your name?"

"What?"

"Your name before. What was it?"

She did not answer. In the silence, Deane felt a burst of shame, as if he'd abused the sacrament of penance. But she had not come here for confession. And there was nothing prurient about her given name. Still, it was the most personal question he'd ever asked her — or anyone.

"Jane," she whispered.

"Jane what?" Deane was not breathing.

"Jane Storrow."

Silence.

When she spoke now, her voice was the whisper of a whisper: "Why do you ask me that?"

Deane shook himself, thinking, the word "seduce" is from the Latin for "to lead apart." In a pointed return to propriety, he said, "Sister, you were right to come here. Dangers abound. You must stay in touch with me. Now more than ever. We must meet."

"No. No. I must collect myself." She pulled back fully into the shadow. But it rang like a verdict when she said, "I will wait until I hear from Philip. I cannot see you now." He heard the swift rustle of fabric as she touched her fingers to her head, shoulders, and breast. When she then said, "Bless me, Father," it was in farewell.

Despite his disappointment at the moment, Deane by now was relieved that she'd put him off. He could engineer but one runaway train at a time. *The priest speaks, and lo! Who but Christ obeys?* With an unselfconscious and habitual grace, Deane bent from the waist to bow and kiss the altar. He turned to face the people, the dozens of old ladies, Roman stragglers, tourists, pilgrims, American soldiers, the random collection that had made its way into the Gregorian Chapel of St. Peter's Basilica, one of the numerous side chapels that filled niches in the vast church.

As he neatly swiveled on his heels, bringing the congregation into his awareness, his unmoored imagination kicked up the grainy old movie of some deranged worshiper rising in slow motion to greet him from the pew with the burst of a Thompson submachine gun, cutting him down in the moment of his sacramental glory — kissing him off. It was a perverse fantasy, one that had teased him periodically since he was a young priest at the altar of Good Shepherd Parish on the northern tip of gangster-ridden Manhattan. But now, in a flash of imagination, he saw a familiar face on the figure holding the gun — Roberto Lehmann, come back to life to finish him off. No. He shook the fantasy away.

"*Dominus vobiscum,*" he said, spreading his arms. The aged acolyte kneeling below him muttered the rote reply, "*Et cum spiritu tuo.*" As if he'd known to look, Deane's eyes went, like the beam of scanning radar, to the figure standing beside the stout marble column in the rear of the relatively small space — not a machine gunner, not Lehmann, but Warburg.

Warburg waited by the column, and after the Mass, Deane found him. Deane had removed his silk vestments and was now cloaked in his red-trimmed soutane and the cappa. He had his breviary under his arm, the obligatory *saturno* in his hand. Warburg was wearing a tan raincoat and carrying his fedora. It had struck him, as he removed his hat upon entering St. Peter's, that the Christian custom of male bareheadedness in church had almost surely evolved from the rejection of Jewish modes.

The men shook hands warmly, as if all were well between them. Using the basilica's hush as a reason not to speak, they walked to the center of the five great portals leading to the exit. Outdoors, Warburg put his hat on, Deane did not. Each man pulled his garment close against the damp wind. Descending the stairs into the great Bernini piazza, Warburg came right to the point. "I've been waiting to hear from you, Kevin. You've put me off half a dozen times."

"Perhaps I've been waiting for you to come to Mass."

Warburg refused the banter. He said, "I know about Father Lehmann's death."

"Yes. Terrible. People here are quite upset."

"Really?"

They crossed into the square proper, heading toward Cleopatra's Needle. Despite the threat of full-blown rain, pilgrims were arriving, vendors were unfolding their kits, stray cats were looking for legs to brush against, and pigeons were wheeling in the air.

"Yes, really."

"I've come here, Kevin, because Lehmann was the source of the material I gave you. I've been waiting for you to identify those bastards. Now that Lehmann's dead, I can't wait any longer."

"You got that stuff from Lehmann?" Deane was genuinely surprised. "I assumed Haganah or something."

"Not that Lehmann knew he was giving it to me," Warburg said. "There are tunnels inside tunnels here, but I didn't expect to be shunted aside by you."

"David, I don't know what you imagine Vatican City is like, but if there are signs attached to the statuary, they decidedly do not read 'This way to the hidden Nazis.'"

"Well, Lehmann's death makes the point, wouldn't you say?"

"What point?"

"He went off the road at the same spot as Lionni's car, the wreckage of which was still down there."

"Lionni's car?"

"You know about Jocko."

"Of course I do. But what are you saying?"

"The wreckage of the car Jocko died in was still in the ravine. Lehmann's car landed on it."

"Good God, David. The papal gendarme's report said nothing about that. It says only that he went off the mountain road, an accident, drunk."

"Which, despite being an account offered by the Holy See, is not true. Lehmann's death was no more an accident than Jocko's was. Surely you see that."

"But Lionni's *was* an accident."

Warburg shook his head.

"Christ," Deane said. He shuddered. "I'm sorry about Jocko Lionni.

I admired him. You know that. He was a hero. But Father Lehmann, I never liked him. He was something of a snake. And I knew he was up to his eyeballs in the *Aussenweg* thing."

"Obviously so, since he made a point of it with where he died. He chose the place."

"If they know that in the Vatican," Deane said, "doors are slamming on all three floors of the pontifical household, drawers being shut, safes locked, cabinets sealed. Like a diving submarine. Get ready for the *magnum silentium.*"

"In Jocko's case it was not suicide. It was murder." Warburg remembered Marguerite's refusal of that word, preferring "combat." But "murder" made it more likely Deane would help. "Kevin," Warburg said, "maybe now you'll work with me. Or are you in the diving submarine too?"

"Look, I carried what you gave me as far as I could. The names, photos, everything."

"You were going to match those names and photos with the new identities."

"But this is more than a Jewish concern," Deane said. "I've had to look at it more broadly than you."

"What the hell does that mean?"

"It means that crimes against the Jews are not to be adjudicated only by Jews. Enraged Jewish soldiers in the British Army have been assassinating German POWs. This Haganah business is assassination, too, but in cold blood. Blatant revenge. Emotional responses are one thing; elaborate plotting is another. I won't be part of that. If there are men at large who oversaw the death camps, then they should be arrested. There are procedures in place for tracking fugitive war criminals, and there is a tribunal, under proper authority, for bringing them to trial."

"I know that. What do you think I'm searching for if not 'proper authority'? Goddammit, proper authority, doing its proper duty, is exactly what I want."

Deane said, "I already took what you gave me to American officials."

Warburg channeled his surprise into a single word, "Who?"

"General Mates."

"Fuck!"

"What do you mean, fuck? The CIC is all about catching these bastards. That's what they do."

"Don't be a fool, Kevin. The CIC is all about the next war, not the last one."

"Hold on, David. I learned from Vatican sources that CIC-Vienna had Ante Pavelic in detention in Salzburg and then let him slip away, disguised as a priest. An outrage, and I felt it as a Catholic because the archbishop of Salzburg was complicit. When I told Mates about it, he hit the ceiling. Mates was more outraged than I was. Enraged at the incompetence in Vienna of his own CIC, suckers for a fake priest. I saw his rage for myself."

"You saw what he showed you. The man is a congenital liar."

"I doubt that."

"The CIC is not incompetent. It's corrupt."

Deane held his ground. "I know Mates well."

Warburg nodded. "Right. In confession with you that day. He tells you all his secrets."

"He worked for us on that Habsburg thing, trying to generate grassroots support for the archduke."

"Where?"

"Vienna, mainly. Catholic clergy."

"And Zagreb?" Warburg asked. "Through Croatian clergy?"

"Yes."

"Nazis, all of them." Warburg heard the anger in his own voice, tried to neutralize it. "You saw the names I gave you. Mostly Croatians. Those men are Pavelic's inner circle, sheltered in Vatican dependencies all over Rome, right now. You *saw* that! And of course I should have seen this, too: General Mates is their protector. Pavelic is Mates's ace to Tito's king. The Ustashe wins the pot. A Catholic counterweight to Bolsheviks. The restoration fantasy resurrected, in cahoots with Nazis, and the Vatican is as complicit now as it was a year ago. Hell, maybe including you."

"No."

"Spellman?"

"Spellman knows nothing. He wouldn't know the Balkans from the Baltics." Deane stopped.

Warburg read the priest's sudden unease. Deane's future was tied to Spellman. It would not do to display disdain for his patron. And, sure enough, Warburg heard the defensive note in what Deane said then: "But why would Spellman know anything about the Croatians? They were a sideshow during the war, and still are. Who in the States has ever heard of Croatia?"

Warburg nodded. "So General Mates needed a Vatican partner who was up to speed on darlings like Pavelic, somebody who would be, how shall I put it, less squeamish than you. Lehmann, obviously."

"In fact, I was the one to tell Mates about Lehmann, last year."

"In that confessional."

"Yes. General Mates checked him out. He came back to me saying Lehmann was clean."

"And?" Warburg poked Deane, not totally without friendliness. "Do the damn arithmetic, Kevin. You knew for certain that Lehmann wasn't clean. Mates all but announced the thing to you. He'd recruited Lehmann somehow. Maybe he offered to help with *Aussenweg*, but for his own reasons. Perhaps blackmail." Warburg stopped. Blackmail about Marguerite? But she'd come late to Lehmann's story.

"What blackmail?"

"Let's think out loud," Warburg said, shifting away from Marguerite. "The U.S. Treasury Department is tracking Nazi loot. I see the reports. At the very end, millions went from Berlin's Reichsbank to various Swiss banks, several accounts held by entities in Rome, including something called Santa Maria dell'Anima."

"The German church."

"Lehmann's church, a simple funnel. Money from Berlin to the Holy See."

"With Lehmann as the teller at the window? Jesus."

Warburg said, "Mates would have had to keep all that from you because you'd have blown the whistle on it. Right?"

"In fact, I did blow the whistle once. There was a stash of Croatian gold in that building over there." Deane pointed at Santa Marta. "Tens of millions. I reported it, and the gold disappeared."

"Disappeared from you," Warburg said. "They just put it someplace else. Good chance General Mates knew about it. Probably knew that you'd done your duty. Which meant that, for his purposes, he couldn't trust you. Not like he could trust Lehmann. After that, Mates had to maintain his distance from you."

"He did. I wondered about that."

"And after Lionni's death, Mates would have realized there were new players in the game."

"Zionists."

"Jews, Kevin. Jews. From Mates's point of view, dogs in the manger, messing everything up, since everything depended on the Nazi killers going free. That's the deal Mates has going — the Austria–Argentina Express, tickets punched to give Pavelic a leg up in Zagreb. And a fresh start for Germans to help build the anti-Communist bulwark. All of it suddenly in jeopardy. After Lionni's death, Mates would have pressed Lehmann. You assume it was Nazis who gave Lehmann reason to drive off that cliff. It might have been Americans."

Deane felt like a mulish pupil unable to keep up with the lesson. Sister Thomas had pushed such questions at him, but this Jew had just dragged the monster out into the light where even a dunce like him could see the thing clear.

Wait a minute. Why "this Jew"?

A brisk wind whipped across the plaza and tore at Deane's cape. He pulled it closer around him. His eyes went to the cross atop the massive Egyptian obelisk. *Jesus.*

"David." Deane spoke carefully, each word a step in a minefield. "I have to ask you. Does your contempt for General Mates start with the fact that he's working with the British against Zionism?"

"Mates told you that?"

"Yes."

"To discredit me," Warburg said. "And you believed him."

"He told me to be wary of you."

"And you have been."

"But is it true?"

"Does it discredit me? My trying to get Jewish DPs to Palestine? Are we back to that? The Church's insistence on the Wandering Jew?"

"Not my insistence," Deane said, yet he himself had just produced a visceral "this Jew."

Warburg said, "You make assumptions, Kevin, without knowing it. I guess we all do."

"Not an assumption now, David, but a question. What do we do with this? We both see it: Americans helping the commandant of Treblinka to escape. The Gestapo chief of Lyon. The others on that list. That's not our America."

"And a Church supporting Pavelic—"

"—is not my Church."

"'Procedures in place,' you said. 'Proper authority.'"

"Yes."

"General Clark," Warburg said. That simply.

"All right," Deane answered, but uncertainly. "And how do we get to Clark?"

"By going to his office."

Deane stared at Warburg.

Warburg said, "Right now."

It took Deane a moment to realize that Warburg was dead serious—and dead right. Deane nodded. "Fast break," he said.

Tugging their garments, they crossed out of St. Peter's Square, out of Vatican City, to Warburg's car on Via della Conciliazione, halfway to the Tiber. They drove to the Palazzo Margherita on Via Veneto, the grand building now commonly referred to, even by Romans, as *Sede*, for headquarters. They arrived just as the khaki-clad enlisted clerks and junior officers were squaring up the folders for the in-boxes of their superiors.

The corridors were crowded with self-important Americans in uniform. Warburg led Deane up the stairs to the second floor, to the palatial office of General Mark Clark, who, at war's end, had been given his fourth star and named commander of Allied forces in Italy. General Clark's executive officer greeted them. The exec, a colonel, knew Warburg, but it was clearly the Vatican official—the cape and red piping, the Roman priest's hat he was carrying—that got his attention. The colonel promised to show them into the general's office as soon as Clark's daily brief was finished.

"Daily brief?" Warburg asked. "Who briefs the general?"

The colonel answered only with a stare, which the stolid Warburg returned. What, Deane wondered, had Warburg just asked? Who cares who briefs the general?

Deane and Warburg sat on a hard bench against the wall. Twenty minutes later, they were ushered in.

Clark's handsomeness was marred by dramatically protruding ears, his gravitas undercut by youth—he was the youngest full general in the U.S. Army. But there was steel in the man, as the Germans knew, and as his own troops could not forget. He had unflinchingly ordered the reduction to rubble of the sixth-century Abbey of Monte Cassino, where Saint Benedict had invented Western monasticism. He had ordered minefields crossed, knowing the mines would be cleared by his own dead. General Clark did not stand when the two men entered his office, made no effort to look pleased, and did not invite them to sit. Nor did Clark flinch as he listened to them from across the minefield of his desk.

No one else was present. Warburg did most of the talking. Deane was impressed as he listened to the summary of what they'd come to, and he reminded himself that Warburg was a trained lawyer. This morning he was the prosecuting attorney.

Warburg's charges built to the climactic indictment of Clark's own Counter-Intelligence Corps, acting—no doubt without authorization—to cooperate with Croatian Fascists, facilitating the escape to Argentina and beyond of some of the most sought-after Nazis. Indeed, the CIC had already allowed the release from Allied custody of the Ustashe commander Ante Pavelic, one of the worst war criminals. That Warburg did not refer by name to General Mates struck Deane as odd, but then he realized that the note of impersonality in his blistering of the CIC was essential. To maintain his damning objectivity, Warburg had to keep a distance from his own loathing.

When Warburg had nothing further to add, Clark sat silently for a long moment, then leaned close to his desk intercom. He pushed the button, but still said nothing. A door behind him opened, a door hidden until then in the panel molding and leading in from a small side office. General Mates strode through.

Mulish Deane suddenly understood Warburg's question about the daily brief. They had interrupted the intelligence officer's morning report. Of course it would be Mates. Warburg had foreseen this.

Clark said, "I believe you both know General Mates."

Neither Warburg nor Deane spoke.

Clark looked up at Mates. "General?"

"Sir, the one point of fact in the nonsense you just heard has to do with the escape from detention of Ante Pavelic. CIC-Vienna bungled that. I investigated, found malfeasance — gross negligence — and have initiated court-martial proceedings to punish the responsible personnel. Pavelic is being hunted as we speak, and I am sure we will capture him. Otherwise, what you heard is a fairy tale. Mr. Warburg has ties to the Haganah, which obviously has its own agenda here. Apparently he has enchanted Monsignor Deane with these fantasies. I have consulted with Vatican officials, and they would be as appalled as I by the implications of these charges."

"Not implications, General," Warburg said, addressing Clark. "Nothing implicit in what I said. I have put before you an explicit case tying the CIC to Nazis."

Clark said, "And tying the Catholic Church to Nazis, no?" Clark turned to Deane. "So what about it, Monsignor? Isn't the Very Reverend Tardini the one who handles Vatican diplomacy? He's the man I do business with. Have you spoken to him? If I asked him to come over here, what would he tell me?"

"I have no idea what he would tell you," Deane answered calmly, but he knew full well what Tardini would tell Spellman. *This Monsignor Deane, how dare he! A violation of sacred Holy See confidentiality!*

Having denounced Deane, Tardini would turn his rage on Spellman himself. And Deane could kiss his own promotion to bishop goodbye. No ring, no next rung on the ladder. Still, Deane's calmness was real.

"Well, Monsignor," General Clark said, "perhaps Tardini's the one you should take this up with. Pavelic, he's a Catholic, isn't he? The whole goddamn Croatian thing, that's the Catholic Church, isn't it?"

Deane said, "The Vatican has its business here, General. Fair enough." It surprised Deane how unfazed he felt. This shit was so much bigger than anybody's being promoted to bishop, himself included. *Let Tardini do what Tardini does.* He said, "But I'm here as an American, because America is ensnared in this rats' nest, too. That's what this whole thing is, a rat*line,* for getting rats off the ship. Off the continent. Rescuing rats, General. Is that what we fought the war for?"

With forced detachment Clark leaned forward slightly as if to say, Who the fuck are you? What fucking war did you fight? But he said, "I think we know what we fought the war for, Monsignor. As for the rats' nest, why don't you leave that to us?" Clark looked at Mates, a curl at his mouth. "Aren't you the rat exterminator, General?"

"Yes, Sir. Selectively."

Warburg waited until Mates looked at him, then said, "And how would the American people react to your selections, General?"

"What are you implying now, Mister?" Clark asked.

Warburg looked steadily at Clark. "Monsignor Deane is friendly with Henry Luce, General. Mrs. Luce is a fervent Catholic. What do you think readers of *Time* magazine would make of your rescue of Nazis?"

Clark snorted. "Rescue of Nazis, no. A first salvo against the Reds, yes. Henry Luce sat in that goddamn chair a month ago, right there." Clark pointed at one of the chairs that had not been offered to Warburg and Deane. "Luce proposed the very thing that has you so worked up, recruiting the Germans who know Stalin's weak points. And Luce's wife? Hell, yes, pious Catholic! She'd take her cue from the Holy Father, and where's his complaint? Anyway, you think there's a publisher in America who'd violate Army censorship? Think again, Warburg."

Deane heard the sneer in the way Clark pronounced Warburg's name.

Still, Warburg stared impassively back at the two officers. It was Mates who flinched slightly. He unbuttoned the flapped breast pocket of his tunic and took out a silk square. He blew his nose—the business of a man covering up his uneasiness. Why, Deane wondered, did Mates seem the one who'd just been thwarted?

When Deane and Warburg left the Palazzo Margherita, they found that the skies had opened, and the rain was bouncing in its own puddles. They ran to Warburg's car. Neither spoke as they returned to the Vatican. When the guard at the sovereign edge of St. Peter's Square peered into the car and saw the red tab at Deane's clerical collar, he waved them through. Warburg pulled into the square, between the Bernini fountain and the colonnade, and stopped. Deane said, "Jesus, David. Henry Luce? A friend of mine?"

"I was scrambling, Kevin."

"No you weren't. You expected that, didn't you? You knew Clark would blow us off. You brought up Luce so that I would get the whole picture."

"Well, did you?"

Deane could not think what to say.

Warburg grabbed Deane by the arm. "Look, I am as thrown as you are. If there's a difference between us, Kevin, it's that I've been trusting you. I've trusted you from the first day we arrived here. You've never trusted me. Why is that?"

Instead of answering, Deane got out of the car. He'd heard the accusation—Jew hatred—and he was sick and tired of it. Then Warburg got out and crossed over to Deane. Once again he seized the priest's arm. The rain pounded them. Deane had finally donned the goofy *saturno* headgear, but only because of the downpour. Warburg was hatless. He had to speak loudly, almost shouting. "Listen to me. With the brush-off from Clark, it boils down to this. The *Aussenweg* network is beyond us, maybe. And the CIC, too. And who the hell knows what's hidden in the Vatican catacombs? I'll tell you what I do know. I know who killed Jocko Lionni, and I need you to help me find him."

Two nights before, Warburg had refused to let Marguerite go alone to Santa Maria della Vittoria. It was after ten o'clock when they'd arrived at the church, time enough for Lehmann to have left his note and gone. Marguerite had the key to the donation box from one of the Cistercian sisters, the women who had raised her at Casa dello Spirito Santo. She opened the box, ignored the few coins it held, and withdrew a folded envelope. Warburg followed her across the darkened church to the bank of blue votive candles, which offered light to read by. He stood aside, letting his eyes drift to the marble face in the candles' violet illumination — an altarpiece statue. A woman, head thrown back, covered by a nun's cloak. It was news to Warburg that a Catholic saint should be so explicitly in the throes of erotic arousal. Ordinarily he'd have been transfixed by such a sight, but his attention remained on Marguerite, even turned away as she was. He resolutely did not intrude upon the space she'd claimed simply by hunching over what she was reading.

A few moments later, she folded the note back into its envelope and led the way out of the church. She was silent during the drive back to her enclosed family villa, now the home for girls in trouble. Before leaving Warburg's car, she turned to him, declaring, "He says nothing about Vukas."

"Slobodan Vukas," Warburg said to Deane now. "A Franciscan friar."

"I recognize the name," Deane said. "He was on the list you gave me."

"Yes. He had taken over the Casa dello Spirito Santo. Now he's gone from there. We thought Lehmann would lead us to him."

"'We'?"

"Marguerite d'Erasmo and me. She knew Vukas in Croatia. He ran a death camp for children."

"A Franciscan *priest?*"

"Yes. The real thing. Pavelic's chaplain. After Lionni on the Via Cassia, he knows he's a target. He knows that the next attack will be smarter. But Vukas is key to the Road Out — yes, what you called it, the ratline. But there's a road *back* in this, too. Vukas runs a group called the Crusaders — the vanguard of the Croatian restoration. Pavelic needs him in Rome, their staging area for the take-back of Yugoslavia. Almost certainly Vukas is holed up in another of the Vatican extraterritorials. How many of those places are there, anyway?"

"Monasteries, convents, schools, institutes . . . dozens."

"I need you to find him, Kevin. I know what you'll say: it's too many places. But narrow it down. Suppose he avoids the obvious Croatian institutions. Suppose, instead, he depends on his fellow Franciscans."

"Or Franciscan nuns," Deane offered. The pull he felt from Warburg, suddenly, was like a magnet. But that presumed some metal in himself. He said, "Vukas would feel safer with nuns. Nuns wouldn't turn away a monk in sandals. Most convents sheltered Jews."

"Even Jews?"

"Do me a favor — spare me the 'even Jews' stuff."

"The point is, Kevin, once you settle on a few places to look, it might be easy. Vukas has a harelip. He drools, which requires a constant handkerchief. Hard to hide that."

Through the rain, so quietly, Deane asked, "What are you after here, David?"

"Justice, Kevin. At least in this one case."

Justice. Deane thought that Warburg could pull such a word out of this thicket of corruption and contradiction and have it seem true. Yet Deane, the contentious friend, was compelled to supply another word. "You mean revenge, David," he said coldly.

And Warburg, coldly, declined to reply.

By now the rain was dripping off the capacious brim of Deane's hat. It was streaming from Warburg's matted hair onto his face. The pigeons were gone from the open square, as were the cats, pilgrims, and vendors. The men were alone in the drenching, womb-like piazza. The only witnesses to the monsignor's moment of decision, now arrived at, were the travertine marbles high on the crown of St. Peter's façade, the twenty-foot-high Christ, and, flanking him, the eleven loitering Apostles. All the Apostles — *lo!* — but Judas.

She had made clear to him her intention that they should remain apart until she'd heard from Philip, which he understood. She needed to sort through her feelings, and he respected that. He had found it possible to let go of his own impulses. But that was before.

Deane's thoughts went from Sister Thomas to the unknowing nuns among whom Vukas might have sought shelter. What were the odds that the mother abbess of a convent in Rome would violate the rules of the Vicariate? Religious foundations of women were allowed to admit to residence male externs such as retreatants, chaplains, and spiritual directors if accommodations could be provided outside the cloister. But the mother abbess was required to inform the cardinal vicar of any such admission. The Vicariate's commission for religious orders had its offices in the warren of rooms at the far end of the corridor off which Deane's own offices were located, and it turned out to be a simple matter for Deane to consult current records there. He found that of the seven Roman convents that had registered male admissions in the past week, only one was Franciscan. A friar named Bruno Pladic, OFM, identified as a professor emeritus of medieval history at the University of Trieste, took up residence in Santi Tre Vergini two days after Lionni was killed. Pladic — a Slavic name, like Vukas.

The convent in Testaccio was named for three Christian virgins martyred by Diocletian. It was attached to a crumbling sixth-century basilica, and was itself all but derelict. The ancient building was tucked into a crowded hillside southwest of Aventino, a gritty area where, for most of a century, squatters' hovels had competed for space with broken-down caravans and with the thrown-together tin huts of Rome's forgotten transients, including Gypsies. The nuns of Santi Tre Vergini had begun as a contemplative presence, but while caring for their impoverished neighbors, they had slowly become impoverished themselves. The adjacent basilica was a dark horror-house of neglect, haunted by homeless desperadoes. Now the convent was defined by its soup kitchen — and also by the stench of sewage, which seeped from

the shantytown above into the rotting walls, fouling the cloister, chapel, and ill-used guest wing with mold. An unlikely place for a distin-
guished visiting friar.

Deane was reluctant to approach the convent alone — an American
priest all too conspicuous, with the mother abbess likely to be skittish.
That was why he'd thought of Sister Thomas. One nun to another, a
shot at really learning something. Setting out to explain the urgency
of her coming with him, he hoped she would see it. Deane went to
the second floor of the Apostolic Palace, to Tardini's suite of offices,
expecting to find Sister Thomas at her desk in the small room from
which she supervised the prelate's communications with his nuncios
and legates.

She was not there. Her assistant was an elderly Italian laywoman,
Signora Palladio, a stenographer and file clerk. If most such positions
in the Vatican were held by men, the prior exception for the crypt-
analyst-nun had required a further exception, since it would not do
to have a female, not even a Cambridge DPhil, supervising a male,
not even a clerk. Signora Palladio's winged typewriter table was in an
alcove fronting the room in which Sister Thomas worked, the way
Deane had seen Thomas's own table tucked into the corner of Cardinal Maglione's office the year before.

The woman knew Monsignor Deane and greeted him warmly. She
explained that Sister Thomas had been at work earlier. "But then an
officer came to see her. She told me to take my *pranzo,* my meal. When
I returned, she was gone." The woman paused. "Perhaps she is ill," she
said, with ample concern.

Deane thought at once of the nun's thinness, emaciation almost,
and felt a rush of worry.

"Officer?" he asked. "What kind of officer?"

"British."

Philip. Deane did not move. Then, as if he would see Thomas there,
he looked past the woman into the office proper. On Thomas's desk he
saw, lying at an angle atop a tidy pile, an unfolded page in the telltale
yellow of a cablegram. The nun was discreet with all kinds of communications, no matter how trivial. What prompted her to leave this one

exposed? Not illness. He pictured her, startled, pushing back from her desk and hurrying away. Why?

"Signora," Deane said, "I'd like to leave a note for Sister."

"*Sì, Monsignor,*" the woman said, and handed a steno pad to Deane. He bent and jotted a few lines.

He tore the page from the pad. "I'll just leave it on her desk." He went from the alcove into Thomas's office. The woman's view was blocked. Dropping his page, he picked up the cablegram. Normally he'd never have taken it, but what was normal now? Feigning a cough, he stuffed it into his cassock. With a brisk farewell to Signora Palladio, he left.

The paper burned at his chest as he made his way back to his office. He closed the door. Leaning at his desk, he smoothed the paper out and saw that it contained digits bunched into perhaps two dozen groups of five. At the top of the page was a mark—the crown, scepter, and unicorn of the British seal, and, in plain text, the heading *H.M. Government Communications Headquarters.* Between the lines of numbers, someone—not Sister Thomas, whose handwriting Deane knew well—had penciled a string of words, an obvious decoding of the encryption: "Explosion Tuesday—Headquarters British Forces Palestine-Transjordan. Killed on duty—Philip Barnes Morton, Major, Royal Signals, Section IX. Details unavailable . . ."

Deane stared at the page as if the numbers and letters would rearrange themselves into some other meaning. He sat down. *Yes, Philip. But not this.* He ran his open hands over the paper, pressing its two creases smooth, as if erasing. Then he picked up the telephone, waited for the operator, and asked to be put through to Sant'Agata, the Vatican residence for consecrated women. There, the portress told him that Sister Thomas was at her Curia office, which Deane knew not to be the case. He could not think what else to do, so he set off.

Santi Tre Vergini was at the upper limit of a lane that was almost too narrow for Deane's car. The road was so badly rutted that his driver muttered unhappily as the undercarriage repeatedly banged. Upended pavement stones competed with mire from the recent rains, threatening to trap them. Finally Deane left the car and continued the climb on foot, soiling his shoes with mud. He kept his eyes up and ahead, on the bell tower that marked the place.

The sun was high in the sky, and played with the tower, momentarily blinding him. The basilica, with its belfry, was on the far side of the compound, with the main church entrance apparently facing a distant street. The church's roof line was jagged. In places the earthenware tiles were gone, with bare slats exposed, suggesting that the church interior was partially open to the sky. As he approached the nearer convent enclosure where the hill plateaued, he could see an opening in the flaking stucco wall. A half-rotted gate hung at an angle off its post. Because the fractured gate was necessarily ajar, Deane could see that, just inside the close, a man sat on a shaded ledge, hat pulled down on his face. He was dozing. Deane slowed, uncertain. In the crook of the man's arm was a shotgun. A guard.

Deane stopped where he was, then backed away. He retreated to an upended crate just out of the guard's sight line. By stepping onto the crate he was able to look over the convent wall and down into the enclosure. He was peering into one of two courtyards, with a corner of the other yard visible beyond the dividing single-story structure. The near courtyard was strung with clotheslines, from which only a few articles of clothing hung. Approximating the human form, a brown garment with long sleeves and full-length legs was pinned at the shoulders on one line, hanging like the flayed skin of a martyr. Deane's old-country father wore such an undergarment—"long handles" he'd called it. On the same line hung a sleeveless undershirt, also male apparel, and a pair of faded gray drawers with fly buttons at the yoke. On another line, carefully arranged in a row and fastened with wooden pins, were a number of white cloths, each one a foot square. Six of them. Deane thought at first they were purificators, the altar linen with which the priest wipes out the chalice, but then it hit him: handkerchiefs. Who would have one undershirt but half a dozen handkerchiefs?

Marguerite climbed the stairs to the fifth floor of the beaten-down building. She moved quietly, an instinctive caution. And sure enough, sounds of voices coming from within the small attic room alarmed her. She had been told that "Malachi," the one-word alias of the commander she was meeting, would be alone. She froze four or five steps from the top of the staircase. She heard three male voices. The heated discussion was in Hebrew, a language she could recognize but barely understand. She waited.

At exactly eleven p.m., the appointed hour, she rapped on the door once, firmly. The voices fell silent. The door was pulled open. She was here to brief them on what Warburg had learned from Deane, and on what she herself had then seen in Testaccio, as the day had faded into night, loitering in and around the basilica of Santi Tre Vergini, with an eye on the adjoining convent. She was still dressed oddly, having pulled together a disguising Romany wardrobe from the stock of clothes left behind by the street women who shared her family villa. Her head was wrapped in a black scarf, knotted to send a slender fall of rough silk to her shoulders. Her layered skirts were broad, bright-patterned, belted with a wide leather strap. She wore a black basque, a fitted bodice that drew in her waist and pushed up her breasts. She stank of musk oil. Inside the half-ruined basilica, she had nicely resembled other women among the squatters who had taken over the place.

Then, at the convent, she had noted the presence of two rifle-bearing guards, one at the automobile entrance to the enclosure and one on the roof of the main of three buildings. Otherwise, she had been unable to confirm what Deane reported. She climbed the bell tower of the basilica, and had been able to look down into the two convent courtyards. The clothesline in the one was bare, and the only figures who'd appeared in the other, apparently cloistered, were brown-robed sisters, solitary walkers in their circuit of postprandial prayer. In the clothesline courtyard, near the door, there was a weary canvas chair and, beside it, a tin bowl, as for a dog. She had seen no sign of Vukas. When the last of the convent lights was extinguished, about two hours ago, she had left.

"I am Miriam," she said.

The man opened the door wide, and she entered.

He and two others had been standing around a small table. They were dressed in rude proletarian clothes. The man who'd opened the door — Malachi? — wore a seaman's cap pulled low over his forehead. A pair of broken cane chairs were against one wall. A cot with a bunched blanket was against another. Under the cot were a pair of wooden boxes of the sort used to carry weapons and ammunition. Spread open on the table was a newspaper, the apparent object of the argument she had interrupted.

The man in the cap addressed her in Hebrew, but she shook her head, replying with the phrase she had often used in Galilee: "You must speak very slowly."

"English, then," the man said.

"Yes."

He gestured at the newspaper. The front page was organized around a photograph of a large building, a corner section collapsed to the street, with interior staircases exposed. Six stories — no, seven. In the foreground were a pair of cypress trees. The banner headline, in Italian, read, "Jerusalem Hotel Destroyed by Terrorists." Looking closely, she saw that it was an early edition of the next day's *Il Tempo*.

"Would you translate, please, in English?" the man said.

So none of them had Italian.

Marguerite stared at the page, unsure what she was seeing. Slowly, focus came, and horrified understanding. She conveyed what she read. Explosions at midday destroyed the King David Hotel, the limestone structure looking across the Kidron Valley to the Old City and Mount Zion. The only luxury hotel in Jerusalem. Half of one wing entirely collapsed. Many dozens assumed to be dead, including hotel staff and clerical workers. The explosion was carried out, the article said, by Zionist terrorists.

As Marguerite looked up from the paper, two of the men resumed their argument in Hebrew. The man in the cap banged the table. "Enough!" he barked. He looked at Marguerite. "Surely it says the hotel was the British military headquarters. Surely it says that."

"No. It makes no mention of British headquarters."

"The southern wing of the hotel, that is the damage?"

Marguerite looked at the story. "Yes. Southern."

"The Secretariat of the Mandate, then. And British Army head-quarters. Including the intelligence office, with its records, all the files on Irgun and Haganah. That is what was destroyed."

"It says a nightclub was destroyed," she said. "A restaurant, crowded. The French consulate across the street was damaged. Passersby were killed."

"Does it mention a warning? There would have been a warning."

Marguerite looked again. She spoke the translation aloud. "The British government spokesman says there was no warning. 'A despicable, cowardly act,' he says. 'All available information is to the effect that the perpetrators were Jews.'" Marguerite looked up from the paper. "Are you Malachi?"

"Yes."

"David Ben-Gurion is quoted here as saying whoever did this is 'the enemy of the Jewish people.'"

"*Merde*," one of the others said.

"An attack at noon?" Marguerite said. "A hotel?"

"Army headquarters," Malachi retorted. "Not civilians."

"British vermin," the third man said. "And the parasites that feed on them."

"Vermin?" Marguerite repeated. "Parasites? Those are Fascist words for Jews."

"Enough!" Malachi commanded, and his sharp tone silenced the two men. "This was an operation of the Jewish Resistance Movement," he said to her. "This has been planned. Much prepared for. Carefully prepared for."

"Hotel staff?" Marguerite said. She would have liked to keep a measured air, but astonishment and anger laced her voice. "Clerks? A nightclub? Passersby?"

"I told you. There would have been a warning. That is always the way. With so many dead, the British certainly ignored the warning."

"Why would they do that?" Marguerite asked.

"To vilify us."

"They would let dozens of people die to vilify the Haganah?"

"Irgun. This is Irgun. This is Gidi."

"Gidi" was the alias of the legendary Irgun commander in Palestine. Marguerite had heard him referred to, but always with lowered voices. It had yet to come clear to her where the Irgun began and the Haganah left off. It wasn't clear to the Irgun, either, or to the Haganah. Perhaps this attack would clarify things.

Malachi folded the newspaper, a decisive signal that its subject was closed. "And you, Miriam?" he said. "You have a report to make?"

Marguerite glanced at the others, a pair of hard men. But of course they would be. She herself was supposed to be hard.

She had told David that, once her report to Malachi was made and responsibility for the final disposition of Vukas handed off to men prepared to accomplish it, she would come to him. She would return ready, finally, to resume what they had begun.

Since the day of Jocko's burial, there had been only interruptions, beginning with the curse of the cryptic message Father Lehmann had left in the donation box, an emotional scrawl. At first, crushed by what she read, she had resolved to show the letter to no one. But then, late the next day, she learned about Lehmann's death. That had taken her immediately to David's flat, overlooking the Piazza del Popolo. When he answered the door, she simply handed him the paper, and watched him read:

Verily I say unto you, all sins shall be forgiven unto the sons of men, and all blasphemies wherewith soever they shall blaspheme. But he that shall blaspheme against the Holy Ghost hath never forgiveness, but eternal damnation.

When David looked up at her, Marguerite said, "These are the words of Jesus. I thought Father Lehmann was using them to condemn me."

"But he was condemning himself."

"That is what I realized when I learned what he had done . . . But I, too, am condemned."

"Such words are heartless," Warburg said. "I thought Jesus was the God of mercy. Where is the mercy here?"

He opened his arms, and she went into them. They found the way to his bed while holding each other. Now, when they made love, unlike before, all was gentle but for the fierce moments in which each one cried out. Mostly, their embrace was merciful, kind, and quiet. Surprised by tranquility, they eased into the forgetting of everything but physical sensation, two minds lost in one body. They held each other for a long time, saying nothing.

The next evening, she returned to David's place. He had just learned from Monsignor Deane about Santi Tre Vergini. Having explained about the posted guard and the handkerchiefs on the clothesline, David insisted on going with her. She replied that it was for her to do alone — to confirm what Deane had seen and to bring news of Vukas's hiding place to Malachi, handing the burden off but also fulfilling her duty to Jocko and the children of Sisak. Because David trusted her, and loved her, he let her go.

She assumed — they both assumed — that she would return very soon. At his door, they kissed lightly. She pulled back. She reached into her bag and withdrew a folded square of cloth. She held it out to him. He took it. She turned and hurried down the stairs, leaving him to stare at the fabric, white wool with black stripes. He opened it, and fringes fell at the corners. A *tallit*.

Malachi expected this Miriam to hand over what she knew of the place where Vukas was hiding, and, resigned to her role, she might have. Jocko's fate had turned her one way, and Lehmann's another. Warburg was showing her yet a different way, and it was the one she wanted. She would be a killer no more, not even of Vukas. She would gladly let Malachi's team take care of the Croatian monster, avenging Abel and his men — avenging the bullet through Jocko's lip. She knew they would.

But how? She was ambushed by doubts tied to what she had just read in *Il Tempo:* Jewish fighters responsible for the wanton killing of innocents. A bomb without warning. Carelessness at the King David to the point of murder. Marguerite took a step back. Considering her words carefully, she said, "My information is less certain than I thought. I went to the place tonight. I saw no sure evidence that Vukas is there."

"You said handkerchiefs."

"I saw no handkerchiefs for myself. But what are handkerchiefs? We must have a sighting of the man himself. I did not see him."

"Where is the place? What is the name?"

"What is the plan?"

"The plan is of no concern to you. Tell me where is the place."

"What is the plan?" she repeated, calmly. But her mind was taken over by a vision of the explosion she had witnessed at the British embassy on Via XX Settembre, the combustion flash that seared her eyes, the wall of heat that hit her, most of a block away, the roar of the falling debris, followed by the eerie silence in the cone of which came the recognition that this conflagration was something *she* had done. It had mattered infinitely, not only to her but to Jocko, that no one had died in the embassy. Jocko had been the one to force on Abel the precautions they had taken, including the sawhorses placed to keep passersby away and the ruse of her own visit to the embassy ahead of time, the reconnoitering that made certain no one would die. That had mattered, in the end, to Abel and the others, too.

But to these men? Would they just topple the Santi Tre Vergini bell tower, bringing down a wall of rubble not only on the adjacent convent but on the abandoned church? Abandoned by all except squatters, thieves, whores, Gypsies. Vermin and the parasites that feed on them. If their plan included taking care to spare such nobodies, not to mention the nuns who'd unknowingly offered Vukas shelter, Malachi would tell her. He knew what she was asking. His refusal to answer meant the plan was another King David Hotel.

"There must be further surveillance," she said. "There must be confirmation. The convent must not be attacked. Only Vukas."

"I told you. The plan is of no concern to you."

"With Abel, the plan was agreed to by the group."

"Abel is dead. And this is not your group."

Marguerite stepped back toward the door. "A good point. You are not my group. I have made a mistake." She turned, half opened the door. But Malachi grabbed her and slammed her against the door, forcing it closed. His face was only inches from hers, reeking of garlic. "Where is the place?" he demanded again. "What convent? What is the name?"

Marguerite answered with nothing but her unflinching eyes.

He closed his fists on the pleated fabric of her bodice and lifted her, pressing up into her breasts. "Tell me, you Gypsy whore."

But she would not. Yes, she thought of Carlo Capra, how he had seized her like this, in rage, but Malachi was not Carlo. Nor was this rage — only the distillation of male dominance. Grasping that she was not going to answer him no matter what he did to her, Malachi roughly released her.

She said, "I am not a Gypsy. If I am a whore, it is a whore for Zion." Then she turned, opened the door, and left. Behind her, a man cursed loudly until, once again, Malachi silenced him with a single, drastic word.

By the hour before dawn, Marguerite was back in Testaccio, now with a beaten leather satchel slung across her chest. The satchel carried, among other things, her own copy of *Il Tempo*. She knew that David would be awake, waiting for her. But perhaps he, too, would have found the newspaper by now. Reading of the bombing of the Jerusalem hotel, he might guess why she had not come to him as planned.

She entered the church by the door she had used the afternoon before, and made her way through the shadows, past the rising and falling hulks of sleepers, to the door of the bell tower. She had jammed it closed with an odd piece of iron and was satisfied to see it that way still. The bell tower was an elevation of sixty winding steps.

Sunrise over Rome was a slow-moving miracle of dazzling reflections, as the golden rays found, first, the dome of St. Peter's, then the lesser domes of other churches, then the ocher tiles of slanted rooftops and the white marble wedding cake of the Victor Emmanuel monument. Closer in were the pointed fir trees of Aventino, their needles ornamented with tiny dewdrops, glistening like diamond dust. The trees called to mind the cypresses in the foreground of the *Il Tempo* photograph, dumb witnesses to the Jerusalem hotel's destruction. In her proselyte's instruction in Judaism, she had been told that King David himself had stood near that very spot, overlooking the valley, when he wept for his wicked son: *O my son Absalom! Absalom! Would to God I had died for thee!*

Once before, she had watched the extravagant light of dawn quicken the glass needles of pine trees. She knew when and where — the knoll above Sisak. She had watched the sunlight slide like a glacier down the slopes toward the derelict racetrack that had been given over to the camp for children. Carlo. Croatia. Now Jerusalem.

Her gaze went to the roof line of the Red Cross palazzo on the Aventine Hill. Once that building would have made her think only of her father, or perhaps of her innocent self long ago. But now, again, it was a David who came to mind, the other David, hers. *O my love, David, David, would to God . . .*

She had not deliberately deceived him, but deception was the effect of what she had done. It was out of the question to have returned to him last night, to have involved him further in her desecrations, to have not come here to finish this one last desecration herself. What this dawn illuminated most clearly was her absolute return to the numbness to which, for more than a year, she had become wholly accustomed.

The numb state was good. And the dawn also gave her the practical light she needed. From Malachi's hovel, she had rushed back to her place in Parioli for this satchel. Now, from it she withdrew and assembled, in practiced sequence, the cut-down rifle stock, the barrel, the bolt, the firing pin, the cheek pad, the wooden hand guards, and the telescopic sight. With the weapon set, she inserted four bullets into the breech, then threw the bolt handle, driving a cartridge into the centerfire. She braced against the belfry wall, back from the ledge. Through the lens of the aiming device, she found the clothesline courtyard, zeroed in on the dog's water dish, and set herself to wait.

Absorbedness transformed time. At some point, as she expected, the courtyard door opened, and the Doberman pinscher bounded

out. The animal dashed with such exuberance from one wall to another, bouncing and leaping, that only then did Marguerite sense how
constricted the yard was. Within a moment or two, the dog trotted
to the dish, looking up expectantly at the door. That was when the
man appeared, dressed only in scrawny long underwear, carrying a
washbasin pitcher in one hand, a handkerchief in the other. He bent
to pour water from the pitcher into the dog's dish. Then, as if taking
commands from Marguerite, the man looked up at the sky, to enjoy
the first splash of morning light, giving her a clear sight of his mouth.

Whatsoever man that has a blemish . . .

The year before, at Sisak, she had locked binoculars on this same
face, and had wished then, without knowing it, for the cold steel inside the curl of her forefinger. Marguerite fixed the crosshairs on the
glistening cleft of the upper lip. Careful. Premeditated. Chosen. How
different this was from the first time. She waited, still.

. . . he shall not approach the altar.

She did not know what she was waiting for until, as the friar continued his casual survey of the surrounding roof lines, his gaze came
to her, perched in the archway of the bell tower. She adjusted her face
away from the weapon, so that he could see her clearly, perhaps to remember her from the day of her visit to that monastery in Zagreb. She
wanted him to sense that she had tracked him from Sisak. In his eyes
she saw an instant's shock of recognition — enough. Gunsight fixed
upon his blemish, she squeezed the trigger, as she'd so gently done on
the firing range in Galilee hundreds of times. As she did in panic in a
urine-soaked alcove, once.

The thunderclap at her ear, the reverberating echo above the surrounding rooftops and out into the city, made her realize that now she
would be a target. The guards. But she kept the crosshairs on Vukas,
following him as he crumpled to the ground. Good. The dog at once
began to lean onto Vukas, licking at the blood pouring from his exploded face. Once, she'd have gladly shot the Doberman, but not now.
No more killing than was necessary. She watched Vukas through the
sight for a further moment, to be sure he was dead.

She placed the gun on the floor, leaving it. She descended the spiral staircase with no thought of escape. Vukas dead—that must be enough. And for the moment, it was. As for the rest of life, that no longer registered as hers. What she had feared before, now she knew: there was no escaping what she had become. Now, simply to hand herself over to it, hopeless.

TWELVE

Vieni! *Come!*

AVID WARBURG SAT looking out his window, unsure what else to do. She had told him midnight, an hour after midnight at the latest. Then it was two hours after midnight, three. The city was dark, with the yet darker silhouette, opposite his window, of what he thought of as the Caravaggio church, for its stunning altar painting of the crucifixion of Saint Peter, one poor old bastard being gut-hauled upside down.

Perverse association. Warburg shook it off, letting his eyes stray to the obelisk in the center of the Piazza del Popolo. The place was named not for the "people," as he'd first imagined, but for poplar trees. He'd read that the obelisk marked what had been, for centuries, the site of public executions in Rome. *Where the fuck is she?*

Again Warburg rebuked himself for letting her go alone. He reviewed it: how she had called it her mission, said it was her last. She was going to the meeting place for the sole purpose of telling the Haganah about Santi Tre Vergini. She was handing Vukas over to what passed, even in Warburg's eyes by now, for proper authority. And then she was coming to him.

Obviously not. Had she lied? He knew that was possible. She had gone down into a darkness of which he knew nothing, and she was still in search of the door to herself. Unlike Jesus — *Verily I say unto you* — Warburg did not condemn her.

Rome had condemned her. The city was her labyrinth, with a slew of monsters, unbridled all. The Croatian. The Pope. The Nazi priest. An American general. Fugitive Fascists. And, why not, also the killer Jews. Warburg realized he'd come to loathe the place. All he wanted at this point was to save her from it.

When the first light of morning kissed the tip of the obelisk, the point of the spear, he stood and went to the bed. He knelt there, searching underneath with his hand. He pulled out the wrapped leather holster he hadn't touched in a year and then left his rooms. He drove the three blocks to the Tiber and turned south, following the river to the far edge of the ancient city, past the ghetto and, on the far bank, Trastevere. He went to Testaccio, the hilly *rione* nestled in the crotch of the Aventine Hill.

What he knew to look for was the towering Romanesque belfry of the Church of Three Virgins, the feature Deane had emphasized in locating the convent on the map he'd brought to their meeting. Now, in the flat early light, Warburg saw the landmark from the river road. He plunged into the neighborhood. Losing sight of the bell tower, he made his choices at every corner by turning toward elevation, since he knew the basilica crowned the hill. The engine of his aged Fiat whined at the steepness of the streets, which, because of the hour, were clear.

He was driving fast already, bumping through rocks and mud, but when he heard the unmistakable report of a gunshot, he pressed the accelerator to the floor.

He came around a last corner. He saw the church and the looming bell tower and the walls of the adjoining convent. In the street ahead stood a man, facing away and holding a rifle at the ready. Opposite the man, in front of the basilica entrance, stood a woman. They were as unmoving as figures on an agora frieze — a Roman hunter, a Gypsy queen. An Ustashe gunman, Marguerite.

Marguerite was facing the gunman as if entranced, making no effort to get away. The man was poised to shoot. Warburg let the car soar.

The machine struck the gunman before he'd really seen it. A brutal crunching of steel on bone knocked him away, while Warburg registered the jolt of the collision in his hands on the wheel. He stopped the car, got out, and raised an arm toward Marguerite. "*Sono io. Vieni!*" was all he said. It's me. Come!

And she did. This choice differed from the decisions she'd made in the tower and on the street because of who had put it to her. David. He was here. *L'chaim.* She rushed toward him. A defining choice.

They mirrored each other in leaping into the car from opposite sides, slamming doors with the sound of one sharp slap.

But before Warburg could get going, a second gunman appeared at the adjacent gate, on Marguerite's side of the car. The man raised his rifle but stumbled slightly, giving Warburg time to reach into his coat and withdraw the pistol. The man leveled his weapon at Marguerite. Warburg brought his gun up in front of Marguerite's face and fired. The man fell.

Warburg looked at Marguerite. Her eyes met his. Now he understood what he had seen in those eyes all along, this depth of pointed feeling. And he saw in her the glint of recognition. They were alike.

Warburg dropped the gun on the seat, popped the clutch, and got them away.

Immediately upon waking, Kevin Deane threw back the covers, rolled out of bed, and dropped to his knees, beginning the day as he had every day for forty of his forty-five years. This morning, though, he had no idea how to start his prayer.

What first to entrust to the hands of God? Usually he called to mind the lost ones whose welfare consumed his working days — refugees and the displaced. They were mostly nameless to him, but he could readily conjure the faces of those he saw on his rounds of visits to camps and shelters. *All you holy men and women, saints of God.* But this morning his devotions were preempted. The intrigue with Warburg, the fate of the Croatian priest, the handkerchiefs, Sister Thomas, the death of her Philip. *Where was she?*

Behind him, on his small desk, were the yellow pages of the long memo he had been drafting late into the night, his summary of the malign machinations in which he'd become ensnared, from the Danube Federation and Father Lehmann to the Croatian Franciscans and the American sponsorship of Nazi escape to Argentina. Oddly, perhaps, he began his account with his day-one discovery that most of the Jews being sheltered from the Nazis in the Vatican had been baptized, *conversos*—a first confrontation with the fact that things in Rome were not what they seemed, not by a long shot. His purpose in writing was to identify each of the moral boundaries that had been crossed, and each of the story's lacunae that could be filled only by actions taken from inside the Holy See, from the criminal appropriation of extraterritorial foundations to the elevation of Cardinal Caggiano to the disappearing Ustashe gold. He was composing, in effect, a report to the Vatican *about* the Vatican.

But that was last night. Now he was kneeling at his bedside. It was, in the liturgical phrase, right and just to be in the posture of a child, since it was with a child's sense of helplessness that the entire unbelievable intrigue had left him. The unspeakable leaves you speechless. In point of fact, it was only at moments of extremity like this that Deane felt any true sense of identification with his Lord. Near despair, Deane most felt his faith. He did believe. *Not my will but Thine* were the only words that came into his mind. He moved his lips around them. He made the sign of the cross, stood, shook himself, and began his day.

Dressed in cassock and collar, he went to the *colazione,* the informal refectory in which senior clergy resident in the south wing of the Apostolic Palace took their light breakfasts. Happily, the men by custom sat apart from one another—three priests present already, but at separate tables. Deane lifted the morning newspaper from its rack and took his usual chair by the window, which opened onto the gardens and a view of the rear façade of the main wing of the palace. As always, his eyes went first to the balconied window across the courtyard, the Pope's library, as if today the Holy Father would show himself. He never did.

The newspaper was fixed to a rod along its crease, the manipulation of which took a certain skill. Deane had it. He lifted the paper, flicked it for the front page, and what he read stunned him: "Jerusalem Hotel Destroyed by Terrorists." Shocking at any time, but staggering now. He scanned the story quickly, looking for the name "Philip Barnes Morton," not finding it. Dozens were killed, a death toll expected to climb.

Sappers clawing through rubble. Hotel workers killed, passersby, various nationalities including British, Arab, French, and, also, Jews. Many wounded. Many missing. There was no mention of "Headquarters British Forces Palestine-Transjordan," but Deane assumed he was reading of the attack referred to in the cable — Philip Barnes Morton, killed on duty. The story said a Jewish paramilitary group was responsible, the Irgun or Haganah or Palmach, a confusion of culprits that squared with Deane's own confusion. Which of these groups was Warburg involved with? Deane instantly put the question another way: With whom has Warburg involved me? What bastards they are, what monsters!

Deane lowered the newspaper, realizing he could have as readily seen a headline announcing the destruction of Santi Tre Vergini, the innocuous Roman convent that he himself had made a target — based on what? A few handkerchiefs hanging on a clothesline? Forget the harelipped Croatian — what would the killers do to the nuns who had hung the laundry? *Roman Convent Destroyed by Terrorists.* How could he have allowed himself to be dragged into this vendetta?

To look away from the news and its guilt-inducing implications, he faced the courtyard, only to fix his gaze upon the Pope's window. *And you, Your Holiness, where are you in all of this?* The blank drawn curtain supplied the answer: *Nowhere. Deus absconditus.*

Deane thought of the unfinished scrawled memo on his desk. To whom was it addressed? Presumably, since it aimed to make explicit a Vatican entanglement in nefarious activities and crimes, such a document would be addressed to the pontiff. There was little point in thinking of Apostolic Protonotary Tardini as its recipient, since there was every reason to think he was already more or less fully informed of the malignity. As to other stalwarts of the Pope's Curia, they would rank suppressing the scandal of Catholic complicity in Nazi crimes in Croatia with advancing the overthrow of Tito — a wash. And both purposes were being nicely served by the rehabilitation of Ante Pavelic. Deane had no doubt that Pavelic's ass was *somewhere* at rest on a velvet cushion with crimson tassels woven *somewhere* on the Third Floor.

Therefore, not to Tardini, not to the Curia. Stir into this already lethal brew the bloody purposes of Jewish revenge seekers and freedom fighters . . . Who besides Deane foresaw the approaching intersection of all these lines, the inevitable train wreck? *Might I have a word with you, Your Holiness?* But the thought of taking such a brief to the Third Floor was ludicrous.

Then Deane saw it — the ingenious character of the Pope's avoidance. By declining to appoint a papal secretary of state to replace Cardinal Maglione, His Holiness had guaranteed that no single figure would have the responsibility to present him with news he did not want to hear, news upon which he might have to act, or even acknowledge.

The Pope's blank window stared back. Deane had to laugh at the thought that His Holiness might ever read what he'd been writing — what, passed along by papal chamberlains, for God's sake? But the real joke was that His Holiness, to be informed of the sewage rising above the floorboards of his own sacred domicile, had need of such a memo in the first place. *The man can smell. He knows.*

Deane looked again at the front page of the newspaper, with its rabid show of what the Jewish resistance could do. Laid bare in this grotesque act of terror was wickedness involving Deane himself. Who the hell are you, he asked himself, to mount the moral high horse? What have you brought down on those poor nuns in Testaccio? For a few handkerchiefs.

He had to find out what was happening at Santi Tre Vergini, which meant he had to get to Warburg. He thought of summoning his car, but it was too early. Vatican drivers weren't on duty yet. He might have phoned over to Sant'Agata, for Sister Thomas, a bold move at this hour, before Terce, but surely not unprecedented, given her work as secretary of ciphering. But she was gone. He had determined late the day before that she had packed her bag and left the sisters' Vatican City quarters for the Angelicum, the Dominican college beyond the Tiber. Cloistered there, she would not see the newspaper this morning. What did she know? What was she thinking?

Deane went back to his room, knowing that he had no choice but to plunge into Rome, a prospect that struck him just then as setting out into an unmapped wilderness. Despite local Church custom, he did not want flailing skirts at his ankles, so he changed from his cassock into his street clericals, black suit and rabat. He tucked his breviary under his arm and left.

There was frost in the air, the start of an overcast, chilly day. At the yawning mouth of St. Peter's Square stood the first of what would become a line of taxis, and he took it to the Piazza del Popolo, to Warburg's place. But there was no answer at Warburg's door. Back on the street, where the morning traffic was picking up, he was at a loss, faltering and bereft. Lately such feelings defined the magnetic field of his preoccupation, how the needle of his awareness, set free, went to her. The Angelicum.

The walk down the arrow-straight Via del Corso took him, within twenty minutes, to the Palazzo Venezia, Mussolini's balcony. A few blocks east was the Pontificium Athenaeum Internationale Angelicum, named for the angelic doctor Thomas Aquinas. A pontifical university, it was also the mother house of the Dominican order. No surprise, then, that Sister Thomas would have gone there.

The main building was a huge structure, typically Roman for the way it displayed its history in mismatched tropes of Renaissance and Baroque architecture, with slapped-on modern fixes. The entrance was up a broad set of well-worn stairs. At the closet-sized vestibule just inside, Deane presented himself to Brother Porter, a white-robed friar, stooped and aged. With crisp authority, Deane asked to have Sister Thomas Aquinas informed of his visit. Long minutes passed. Deane leaned against a wall, opened his breviary, and ran words of the appointed psalm through his lips, like rounds through a Gatling gun. Then an ageless nun appeared in the foyer, garbed like Sister Thomas, but stout. She spoke Italian with an accent Deane placed as French.

Sister Thomas, the nun said with resolute brevity, was not in residence. No information about Sister Thomas was available, nor would
information about her become available. *Fermo.*

Deane resumed walking, back in the direction of the Palazzo Venezia and the Vatican beyond. But as he crossed into the first square
he came to, a plaza opening out toward the massive ruins of Trajan's
Market, he hit upon a newsstand and glimpsed yet another headline
featuring the word "terrorist"—a later edition of *Il Tempo.* He bought
the paper, took a table at a nearby café, ordered a cappuccino, and lit
a cigarette. In an updated story, he read that, indeed, the King David
Hotel did house the headquarters of the British Mandate Authority
and the British Army. Casualties were expected to be well in excess of
one hundred, the vast majority civilians. The bombing was thought to
be a Jewish retaliation for British raids on offices of the Jewish Agency
and the British confiscation of documents tying the agency to underground groups. Most of the dead were hotel workers, but dozens
of British military officials were also killed. The British Army commander for Palestine, a General Sir Evelyn Barker, called for a retalia-
tory boycott of all Jewish businesses, to "strike the Jews in their pockets," which was where Jews most hated to be hit. *Jesus.*

In a sidebar to the wire-service story was a short article quoting a
Carabinieri official to the effect that the Jerusalem bombing was carried out by the same Jewish terrorist cabal that had attacked the British embassy on Via XX Settembre, a group calling itself the Irgun.
The official reported that the investigation by Roman authorities into
the embassy bombing was progressing, with suspects expected to be
apprehended soon. That there had been no casualties in the embassy
bombing, the official said, was a tribute to the prompt response of the
Roman police.

As Deane read, a subtle perception tugged at his attention, a sense,
perhaps, of being observed. There were others at the café, and a waiter
was floating among the tables, balanced by his tray. A hint of sandalwood came to his nostrils. He raised his eyes, and at once they found
their point of focus on a distant figure onto whom a break in the clouds

was sending a shaft of light. A laywoman coming from the direction of the Angelicum.

As she entered the square, her stride was purposeful. Her posture was erect. She seemed indifferent to the scene around her—the remnant Roman Forum, Trajan's broken glories, the most dramatic ruins in the city. She seemed to be walking toward the corner where ancient Rome intersected a mundane district of modern commerce, beginning with the café at which Deane was seated. She seemed, that is, to be walking directly toward him.

As she drew nearer, he saw that she was modestly dressed in a plain brown skirt reaching below her knees, a white blouse, a brown woolen sweater-jacket. She had the wholly unglamorous appearance of the practical women who ladled soup into the tin bowls of camp dwellers. But her sweater was open, showing the belt at her waist, which emphasized not slenderness but extreme thinness. In her right hand she carried a cloth satchel. Her left arm hung free, swinging as she walked. The sweater sleeve was bunched at her wrist. She was bareheaded, with salt-and-pepper hair cropped so close to her scalp that Deane thought of the shaven-headed young woman of the year before.

She wore sandals. As she drew nearer, he saw that her legs were unshaven. Legs, he realized only then, that he had never before beheld. Her legs.

Deane was wrong to assume that Thomas was headed to his table, that she had seen him at all. He was so aware of her it seemed impossible she had no idea that he was sitting there, an ordinary priest with his coffee and morning paper, a figure, above all in this city, to ignore. Her gaze was fixed on the middle distance, as if drawn by Mussolini's palace. She drew close to the café, veered slightly and automatically to avoid the tables, and made as if to walk on by.

Deane stood. "Sister," he said.

Seeing who it was addressing her, she leapt back, nearly stumbling into the street. By the time she regained her balance, her face was flushed.

He saw that her eyes were red, bloodshot. He stepped toward her.

"Sorry to startle you. I was startled myself to see you. I spoke without thinking."

"What are you doing here?" she asked.

"I was at the Angelicum," he answered, pointing toward it. "I was looking for you. They turned me away. And then—" He gestured at the newspaper.

When she took in what he had been reading, she reached into her bag, withdrew a copy of the same newspaper, and dropped it on the table so it covered his. There was anger in the act, and something else.

"I am so sorry, Sister," he said, gesturing again at the paper.

"Don't call me Sister." Her face was wrecked. Her free hand went to her lips, trembling. But her burning eyes challenged him.

"I mean about . . ." But he could not say it. He gestured at the newspaper, the story it told. Deane felt as if he had been transported into some other reality, a dream state or hallucination. This was Thomas, his familiar friend, but this was also a hostile stranger who'd taken deep offense at him, as if he were the one who'd placed the Jerusalem bomb. But why was she dressed like this?

"Will you sit?" he asked, indicating the nearby chair.

At first she didn't move. That he met her immobility with immobility of his own seemed to be what she required, and she sat. When he was seated, he put out his cigarette and raised a finger toward the waiter, saying to her, "Will you have coffee?"

"No." A firm refusal. To his surprise, she reached for his cigarettes and took one. She held it at her lips as he offered a match. Still her hand trembled. Something told him to make no comment. She inhaled expertly, an old habit. She put her hand on the newspaper. She said, "You told me it was Nazis who caused Father Lehmann's death. It was these Jews. Here in Rome. The Jews who blew up our embassy."

"And now they've killed your Philip."

Surprise showed in her face, that he knew. All she said was "Please don't call him that. He wasn't mine."

"But tell me what has happened. You are . . ." He raised his hand, indicating her clothing, her cigarette. The thought vaulting into his mind was *But you are beautiful.*

"I have left the order," she said. "I will apply for dispensation from my vows. It all became very clear, very quickly. Not unlike seeing in an instant the key to a cipher. I should never have taken vows. I have been dishonest. That is what I just saw — yesterday, through the night."

"Because of Philip?"

"I loved him, as I told you. When I couldn't have him, I thought I would have God instead. It was an unworthy motive. My vocation was based on rejection. Like a rebound love affair. Nothing real about it."

"That's not true. Whatever prompted it, your vocation became real. I saw that for myself."

"You do not understand, Monsignor." At this, a faint smile crossed her face. "You do not see what's real, right in front of you."

"What do you mean?"

"Our Sherlock Holmes bit, what we were trying to parse, you and I — what we found! The beeswax candles. Caggiano. Looted Croatian gold in the Holy See. Holy Mother the Church, in the end — how else to say it? — in bed with Nazis. Pavelic, Lehmann, Stangl the Treblinka commandant, for the love of God! Living in our religious houses. Nazis in monasteries and convents. Vichy collaborators protected. The protectors promoted. Gestapo killers with Vatican passports. The Church welcoming them in Argentina."

"We did parse it, you and I. And I am drafting a report, laying it out. All of it. It's on my desk right now."

"A report to whom? They all know! Tardini knows. The Third Floor knows."

"A report to you. You were going to be my first reader."

"And probably your last," she said. "There's too much. Too much to be the work of functionaries, rogue priests, the odd Fascist bishop. This bile is the work of the Church. How can you be part of that?"

"It isn't 'the Church.' *Members* of the Church, yes. Even officials. But not 'the Church.' And I am not part of it, Sister."

She slammed her hand onto the table — "Don't call me that!" — making the spoon jump off the saucer of Deane's demitasse.

He said, "I'm sorry, I —"

But her fury was loose now. She snapped her cigarette toward the street. "That's who these Jews should be blowing up, the fugitive Nazis! And the monasteries and convents where they are sheltered. Stangl, blow him up! Nazis! Not British soldiers! Not the valiant men who defeated Hitler! Why are the Jews blowing *us* up? Although if the Jews killed Lehmann, I say jolly good for them." She shocked herself with that, and fell silent.

Deane recalled her scruple from before, her not wanting to be party to revenge. The *Jewish* God of vengeance, she had said.

But what if Jews were defending themselves? That's what he should have answered her. Not revenge, but survival. He had no use for bombs, but clearly their war was not over. That was the point. It was in the Jerusalem news story: . . . *retaliation for British raids.* The Jews were still at war. Yet he had no way to speak of that with her.

For a long time Deane matched her silence. Then he said, "I don't think the Jews killed Lehmann. I think he killed himself." Deane recalled her asking if Lehmann had been murdered, but he saw now, in the jolt of her reaction, that she had not thought of suicide. Her face softened, which prompted him to add, "Whatever Lehmann did or was doing—that's still sad, if he killed himself. Don't you think?"

She nodded, chastened. "Yes. Very sad. I'm sorry for saying what I said. I've been . . . very upset." She touched the newspaper. "Did you read this? The story says that on the radio in Palestine, the Irgun announced they would 'mourn the Jewish victims, but not the British ones.'" She was shaking her head, as much from incomprehension as disapproval. She went on, but quietly, "How dare they! And what about the Arab victims? The largest number of dead at that hotel were Arabs who have nothing to do with the Jewish complaint against us."

Deane was mystified by her—a woman whom he knew so well yet who seemed a stranger, a woman enraged but also grief-stricken. One moment she seemed mad, railing at Jews, at the Church, at him; then an out-of-the-blue identification with Arabs. All tied to the harsh fact of Philip Morton's death, and how could she possibly have reconciled her feelings to that?

Deane knew that if he himself were to give vent to what was bottled inside him, his expressions would carve a similar arc from rage to desolation, with no more consistency or restraint than she was showing. But wait. Had she just advocated what he dreaded most that morning, a convent being blown up as long as bad men die? *Jolly good for them!* Deane himself had set Jewish warriors loose to kill the harelipped Ustashe priest—and to kill whom else? Again he asked himself: Were innocents to be slaughtered now because of him?

And why shouldn't such questions make a person mad? The difference between him and her was that she had thrown off the sanctifying cloak, literally uncovering herself, exposing the emaciation less of flesh than of virtue. Good Sister Thomas, with the dropping of a veil, was simply gone, replaced by this harried, tortured—and yes, anti-Jewish—woman. As for Monsignor Deane, he was still primly vested, his breviary squared neatly on the table with newspapers bearing the grotesque report from Jerusalem. His breviary his shield. Shielding him, but no one else.

Shielding him from her.

"Jane," he said, but so tentatively that she might not have heard. He waited for her rebuke. When it did not come, he went on. "Tell me what you learned about Philip."

"A captain from Group Six came to my office yesterday. He brought the first cable they'd received, earlier."

"You read it at your desk." Deane reached into his coat pocket and gave her the folded yellow paper. "I took it. It's how I knew."

She opened the cable flat on the table, stared at it, saying, "Philip was officially attached to Signals. The bomb was shortly after noon. He was in his office, three floors above the basement room where they brought in the cans. Milk cans, can you believe it? Filled with chemical explosives, nitroglycerine probably. His office was in the dead center of the collapse. His body was one of the first identified."

"I am so sorry."

She looked at Deane, seeming entirely sane now. She said, "He lied to me."

"What?"

"He told me, when we met here in Rome, that Edith was dead. I spoke of that to you."

"Edith?"

"His wife. She was dead. Then yesterday the captain said Philip's body was mangled but that his wife had come at once and identified it. 'His wife?' I said to the captain. 'Yes,' he said, 'Edith Morton.' She'd come from England to be with him. They lived a block from the King David, she heard the explosion, was there on the instant. Poor Edith. Philip had lied to me, thinking that I would be at his mercy if he were widowed. Thinking, pathetic woman that I am, that I would work for him, his lovesick Vatican spy."

"Good God, that's —"

But she went on, "What if I had said yes? How long would he have kept it up, the lie that Edith was dead? How would he have done that? Was such deceit peculiar to Philip, or is it universal now? Your fellow General Mates lying to you about Father Lehmann. The Jews lying about being mere victims. German lies — of course. But also British lies. American lies. Catholic lies. There you are. That's the report on your desk. This continent awash in lies, swamping even the Church. That is why I went to Mother Superior last night, having seen *my* lie. I could not go on with it."

"Philip's death made you see how much he still meant to you? That you had always loved him?"

"No. Not at all. I reckoned with Philip back when I said no to him, here in Rome. That was when I began to face the truth."

"What truth?"

"It wasn't Philip I loved. It certainly wasn't God. It was you."

Deane could not think what to say. Opposite him, she was poised, stripped-down, decisive, lean. By contrast, Deane was hamstrung, tired, humbled by a lifetime of indirection. Around them people were paying their bills, heading off to jobs, boys with schoolbooks, trams in the street, a sharp smell of truck exhaust, a beggar approaching, and, in the distance, a pair of wing-hatted nuns crossing the square, unaware that the tortured priest and exclaustrated sister even existed.

Finally Deane said, "Jane . . . May I call you that?"

"Yes."

He said, "Our friendship has been so important to me. But it depended on neither of us using the word . . . love."

"I know. And I don't use it expecting your reply."

"But lies everywhere . . . universal? Jane, have there been lies between us?"

"No. No."

How relieved he was at that.

She said, "I know what makes us different, you and me. You believe in God."

"Yes, I do," Deane said, words that came from his very depth. He gently placed the flat of his hand on the black leather of his breviary, the wife.

"And I do not," Jane said. "God has nothing to do with me."

"That cannot be true."

She shrugged.

God was in the eye of the bird, there, watching them. God was in the crust of bread on the waiter's tray. God was in the water glass. God was in the corruptions that had seared this woman's conscience. God was the breath that had shut itself up in Deane's lungs, like a beast in its cage. God was terrible, which was how Deane knew that He was real.

He said, "What do you need?"

She laughed. "Nothing. Nothing at all. I have train fare to London. I have a hundred pounds. I have the rest of my life." She lifted her bag. Then she asked, "And you, Monsignor, what do you need?"

He stopped himself from saying "Nothing." That, indeed, would have been his uncouth lie. He said, "I need for you to be well and happy."

"And for yourself?"

"I need to be what I am."

"That's happiness, then," she said.

"I suppose."

"If you need to be promoted to bishop, you'd better forget that Vatican scandal report you're writing."

, "I'm giving it to Mother Pascalina and to Cardinal Spellman."

"They will bury it."

"I know."

"And then *you'll* be buried in some parish in — what's that awful place in New York?"

"The Bronx."

"Right."

"The Bronx, Jane . . . it's the Irish Riviera. As for being bishop, why in the world would I want that now? I'm a priest. A priest, that's all. I'll do the sacraments. The Mass. Bread for the hungry, not the well fed. I know what it can be for people because I know what it is for me."

"Broken servant to a broken world."

"I guess so."

Jane's red eyes welled as she looked at him. "What I see in you is wholeness."

He shook his head.

"That you don't see it makes it real." She stood. "May I call you Kevin?"

Deane did not move. "Yes," he said.

"Goodbye, Kevin." She hoisted her bag, leaving the newspaper and its burdens behind.

He watched her go until she disappeared.

When Deane got back to his office, there was a message waiting on his desk: "Call Father Boyle at NAC."

Terry Boyle was the young Brooklyn priest Spellman had sent over from New York to manage the restoration of the North American College, once the refugees had been cleared out of it. Fumigation. Fresh paint. Kitchen refurbished. Lawns reseeded. Chapel reconsecrated. Now the college was up and running, the red-cheeked seminarians were back, reading Aquinas in Latin, and Boyle was the officially designated father procurator. Deane called him.

"There are a couple of people here, Monsignor," Boyle said. "They say they're friends of yours. They are waiting to see you." Boyle's tone was respectful. Deane knew that Boyle had been one of the young jocks who'd called him Auntie behind his back a long time ago. Now Boyle went on, with a curl of disapproval in his voice, "The man is outside shooting baskets. The woman is watching him."

Less than half an hour later, Deane was there. Because it was morning, the seminarians were all in class, and the public spaces of the former palazzo were deserted. Deane cut through the marble-rich first floor toward the French doors that marked the building's far wall. He moved swiftly, a couple of brisk pivots around columns, as if the breviary under his arm were a football.

When Warburg saw him approach, he ignored the basketball's last bounce off the rim, went to the bench, took Marguerite's elbow, and they walked toward Deane. In the distance, bright in the east across the Tiber, sunlight washed the panorama of bell towers and domes — a sight to which all three were now indifferent.

They met on the lawn, not far from a freshly installed statue of Mary, a small shrine to Our Lady of Lourdes that Spellman had ordered erected in thanksgiving for his Red Hat. Arranged before Our Lady in a small semicircle were kneelers and benches. Deane was all business as they greeted one another. He gestured at the benches. They sat, Warburg and Marguerite on one bench, Deane facing them on another. "What happened?" he asked.

"Vukas is dead," Warburg answered.

"An attack on the convent? What?" Deane could not keep the urgency out of his voice, an edge of panic. The headline he had imagined. Explosions.

"I shot him," a subdued Marguerite said, apparently understanding what Deane needed to know. "I acted alone. One shot." She did not say she had loaded four bullets and left three behind in the rifle, on the floor, not caring whether she lived or died. Now she cared.

"There were two guards," Warburg said, "as you warned there would be. I ran one over with my car, shot the other. They're both dead."

"Good God, David." Deane had assumed he'd left surprise behind. Not so. "And the Irgun people?" he asked. "Haganah? Whoever the hell they are."

"They were not involved," Marguerite said. "They were never told of the convent. Vukas now comes off their list. The Franciscans will have removed his body. The Church, wanting no notice drawn, will control the police."

Deane said, "But the Ustashe will notice. The Crusaders — whoever the hell *they* are."

"Which is why we have to leave," Warburg said. "To make sure it ends here. As if none of this happened."

"But it did happen," Deane said.

"A lot happened, Kevin," Warburg said. "You broke your leg."

"A long time ago. An innocent time."

"The time of Fossoli?" Warburg said. "Innocent? That was when the Vatican newspaper canceled its edition rather than mention Jews being slaughtered."

"Did you bring me up here to break my bones again?"

"No. Only to report. To thank you, and to say goodbye."

"You know about Jerusalem," Deane said. "The King David Hotel."

"Of course. It's why we must go there now."

"What?"

"Did you see the reaction from London?" Warburg asked. "Churchill deplored the bombing, but said it was time to let the Jews emigrate to Palestine."

"So you're saying the King David bombing worked?"

"No. It was a brutal, unnecessary, and criminal act. It must not be repeated. From what I hear of Jewish reaction, it *will* not be repeated. But the time for the Jewish nation has come. We're going to be there."

"A Jewish nation born in blood?"

"A nation, therefore, like every other nation, Kevin. That was always the only Zionist dream." Warburg put his arm through Marguerite's. "I sense your Catholic skepticism."

"No. If there's one thing I've left behind, it's the Wandering Jew bullshit. I'm with you as far as the Jewish homeland goes. Refugees deserve refuge. But"— he thought of Thomas, Jane Storrow —"the Brits brought trouble on themselves in Palestine. Not so the Arabs. What about them?"

"The Arabs will be respected, Kevin."

"It would be lovely to think so, David. But the Arabs are screwed."

Warburg said nothing to that.

Deane asked, "What about America?"

"That's a Jewish homeland too," Warburg said. "Thank God for it."

"General Mates and all? Americans helping Nazis escape?"

"Yes. Not so different, I gather, from the Catholic Church, Pope Pius and all. No question anymore of the Church's being sinless. At least that's cleared up."

"So the Church is"—Deane paused to let the word echo—"a homeland."

"For?"

"Sinners," Deane said.

"Like you," Warburg said with a slow smile.

Deane again thought of Jane Storrow. He said, "In point of fact, yes."

After a moment Warburg asked, "What will you do now, Kevin?"

Deane shrugged. "I've written the whole thing up. A report. The whole damn thing. *Accusatio.* Italian for *J'accuse.*"

"Report for whom? Clark was right. Henry Luce wouldn't touch it."

"I'm giving it to Spellman."

"He's the Pope's lapdog."

"I know. And to the Pope's Doberman pinscher—I'm giving it to her, too. It's all I can do."

After a moment's thought, Warburg said, "Roncalli."

"What?"

"Archbishop Roncalli."

"The papal nuncio?"

"You know what he did for us in Budapest. He's still helping us. The only Catholic bishop in Europe who has agreed to the return of Jewish children."

"What children?"

"The ones who were hidden by Catholics when their parents disappeared. Most were subsequently baptized, but Roncalli accepts that they are still Jews. Orphans, obviously. To let the Jewish community take care of them, he has to operate under Vatican radar. The guy has guts. Get your report to Roncalli. Forget Spellman."

Deane took this in, then said, "I'll get it to both of them. Roncalli to do something, maybe. Spellman because I owe him the truth."

"Spellman will screw you."

"Nothing he can do will touch me, David. I'm beyond that bullshit. I apologize for it."

Warburg gently put Marguerite's arm aside and stood. From her bag he took the folded white cloth with black stripes and held it out to Deane. "Would you bless this for me?"

"What?" Deane stood.

"This *tallit*."

"I know what it is. But surely, I—"

"Who has been my rabbi, Kevin, if not you?" Warburg held Deane's eyes.

Deane took the shawl, opened it, let its folds and fringes fall from his left hand. His right hand hovered above. After a long silence, the priest said, "Blest art Thou, Lord God of Abraham, Isaac, and Jacob. Blest art Thou. From Thy goodness comes this *tallit* with its *tzitzit*. May the one who wears it do justice, love mercy, and walk humbly with Thee."

Deane lifted the shawl, kissed it, and, with Marguerite helping, draped it across Warburg's shoulders. Firmly pressing Warburg's upper arm, Deane said, "Through . . ." But he paused, the point in every blessing at which a priest invokes the name of Jesus and signs the cross. Instead, he said, "Through Thy commandments we are sanctified." Then he added "Amen," a word that David and Marguerite softly echoed.

Author's Note

The lines of this book are fiction, but the dots they connect are history, from the War Refugee Board to the Vatican ratline. The novel's main characters and their story are inventions of my imagination, though nothing in the account contradicts what happened in Rome at the end of World War II. If actual events or figures are referred to, it is in ways consistent with the historical record.

Many years ago I began a novel set in wartime Rome. Realizing that I knew too little about the true relationship between Christians and the Holocaust, I abandoned that work. Instead, in nonfiction, I took up the question of the Church's long conflict with the Jewish people. I acknowledge all of the scholars, religious figures, and dialogue partners whose work has informed my own over the years. Christian self-criticism for the crimes of religiously justified anti-Semitism has been powerful in the decades following the war. It was advanced by no one more forthrightly than Pope John XXIII, who, as Angelo Roncalli, was papal nuncio to Turkey during the Holocaust. His brave support of Jewish survival is noted on the margins of this novel. My conceit is that Monsignor Kevin Deane forwards a copy of his final *J'accuse* to Roncalli. In fact, Roncalli knew enough of the Church's failures to force a reckoning with them as Pope. For that, above all, I acknowledge John XXIII.

· · ·

I am grateful to the many people who helped me with this book. Donald Cutler was the first person with whom I discussed it, and a first reader. His support, over many years, remains precious. Early readers of my first drafts included Bernard Avishai, William Phillips, and Roberto Toscano, each of whom helped me in important ways. Thank you, dear friends.

Thanks to my colleagues and students at Suffolk University in Boston, where I am privileged to be a scholar-in-residence. I especially acknowledge Dean Kenneth Greenberg, Fred Marchant, George Kalogeris, Jennifer Barber, Gregory Fried, Bryan Trabold, Nir Eisikovits, Marilyn Plotkins, Wesley Savick, and my fellow scholars-in-residence, Robert Brustein and David Ferry. As an associate of the Manhindra Humanities Center at Harvard, I have received generous support from Homi Bhabha, Mary Halpenny-Killip, Kiku Adatto, and Michael Sandel. At Houghton Mifflin Harcourt, my editor and friend Deanne Urmy brought this book to life. Ashley Gilliam and Larry Cooper aimed their laser focus on the manuscript, helping improve it a lot. The Houghton Mifflin Harcourt team brought the book to the world with style. I am profoundly grateful to you all. And thanks to Tina Bennett for sage advice.

At the center of my life and work is my family. Patrick, Lizzy, James, and Annie define my happiness and hope. My wife, the novelist Alexandra Marshall, deserves special thanks for being my first and most careful reader. But that's the least of what she gives me. I dedicate this novel to Lexa, with love.

• • •

Among the works from which I drew instruction for this novel are:

Aaron, Mark, and John Loftus. *Unholy Trinity: How the Vatican's Nazi Networks Betrayed Western Intelligence to the Soviets.* New York: St. Martin's Press, 1992.

D'Este, Carlo. *Fatal Decision: Anzio and the Battle for Rome.* New York: HarperCollins, 1991.

Eizenstat, Stuart E. *Imperfect Justice: Looted Assets, Slave Labor, and the Unfinished Business of World War II.* New York: Public Affairs, 2003.

Godman, Peter. *Hitler and the Vatican: Inside the Secret Archives That Reveal the New Story of the Nazis and the Church.* New York: Free Press, 2004.

Gruber, Ruth. *Haven: The Dramatic Story of 1,000 World War II Refugees and How They Came to America.* New York: Three Rivers Press, 2000.

Hilliard, Robert L. *Surviving the Americans: The Continued Struggle of the Jews after Liberation.* New York: Seven Stories Press, 1997.

Judt, Tony. *Postwar: A History of Europe Since 1945.* New York: Penguin, 2005.

Katz, Robert. *The Battle for Rome.* New York: Simon & Schuster, 2003.

Kertzer, David I. *The Pope and Mussolini.* New York: Random House, 2014.

Morgenthau, Henry, III. *Mostly Morgenthaus: A Family History.* New York: Ticknor & Fields, 1991.

Phayer, Michael. *Pius XII, the Holocaust, and the Cold War.* Bloomington: Indiana University Press, 2007.

Wyman, David S. *The Abandonment of the Jews.* New York: Pantheon, 1984.

Zimmerman, Joshua D., ed. *Jews in Italy under Fascist and Nazi Rule, 1922–1945.* Cambridge: Cambridge University Press, 2005.

Zuccotti, Susan. *The Italians and the Holocaust.* Lincoln: University of Nebraska Press, 1988.